# Across the Divide

## A novel

### Jan Gabrielson

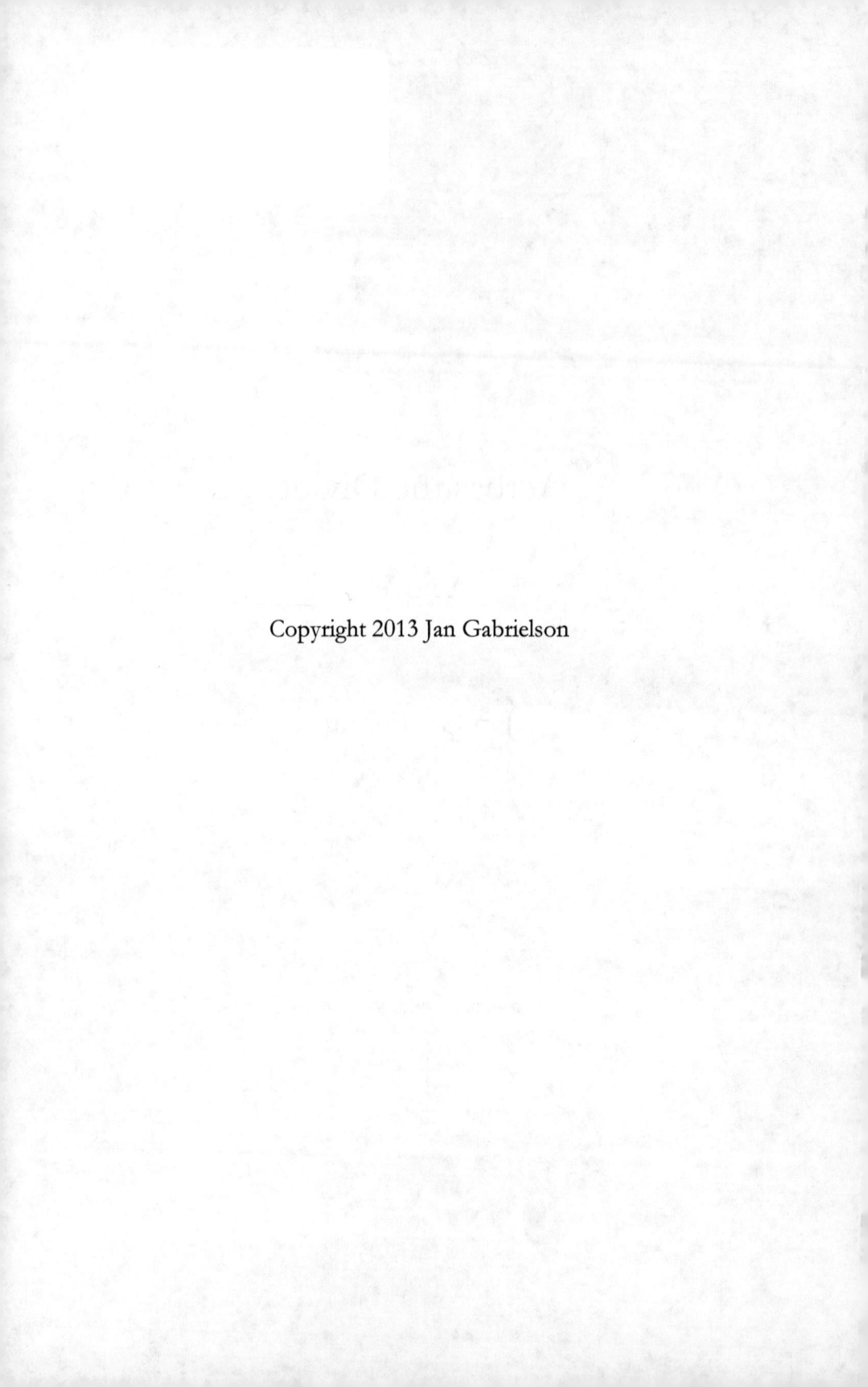

# TABLE OF CONTENTS

# ACROSS THE DIVIDE

## Chapter 1: A Bookstore in Brittany

*Auray, France*

Anne heard the door of the bookstore open and looked up from behind the counter.  A man entered and stood facing her while the door closed behind him.  He stared at her for a moment before responding to her *bonjour,* then turned to browse among the display tables.

Something set him apart from the morning's run of customers: his hesitation perhaps, a trace of an accent.  Or something else.

She watched him as he picked up books, thumbed through them and put them down.  There was no apparent pattern to his browsing, which was not unusual; people often came in, browsed a bit and left.  Others bought a book on a whim, and for them the displays were arranged to turn browsers into buyers.

When the man had entered the store with the window light behind him, Anne had seen his face only well enough to know she wanted to see it again.  She resumed her work and after a minute looked up to find him staring at her again.  He turned quickly to a bookshelf against the wall.  Scanning the titles, he pulled out a book, examined it, put it back and pulled out another.  The fiction section, she noted.  Authors whose names began with H, now L.  Now the travel section.  It was too soon to approach him.  Her customers wanted service when they asked for it, but until then preferred to be left alone to the randomness of browsing, the pleasure of finding the right book by chance.  But if she left him to browse on his own, he could leave without ever speaking to her.

She moved from behind the counter to a shelf near him and busied herself straightening books, daring to peek at him from time to time.  He wore blue jeans and an open-collared shirt, was tall and mildly handsome with an otherwise unremarkable face, from what little she could see of it. Yet something about it appealed to her. He appeared to be her age or slightly older, perhaps in his mid-thirties.

He turned and caught her eye. She was too close to pretend she had not been looking at him. "Do you need help finding something?"

"I'm looking for a novel—with some substance but not too obscure. What can you recommend?"

Excellent French, she observed, but a definite accent.

"What kind of novel do you like? Classic? Contemporary? Popular?" She was more comfortable now, helping a customer instead of spying on him.

He named some French novels he had liked, most of them not known for their enduring literary merit. But he was a foreigner, so lighter reading outside his native language, whatever it might be, was forgivable. She showed him three novels that met his criteria, ones she had not read but her customers had enjoyed. He looked briefly at them, then asked her for Voltaire's *Candide*, adding almost apologetically that although he had a college degree in French, he had never read it.

She found it, pulled it off the shelf and handed it to him. She was not ready to end the conversation, such as it was, but saw no way to prolong it short of asking an indiscreet question. "If it's not too personal," she ventured, "Where did you get your degree?"

"In California and at the University of Bordeaux."

*California?* From his accent and general appearance she had expected him to say England or Canada. She could not imagine how a Californian had found his way to Auray. "Are you in Brittany on vacation?"

"I moved into a house in Sainte-Anne-d'Auray a few weeks ago. I plan to live here as long as I can."

"You'll have time to read," she said. "Once you've seen the Basilica, there's not much to do in Sainte-Anne."

"That's one reason I like it." As he spoke, he shifted from side to side and played with the books in his hands. She tried to read his demeanor: not exactly shy, but seemingly uncomfortable in her

10

presence.

Sainte-Anne-d'Auray, a fifteen-minute drive north of Auray, struck her as an unlikely place for an American expatriate to settle. To Anne, the village was just a destination for Catholic pilgrims, a place where Saint Anne, the patron saint of Brittany and mother of the Virgin Mary, once appeared to a peasant. Why would anyone move from California to Sainte-Anne-d'Auray? She might never find out. He could pay for his books and leave the store and that would be that.

As her curiosity increased, so did her sense that she was out of line nosing into a customer's private life. She excused herself, went across the room and picked up some books that had escaped from their shelves, still thinking about the man behind her, resisting the urge to turn and resume spying on him.

She drew on little more than movies and stereotype to support her impression of Americans: superficially friendly, quick to smile and strike up a conversation, moving on before any real friendship could take root. Her one experience with an American seemed to confirm the stereotype. An outgoing American girl sat next to her one time in a university class, struck up a conversation and suggested they go to a café to continue their discussion. Anne enjoyed the chat in spite of the girl's bad French, but that was the last she saw of her.

This man seemed different. For one thing, he was not especially friendly. Nor did he smile much.

She heard him approaching and turned to face him.

"Do you have a book that explains the traffic laws?" he asked.

"I should have one or two." He followed her to the back of the store where she pulled out two volumes and showed them to him. A regular customer entered, a woman who liked to chat. Anne tossed a *bonjour* over her shoulder and turned back to him. "This one is more compact in case you want to keep it in your pocket or your car. This one has better illustrations." Showing him the books gave her cause to stand close to him.

He reached toward her and took the one with better

illustrations, allowing her to glance at his ring finger and find it bare.

Looking quickly at him and down at the books he was holding, she asked, "Do you find it hard to drive in France?" Although her sense of propriety told her not to get too personal, she wanted to prolong the conversation, to hold him there for interrogation. So far, he seemed a willing victim. In fact, it almost seemed he was prolonging it himself, coming up with more books to ask her for.

"No, not at all. The roads are good, and the French are good drivers. I'd rather drive here than in California. Drivers there are getting worse." He took a quick look at his watch. "What are your hours?"

"9:00 to 12:30, and 2:30 to 6:00. We're closed Wednesday and Saturday afternoons and Sunday."

He glanced across the room at the other customer, turned back to Anne and said, "May I take you to lunch?"

Rarely was Anne at a loss for words, but now, without warning, the boundaries had shifted. She stumbled for an answer. *Decide, quickly. Say something.*

Before she could answer, he said, "I'm sorry. I didn't mean to put you on the spot. Would you like to think about it?" He was looking directly at her now, more confident. It was her store, her language, and her country, but he had taken charge.

She regrouped quickly, hoping she had not given the impression that no man had ever asked her to lunch. "No. That won't be necessary. Today, you mean?"

"Yes. At 12:30, after you close." There was something paradoxical in his voice. It was as if he wanted nothing more in the world than to have lunch with her, but would not give it another thought if she declined.

"Sure. Why not?" Not knowing what else to say, she retreated to safer territory. "Did you need anything else?"

"These should last me a while." He handed her the books and followed her to the counter, where she scanned the bar codes and ran his credit card. She set the charge slip on the counter with a pen, taking care not to look straight at him, lest he sense she was entertaining thoughts unrelated to selling him books. While he signed, she slipped his books and receipt into a bag and handed it to him over the counter. He said, "See you in a few minutes," and walked to the door with the sure step of a man in good shape. She gave him a quick scan from behind and liked what she saw.

She watched the door as it closed behind him, puzzling over what had just happened. She had done her businesslike best not to let on that she was attracted to him. For his part, he had kept a polite distance like any other customer, then out of nowhere asked her to lunch. Whatever his motivation, she wanted to hear more about California, more about him. And it was all quite harmless. They would have lunch and talk—about books, about California. Her curiosity would be satisfied, and if he came to the store again, they would chat briefly about what books he should buy. It mattered little that she felt strangely drawn to him. A foreigner, after all, was not husband material.

While the other customer perused paperbacks in the romance section, Anne examined his credit-card slip: "John L. Becker." Strange, those Anglo-Saxons with their middle initials.

He reappeared at 12:30 sharp, while she was rolling a rack of postcards inside and changing the OPEN sign to CLOSED. He asked her about restaurants, and she suggested La Crêperie Alréène. They set out on the narrow sidewalk bordering the Place de la République, cars hurrying past them in the street. They walked side by side when space on the sidewalk permitted, mostly in uneasy silence. When throngs of people making their way home or to a restaurant forced them to walk single file, he motioned for her to pass in front of him. She sensed his watchful presence behind her.

Anne was not timid by any measure. But now, in a restaurant with a foreigner she had just met, she found herself searching for words. He did not even know her name, and it seemed awkward to introduce herself now. She wanted to say "Tell me all about California," but that sounded inane and provincial, as if she had never been out of Brittany. She was relieved when he took the lead.

13

"It feels a little strange. Here we are having lunch together and I don't even know your name. Mine is John."

"Anne."

"A good name for a Bretonne."

It impressed her that he seemed to know some local history. Not only was Saint Anne the patron saint of Brittany, Anne de Bretagne was a revered historical figure, whose loyalty to Brittany had not wavered despite her marriages to the heir to the Holy Roman Empire and two successive kings of France.

"How are you so sure I'm Bretonne? Am I speaking with an accent?"

"No, but *I* am."

"Barely."

"Thanks. I'm doing my best."

He opened the menu and while he studied it, she allowed herself her first good view of his face. He seemed even more serious now, almost humorless.

"What's good here?" he asked.

"Just about everything. I think I'll have a *galette complète*."

"What is that exactly?"

It was time to find out if he had a sense of humor. "It's something you'd better learn to like if you plan to live in Brittany: a buckwheat crêpe with ham, cheese, and a fried egg. It starts out round, but they fold the edges in until it's square. That leaves an opening in the middle for the egg. When they serve it, it looks like a big yellow eyeball staring at you. At least that's what I used to think when I was a kid. A bowl of cider goes well with it."

He shot her a perfunctory frown, like a parent whose child has just said a mildly bad word. "That sounds, uh, quite appetizing. I think I'll have the same thing. That way you won't have to tell me what organs the other items on the menu make you think of."

A quick peek at him revealed a smile that might have a laugh behind it trying to escape. There was hope for him.

After the waitress took their order, he told her he was a lawyer with a firm in Los Angeles. "They let me work at home, but it remains to be seen how long I can do it at this distance. When

14

people arrive at the office, it's already six in the evening here. So I work a lot at night."

"How do you pass your time during the day when you're not working?"

"I take care of the house and the garden, trying not to kill all the plants. Once or twice a week I take a drive somewhere. Now that I'm organized and have some books, I plan to read. That's about all there is to tell about my life right now. I imagine yours is more interesting."

She was starting to think they would spend the whole lunchtime each trying to keep the other talking.

"If you think I'm going to tell you what an exciting life I lead so you can enjoy it vicariously, you're going to be disappointed. For one thing, I've never lived in a foreign country—or outside of Brittany for that matter." May as well let him know now that he was having lunch with a provincial, small-town bookseller, in case he expected something more.

The waitress arrived with two cider bowls and filled them. He thanked the waitress and turned back to Anne. "We might have different ideas about what's exciting. You're French. That's a good start."

"The last time I checked, there were almost sixty million of us. How much excitement can you handle?"

"Let's just start with you. The other fifty-nine million plus will have to wait their turns." He covered a little smile by raising his cider bowl to his lips and taking a drink.

*That's it!* His lips. That was what gave his face its distinctive appearance. His lips turned down slightly at the corners, giving him a serious look that was not quite a frown, so that when he smiled, the dramatic change added to the warmth of his smile. He had not smiled much so far, so it had not been obvious. But now, he seemed to be relaxing.

Trying not to gaze too long at his lips and imagine how well they would fit on hers, she told him she had grown up mostly in Rennes and gone to college in Nantes. "I got my degree in French, like you. After college, I got a job at a bookstore in Nantes and

15

worked there a few years."

"How does a woman from Rennes go to college in Nantes and end up in Auray? If it's not too personal."

"It was time to move on. My mother had the bookstore here and invited me to come work with her, and I had lived here for few years before I left for college. How does a man from Los Angeles move to Sainte-Anne-d'Auray? If it's not too personal."

"It was time to move on."

The brevity of his reply told her it was too personal. Time to change the subject. "Tell me about Los Angeles."

"French tourists don't usually like it. I'm tired of it myself. Traffic is bad and getting worse, there's graffiti and litter everywhere."

"That surprises me. When I think of Los Angeles, I picture big, fancy cars, palm trees, sunshine, surfers, movie stars, carefree people enjoying life."

The waitress arrived with their *galettes*, and they started to eat. She noticed his impeccable table manners; he even wiped those cute lips with his napkin before drinking. "Have you been to California?" he asked.

"No, but I see it in books and movies. And it's in the news here from time to time. You know, wildfires, landslides, floods, earthquakes. One day they show us the state being destroyed, and the next day it's the Oscars, as if nothing bad had ever happened."

As they ate and talked, she began to wonder if he would want to see her again. Would an American consider it too aggressive if she suggested it?

After lunch, he walked her back to the store. He shook her hand and said, "I enjoyed getting to know you. I'll read my books quickly, so I'll have an excuse to see you again."

"You don't need an excuse. You know where to find me." She unlocked the door of the bookstore, said goodbye and went in, worrying that her parting line might have been too forward or too flip. She had intended to tell him she would be happy to see him again, but what came out did not sound inviting. As she put up the "OPEN" sign and turned on the lights, she scolded herself for

16

sounding sarcastic, even cold. Would he come back to the store? Did he find her boring and provincial and regret having asked her to lunch?

It was comforting to be back in her store, where she was in charge, where relationships and expectations were clear, where everything was in its place.

The store was compact, its interior arranged to display as many books as possible. An L-shaped counter faced customers entering the store, the small end of the L near the door and attached to the wall. Light from windows across the front of the store helped illuminate shelves of books on three walls and a maze of display tables in between. On slow days, Anne sometimes scanned the shelves, knowing exactly what was where. All that knowledge, all that thought at her fingertips. There was always something new to read, something new to learn.

They carried books of all kinds: children's books, books on Brittany, picture books, nonfiction, fiction, classics, mysteries, romances. Today, Anne's eyes wandered to the romance section on the wall opposite the counter. From time to time she thumbed through a romance novel but had no patience for their superficiality, their mediocre writing and improbable plots: innocent heroine meets man from some exotic place, usually Spain, Italy, or Africa. The hero was never an American. If he were, the heroine would meet him in the first chapter, and in chapter two he would say, "It's been nice knowing you" and disappear forever. If the story followed the stereotype, it would be a very short book.

"I enjoyed getting to know you," he had said. In truth, he had gotten to know very little about her. She had read that Americans say such things whether they mean them or not and that if an American tells you, "We'll have to get together again," that is the last you will ever hear from him. *What strange people*, she thought, a notion which only whetted her curiosity.

She went to the computer and, launching a search engine, typed "'John L. Becker' lawyer California." One of the hits appeared to be a newsletter of a bar association. She clicked on it, scrolled down and found a photo of him in a dark suit and blue necktie,

17

standing with three others, exuding the self-assurance of a man in his element. She could see he was smiling, but the photo was too small for a good view of his lips. The caption revealed the men in the photo with him to be a Justice of the Court of Appeal, a member of the City Council, and the president of something she could not translate. Seeing John in California among important people left her feeling distant and insignificant. Yet he had struck her as simple and natural, not at all like the big shot in the photo. And however important he might have been in his former life, he had left it behind and moved. Why? Why did he abandon paradise and move to Brittany? He said he was tired of Los Angeles, but who does not tire of home from time to time?

Changing to the online telephone directory, she punched in his name. The result, with his phone number, displayed on the screen: "BECKER, John, Rue de Locmaria, 56400 Sainte-Anne-d'Auray." She knew the street, a rural road next to the grounds of the Basilica. A cluster of houses on Rue de Locmaria marked the edge of the village, just north of the Basilica complex. The stores in the center of town were a short walk away. She decided his house must be one of those.

She went next to a map site, typed in "Auray, France" and hit Enter. From the map of Auray that appeared, she zoomed out, first to all of Brittany, then higher. The outside came world into view: the rest of France, Great Britain, the rest of Europe. She navigated westward across the Atlantic, across the United States to California, and descended to Los Angeles, where she contemplated a vast grid of streets ending at the Pacific Ocean. Switching to the satellite view and descending further overwhelmed her. Buildings, streets, highways, dark areas that appeared to be mountains. The size of the city was staggering. Switching back to the map view, she calculated its expanse as 130 kilometers in each direction.

The door opened. A customer entered, bringing Anne back down to earth in her little corner of Auray in her little corner of Brittany in her little corner of France.

# Chapter 2: *La Belle Californie*

At 6:00 Anne closed the store and went upstairs to the apartment she shared with her mother. She changed to blue jeans and a casual sweater. Jeans buttoned and shoes tied, she lifted a book from a closet shelf and laid it on her desk. On its cover the title *La Belle Californie* stood out from a photograph of a boulevard whose sidewalks were adorned with rows of stars. She opened it and turned its pages as she had done so many times, looking yet again at photos of an orchard of orange trees bathed in sunshine and stretching to the foot of snow-capped mountains, deserts covered with wildflowers, smiling people cruising along the beach in a red convertible. And Hollywood. Rows of stars along glistening sidewalks, each bearing the name of a movie star.

The book was her favorite of the many her father had given her, this one for Christmas when she was ten years old, shortly before he moved out. It was a dismal time in her life, a time when Brittany was cold and gray. Over the years she looked at the book again and again, studying the details of each picture and rereading the captions. California became her paradise, her escape. In California, every day was sunny, and nobody had a care in the world.

Even now, as an adult, she could not imagine why someone would leave such a place and move to Brittany.

At dinner with her mother Brigitte, Anne did not mention John. She saw no reason to feed her mother's unspoken concern about whether Anne would ever marry and live a normal life. In her mother's generation, a woman still single at thirty-three was assumed to be on her way to permanent spinsterhood. Her mother had married at twenty and had her first child, Anne's brother Bernard, at twenty-one. Now fifty-five, neither her divorce nor the passage of years had diminished her elegance. She was slim and graceful, her hair the color of shifting sand that French women often opt for when they start to gray.

Although Anne considered herself close to her mother, the two women were careful to respect each other's privacy. Years of living and working together had fostered a sense of what not to ask.

After dinner, Anne picked up a novel she had been reading about a priest who hid Jewish children from the Nazis during the Occupation. Unable to concentrate, she set down her book, went to her bedroom window and looked out over the gently sloping town square where she lived and worked. From the uphill end of Place de la République, the facade of the City Hall looked down a hundred meters to a row of half-timbered buildings next to where the Rue du Château began its steep descent to the fifteenth-century port of Saint-Goustan. Anne's building was typical of those on the square: four stories with shops at street level and apartments above. Some buildings were trimmed with the hewn stone of French villages while others yielded to the economy and convenience of tinted stucco.

Opposite her window, red-orange poppies and multicolored pansies set in a sea of green brightened a traffic island separating the two streets that ran through the square and converged near the bookstore. In the evening the square was quiet, but during the day, cars, trucks, and pedestrians hurried about. Like other French towns, Auray strived to maintain its character while adapting to the demands of a modern economy.

She tried to see her town as John might see it. To him, coming from America, it must seem small and forgettable. To her it was a comfortable place to live, but at times confining.

She had traveled some, to England, Spain, Italy, Germany—nowhere far or exotic. California excited her in spite of John's dismal description. If they became friends, she could visit him there and see for herself. She imagined arriving at his house. He shows her to a separate bedroom. No, to *his* bedroom. Two weeks of passionate lovemaking, then returning to her chaste and sometimes lonely life in Auray. *This is insane. I sold him some books and we had lunch. That's all.*

Yet she could not stop conjuring up scenarios of how they might meet again. How long would he need to read three books and come back for more? *Candide* alone could take weeks. Maybe he thought she did not like him. Perhaps she gave him too much credit, assuming he understood how the French behave with people they have just met, maintaining a polite distance and avoiding private subjects. How could she let him know discreetly that she was not indifferent to him? She thought of businesslike reasons to call him. Wait a week, then call to tell him they just received another book by the author of one of the novels she sold him. Too pushy. Or she could read one of them and suggest they meet at a café to discuss it. Even pushier. How would an American man react to such an overture?

*If I were American, I would know what to do.* She resolved to check her catalogues for etiquette books written for French people who go to live in America. But even if she found a book that assured her American women call American men and ask them out, and she called him, and he accepted, then what? They might see each other for a while, maybe even sleep together, then one day he could announce, "It's been great, but it's time to go home. Come see me in Los Angeles someday."

No, she thought, it would be best if she never saw him again. At thirty-three years old, with her college degree and a satisfying job, one piece was still missing from what she considered a complete life. As much as she liked to think of herself as a modern, self-sufficient woman, it was time to give up some of her independence, to marry and have children and recapture the family life she had enjoyed too briefly as a child. As the years passed and the pool of potential husbands dwindled, one more dead-end romance was the last thing she wanted.

## Chapter 3: Jean-Louis

The summer after graduating from *lycée,* Anne and her mother and brother joined her uncle and his family for the month of August in a rambling house near the beach at Perros-Guirec, on the northwest coast of Brittany. In the past, she had looked forward to summer vacations with her extended family, enjoying her status of prima donna among her younger cousins. But this year, preoccupied with an impending change in her life, she had become an outsider. She was starting to see herself as a young adult, and her cousins were still children.

Walking alone on the Sentier des Douaniers, the path along coastal hills to the pink granite boulders of Ploumanac'h, she tried to imagine the following month when she would go alone to Nantes for her first year of university. She had stopped at a viewpoint and was staring idly at the ocean when a young man came up to the railing next to her and said, "Why aren't you on the beach like everyone else?"

"I'm tired of the beach. It's for kids. Why aren't you?"

"Same reason."

He seemed a little older, more poised than boys her age, his manner relaxed and friendly. She was lonely and happy to have someone to talk to, and since she would never see him again, a little conversation was harmless.

"You seem to have something important on your mind," he said.

How did he know? She turned toward him, but he was leaning on the railing, facing the ocean. "Are you a student?" she asked.

"I graduated from college in June. I just started working in the family business in Tours. My parents assumed I would come on vacation with them again, I suppose because I'm still living with them. But this is the last time. And you?"

He was already out in the world and she had not even started college. It would not be long before he resumed his walk by himself. "I start at Nantes next month. That's what I was thinking about. I'm excited, but I'm nervous. It's only an hour and a half from home, but it seems far away."

"I was nervous too, even though I stayed living at home with my parents." He had turned toward her, and she could see his face more clearly, mature but youthful. "It's a big change; I know, and it's a little scary, but you'll love it. Where's home for you?"

"Auray."

"Where's that?"

"On the north shore of the Gulf of Morbihan, west of Vannes." A Bretonne from a small town, he was thinking. If he was trying to decide whether she was worth talking to, she had just made his decision easier. He would wish her well and go on his way.

But no. "I was walking toward Ploumanac'h too. May I join you?"

How would he know she had been walking that direction unless he had been watching her before she stopped? She was warming to his company. "Sure. Let's go."

As they walked, he told her about university life. By the time they reached Ploumanac'h, the prospect of leaving home to go to university was not so daunting.

On the walk back, he said, "I was planning on going to a movie tonight. Would you like to come with me?"

She said yes, and they talked about cinema all the way back to Perros-Guirec. Just before they parted company, he asked her name.

"Anne."

"I'm Jean-Louis."

His handshake was firm and masculine but still gentle.

That evening after the movie, as he walked her back to her house, she braced herself for what she feared was coming: the sloppy, aggressive kiss, the groping hands, the moment of betrayal and disappointment when he, like others before him, would reveal what he was really after. To her surprise, he shook her hand and said, "I'd like to see you tomorrow if you're free." They made plans to meet, and he waited at the gate until she was inside the house. She went to the window to see him still standing outside the gate, looking at the front door until he turned and walked away.

As she thought about seeing him the next day, she began to fret that at the end of vacation, he would leave her and go home to Tours. But by the time she fell asleep, she had resolved not to think about it. It was a long way off.

They met the next day, and the next, and every day and every night for the weeks that remained of vacation, strolling on the beach together, talking, going to movies. He seemed in no hurry to get physical, and as she began to trust him, they progressed from holding hands to kissing. Then, on a day when his parents left to go sightseeing, Anne, without really thinking through her motives, asked Jean-Louis if he would show her the villa his parents had rented for the month. He obliged, taking her to a white house nestled among trees on the hill separating the beaches from the port.

After a quick tour of the villa, they lay on the couch, talking, kissing, and caressing each other. She felt safe with him, trusted him—enough to venture with him into the alluring unknown, to try for herself what she had only heard and read about. Between kisses, she asked him timidly, "Do you want to make love?"

"Are you sure you want to?"

"I'm sure," she said, "but . . . ." Her eyes drifted to the window, to the trees outside. She was afraid she would do something wrong and ruin it.

He stroked her hair. "Are you nervous?"

"A little. It's my first time, and . . . I don't . . . I don't know what to do."

"Don't worry, you'll be fine," he said, kissing her on the cheek. He took her by the hand into his bedroom, where a jay was squawking in the yard outside the window.

He was patient and sensitive and took the necessary precautions. It did not hurt as much as she had expected, nor did it give her much pleasure, until afterwards when he held her and kissed her and told her that giving him her virginity was an act of great generosity. The jay had flown on to other trees and other yards. For years after, whenever she heard a jay, she thought of Jean-Louis.

24

The next time was better, and the next even better. For the rest of vacation, they made love at night on secluded beaches and wherever else they could go to get away from their families. She could not get enough of him.

Toward the end of vacation, she said, "In a few days, you'll be going back home. I'll bet the girls in Tours are smarter and prettier than the girls in Brittany. You'll wonder why you wasted your time with me."

"Anne, why do you talk like that? I tell you I love you, but you don't believe me."

"I know you mean it," she said, "but I can't understand why."

"I understand why. I can't imagine my life without you."

Jean-Louis's home in Tours was two hundred kilometers up the Loire River from Nantes, in the heart of the château country, where, it is said, the purest French is spoken. They managed to get together several times in her first months of college, as inconvenient as it was. Jean-Louis lived with his parents, so Anne had to stay in cheap hotels and he had to concoct excuses for staying out all night. The train, the hotel, meals together, all were expenses they could ill afford. It was no better when he came to Nantes. Although she had a dormitory room to herself, coming and going were awkward, and he could not eat with her in the student cafeterias.

More and more, when he was free, she had exams or an assignment due. When she was available, he had family or work obligations. She got into the student life, made new friends, and started noticing other men. And when Jean-Louis talked about the family building-supply business, she found it hard to pay attention. She began to realize they lived in different worlds. They wrote letters and talked on the phone, but their visits, their calls, and their letters became less frequent.

Finally, he called her and said what she had not wanted to face. "It's just not working. I love you and I miss you, but our lives are passing us by. I think we should agree that you can see other men and I can see other women. And we'll get together when we can."

Upon hanging up, she stared at a movie poster on the wall and soon fell onto her bed and lay motionless the rest of the evening, too numb to cry. She knew she would not see him again.

Two days later a letter arrived.

Dearest Anne,

It broke my heart to hear the sadness in your voice when we last spoke. It was the hardest thing I have ever had to say. I wish we lived in the same city or were at a different time in our lives. You are a wonderful woman, intelligent, beautiful, sensual. I am richer for having shared a part of my life with you.

I hope you learn to appreciate yourself as much as I appreciate you. I remember when you said you didn't understand why I loved you, as if you believed there was some reason not to. Such nonsense.

I will always love you.

Jean-Louis

She lay on her bed, holding the letter, staring at it, rereading it. She had allowed him to penetrate her facade of self-confidence to the self-doubt she tried so hard to hide, and he loved her just the same. She rolled over onto her back and stared at the ceiling.

A year after graduating from college, she wrote to Jean-Louis. Half-formed hopes of seeing him again were put to rest by his response: a sweet letter telling her he was married and his wife was pregnant and that Anne would always be one of his fondest memories.

## Chapter 4: Business Is Business

The day after her lunch with John, Anne's work day ended at 12:30. She paced around the apartment, pondering how to spend her afternoon off. She toyed with the idea of calling John but promptly rejected it. She had dropped a hint that she was willing to see him again, so the next move, if there was to be one, was his. For now, the best she could come up with was shopping in Vannes, which, if nothing else, would get her out of Auray.

Anne had been to Vannes so many times she barely noticed its antique charm. But today, she imagined walking through it with John, showing him its beautiful old city center, bordered on the east by a château and ramparts overlooking a formal garden. She would show him the Marle River flowing through the garden and its lawns, flowers, and walkways, and passing in front of a thirteenth-century wash house, where the women of Vannes once met to exchange news while doing their laundry. She was sure he would be enchanted by the storybook half-timbered buildings that graced the quarter around the Cathedral of Saint-Pierre.

At one of her favorite clothing stores in a dressing room trying on tank tops, she had just taken off her sweater and bra when her mother called to tell her that someone named John had called the store and asked for her. Anne was curious why her mother had called rather than leave a note as she usually did. But this was not the time to ask; she would wheedle that out of her later. For now, she amused herself with the thought of returning John's call in her present state of undress, spinning up a playful fantasy in which he figured out from her voice that she was half naked. She emerged from her fantasy, dressed, and walked to a nearby park, where she sat on a cast-iron bench away from the street.

Two women sat on a bench across from her, peeking occasionally at their babies in strollers next to them. She watched and listened to them for a moment, then punched in John's number. He answered.

"This is Anne from the Librairie Renaud. I got your message." Too formal. How many women named Anne could he have called?

After an exchange of pleasantries, he said, "I was thinking of getting a boat and exploring the Auray Estuary on Saturday or Sunday. Would you be interested in coming with me?"

*Yes! Careful. Don't sound too eager.* "Let me think a minute. I don't have my calendar with me. I know I have a family dinner on Sunday. I could go Saturday afternoon after work." One of the babies awakened and started screaming. Anne turned away and covered an ear.

"Where should I pick you up?"

"At the bookstore. I live right above it."

On hanging up, she sat for a moment, watching the two women and their babies, and turned to thoughts of Saturday. The prospect of seeing him again left her excited but strangely uneasy.

After graduating from college, Anne stayed in Nantes where she worked in a large chain bookstore that filled several stories of a historic building in the center of the city. She lived alone in a small apartment on Rue Gambetta, across from the Botanical Garden. Men who shared her interests—books, cinema, music, history, nature—were not hard to meet. Her new relationships were always promising; several started out gloriously. Two of her lovers even broached the subject of marriage. But Anne found some insurmountable flaw in each of them, some plausible, compelling reason to break it off. One turned out to be a boring twit, another an egocentric snob. One had too little education; another was selfish in bed. As the years passed and her friends married off, she remained single in a world of couples.

She went to Auray twice a month to see her mother and help in the store on Saturday mornings. Those visits helped assuage her occasional moments of guilt for staying in Nantes and leaving her mother alone in Auray. When Brigitte went so far as to muse out loud about how the store might become a joint enterprise, Anne took a hard look at her life.

The idea of moving back to Auray to live and work, while tempting, clashed with Anne's idea of herself as a modern, independent woman. But Auray was a comfortable town with its own understated small-town charm. And for any stores or services that might not be available in Auray, Vannes was barely fifteen kilometers away.

Pondering how leaving Nantes might affect her love life, Anne concluded that even in Nantes, the good men her age were either married or gay and that her prospects could hardly be worse in Auray. She went so far as to imagine that while the pool of eligible men might be smaller in Auray, the quality of prospects might be higher. City men, if she allowed herself to generalize, were too full of themselves. She accepted her mother's offer of a job in the bookstore and moved back to her old bedroom in her mother's apartment.

Once settled in Auray, work, family, friends, and an occasional date occupied her. Some of the men she met seemed to have potential, but she soon tired of them. As time passed, she often found herself staring out her bedroom window, wanting to escape from the apartment, from Auray, and having nowhere to go. By train, she could be in Nantes or Rennes in an hour and a half or even Paris in three and a half hours. But she had spent enough of her life in Nantes and Rennes, and as for Paris, in spite of all there was to see and do, for a single woman visiting alone it could be the loneliest place in the world.

Those were the times her life seemed to have stalled.


At dinner, she knew her mother was curious about the man who had called but would respect their unspoken rule not to pry into each other's business. For her part, Anne still wanted to know why her mother had gone to the trouble of calling with the message. Perhaps, she thought whimsically, he had said, "Your daughter is bewitchingly beautiful. I must talk to her immediately!" Not likely.

Doing their awkward best to avoid the subject of John's call, they ate and talked about the bookstore until Anne could no longer restrain her curiosity. "The man who called today, did he ask you to call my cell phone with the message?"

"No. It just seemed right to call you rather than leave you a note, that you might want to talk to him right away. I don't really know why."

Anne knew what was coming: a subtle probe for more information. As expected, Brigitte added, "I noticed he had a slight accent—maybe Canadian or Belgian. I don't know."

"He's American," Anne said, hoping for a reaction from her calm, predictable mother that would betray her surprise.

"Really!"

Bull's-eye! "Is that a problem?" Anne took a sip of cider and looked idly across the kitchen, doing her best to appear indifferent to the whole incident.

"Well, no. But an American? How did you meet him?"

"He came into the store yesterday to buy some books and we had lunch together. We're going boating on Saturday."

Brigitte set down her fork and looked across the table at Anne, who was acting as blasé as she possibly could, studying a piece of chicken as if she were the Curator of Poultry at the Auray Museum. Brigitte said, "You always find new ways to surprise me. I was back to blaming myself for keeping you here in this little town instead of encouraging you to move back to a city where you'd meet more men, and you come up with this." It was a subject they usually avoided, but this time, her mother could not help herself.

"Easy, Mom. Don't start sewing my wedding dress just yet. I've known him for one whole day. I don't even know for sure if he's single, although he seems like he is, and he wasn't wearing a ring."

"And if he's married?"

Another opening, too good to pass up. "If he's married and looking to get laid, you know how I feel about that."

Brigitte frowned. "With all your education, you can't find a more elegant way to make your point?"

"Apparently not." Anne was amused by her mother's perfunctory attempt at parental disapproval. "But married or single, he doesn't strike me as a pickup artist."

"He asked you to lunch," her mother said, adding hastily, "Not that there's anything wrong with that."

30

"How do you know *he* asked *me?*"

"Because my daughter and partner doesn't hit on customers."

Anne laughed. "Maybe I should start."

Brigitte picked up her fork. "As long as you get their money first."

"Don't worry, Mom. Business is business. Lunch is lunch. This chicken is excellent. Where did you get it?"

There was only so much to say about where to buy chicken, and when that subject was exhausted, Anne was ready to talk more about John. If her mother had any misgivings about her dating an American, she kept them to herself, which was no surprise to Anne. Anne had made it clear that if she wanted her mother's opinion about how she was living her life, she would ask for it.

Later, while getting ready for bed, Anne tried to imagine their upcoming outing. Exploring the Auray Estuary by boat, while nothing new for her, would give them several hours alone together, during which they were not likely to discuss chicken-shopping. He would have to reveal more about himself.

## Chapter 5: A Sailor in Distress

Saturday afternoon he picked her up and drove to the dock with the confidence of someone who had lived in the area all his life, leading her to think he had driven the route before to avoid the embarrassment of taking a wrong turn or having to ask Anne for directions. The man at the dock already knew John, who, it was starting to seem, left little to chance. The man reviewed with them how to put on a life vest and the operation of the outboard motor, controlled by a helm and throttle at the pilot's seat on the port side. Anne asked some questions about the controls to be sure they were similar to those in other boats she had piloted. She thought she might offer at some point to take over the helm so John could enjoy the scenery.

The man steadied the boat while John stepped across to the pilot's seat and Anne took the seat next to him. While untying them, the man warned them not to go too far up the Estuary or down into the Gulf after 4:30 when the tide would be going out. The water rose and fell dramatically in the Estuary as Brittany's notorious tides rushed in and out of the seaward entrance to the Gulf, filling and draining its adjoining waterways.

"I thought we could go up toward Saint-Goustan," he said, "and when we get there see how much time we have left. How does that sound?"

"Aye-aye sir!" His smile told her that her silliness had landed well.

They headed into a gusty breeze. As they picked up speed, the putt-putt of the motor smoothed to a hum. The water sparkled, its ripples scattering the sun and lapping softly against the side of the boat. A flock of gulls congregated around them, anticipating bait to steal. Anne took a deep breath of the damp salt air, happy to be out of the apartment, out of the bookstore, out of her routine—in the company of someone new and different.

They cruised upstream along wooded banks, sharing the channel with other boats, to where the navigable part of the estuary ended and other boats were turning around.

As they headed back down the channel, he made a sweeping gesture at the scenery and said, "You're lucky to live in Brittany."

Anne shrugged. "I've always thought people were lucky to live in California."

"Maybe I lived there too long."

An opening. "Is that why you moved?"

"Not really."

Try another tack. "How long do you plan to stay here?"

"As long as I can, but you never know. My parents are young and in good health, but that could change. I'm at a point in my life where I want to find some happiness other than living and working in Los Angeles, but sometimes I feel a little guilty for moving so far away."

He was starting to open up. How long could she keep him talking?

"Do you expect to find happiness living in Brittany?"

"So far, so good. I'm happy right now." He glanced at her and smiled, as if to let her know he was happy to be with her. At least that was how she chose to take it.

Cracking through his reticence had become a challenge. "It's hard for me to imagine moving to a foreign country and starting a new life. I expect it could be lonely at times." It came out sounding like she thought he had asked her out just because he was lonely, which would be insulting to both of them. She regretted saying it, but it was too late.

He did not seem to mind. "It's lonely at times, but I have friends here. I've lost touch with some other people I knew from before, including my ex in-laws in Bordeaux."

Ex in-laws in Bordeaux? A French ex-wife? If she expected to hear more, she was quickly disappointed. He turned the conversation back to her.

"And where do you find *your* happiness?"

She reflected a moment, not just about her search for happiness, but whether to tell him more. Perhaps if she opened up a bit, he would too. "It's been said that happiness only comes to people who don't think too much about it, so I don't. I see friends,

33

family. I exercise. I read. I go to movies and concerts. I work. Unlike most people I talk to nowadays, I like my work."

"You describe a life most people would envy."

It sounded like an invitation to tell him what was missing in her life, something she knew too well and was not about to share with him. The conversation, now that her life had become the subject, was getting too personal.

The wind across the water picked up and began blowing her hair. She reached into her purse for a barrette and fastened her hair back, welcoming the break in the conversation. Sitting back in her seat, she gazed off over the starboard bow. A small sailboat, piloted by a young woman alone, glided into Anne's field of view. Suddenly the sailboat turned sharply in a strong gust of wind and capsized, pitching the woman into the water.

Anne touched John's arm and pointed. "Look!"

He turned the boat and opened the throttle. They slowed next to the woman, who was desperately treading water five meters from her boat. He asked Anne to counterbalance while he helped the woman aboard. Even with Anne leaning to starboard, they rocked sharply as he pulled the woman up and over the side. The dripping woman crawled to a space just behind the seats, and John steered to the end of the sailboat's floating mast. He caught a line at the end of the mast.

As he held the line, he said, "Anne, can you take over the helm? I want to try raising the mast to right the boat before it sinks."

"Stand up. I'll slide in behind you."

With one hand on the top of the windshield and the other holding the line at the end of the mast, he stood and stepped gingerly to the center of the boat, while Anne slipped behind him into the pilot's seat. "OK," he said, "Give it some gas."

He grappled with the mast, which was weighted down by the wet sail, raising it little by little while she carefully opened the throttle. He balanced as best he could as their boat teetered.

Anne maneuvered closer and closer to the sailboat, and he pushed up on the mast. Just when the mast was as far up as he could reach, the sailboat righted itself, rocked in the wind, and started to

34

drift rapidly away from them. "Hang on!" Anne shouted, accelerating to catch up to the sailboat. Too late. He lost his balance and fell into her lap. "Sorry," she said, putting a hand briefly on his back to help him up. As she swung to port at the bow of the sailboat, he knelt on the starboard seat, reached out and grabbed a line dangling from the bow. He worked his way to the stern where he could hold the bow line while Anne piloted. As he stepped over the shivering woman, he said, "Go sit in the front where you'll have some shelter from the wind." By now they were close to their dock and agreed it was best to tow the boat there.

When Anne noticed the woman's lips were blue and her teeth were chattering, she reached for John's jacket and handed it to her. "You have a liter of cold water in your sweater. Why don't you take it off and put on the jacket?"

"O.K. Thanks."

"What's your name?"

"Chri – Christine."

"I'm Anne. He's John."

Christine glanced at John, whose eyes were fixed on the sailboat behind them, pulled off her sweater and put on his jacket.

Now, Anne had time to think about how good it felt to touch him.

At the dock, the man told them he would pump out the sailboat and keep it there until Christine could retrieve it. John and Anne turned their attention to Christine. John offered to drive her home.

"If you could just take me to my car, I can warm up there and go home and change."

They drove her to her car, where John insisted she keep his jacket and return it to him later. Anne suggested she drop it off at the bookstore, realizing as she said it that her possession of his jacket would assure she would see him again.

They waited for Christine to drive away. As they sat in the car, John seemed withdrawn, perhaps at a loss for what to do next. The day had not gone as he had planned, and the excitement of rescuing Christine and saving her boat was over. A little teasing might cheer him up. "Did you arrange all that to impress me?" she asked.

"No, I arranged it so *you* could impress *me*. You're an excellent pilot."

"It's impossible to live on the coast of Brittany and not know something about boats. Actually, I thought we made a pretty good team."

He nodded. "I was thinking the same thing."

"There's a lot of afternoon left," she said. "What would you like to do?"

"I'm not ready to take you home. Shall we go someplace for coffee?"

"Anywhere but Auray." Anne was not ready to go home either. Far from it.

"Find me a café in a quiet village," he said, "with a shaded terrace on a town square where old men play pétanque."

"Where do you think you are? Still in Bordeaux? Do you want to become a Breton or not?"

He reached for the door handle. "Shall I get my bagpipe from the trunk and give you a recital?"

"An American playing a bagpipe? Don't scare me like that. Let me think. I know. Let's go to Plumergat. It's north of Sainte-Anne-d'Auray. Just head toward home and instead of going left at the roundabout, keep going straight."

Another route to Plumergat would take them into Sainte-Anne-d'Auray, then north on his street. She thought it best not to go past his house. He might offer to show it to her. Once in his house, she would be tense, wondering what was next. Even with French men, these little games were tiresome, but with an American, Anne could only guess what to expect.

In Plumergat, they sat outside at a café across the square from three churches. She wanted to explain to him why such a small village had three churches on the same square, but she could not remember the story. After they ordered coffee, he noticed a *pâtisserie* across the street and said, "I'm hungry. I'd like to get a pastry. May I

36

get you something?"

"No thanks. But go ahead."

He returned with a piece of *far*, a Breton prune pudding, which he proceeded to eat with his coffee.

"Is this the American equivalent of teatime in England? Late-afternoon coffee and pastry?" she asked.

"No," he said, "It's just a habit of mine. I have a weakness for French pastry. But I don't indulge it every day. I don't want to end up overweight like a lot of my compatriots."

"So far, so good," she said, pointedly scanning him from head to foot, "as near as I can tell, anyway." *Until I see you naked.*

While he was finishing a bite of *far*, it seemed up to her to restart the conversation. She stopped trying to imagine him naked and fumbled for a safe topic, one that would not give a hint of what she had been thinking.

"I hope you won't need your jacket right away. I should have asked you before I offered it to Christine."

"You did the right thing, including stopping with my jacket. My shirt and blue jeans wouldn't have fit her."

She was surprised at a remark that seemed out of character. Up to now, he had been polite and proper, almost distant. She could not decide whether to engage him with a snappy comeback or let the comment pass.

"Is running a bookstore as much fun as it seems?" he asked.

She welcomed the return to an innocuous subject. "Most of the time it is. I know my customers. When it's not too busy, they look at a book and ask me about it. After they buy it and read it, we talk about it again. I get a sense of their taste, so I know what to recommend, and I get ideas of books to read myself. When it's too busy to chat, we make more money, so it's good either way." *Too much detail. Don't bore him.*

"I didn't see your mother in the store when I was there," he said, pushing aside the remains of his *far*. "Do you take turns working?"

"Usually. But if it gets really busy and the other's available, we aren't shy about asking for help. That's one advantage of a family

37

business; we don't count every minute we work."

"I don't think I could work with one of my parents. We get along fine as long as we don't see too much of each other."

Was he serious? Was getting away from his parents one of the reasons he moved to Brittany? He had a perplexing way of dropping little comments and not following up, leaving her with the impression that the subject was not one for further discussion. Like when he had mentioned his ex-in-laws.

"I get along with my mother most of the time, partly by necessity. When two people work and live together, they don't have a choice. They have to get along."

*Damn! I was not ready to tell him I live with my mother. Does he have any idea how disarming he is?* She played with the wrapper from a sugar cube, trying to figure out how to change the subject.

He came to her rescue again. "If you want to read a book, do you just pull it off the shelf and read it?"

"Of course."

"And when you've finished, do you put it back on the shelf and sell it like it's new?"

"Not if I've taken it home and read it." Was he serious or just teasing her? Either way, she did not want him to think she would sell a used book as new. "Don't worry, the books I sold you were pristine. But I'm always thumbing through books and reading parts of them. How do you think I'm such an expert on California, even though I've never been there?" Great segue, she thought. Now he would have to talk about California and why he moved.

But no. He turned it back to her again. "Have you ever thought of traveling there?"

"Yes, but it's a big expense. And . . . " Too late.

"And what?" he asked.

She stalled by lifting her cup to take a sip of coffee and finding it empty. Setting her cup down, she said, "It's not a trip I would want to take alone." She regretted leading them into a subject she preferred to avoid: her displeasure at being single.

"If I thought I would be there, I'd offer to show you around. Of course, I'll have to go back someday for a few weeks to visit my parents and make an appearance at my firm. You could time your visit to coincide with mine."

The invitation seemed too generous for the short time they had known each other, which made her suspect he offered knowing he would never have to deliver. But if that were so, why say it? *I don't understand these people.* "Be careful what you promise. By then you won't even remember me."

"Don't be so sure. I have to buy my books somewhere. And if I can judge by one visit, the service is excellent at the Librairie Renaud. You're likely to see more of me whether you want to or not."

By now she knew she wanted to see more of him—in more ways than one. "You'd better read your books before you say that. What if you don't like them?"

Another awkward pause, and once again, he rescued her. "Would you like another coffee?"

"Yes. Please."

He gestured to the waiter.

In spite of its uncertain beginning, the conversation began to flow, moving from one common interest to another. She noticed that when either was speaking, he looked her in the eye and that often, when it was his turn to speak, he gazed briefly across the square, no doubt assembling his thoughts and searching for the right words before turning back to her. She felt his attention, his presence in a way she had not felt with a man in years. So many men, it seemed, would look past her at the soccer game on the screen behind the bar or sneak looks at other women. When she next looked at her watch, she was surprised to see that an hour and a half had passed.

As they walked back to where they had parked, a little tease seemed in order. "How's the trunk space in this car?" she asked.

"I'll show you." He opened the tailgate and the trunk.

She looked into the trunk, then sternly at him, waiting for a reaction.

He knew he was cornered. "Go ahead. Say it."

"No bagpipe."

He smiled. "From now on, I'll watch what I say around you.

You don't miss anything.  I'd better take you home before you ambush me again."

As they arrived at the bookstore, a car vacated a parking space.  He pulled into it, turned off the motor, and turned to her.  "I'd like to see you again soon.  I'll call you."

Now what?  More guessing games?  Would he live up to the reputation of Americans and just disappear?  Did he expect her to sit next to the phone and wait for him to call?  Did she have nothing to say about it?  Not acceptable.  "In America, is it always the man who calls?"

He appeared surprised by the question.  "Not necessarily.  Over there, women call men and ask them out.  But many women are more traditional and prefer to be asked.  And here?"

"The same.  Would it bother you if I called you?"

"Not at all.  Call me for whatever reason or no reason.  Call me just to say hi and talk.  You don't need an excuse."  He had noticed and remembered her impulsive comment after their lunch.  One more connection.  They shook hands, and while their hands were still touching, Anne indulged a fleeting fantasy in which he took her in his arms and kissed her.

But she knew he would not kiss her today, no matter how much she hoped he wanted to.

# Chapter 6: My Best Friend

She went up to the apartment, to a shallow wicker basket on a cabinet in the hall where she had dropped the mail after coming up from the store. A busy morning in the store followed by getting ready to go out with John had left no time to deal with it. Now, while sorting the mail, a letter bearing her father's name and return address caught her eye. She could not recall how long it had been since he had last found time between working and chasing skirts to write to her. And heaven forbid he should actually pick up the phone and call her.

Inside the envelope, she unfolded a short letter and two pages of cross-ruled paper: a composition she had written for school when she was nine years old.

Dear Anne,

Going through storage boxes, I found this. I thought you might like to see it again. If you don't want to keep it, please give it back to me.

Love,

Dad

She went to her bedroom, sat down at her desk, and began reading her old composition. Its title: "My Best Friend."

"My best friend is my father. We do everything together. . . "

She stopped reading and sat staring at a drawing on the wall in front of her. The drawing depicted the Parlement de Bretagne in Rennes, a building beloved by the people of Rennes and carefully restored after a destructive fire in the 1990s. She folded the two pages and reached for the envelope, stopped, unfolded them again, and resumed reading.

When Anne was eight years old, she encountered her father fixing a broken door latch and asked if she could help. He showed her how to reassemble the parts and screw them together. When she completed the job with his guidance, he complimented her on her dexterity.  After that, whenever he had a home-repair project, he asked her if she wanted to help.  If he needed a tool or a part, he took her with him to Mr. Bricolage, a superstore for do-it-yourselfers, followed by a stop for ice cream, which they ate while discussing the project at hand.

At the end of a day of working together, they reviewed their work and congratulated each other.  When he tucked her in bed, she kissed his bristly cheek and inhaled a familiar musty, soapy aroma of old wool and shaving cream.

Her composition still in her hand, she sat staring out her window at the cars and pedestrians bustling about in the Place de la République and wondering why he sent her the composition.  To remind her of how close they once were?  If she called him to thank him, he might say something about why he had sent it.  No.  It was better not to stir things up.

She took out a piece of stationery and wrote:

Dear Dad,
>Thanks for sending the composition.  I'll keep it for now.
>Say hi to Florence.
Love,
Anne

She slid his letter and her composition back into the envelope and stored it in a desk drawer, all the way in the back.

## Chapter 7: See Him Again

Her mother was away for the weekend visiting Charles, her gentleman friend in Nantes. Charles's wife, one of Brigitte's best friends, had died five years before.

Now alone with her thoughts, Anne sifted through her mixed feelings about John, all the while resisting the urge to call him as she had hinted she might. She had seen him only twice and already knew him well enough to miss him, even sensing that seeing him again could lead to something she did not want to face.

She ate a quick dinner of leftovers, opened a book, put it down, turned on the television, turned it off, and picked up the phone.

She caught Sophie about to go out with her husband. Anne had known Sophie since middle school and shared with her the intimacy of having stumbled through puberty together. Some were put off by Sophie's uninhibited exuberance, but Anne found it refreshing and entertaining—most of the time. "Hang on," Sophie said, "I have to let the babysitter in." On returning to the phone, she added, "Michel has just decided he has to shave before we go, so I have a few minutes. What's up with you?"

"I met a man," Anne said, "We've gone out twice."

"Excellent! Tell me about him."

"Well first of all, he's American." She braced herself for Sophie's reaction.

"American! I am impressed. You are so cosmopolitan! Does he speak French, or do you talk to him in English with a cute little French accent? I hear Americans love French accents."

"He speaks excellent French. I hope he never hears me try to speak English. 'Cute' would not be the word."

She told Sophie about how he had asked her to lunch, how she had accepted on a whim, about rescuing Christine, about losing track of time in the café.

Sophie said, "You must absolutely see him again and tell me everything in great detail. What an adventure!"

Sophie seemed to have an insatiable appetite for tales of

Anne's single life. But at times, talking to Sophie about men reminded Anne that where she was in her life was not where she wanted to be. Anne protested impatiently, "I don't have time for an adventure. I'm ready for a family, a husband and kids—like yours." She said it with no sarcasm or bitterness, just a touch of envy.

"What does this guy – what's his name?"

"John."

"What does John have to do with having a family? You'll have a family soon enough. Here's what'll happen. After your kids have gone to bed, you'll be in the kitchen washing dishes while your sweet little husband watches rugby on TV. You'll finish the dishes and look around and say 'now what'? That's when you'll start thinking about John again and imagining all the excitement you missed. But it'll be too late."

As well as they knew each other, Anne was not always sure if Sophie was serious. "If life with a husband and children is so bad, why don't you ever complain?"

"What's to complain about? I have a great life. So do you. You just don't realize it. You keep waiting for another Jean-Louis to come along. Hey! Isn't John the English version of Jean? Maybe it's a sign. What's his middle name?"

"I don't know, but it starts with L."

A sign? Anne had learned over the years that behind Sophie's chatter, little gems often lurked.


Sunday morning. Anne was to meet her mother and Charles at noon at Bernard's home near Nantes for a family dinner. Thoughts of John distracted her as she dressed. Even after hinting she might call him, she wanted him to call her so she would know he wanted to see her.

What had provoked his move to Brittany? She did not expect him to tell her; it was not her business. Nor was she ready to tell him of her lingering childhood fascination with California. He might find it silly and provincial.

She thought of their long conversation at the café in Plumergat and how he looked away from her while gathering his thoughts but looked her in the eye when talking or listening to her. As mysterious as he was, something in his tone, his eyes, the way he responded to her made her feel alive and appreciated.

But as she inventoried all those things that attracted her, she felt herself losing control, exposing herself to disappointment. And for what? At best, they might become lovers, then break up in a few months or continue into a turbulent life of long separations, of family disapproval, of what else she could barely imagine.

It was 9:45. She had to leave for Nantes at 11:00. Just enough time for ten-o'clock mass. She finished dressing and walked up the street to the Church of Saint-Gildas. Anne's disdain for Catholic dogma did not stop her from attending mass occasionally, where the ritual, music, and grandeur brought her calm and perspective. But whenever a sermon denounced the evils of contraception or sex outside of marriage, she yawned visibly, hoping the priest would notice and expect her to rethink her sinful disrespect and come to confession, only to be disappointed when she failed to show up and recount the lurid details of her love life.

Father Kerbol was around Anne's age, with bushy black hair, a square jaw and steely eyes. Anne remained unconvinced of his priestly indifference to the world of the flesh. On the rare occasions when she went up to the rail for communion, she flashed him a subtle smile, which always made him look away. After one such episode, Anne, now safely back in her pew, imagined slipping into his compartment in the confessional and sliding a hand up under his cassock to give him an idea of what he was missing. Nobody in Auray, least of all Father Kerbol, would ever imagine Miss Proper Unmarried Bookseller harboring such evil fantasies.

Entering the church, she took her usual aisle seat on the right, in front of a painting of Saint Anne as she is often depicted: instructing her daughter Mary, preparing her for her unique destiny. Anne drew comfort from her saint, all the while harboring serious doubts about her existence—in Anne's view a harmless inconsistency.

Sometimes while contemplating the painting, she related silently what was happening (or more often not happening) in her life and tried to discern her saint's response. But not today. Anne's own misgivings were already strong enough without an imaginary lecture from a saint.

During mass, Anne pictured her extended family around the table later that day. She looked forward to seeing her cousin and lifelong friend Jocelyne, who was about to marry, and telling her about John. Her mind wandered from Jocelyne's wedding to imagining herself marrying John and leaving them all behind to go live in California, as if such a rash act were her only escape from the fate of ending up her family's spinster aunt, treated with outward respect but silently pitied.

For some reason, finding herself still single at age thirty-three bothered her more than it did other women her age.

Dinner that afternoon was much like any other French Sunday family dinner: an assortment of parents and children, aunts and uncles, cousins and grandparents, and often close family friends. The guest list varied from week to week as people went to dinner at the homes of their in-laws or were away on business or for long weekends. Today, Anne sat patiently through the endless courses and conversation, waiting for the moment when she could escape and take a walk with Jocelyne, away from prying ears.

Anne and Jocelyne shared a long history of standing by each other through the ups and downs of their love lives. Jocelyne was a philosophy teacher in a *lycée*, and even in her personal life was more likely to ask provocative questions than to volunteer advice. Best of all, she could be trusted not to broadcast to the rest of family whatever Anne might tell her.

They walked along a quiet street in the clean and carefully landscaped suburban housing tract, the sun muted by a light overcast. Anne told Jocelyne about John, fully expecting her to respond with the sensible thing: don't waste your time with an American.

Typical for Jocelyne, she offered no comment until Anne had finished. They walked another minute, then Jocelyne said, "He must be so different from any other man you've known." She sounded intrigued.

46

"He is different, and not just because he's American. He reminds me a little of Jean-Louis. He's about his age and every bit as sweet."

"Do you think you'll see him again?"

"Part of me wants to, but we could get too involved and he could pack up and go back to California. It's 9,000 kilometers away. I looked it up."

"A man who lives *nine* kilometers away could pack up and leave."

Jocelyne's reaction was not what Anne had expected. "Most men who live nine kilometers away don't have their family, friends, and job on the other side of the world."

"What do you have to lose?" They had reached the end of the street and stopped just short of where two boys were kicking a soccer ball back and forth.

"Time. That's what I have to lose," Anne said. With her wedding imminent, Jocelyne had already forgotten what they had often talked about: the relentless advance of age, their biological clocks ticking. "I don't have time for a fling. You know how old I am." The soccer ball went astray and rolled to Anne's feet. She picked it up and threw it to one of the boys.

"You talk like going out with him a few more times will ruin your chances, as if all the eligible men will hear about it and run the other way." They started walking back toward the house.

What was Jocelyne telling her? Was she encouraging her to keep seeing John, or help her see all the reasons why she should stop? Time to get to the point. "What would you do in my place?"

"I think I'd see him again and get to know him better. It's a chance to try something different. You don't have to marry him."

True. She did not have to marry him. Of course not. As obvious as it was, Anne had been too busy spinning up elaborate fantasies to realize it.

Encouraged by Jocelyne's simple wisdom, which concurred for once with Sophie's boisterous enthusiasm, Anne resolved to call John as soon as she got home. Jocelyne was right. To see him again was no risk. She could stop it anytime.

47

Driving back to Auray, she half listened to her mother's commentary on how well all the in-laws, including Charles, fit in the family. Anne almost asked her how she supposed an American son-in-law would fit in. It was not just another of her post-adolescent urges to needle her mother. Anne wondered herself.

Brigitte said, "I didn't have a chance to talk to Jocelyne. How are her wedding preparations coming?"

"We don't talk much about the wedding ever since I told her I'd rather not be a bridesmaid. Mostly we talked about John. She encouraged me to see him again. So did Sophie. I wonder what my engaged and married friends will do for their vicarious thrills if I ever get married."

As Anne expected, her mother did not comment. Brigitte rarely mentioned Anne's marital status, which was fine with Anne.

Suddenly Anne wanted to get away from her mother, to escape from the eternal sameness and loneliness of her life. She imagined dropping her mother at home, driving to Sainte-Anne-d'Auray and walking up Rue de Locmaria, knocking on doors until she found John, and dragging him into bed.

"You have a message on the answering machine," her mother called down the hall. Anne tried not to run.

"Hi Anne. It's John. Would you please call me when you have time. I hope to talk to you soon," followed by the machine's monotonic: "Call received today at17:47."

She went to her bedroom, closed the door, and called him. When he answered, she blurted out, "I'm glad you called. I was about to call you."

"What were you going to tell me?"

"That I wanted to see you. But you called first, so go ahead." She started to chide herself for having said too much, but realized that her opener, however impulsive it may have been, had been purposeful.

"I'd like to put our budding friendship to the test by asking you to reveal one of Brittany's deepest secrets."

Budding friendship. Was that what it was? "And what secret would that be?"

"How to move the Trembling Rock at Huelgoat."

"I, uh, why? Have you tried it?"

"Yeah, but I couldn't figure it out."

An American was actually talking to her about visiting a remote village in the interior of the Finistère, the westernmost county of Brittany. A snappy comeback was in order, if only to conceal her embarrassment that he had been there and she had not. "And after I show you how to move the Trembling Rock, shall I explain to you who put up all the megaliths and why? I haven't told anyone else, so it'll be our secret."

"Let's save that for another day. But I'll hold you to it. I thought we could also go to the Roc Trévezel in the Monts-d'Arée and Saint-Herbot."

"Sounds like fun," she said. "So when do we take this trip, Mr. Tour Guide?"

"How about tomorrow? I could pick you up at 10:00."

"Hang on," she said. "I'll be right back."

She found her mother in the kitchen. "Mom, can you cover my shift tomorrow morning? It's very important!"

"I think so." Barely suppressing a smile, her mother checked her calendar. "Yes. That's fine. Go ahead. Send me a postcard from California."

"We're not going to California. I think he's saving that for our fourth date."

How to move the Trembling Rock at Huelgoat. The answer had to be somewhere in the Brittany section of the bookstore. She was determined not to disappoint him.

## Chapter 8: I'll Take Care of You

By the time Anne was ten, her father had changed. More and more, when she asked him on a Saturday if they could do some project together, the answer was, "Not today. Maybe next week," and he went out, sometimes for hours. She coped with her disappointment by helping her mother in the kitchen or reading in her room. She began to notice that her mother did not smile as much as she used to.

Anne could only protest to her mother, powerless against whatever was taking her father away from her. She did not dare ask him. No matter what he said, his words or his tone might confirm her suspicion that he was tired of her, tired of spending so much time with her.

Her mother tried unconvincingly to explain away her father's absences with excuses that were all variations on the same theme: "He's very busy at work."

And then one day the excuses stopped.

Her mother asked her to come into the living room. "Dad and I want to talk to you and Bernard." The gravity of her tone gave Anne a strange feeling in her stomach. Something was wrong. Something terrible had happened. Entering the living room, she saw Bernard in a chair next to the television. She sat across the room, on the couch next to her mother. The lights were on and sunlight was filtering through sheer curtains covering the windows, yet the room seemed darker than before.

Her father shifted uncomfortably in his chair, beads of sweat appearing on his forehead. He began haltingly. "Mom and I have reached a decision. We are going to separate. I'm going to move out. This is not her fault. It's mine. It has nothing to do with either of you. Nothing will change between us."

Anne stared at her father, still absorbing what he had said. She turned to Bernard to see his reaction. Bernard's face revealed nothing. She turned to her mother, trying to make sense of what was happening. She saw only sadness.

Her father said, "Do you have any questions?"

Bernard jumped up and stormed out of the living room and out the front door, slamming the door behind him.

Anne shook her head, afraid of the answers she might hear. This could not be happening. It was not real. It was all a mistake. In a few seconds she would wake up, and all would be as it was. She got up and walked slowly to her room, shutting the door behind her.

A book her father had given her lay on her desk. She grabbed it and threw it as hard as she could at her bedroom door. It hit the door and fell to the floor. A few seconds later she heard a knock. The door opened, pushing the book aside. Her father took a step into her room toward her. He said, "Anne, I want to – "

She screamed at him, "Get away from me! I hate you!" and fell face down on her bed, covering her head with her pillow. The door closed quietly.

Minutes later, her mother came into her room, sat down beside her and rubbed her back, saying nothing. Anne turned over to face her mother. As far back as Anne could remember, her mother had been cheerful, quick to smile, always knowing the right thing to say. Today, that smile was gone, and the comforting words Anne expected to hear did not come. Nothing her mother could say would make this disaster go away—for either of them. Then and there, Anne decided it was up to her to help her mother any way she could.

"It's OK, Mommy. He was never here anyway. We'll be OK. I'll take care of you."

Her parents' sparse explanation for their breakup and her father's attempt to assure his children that they were not the cause were little comfort to Anne. If the family bored her father so much that he had to leave, it must have been her fault. The truth was now apparent: he had only pretended to enjoy her company. She was not good enough, not worthy of a man's attention, not even her father's.

## Chapter 9: The Dragon's Mouth

Monday morning, she tried on several pairs of pants and asked her mother which was the most flattering. Her mother was not very helpful. All she could offer was, "With a figure like yours, you can wear almost anything."

Anne finished making sandwiches and packed them in a picnic bag. After dropping off the bag in the bookstore, she took a walk through the weekly open-air market, which filled the Place de la République to her doorstep, spilling into adjoining streets. The streets, closed to traffic, were crowded with locals and tourists. Clothing vendors draped their booths with shirts, blouses, shawls of lace. Colorful displays of melons, artichokes, pears, lemons, oranges, and tomatoes drew the eye across the spectrum. *Charcutiers* chatted up anyone within range, deftly slicing off and offering samples of andouille.

The music man held his usual position behind racks of CDs in front of a huge *Gwenn Ha Du*, the white and black Breton flag. Today, she noted its resemblance to the American flag. Another sign?

As ten o'clock drew near, she returned to the store and found John inside, engaged in polite small talk with her mother. As Anne approached them, her mother was saying it was a perfect day for a drive; the sky was mostly clear, and mild temperatures had been forecast.

Anne picked up her bag, and they said goodbye to her mother. As they walked to his car on a back street to avoid the crowds at the market, he said, "Your mother is very nice. She asked me to call her Brigitte. She said *Madame* makes her feel old."

"She gets it from me. I hate it when someone calls me *Madame*." Anne was in a playful mood and for the moment did not even mind joking about her age.

They arrived at his car in Place de Keriolet. He opened the door for her, and while he went around to the driver's side, she reached into her bag and pulled out a package. "Before you start

52

driving, I have something for you." She handed it to him.

He opened the brown wrapping paper and pulled out a book: *Gardening for Dummies.* He smiled. "Thanks."

"I hope you're not insulted."

"Not at all. You just saved the lives of twenty innocent plants." Staring at the cover of the book, he added, "Every time I admit to some incompetence, are you going to give me a Dummies book?"

"Do you have a lot to admit to? This could get expensive, even at wholesale." There was something about him that begged her to tease him.

"That, *Mademoiselle*, you'll have to find out for yourself." He turned around and set the book and wrapping paper on the back seat. "We'd better get going. We have a lot of ground to cover."

Heading west on Route 165, they chatted casually about innocuous subjects until a construction zone took over John's attention. Red and white cones and barricades marked the roadway while yellow signs guided motorists through altered traffic patterns. Just west of Lorient, a sign next to the highway announced they were crossing into the Finistère. The sign reminded Anne of a startling discovery she had made when she was eight years old while studying a map of Brittany. She had run to tell her mother about it. "The west end of Brittany is the head of a dragon! Look!" she said, pointing at the map. "The Léon north of Brest is its nose, the Pointe du Raz is its lower lip, its chin is the Penmarc'h Peninsula, and the Crozon Peninsula is its tongue. See how it's forked? That's why it's called the Finistère. It's a code. It means dragons live at the end of the earth."

Her mother looked, smiled, and said, "It certainly looks like a dragon to me."

Two weeks later in school, Anne's teacher pointed to a map of Brittany and said, "The county at the west end of Brittany is called the Finistère, from the Latin *finis terrae*, the end of the earth." Before Anne could raise her hand and tell the teacher about her discovery, he added, "It's shaped like a wolf taking a bite of the Atlantic

Ocean."

Anne grumbled to herself, "It's a dragon!" Her discovery, it turned out, was not original. Others before her had noticed that the west end of Brittany resembled a ferocious animal. Her mother must have heard it before but did not want to disappoint her. Anne learned a lesson in school that day, but not the one her teacher had intended: Parents are not above hiding things from their children to protect them from disappointment.

With the construction zone behind them, John turned his attention back to Anne. "Have I managed to dismantle your stereotype of Americans, or do I have more work to do?"

"My stereotype of Americans? What makes you think I have one?" She thought it best to evade the question. What she had heard about Americans was not flattering.

"Maybe you don't, but most French people seem to. You know exactly what I'm talking about. We're a bunch of overgrown children, friendly but superficial. We make friends too fast, then move on. All we care about is money. We're loud. Let me know if I forget something."

He was chattier today, more relaxed. And by now he knew her well enough to expect a parry and riposte. "I hope you're not going to tell me Americans don't stereotype the French. Don't say anything; let me see how close I can come. We're snobbish. We're rude. We refuse to speak English to Americans even if we're fluent. All we do is eat, drink, sit in cafés and smoke, and sleep with someone else's spouse. How am I doing?"

"Totally accurate. I couldn't have said it better."

She tried her best to sound indignant. "Is that how you think we are?"

"Yes and no. French people like to eat and drink and smoke in cafés. But if I'm polite to them, they're polite to me. As for refusing to speak English, how would I know? I don't speak English in France."

It did not escape her notice that he had said nothing about sleeping with someone else's spouse. Perhaps the omission was intentional. She assumed he had been married to a French woman

54

and they had divorced, so perhaps for him as well, the subject was too close to home. Time to nudge the conversation in a different direction. "Shall we go on to stereotypes about Bretons?"

"I can't help you there. Americans don't have any. They don't even know you exist. When I tell Americans I've moved to Brittany, they ask, 'Is that somewhere in England?'"

"Maybe it's just the rest of the French who stereotype us. They think we're simple-minded and snub anyone from outside who dares to move here."

"You're hardly snubbing me. As for simple-minded, whatever your frailties might be, that doesn't appear to be one of them."

She appreciated the roundabout compliment. "Thanks. But back to your question, yes I've heard all those stereotypes about Americans, and you don't seem to fit any of them." More cautious now, she was going to stop there, but could not resist adding, "So far, anyway. My opinion could change, so watch your step."

"Don't get your hopes up. I'm not a typical American."

"So I gathered." In fact, he did not appear to be a typical anything.

"Maybe to be safe I should buy a French etiquette book, so I can learn how to behave. Do you know a good bookstore?"

She gave him a playful thump on the arm. Not only could he take some teasing, he could dish it out as well.

By now the sky had clouded over and a light rain was falling. He turned on the windshield wipers and asked, "Do you think it'll rain all day?"

"Probably not. The weather in Brittany changes constantly this time of year. Whether it's stormy or fair, warm or cold, it never lasts long."

"Does that apply as well to the women of Brittany this time of year?"

"That, *Monsieur*, you'll have to find out for yourself." *Gotcha!*

He was not ready to concede. "I can imagine what's coming next: *French Women for American Dummies*. On second thought, maybe I should go buy it myself from another bookstore so you won't know

55

I'm reading it. I could pick up that etiquette book at the same time."

"You wouldn't dare. We have a business relationship now, and you're stuck with it."

"I don't know what came over me," he said, feigning contrition. "I would never betray our relationship."

She was sure it meant nothing that he left out the word "business." What other kind of relationship could he have in mind? How could they ever be more to each other than casual acquaintances?

The highway led them across rolling hills of green farmland and forests, the bucolic vista interrupted from time to time by an industrial park or tract of identical white houses. As much as she was enjoying his company, she assumed nothing about the days, weeks, or months to follow, whether they would become friends or something more and fade out of each other's life when the novelty had run its course. She could only imagine he was thinking the same thing.

By the time they arrived at Sizun, the rain had stopped and the sky had turned a pale blue. They parked in the village's modest commercial area, which was separated from a churchyard by a triple arch. He pulled a guidebook from his glove compartment and handed it to her. She glanced at the guidebook and turned to him, her eyebrows raised in disapproval.

"Relax," he said. "I bought it before I met you."

They walked under the arch into the churchyard. The triple arch, topped with Corinthian capitals and sculptures of the crucifixion, seemed almost too grandiose for such a remote village. While Anne read from the guidebook and pointed out architectural features, John said little. She turned to see if he was listening and caught him staring at her, on his face a beatific little smile. She asked, "Are you listening?"

"I'm listening—and looking."

"Looking at what?" Apparently not the architecture.

"The wonders of Brittany."

His flirtatious foray gave her a little tingle. His pursuit of her, if that was what it was, had been cautious. In fact, the way he kept a certain distance had intrigued her. But now he seemed to be warming up, willing to come closer.

Leaving Sizun, they headed east, past the turnoff to the village of Commana, into the Monts d'Arée, a range of low mountains dominated by the Roc Trévezel, at 384 meters one of the highest points in Brittany. As the road rose along a ridge, forest and farmland gave way to scrubby heath, punctuated here and there by jagged rocks.

They parked in an unpaved lot across the road from the trailhead and ascended the short path to the rocky ridge. Near the top, he stepped up to a ledge and reached out to help her up. She needed no help, but took his hand anyway. As she stood beside him on the ledge, the moment for him to let go of her hand came and went.

At the crest of the ridge, a panoramic view stretched to the horizon. They stood alone, a mild early-August breeze blowing. To the south, a road disappeared over a barren hill, as if leading off the edge of the earth. To the north, a towering antenna stood as a sign that the modern world was not far away. Anne did her best to appreciate the view, all the while distracted by his warm, tender grip on her hand.

He said, "I love this place, as desolate as it is. But it's not a great place to come alone."

"You're not alone now," she said.

"Neither are you."

Still holding her hand and standing close to her, he turned to face her. She looked into his eyes, then her gaze drifted irresistibly down to his lips. They drew closer to each other, closer, coming together. He was soft and warm and gentle and tasted so good. She slid her tongue between his lips without thinking, then retreated, unsure of what he wanted. He responded, probing tentatively, seeking acceptance, finding it. When their kiss ended, she wanted to say something to him, anything, but no words came.

He broke the silence. "I like the way you kiss." He had switched at the right moment from the formal *vous* to the familiar *tu*. His manners, as always, were impeccable.

57

"I wasn't sure what to do," she said. "You're the first American I ever kissed."

"If I have my way, I'll be the last one." He let go of her hand and put his arms around her.

With her hands on his shoulders and her cheek against his, the rocks and hills below them seemed to blur and vanish. She was aware only of him, lost in the wonder of what was happening between them.

## Chapter 10: The Virgin and the Devil

Huelgoat—the Tall Wood in Breton—nestled in a gentle valley barely fifteen minutes by car from the stony outcroppings of the Roc Trévezel. As the road descended into the valley, the landscape changed dramatically from treeless, windblown heath to forests and glens. While she thumbed through his guidebook, they passed through the village and across a bridge next to a lake and up a short hill to a small parking area in a forest, little more than a wide space in the road, with room for five or six cars to pull straight in.

She finished reading about some of the sights at Huelgoat: the Trembling Rock, the Virgin's Kitchen, the Devil's Grotto, then slipped the book back into the glove compartment and got out of the car. A breeze whispered through the trees, the voices of sylvan spirits, she thought, standing guard over ancient traditions. It was not an idea to share with him. His country was practical and efficient, its people more at home in the material world. Yet he had been to this place before and for some reason wanted to bring her here.

At the end of a short path through the woods, a boulder the size of a house trailer stood alone in a level space on the side of a hill behind a sign announcing La Roche Tremblante, the Trembling Rock. After a moment's contemplation, she walked up to the end of the boulder and pointed. "Stand with your back in this crack and push up with your legs." He obliged. When the rock moved a centimeter or two, she said, "There, now you know all my secrets."

"How many times have you come here?"

"It's my first time."

He looked puzzled. "How did you know how to move the rock?"

"You're either Breton or you aren't."

"How long will it take me?" he asked, stepping away from the rock.

"Oh, I don't know," she said, raising a hand as if to examine her fingernails, then gazing off into the forest. "If you buy enough books from me, I might put in a word for you."

59

"When I'm ready to apply, you'll be the first to hear. Shall we go on to the Virgin's Kitchen?"

She feigned surprise. "Are you taking me home already?"

He turned to her as if to be sure he had heard her correctly and was met with a mischievous little smile. She could see he was amused.

They started down the path, their arms around each other. As they walked, an unfamiliar contentment washed over her, a sense of living richly in the moment, of comfort and ease in his presence. She wanted to share it with him. She asked him, "Are you happy?"

"Right now, I'm as happy as I can ever remember being."

"So am I," she said, pleased to feel so good with a man she had known for so few days, hoping the feeling would stay with her, fearing it would pass too quickly.

They walked on a path through the forest toward the river to the Ménage de la Vierge, the Virgin's Kitchen, a striking jumble of moss-covered boulders that were said to resemble the Virgin Mary's pots, pans, and furniture. The river appeared from under the boulders and disappeared again, the moss on the boulders highlighted here and there with a patch of wildflowers illuminated in sunlight diffused by the trees.

He said, "We've visited the Virgin. Let's go to the Devil."

"Sometimes when I'm sitting in church, I think that's where I'm headed," she said. "I may as well get a preview."

"Oh really?" he said. "Are you going to tell me what terrible things you've done or leave it to my imagination?"

She smiled. "Someday when we know each other better, you can tell me what you imagined."

They descended a steel ladder into the Grotte du Diable, the Devil's Grotto. In a chasm between massive boulders in the river bed, dark, damp rock faces surrounded them. Below, the river rushed between the rocks, as if the Grotto were the source of the Ellez, the river of the dammed in Breton legend. Cold air rose, stirred up by the torrent.

"It's a little chilly," she said. "Shall we go back up?"

60

He gestured toward the ladder, no doubt thinking it would be impolite to go first.

She climbed the ladder as gracefully as she could, apprehensive but hoping he was enjoying the view. She stepped off the ladder and watched as he bounded up with the agility of a twelve-year-old.

He planted himself in front of her. "Would you permit me to make an audacious observation?"

"Go ahead." With that lead-in, what could he possibly say?

"You have a fabulous ass." His tone was more reverent than lascivious, as if he were admiring a work of art in a museum.

Although his comment strained the bounds of etiquette for the short time they had known each other, Anne was pleased he had noticed and that it met with his approval. She started to acknowledge the compliment, but the words did not come. Instead, her face warmed with embarrassment. She looked down, away from him.

He set his hand lightly on her shoulder and said, "I'm sorry. I shouldn't have said that. It was out of order."

"Even if it was, it was a great compliment. Don't think you have to censor what you say to me." But even as she tried to reassure him, she felt conflicted, wanting to pull away from him but not understanding why.

"Come with me," he said, and led her to a nearby amphitheater surrounded by forest. They sat on the edge of the concrete stage. He looked forlorn.

"Are you aware that you're frowning?" she asked.

"I'm aware that we were having a good time until I ruined it. If I'm frowning, that's why. Now you must think I'm like every other man, interested in only one thing."

"It's not a crime for a man to notice a woman's body. And I meant what I said. It was a great compliment. I just didn't expect it." He had said too much too soon, but she would never tell him that. There was no need. He knew.

"It was bad manners. As simple as that. Will you just forget I said it?"

"No. I will not forget it. I intend to remember it and think about it often. Women need all the reassurance they can get on that subject."

He smiled sheepishly. "Well, even if I'd never said it, it would still be true."

She smiled back. How could she be offended by someone so sweet? Yet she could not quell her rising anxiety. Their day so far had been magical. They had kissed for the first time and were calling each other *tu*. But the uneasiness she had felt at the beginning had returned. His comment, however generous and well-intentioned, had stirred up all her misgivings about him, about them, about the impossibility of the two of them staying together for long.

As she looked out at the terraces of the amphitheater and to the woods and boulders around them, her mood darkened. She did not blame him and did not want to leave him thinking her gloominess was his fault; he was distressed enough already. She had to tell him the truth.

"John, I like you, but I'm not sure it's a good idea for us to keep seeing each other." It sounded too abrupt, almost brutal.

He looked dismayed. "Why not?"

"I don't know where this is headed. It worries me. I'll like you more and more, and someday you'll leave. Then what? I feel like I'm getting into something that could end badly." It was more than she wanted to say, but by now there was no decent way not to say it.

He nodded, his dismay turning to resignation. "I understand. I'm aware I have that handicap. I hope I can stay here, but it's too soon to know. Why can't we just take it a day at a time? I like you very much, even after knowing you only a few days. And it's a risk for me too. The same thing could happen to me. I could like you more and more and have to leave."

The mere mention that he might have to leave Brittany set her off again, started her thinking that seeing him might cause a serious suitor to pass her by. But she was not about to talk about marrying and starting a family. That was too much to share.

"I hope we can keep seeing each other," he added. "I feel good when I'm with you. I haven't had a day like this in a very long time."

He must be lonely, she thought. Why else would he want so much to keep seeing her? If it was sex he was after, it was not obvious. She decided it was all too complicated and the conversation too intimate for relative strangers. It was time to change the subject completely. "I'm hungry," she said. "Let's have lunch."

They sat at a picnic table next to the parking area. She reached into her bag and handed him a bottle of Plancoët water and a sandwich of fresh baguette filled with sliced hard-boiled egg, tomato, olives, and ham. As they ate, she berated herself silently for ruining the afterglow of their first kiss and the glow of contentment they had shared. It was her fault, not his.

Was this how American men and women got to know each other? Had his comment been too aggressive? Not really. If he were French, he might have done more than just look and comment. In fact if he were French, she might have insisted he go first up the ladder.

Neither spoke during the short drive from Huelgoat to Saint-Herbot. She reflected on the highs and lows of the previous two hours, trying to sort out how she felt about him and whether to keep seeing him, at the same time imagining he was still regretting what he had said. The silence was awkward, but speaking could restart the discussion that she had terminated by suggesting lunch.

The square bell tower of the church at Saint-Herbot appeared among the trees. To Anne, the tower resembled those of churches in rural England and seemed almost out of place in the back country of Brittany. Outside the church, they looked at a granite sculpture of the crucifixion atop a narrow column then went inside.

As they left the church, he said, "It's probably time to head home. What do you think?"

"I think so." Sensing he needed reassurance, she stopped outside the church and turned to him. "I had a good time today. I'm glad we did it."

"Me too."

If it was true that Americans said such things whether they

63

meant them or not, would he doubt her sincerity? She added, "I really meant that. I'm glad we came here together."

He looked puzzled. "So did I."

They walked back to the car.

After a few minutes on the road to the main highway, he pulled onto a dirt road into a forest and stopped.

"Why are we stopping?" she asked.

"I want to kiss you here so we don't make a scene in front of your apartment."

Another sign of his manners, she thought, to think that far ahead and not want to embarrass her. And not only was she pleased that he still wanted to kiss her after those uncomfortable moments, she knew she wanted to kiss him again.

He turned off the motor and leaned across the console. His kiss was tender and restrained, more affectionate than sensual. The stuff of cheap romance novels, she thought: kissing a handsome foreigner in a secluded forest. She understood now why she sold so many of them.

At that moment when a modest kiss should end, she felt him start to pull away and knew she was not ready; she wanted more. She slid a hand behind his neck and nibbled at his lips, probed him with the tip of her tongue. She was tempted for a moment to let go, to let their desire sweep them along and take its course. But it was too soon, too risky, too much out of her control. Reluctantly she eased away from him and caught her breath. "I'm sorry," she said. "I got a little carried away. I think we'd better stop there," then added, "for now."

He said, "Anne, I . . . "

"Yes?"

He looked away, at the steering wheel, at the key in the ignition. "Nothing. Never mind. We'd better go."

During quiet moments on the way home, she thought about the sentence he had not finished. "Anne, I . . . " What was he going to say? "Anne, I've never met a woman like you." Not likely. "Anne, I love you." Even less likely. It must have been something else. But what?

When they arrived in front of her apartment, he started to open his door.

She said, "Don't get out." They sat for a moment. "It's been quite a day."

He took her hand in his. "Yes it has. When can I see you again?"

"How about later in the week? Did you have something in mind?"

"Nothing in particular, maybe a movie or a concert. I'll think about it and call you later, maybe tomorrow."

"Unless I call you first." She squeezed his hand, kissed him on each cheek, and got out of the car.

A message from Sophie was waiting for her. Her husband was away on business and her children were spending the night with his parents. Anne called her back and, after explaining briefly where she had been all day, arranged to meet her for dinner at a *crêperie* in Landévant, a village just off the highway, halfway between Auray and Sophie's house in Hennebont. Although Anne could guess Sophie's reaction, she looked forward to talking about her day.

Sophie was waiting in the restaurant, her rusty red hair quickly visible from across the room.

After the waitress had taken their order and picked up their menus, Sophie turned to Anne. "I'm so glad you have a man in your life! Now let's hear it all. You get into a car with a mysterious American, you go off together for a whole day to the middle of nowhere in the Finistère. Don't try to tell me nothing happened. I want every detail."

When Anne described their first kiss atop the Roc Trévezel, Sophie said, "He sounds really romantic. Most men would just kiss you anywhere and not stop there."

"Yeah. Almost too romantic. He didn't just kiss me. *I* kissed *him*."

"That's what I mean. He took his time until you wanted to, and he picked a great place. "

"Not only did I kiss him, I didn't want to stop."

"I bet he didn't want to stop either. It's obvious he's madly in love with you."

However outlandish Sophie's dash to romantic conclusions might seem, Anne knew better than to dismiss her brash pronouncements too quickly. "Madly in love with me? I don't think so. I hope not anyway. If I keep seeing him, I'm doomed."

"If you put it that way, you're doomed no matter what you do. If you stop seeing him, you'll be alone again. Think of all the fun you'd miss—and all the fun I'd miss hearing about it. Hey, I've got the perfect solution for you."

"Let me guess. Sleep with him. Right?" Sophie's advice to Anne about her love life was rarely a surprise. If they had not been friends for so long, Sophie's voyeurism might have been disturbing.

"How did you guess? That's exactly what you should do. It'll clear up everything. Then tell me all about it. I'm dying to hear how Americans do it."

"Maybe I can find you a book that'll satisfy your curiosity. Don't expect to hear about it from me."

Sophie was undaunted. "Let's get to the important stuff. Does he turn you on?"

Anne thought of their interlude in his car in the forest. "Does he ever. Right after he dropped me off, I started thinking about how long it's been since – "

"So screw him. And stop worrying about what happens after that. It'll do you good. You're always happier when you're getting laid."

Anne glanced around the room at the other customers, sure that someone had heard. Nobody was looking at them, from which Anne concluded everyone had heard.

Exasperated, she turned back to Sophie. "You are incorrigible!"

## Chapter 11: The Concert of Despair

John called Tuesday morning, and they made a date to attend a recital of Celtic harpists in Lorient Friday evening. She wanted to talk more, to banter with him a bit, but was ill at ease on the phone, as if it were wrong to take any pleasure from him. Even making the date felt deceptive. But breaking it now would require a decision, and she was not ready to take such a drastic step without first seeing him again.

Over the years of their friendship, Anne had found Sophie's lascivious chatter amusing, even refreshing in its simplicity. From Sophie's point of view, Anne's life was an adventure, her future an unlimited wealth of possibilities. Anne's view of her own life was another matter, especially in contrast to Sophie's. Sophie had it all: charming, healthy children, a faithful husband, soft-spoken in public, but according to Sophie, a tiger in bed. But as devoted as she was to her family, whenever Anne needed her, Sophie would drop everything and come running.

Sophie's solution to the John dilemma was too simple. Yes, she could sleep with him for the carnal pleasure of it. His gentle strength, the warmth of his kisses, and his sensitivity all told her he would go along willingly and be a fine lover. And when the exotic thrill of an affair with a foreigner had run its course, she could ease away from him, telling him its end was inevitable.

But if what John felt for her was as strong as Sophie suspected, to sleep with him to satisfy her own needs of the moment then leave him would be selfish, even cruel. And for Anne herself, coming closer to him would make ending it later even more painful. The more she imagined making love with him, the more she wanted to and the more it was out of the question. No, they were both better off ending it now. How hard could it be to end a twelve-day relationship? Better to brave some brief discomfort and get it over quickly, like pulling a bandage off a wound.

Friday afternoon, Christine, whom Anne and John had

rescued in the Estuary, stopped by the store to return John's jacket. "I'm sorry I took so long to return it. It was full of salt water, so I had it cleaned." She gave Anne a box of chocolates for her and John and a note in an envelope. Anne opened the envelope and read the note:

John and Anne,
    Thank you for saving my life.
Kind regards,
Christine

Anne slipped the note back into the envelope, thinking the words were too strong. "We didn't exactly save your life."

"Don't be so sure. I can barely swim, and I wasn't wearing a life vest. I'm not usually so stupid." Christine said, then added, "If it's not indiscreet, where's he from?"

"California." A peek at Christine's ring finger supported Anne's impression that she was probably available.

"California? Since when do men from California come to Brittany and rescue drowning women? Is he here on vacation?"

"Sort of a long vacation, I think. He plans to stay a while, but I don't know how long." And that, of course, was the problem. Not something to share with Christine.

"Oh. I thought you were a couple."

Were they a couple? Enough of a couple that she would have to explain to him why they could no longer see each other. Enough of a couple that just telling him she was busy the next time or two he called would not end it properly.

Anne found Christine to be poised and charming and far more attractive than the drenched, frightened woman they had pulled from the cold water of the Estuary. She almost told Christine that John would be available shortly. Give him Christine so he could forget Anne. But decency and decorum prevented her from telling anyone else before telling him. That and a stab of jealousy.

After Christine left, Anne stared at the box of chocolates, then resumed her work. Each time she saw the box, it reminded her that she and John would not have a chance to share the chocolates. She put it in a cupboard out of sight.

Friday night when he picked her up, she gave him his jacket and Christine's note, but said nothing about the box of chocolates. It seemed simpler not to open a discussion about how they would share them. She sensed a reticence about him, which made her think he was responding to her mood. She felt dishonest, that she should tell him now. But why ruin the evening for him? Bad enough it was already ruined for her. Let him at least enjoy the concert. But they could not go on like this. She had to talk to him. Soon.

As they sat and listened, he took her hand in his, not knowing it would be for the last time. The gentle strength of his grip and the softness of his skin stirred up memories of the two of them standing together on the Roc Trévezel.

When they stopped in front of her apartment, he asked, "Can we talk sometime tomorrow?"

She could not bring herself to look at him. "I'm working in the morning and I'm not sure about the afternoon. I'll call you." Was there a reason he had said "talk" and nothing more? Her call would not be about their next date. Tomorrow would be the day.

"I should be home most of the afternoon. I'll expect your call." He leaned over the console and kissed her goodnight—on the lips, but with great restraint. She was starting to think he suspected what was coming.

In the store Saturday morning, preoccupied with what she was about to do, Anne plodded dully through her work. At 12:30 she closed the store, and without even a thought to lunch, called John and asked if she could come see him. He gave her directions, as if to someone delivering furniture.

She found the house easily. It was where she had thought it was when she first looked him up, almost in the shadow of the lofty nave and bell tower of the Basilica. When she arrived, his door was ajar. He opened it and motioned her in.

The front door opened directly into a light and airy living room, decorated like a summer rental: nondescript furniture and on the walls the usual prints of Breton seascapes. Unlike a typical French home where company is expected, both doors into the living room were open, one leading into a hall and the other through the dining room and kitchen to what appeared to be a veranda in back. A kiss on each cheek let her see up close how somber he looked.

He invited her to sit on the couch. On the end table, she saw the book she had given him: *Gardening for Dummies*. Pieces of paper marking several pages told her he had started reading it. He sat down next to her, a respectable distance away, and turned part-way toward her.

She was anxious to get it over with and laid it out quickly, as she had rehearsed it. "We have to stop seeing each other. The longer we put it off, the harder it will be."

He turned away from her and looked down. This was not going to be easy.

She went on. "I told you at Huelgoat I wasn't sure we should keep seeing each other. I need to explain why; you're entitled to know. I like you and I enjoy your company, but I'm thirty-three years old and I don't have the luxury of just doing what feels good now with no thought to the future. I have my education and my career. Now it's time to get married, to have children, and my time is running out. I – ."

"We've seen each other four times, and you've already decided that seeing me will keep you from finding a husband. Don't you think that's a little premature?" There was an edge to his voice that she had not heard before.

"Please let me explain." She was afraid he would derail her, make her forget what she had planned to say. "It has nothing to do with how I feel about you. I know that sounds phony, but it's true. You'll make a wonderful husband for some lucky woman. But it won't be me. It can't be. I mean, let's be realistic. Your family is in California. Your work is in California. Your roots are in California. You've said yourself you don't know if you can stay here. The more involved we got, the more I would dread the day you had to leave.

70

That's no way to live—for either one of us."

He had turned back toward her and was looking at her, hurt perhaps, skeptical, trying to make his own sense of what she was saying. "I wasn't exactly on the verge of proposing, but it's disconcerting to learn that I was disqualified before you even got to know me."

She glanced his direction and turned to stare across the room at the window next to the front door. "It would never work. What if one of your parents got sick? What if you decided you were too much an outsider here and didn't want to stay? You aren't one of us. I'm not one of you. You've never heard me try to speak English. Believe me, it's not pretty."

"Is that the only problem? That I'm American? Tell me the truth. If I've done something wrong, I want to know." He was leaning slightly toward her, not ready to disengage.

"That's the only problem. And it's huge. You've done absolutely nothing wrong. Nothing." *It's so simple, so clear, but he's not buying it. He thinks I don't like him.* "This is so hard for me. Please don't make it harder."

"It's hard for both of us. Maybe it doesn't have to be. Suppose we just meet occasionally for lunch or coffee?"

That would be an easy out, but the prospect was overwhelming, like she could not see him and stay in control. A clean break was the only way she could do it. "Not now. It would be too hard to see you and not . . . " This was not going according to plan.

"And not what?"

She had already said too much, and he was not going to let it drop. "And not remember all that happened on Monday."

"You mean what I said about – ?" He glanced down for a split second to her waist and below, probably not even aware he did it.

"No. No. Forget that! It was nothing. I overreacted. I mean the Roc Trévezel. I mean the dirt road in the forest. We can't just sit across the table from each other in a café and pretend that never happened. I don't go around kissing men like that and forgetting it the next day. Maybe someday we can be friends again. Not now."

She looked away from him, at the book on the end table. What she was trying to explain to him was so simple, so logical, so sensible, but it had gotten away from her. It was not so simple or logical or sensible to him. What had she expected him to say? "OK, no problem. It's been swell."?

"Those kisses meant a lot to me," he said. "It sounds like they meant something to you too." A change of tone, a softer expression, not moving, showing little, like an Englishman. If he were French, he would be up and pacing by now, waving his hands.

She clasped and unclasped her hands. "Please. Let's drop it." It was getting worse. He was getting to her. He was not going to let go of her easily. She looked away from him, toward the front door. "I've already said too much. I'd better leave now."

"Just like that? 'You're fired. Goodbye'? This may be the last time we ever talk. Will you stay a minute and listen to me? It won't take long."

"Of course. I'm sorry. Say what you want to say." She could guess what was coming. He would try to dissuade her as he had at Huelgoat. Better to hear him out, let him say it and get it over with. She owed him at least that much. Turning toward him, she saw his eyes reflect the light from the window.

"You warned me this could happen. All week I didn't dare ask what was going on with you because I knew and I didn't want to hear it. I tried to hope I was wrong, that you just needed a few days to yourself.

"If you don't want to see me, of course I'll respect your wishes. But I don't want to look back in a month or two or six and regret having let you leave with no idea how I feel about you. I refuse to slip into your past as just another fleeting acquaintance. Even if we never see each other again, I don't want you to forget me."

Now she knew he had been ready for her. Over coffee in Plumergat he had told her about how he prepared to argue in court. He did not script what he would say. Rather he outlined the points, picked the right words, then said it naturally. Otherwise the power of the words would be spent before they were said. Before she arrived, he had anticipated what she might say and thought of how he would respond.

She noted with relief that the edge in his voice and the hurt look were both gone, nor did it seem he would try to dissuade her. He would be gracious, tell her he liked and respected her and was sorry it did not work out. He would let her go, saying the right things as she left, leaving them both feeling fine. Twelve days. No time at all.

"You're telling me it's over," he said, "so I may as well just tell you the truth. I have nothing to lose. I don't know if you care, but I have to say it." He took a breath and went on. "I can barely find the words to tell you what a loss I feel. You're an extraordinary woman. You have it all: beauty, intelligence, humor, a radiant personality. You don't even seem to realize how attractive you are, and that makes you even more attractive."

She looked away, at the window, at the doorway behind him, anywhere but at him. *He can't mean this. Why is he saying it?*

There was more. "When we were on our way to the Monts-d'Arée, talking and teasing each other, I felt such a connection with you. I thought it meant something more than just a few minutes of fun. I was starting to think we were made for each other. I don't know if that makes sense. I wish I could explain it better."

There was no need to explain. She had felt it too, but this was not the time to tell him.

"I can guess what you're thinking," he added, "that I'm naive, that I barely know you. Maybe I'm wrong about you, about us. I don't know. All I know is how I feel right now."

In spite of his distress, he was poised and eloquent. Now, even more, she understood why she was so drawn to him. Now, she wanted to hold him, to take it all back. No man since Jean-Louis had spoken those words to her. John could have said them to any of thousands of receptive women, but he was saying them to her, saying the words and letting her go, expecting nothing in return. Sophie was right after all. In so few days, they had already gone too far. All the more reason to stay the course and get out now, before it really was too late. There was no turning back.

"I won't call you," he said, "And I won't come to the bookstore, if that's what you want." He turned his gaze away from her, to the floor in front of them. "You can go back to the pleasant, unthreatening life you were leading before I came along and tried to mess it up." He turned to her. "I'm sorry. I shouldn't have said that." Although he was trying hard to be gracious, his hurt was starting to show.

"I don't blame you for being bitter. I led you on. I was wrong to do that. I should've known you'd be mad at me."

"I'm trying not to be. I'm trying to accept that you know what you want in your life and that I won't be part of it. I don't like it. I don't like it at all, but I'll have to live with it."

She got up and started toward the door. He followed her to the door, opened it for her and said, "If you ever change your mind, don't be too proud to tell me. You know where to find me."

As she started out the door, something stopped her. She turned and looked at him. His face betrayed a mix of emotions: disappointment, sadness, resignation. How could she make him understand? Stepping back toward him, she put her arms around him and hugged him. She felt his arms around her, starting to pull her close, then letting her go.

As she drove away, she imagined he was standing at the door watching her, but she kept her eyes fixed on the road ahead of her. She stopped at the end of his street, torn between the urge to turn around and go back to him and the compulsion to leave him far behind. Left would take her back to Auray, back to her life before John. Instead, after a moment's reflection, she turned right and parked next to the Basilica. Leaving her car and entering the Basilica grounds, she walked across the courtyard into the Basilica and sat for a moment in the quiet sanctuary in the presence of her saint, trying to understand what had just happened.

She had often daydreamed about being married in the Basilica, seeing herself standing with her groom in front of the altar.

Today, as she tried to picture his face, all she could see was John.

## Chapter 12: Turning the Page

Sunday morning, Anne lay in bed trying to make sense of what she had done, trying to fathom his reaction, trying to understand her own. How could he have such feelings for her after so short a time? Perhaps he was lonely, desperate for company. But he never seemed desperate, even when he knew he was losing her.

She arose and put on a robe. Even now in late summer, mornings were chilly. Opening the window and the shutters, she surveyed the Place de la République, where she lived and worked, the center of her world. What was there to see that she had not seen many times before? Aside from some early risers returning from the *boulangerie* with fresh bread and croissants for breakfast, the square was empty.

Ending a relationship with a man was nothing new; she had done it many times—too many times, followed sometimes by a touch of regret, a bout of loneliness. But never since Jean-Louis had she been left with such a sense of loss. Was it because of John or the hopelessness of her whole life?

"Now you can go back to the pleasant and unthreatening life you were leading before I came along and tried to mess it up," he had said. In spite of his disappointment, he had tried hard not to be bitter, done his best to let her go without a scene. But he did not believe her life before him was so satisfying. Nor did she. Floating along on a fantasy of meeting Mr. Right and living happily ever after had not been much of a life. And now, it occurred to her that she might have met Mr. Right and rejected him less than two weeks later.

No. That was nonsense. John was not Mr. Right. Her instinct was correct: a man who could pack up and move thousands of kilometers away at any moment was not for her. She had regained control of her life. It had been her decision, made for good reasons, carefully thought out—a rational decision, sensibly done to save them both from heartache.

So far, it was not working.

The next day, Sophie called. "Well?" she asked, "Did you do

it?"

"I told him we had to stop seeing each other."

"Anne! I can hardly keep up with you. Why did you do that?"

Anne went through it all again for Sophie, hoping at the same time to convince herself that she had made the right decision.

When Anne had finished, Sophie was unusually serious. "What he said doesn't surprise me. From the way you described how he was with you, I could have guessed he wouldn't take it well."

"I'm not taking it so well myself." Not well at all, in fact.

"What am I going to do with you? I try my best to fire up your love life, but you manage to stay one step ahead of me. Do you want to get together this weekend?"

"I don't feel very sociable right now. Let's talk later in the week."

Friday morning Sophie called and invited Anne to dinner that night. One of her husband's colleagues was invited, along with another couple that Anne had met. Sophie assured her the colleague was single and attractive and said Anne could fake a headache if she wanted to leave early.

The postman delivered the mail. Among the usual invoices and catalogues, Anne found a letter hand-addressed to her, its return address: J. Becker, Rue de Locmaria, 56400 Sainte-Anne-d'Auray. She opened the envelope, unfolded a single sheet of paper and read,

Anne,

I miss you.

John

She turned the letter over and looked again in the envelope. That was all. He had promised not to call her and not to come to the bookstore, but had said nothing, perhaps purposefully, about not writing to her. She had known him for twelve days and spent the next six trying to forget him. She told herself yet again that she had made the right decision.

Why then, she wanted to know, was her heart pounding?

That evening, as she drove to Hennebont to Sophie and Michel's house, she resolved to put John out of her mind and do her best to have a good time, to meet Michel's colleague and try to like him.

Anne was the last to arrive. Sophie introduced her to Paul, who was about Anne's height, with sandy brown hair and a craggy face, which would have been handsome but for a self-important grin. As he shook her hand, instead of looking her in the face, his eyes darted down to her legs and back up again. Not a good start. Was John the only man left in the world who would look a woman in the eye and perceive a brain behind the face, a person and not just a body?

Sophie seated them together in a corner of the living room and, after serving them each a glass of cider, went to sit across the room with Michel and the other couple.

Paul wasted no time. "I hear you work in a bookstore. I'm planning a vacation. Do you have a good travel section?" He addressed her as *tu*, which was not appropriate for adults who had just met. Even John, whose native language made no such distinction, knew not to do that.

"Good enough for visitors to Brittany. Not many people come to Auray looking for guidebooks to far-off places like California." She saw Sophie glance at her and turn back to her own conversation. Only then did Anne realize what she had said.

Paul continued, "Interesting you should mention California. I was there two years ago. I could have skipped Los Angeles, but the drive up the coast wasn't bad." He launched into a monologue about his travels, displaying a stunning lack of real interest in the places he had visited. His concept of travel seemed to consist of browbeating flight attendants to get a better seat and sneaking contraband past customs officers. At another time, Anne might have taken him on and, with a few cutting remarks, put him in his place. But tonight, as Paul yammered on, feeding his voracious ego, she sat quietly, pretending to listen, thinking of how satisfying it had been to have a

78

conversation with John—a real conversation.

At the end of the evening, Paul walked out to her car with her and suggested they go somewhere for a drink.

She pointedly looked at her watch. "It's late. I have to work tomorrow," she lied.

"I'll call you."

She took her car keys from her purse and opened the door. "It's best you don't."

"Are you seeing someone?"

"Yes," she lied again, getting into her car without even bothering to shake his hand. "Goodnight."

## Chapter 13: At the Market

While dressing the next morning, Anne found herself brooding yet again over the sorry array of men still available at her age. Most of the straight and single men were egotistical creeps, like Paul. Or they were divorced and burdened with children, support payments, and hostile ex-wives. Anne had resolved long ago never to marry a man with children. When she had been made a stepdaughter with no say in the matter, she vowed never to impose that role on any child.

Now, after a week of trying to forget John, she could think of nothing but him. She picked up his letter and reread it. "Anne, I miss you. John" So refined—telling her how he felt but not insisting. She turned away from thoughts of their first kiss, up on the mountain, the highest part of Brittany. Right now, she felt like the lowest part of all France.

She did her best to make cheerful small talk over breakfast, wishing she could allay her mother's concern about her, knowing the effort was futile. Anne and her mother knew each other too well. But whatever concerns her mother might have, she was careful not to intrude.

Brigitte left the table to finish dressing for the morning shift in the store. A glance at the clock told Anne it was time to stop fretting and go to market to buy fresh fish and fruit and vegetables for lunch at home with two of her mother's friends.

She picked up her shopping bag and walked to the upper end of the Place de la République to Les Halles, the covered market in the City Hall building. As in many French towns and villages, shopping at the public market was a reassuring constant in a fast-changing world. Merchants and shoppers took time to chat—about cauliflower, artichokes, and apples, about the invasion of rich Parisians buying second homes in the area.

As she entered the market hall, the smell of fish overpowered the more subtle fragrances of fresh fruit. On busy days like today, voices blended together and rebounded harshly from the hard tile surfaces. She went from counter to counter, weaving among other customers, exchanging greetings with vendors and buying what she needed.

Leaving the fish counter with her package of John Dory, she glanced around at the various vendors to be sure she had not forgotten anything. Something caught her eye. On the other side of the poultry counter, talking to a farmer across a display of Plougastel strawberries stood John.

Now what? Turn and leave? Go over to him, say hello and make inane conversation about the weather? Tell him she missed him? He turned to put his wallet away and saw her. They stood motionless, their eyes fixed on each other, oblivious to the people walking between them with their bags of groceries.

She dropped her package into her bag. He put his wallet in his pocket and walked over to her, stopping barely a meter away. He had said he would stay away from her, but now, here in a public place in a chance encounter, she was fair game.

"*Bonjour*, Anne." Simple and polite.

"*Bonjour*, John. Are you well?"

"I've been better."

What had she expected? A perfunctory exchange of pleasantries?

"I got your note," she said.

"I hope you're not upset that I wrote you."

"No. I'm glad you did. I've missed you too." She looked away, back toward the fish counter, groping for what else to say. As pleased as she was to see him, it was hard to face him. She thought of where she had been the night before, trapped with Paul, yearning to be with John. "I'm not sure I did the right thing." He had not lost his talent for getting her to blurt out what was on her mind.

"You already know what I think. I understand why you did it, but I'm still having a hard time with it."

Her bag was getting heavy; she shifted it to her other hand. "The problem is still there," she said. "I don't know what to do about it." As she spoke, other shoppers stepped around the two of them, paying them little attention, unaware of what was happening between the man and woman who were blocking part of a passage between two counters. Anne herself barely knew.

"It's all still there," he said, "the problem, as you put it, and everything else, everything good between us. Seeing each other was risky for both of us, not just for you. Both of us might have had to make sacrifices. Everything worthwhile has its price. Like right now. I got to have one more look at your beautiful face, and now I'll go home and miss you even more." Yet again, he was eloquent in his distress.

"Is my beautiful face as red as it feels?" she said.

A brief and feeble smile passed over him. She had seen that smile on someone else, somewhere before, but could not remember where.

"John, I'm so confused right now. I need time to think. I'll call you. I promise." She took a step toward him and kissed him on each cheek, adding, "Don't forget your strawberries." He looked back at the strawberry counter where the smiling farmer pointed to John's package at the edge of the counter.

She went out the glass double doors of the market hall to the porch, down the steps and across the narrow street to the sidewalk. After passing several stores, she stopped and turned, not surprised to see him at the railing on the porch just outside the market, watching her. She looked back at him for a few seconds and turned to walk the short distance home, aware of his eyes still on her.

She took some pleasure in imagining where his gaze was most likely fixed.

At the door to the apartment, it came to her where she had seen that feeble smile: on the face of a beggar outside a church. Anne had given him one euro. He was letting her know he was not ungrateful, but had hoped for more.

Taking the groceries to the kitchen, she unwrapped the John Dory, rinsed it, dried it, put it on a plate, and covered it with a paper towel. She put the plate in the refrigerator next to the *crème fraîche* and checked the other ingredients, which her mother had left in a tray on the counter: salt, pepper, white wine, butter. As she took the leeks out of her shopping bag, she sensed something was missing from the ingredients. Should she add some sorrel? Such an important decision would have to wait for a conference with her mother.

Trying hard to keep her mind on what she was doing, Anne cut the green stalks off the leeks, sliced and washed the white parts. After washing and drying lettuce for the salad, she went to the dining-room cabinet, got out a tablecloth and unfolded it on the table.

She would keep her promise to call John, as soon as she could figure out what to say to him. She thought of what he had just said about risks and sacrifices. Had she been selfish to think only of her own risk, her own inconvenience? But what possible future could they have? Marriage was out of the question. How could she ask him never to leave Brittany? His sense of responsibility to his family was part of him. She respected him for it. And what about his work? What if his firm decided he had to return to the office or quit?

Spending part of the year in Brittany and part in California was equally fanciful. However enticing the thought of visiting California someday, she knew that living there was out of the question. The basic English she had learned in school barely equipped her to order lunch in England. When she watched American movies, she understood little. She would always be an outsider, far from her family and friends.

Then she imagined the worst: suppose they married, had children and he left? Children should not grow up without a father in the home. She thought of her brother Bernard and how he had turned rebellious after their father moved out, and of her own despair.

She emerged from her reverie to notice she had put out the wrong tablecloth. Time for a break. She went to her bedroom and called Jocelyne.

She told Jocelyne how she had stopped seeing John, about his letter, their chance meeting at the market, and her latest litany of impossibilities. "I was thrilled to see him, then I started in again with all the negative stuff."

"You like him. You enjoy his company. What's the harm?"

"As long as I'm seeing him, I won't meet other men. I'll be

83

too comfortable and everyone will assume I'm not available. Not only that, I'll compare any other man to him, and nobody will measure up."

"You've known him barely two weeks, he's become your gold standard, but you don't want to see him. What am I missing here?" Anne thought she detected some impatience in Jocelyne's voice.

"I'm afraid of what might happen if I keep seeing him."

"You might like him more, or you might lose interest. What does it matter? You can end it whenever you want."

"To see him knowing I'm going to end it would be dishonest, like I'm taking advantage of him." Appeal to Jocelyne's basic integrity. That would convince her.

"It's not dishonest if you tell him and he agrees." Jocelyne had not even met John and seemed to be defending him. Her logic was compelling.

Anne heard the front door open and close.

"I have to go. Mom just came up from the store. We're having company for lunch and I need to help her."

Anne hung up and went back to the kitchen. Her mother had already picked up where Anne had stopped.

"I'm sorry. I was talking to Jocelyne."

"How is she? Nervous about the wedding? Hand me the leeks."

"No. She's fine. I'll finish setting the table." Anne started back to the dining room.

"Did you shuck the oysters?"

"I forgot. My mind is elsewhere."

"So it seems. Finish setting the table. I'll do the oysters." Her mother was rarely so directive with Anne. She must have known that Anne's mind was likely to linger wherever elsewhere might be—not that it was any great mystery.

Marie-Josephe and Gabrielle were two of Brigitte's closest friends. Anne had known them all her life and sometimes thought of them as her mother's counterparts to Sophie and Jocelyne. Marie-Josephe was simpler, quicker to say what was on her mind. Gabrielle tended to be more thoughtful and less inquisitive. Because Marie-

84

Josephe had two sons and Gabrielle had no children, Anne's life was always of interest to them, as unorthodox as it might seem at times. Nonetheless, both tended to be circumspect when making conversation with Anne. Brigitte must have told them that asking Anne about her love life risked a sharp retort.

After all were seated at the table, Gabrielle asked, "Anne, I haven't seen you in a while. What have you been up to?"

"Nothing much. I went boating in the estuary. A sailboat capsized and we went to the rescue. That's about all."

Marie-Josephe asked tentatively, "Were you with your American?"

"He's not 'my American.'" Anne found the question mildly irritating, as if John were a curiosity and not a person.

"You're no longer seeing each other?"

"No. We went out three or four times. That's all."

Brigitte passed the platter of oysters to Gabrielle. "Go ahead and serve yourself."

Marie-Josephe continued to chatter. "I don't know any Americans. I hear they're friendly but superficial, that they move on before you have a chance to really get to know them. Of course, we have to be careful about stereotypes, don't we?"

"We certainly do. He's not at all superficial," Anne said as Gabrielle passed the platter of oysters to her. It did not escape Anne's notice that Marie-Josephe was pursuing the subject by talking in generalities. But Anne was warming to the idea of talking about John, and she could turn it off if it seemed to be going too far.

"Did he go back to America?"

"No. He has a house in Sainte-Anne. He plans to stay indefinitely."

Gabrielle tried to rescue Anne from Marie-Josephe's interrogation. "You don't have to talk about him if you don't want to. You know we love you, so we're interested in what's happening in your life."

"It's no secret. I stopped seeing him. It was my decision."
*Some decision.*

"What was he like?" Gabrielle asked, now indulging her own

85

curiosity about this mysterious American.

"He's sweet, strong, handsome, polite, intelligent, honest." Anne could hardly believe what she heard herself saying. Why would any sane woman stop seeing a man of that description?

Gabrielle must have been thinking the same thing. "With all that to recommend him," she asked, "you stopped seeing him just because he's American?"

"In effect, yes. That sounds terribly provincial, doesn't it?" Anne realized she was holding an oyster shell and gesturing with it. She set it down on her plate.

"Do you think you'll ever see him again?" Gabrielle asked.

"Yes," Anne said. "I will. I'll see him again."

## Chapter 14: A Second Chance

The conversation turned to other topics. While her mother chatted with Gabrielle and Marie-Josephe, Anne got up to clear the plates and serve the salad, lost in thoughts of what she would say to John and how he might react.

Gabrielle and Marie-Josephe left. As she washed the dishes with her mother, Anne asked as casually as she could, "Mom, do you need the car this afternoon?"

"Not until seven. I'm going to Aunt Gilberte's for dinner, remember? You're still welcome to come if you want to."

"I have things I need to do. I'll have the car back before seven."

"I'll finish the dishes. Go do what you need to do."

Anne glanced at her mother, who was busily washing dishes, and saw a familiar little smile, a look of understanding that she had seen many times before. Anne took off her apron, hung it up, and left the kitchen, silenced by a touch of embarrassed pleasure at her mother's encouragement. So far at least, her mother did not seem to share Anne's misgivings about John.

She went to her bedroom and stood contemplating her space, a microcosm of her life—secure, small, and unchanging. Books she had read as a child remained neatly arranged on her shelves. Only recently had she given her Tintin and Astérix books to her niece and nephew, but she could not let go of her collection of Anne of Green Gables, which she had read and reread. As a child, she identified with the mythical Canadian Anne, especially her penchant for talking herself into–and out of—trouble.

On her dresser, a mahogany frame displayed a photo of her family, all four of them, taken not long before her father moved out. From time to time over the years, she picked up the photo and stared at it, losing herself in fond memories of when she was part of a real family. In the photo, eleven-year-old Anne smiles impishly at the photographer, proud of some quip she has just made, pleased at his response to her childish flirtation. Bernard frowns, fidgets, wants to get done and go join his friends at the café. Her mother, the central pillar of a structure on the verge of collapse, puts forth her bravest face. Her father smiles as if all is well, there in body only, his heart already out the door. Why did he leave? What was missing from his family life? Anne was determined not to repeat her mother's mistake. She would find a faithful husband—one who would not cheat and abandon her.

Anne studied her face in the mirror. She saw no signs of aging, but for how much longer? Makeup added little to her eyes, and the classic shape and color of her lips allowed her to dispense with lipstick most of the time. And if she could judge by the way John responded when they kissed, her lips seemed to meet with his approval.

For a few playful seconds she imagined going braless to see him. The idea was exciting, but the look too brazen. She pulled off her top, slipped off her bra, and looked in the mirror again. What would he think of her breasts? Would he ever see them? She tried to discern if they hung lower than they used to. Still firm and shapely but not large. Good enough. She put her bra back on and a different top—light blue and clingy.

She opened the window and looked out over the square. It was quieter now than in the morning. Many townspeople had finished their work week and were home enjoying a leisurely lunch followed by a nap. She went to the phone, took a breath, and punched in his number.

When he answered, she said, "John, it's Anne. I want to come see you. "We need to talk."

"When?"

"Right now?"

"I'll be here."


As she drove out of Auray toward Sainte-Anne and rehearsed her speech, she thought he might be put off by what she was about to propose. She reconsidered how she would present her presumptuous idea to make it more appealing. Break the ice, give him a taste of what could be his, then talk.

She parked in front of his house. The front door was ajar. This time, free of the gloom that shadowed her first visit, she noticed purple hydrangeas in pots next to the door. They looked healthy. He must have been studying *Gardening for Dummies*. He appeared in the doorway, looking receptive but restrained. She looked over the car at him and smiled. What did he think she was planning to say to him?

He stood aside and motioned her into his living room. As she entered, she dropped her purse on a chair near the door. He closed the door behind her and turned to her. She stepped close to him and ran her hands up his arms, feeling his muscles under his shirt. He looked quizzically at her, waiting for her to say what she had come to say. Instead, she kissed him, confident this time that she knew what he wanted, determined to bring him under her spell. When she slid her tongue between his lips, he pulled her close to him and responded in kind. She felt his hands on her back, the warmth of his body against hers, so close now she felt him getting hard. There would be time to talk later. Right now –

Abruptly, he let go of her and stepped back. "You wanted to talk," he said, catching his breath. He must have sensed she would have followed him straight into bed, but he had not forgotten her reason for coming to see him. He was not like other men she had known. Whatever it might be that drew him to her, it was something more than sex.

He led her to the couch and sat down next to her, closer than last time. He turned toward her, waiting for her to speak.

She tried to remember what she had prepared so carefully to say. Instead of bringing him under her spell, she had fallen under his. She began haltingly, "I think you know what I've been struggling with." She looked at him, as if asking for confirmation.

"You made it clear. You want to get married, and if I'm around when the right guy comes along, you'll miss your chance." He sounded skeptical.

"I'm willing to take that risk now."

"What changed?" He still sounded skeptical.

"I thought if we stopped seeing each other, we'd both get

over it quickly and move on. But it didn't work out that way. The longer we were apart, the more I missed you, the more I wanted to see you. After I read your letter yesterday and saw you this morning, I started thinking of how we could see each other again." No need to mention her ordeal of the night before, stuck with Paul, wishing she were with John.

He took her hand in his and looked down at it, as if examining a piece of merchandise and deciding whether to buy it. "I can't imagine you've suddenly changed your plan for your entire life just for me, a man you barely know." He sounded suspicious, like it was too good to be true, that there had to be a catch.

And in fact there was a catch. Now, the moment of truth. "I'm embarrassed to say what I have in mind. It's a little selfish. I want – Would you be willing to see me with the understanding that it's temporary?"

"And when you meet a man who meets your specifications better than I do, it's over. Is that it?"

"I have to be honest with you, and I don't want to hurt you again, especially after what you said last Saturday." She turned his hand over on the couch between them and put hers on top of it, interlacing her fingers with his. "I didn't expect you to say what you did."

"I said way too much last Saturday. I thought I'd never see you again. I must have sounded pathetic."

"No. Not at all. I thought you were eloquent, like you probably are in court. Listen. As much as I like you and want to be with you, there's only so much I can give you. I know what I want in my life. I don't know what you want in yours. Maybe this won't work for you." Yet again, she had gone beyond what she had planned to say. When he did not respond, she added, "Are you willing to see me under those conditions?"

He looked down at her hand in his, then toward the window.

*He's going to say no, that it's all or nothing. I don't blame him. What a stupid idea. Why would he accept terms I would never agree to myself? Try to save face before he tells me how selfish I am.* "If the answer is no, just tell me, and I won't waste any more of your time."

"If it means I can see you again and this is the way you want it, I accept, but with some conditions of my own."

Maybe her idea would work after all, if she could live with his conditions. "I'm listening," she said.

"If you meet another man, don't keep it from me."

He was not asking for much. "Of course. I would never see you and someone else at the same time without telling you. What else?"

"If you decide again to stop seeing me, don't tell me we can't stay friends. Even if you meet another man and marry him, I can't let you go completely."

Now she realized what had been missing from her brilliant idea: what would happen when it ended. When she had imagined a carefree, just-for-now relationship, she had not permitted herself a glimpse of its inevitable end.

"OK," she said. "It's a deal." Now, when Mr. Right came along and she had to tell John it was over, they would stay friends and not lose each other. Suddenly it was all so simple, so easy, so free of risk. But the rules had to be the same for both of them. "And if you start seeing another woman, you'll tell me?"

"The only woman I want to see is sitting next to me."

He looked at her like it was her turn to speak, but she was done talking for now, eager to resume where they had left off, to follow her friends' advice and live for the moment. Her hand found its way to the back of his neck. She gave him a little tug and they were kissing again, his arms around her. He allowed a hand to drift down to her waist, lingering there, perhaps deciding what to do next, as if there were anything left to decide. In case he had any doubt, she murmured, "I want you."

He gazed at her with his amber eyes, narrowed, intense. Then a little smile and a nod, sliding his hand back up, this time under her top. He unhooked her bra and moved his hand to her breasts. She quivered as he caressed her. She stroked him everywhere she could reach. They stood up and started toward his bedroom, stopping on the way to kiss and fondle each other. One item of clothing after another fell to the floor, marking their path from the couch to his bed.

They lay side by side in each other's arms. Minutes of silence, an occasional smile, an occasional kiss—some quick and affectionate, some long and sensual. A glow of contentment warmed her, even stronger than what she had felt on the path at Huelgoat. In his presence after making love with him, she was relaxed and happy, suffused with a sense of having found something she had been seeking, of coming to rest where she belonged. Occasional thoughts of all the adoring things he had said to her a week before added to the glow.

Suddenly he threw back the sheet and blanket, raised himself on an elbow, and ran his eyes the length of her naked body. "I've been lusting after you ever since I watched you go up the ladder at Huelgoat. You can't imagine how much I wanted to grab your gorgeous little ass. But I didn't dare imagine we'd ever get this far. How did I get so lucky?"

"Maybe I should have played a little harder to get, so you wouldn't think I was too easy." It had occurred to her that an American might think they had not known each other long enough to be in bed together. But her eagerness to make love with him did not seem to present a problem for him.

"You played hard to get for a while."

But no longer. More on her mind now was basking in the present, flirting with him, making love with him again. "So now that you've seen me naked, does my body still meet with your approval?"

"It's a work of art." He ran his eyes down to her feet and back again.

"I'm still not sure about yours. I need to examine it some more." She rolled over, pushed him down on his back, and set about stroking and kissing him, sparing no part of him. He pretended for a moment to struggle, then submitted.

Their desire began to stir again, but Anne glanced at the clock and saw it was 6:25. She sat up. "I have to take the car back to my mother right away. What are you doing tonight?"

"If I had any plans I'd cancel them and beg you to spend the night here. I hate to be seduced and abandoned."

She got out of bed and began to gather her clothes and remembered that some were still on the living-room floor. "Suppose I make you dinner at my apartment? Will that reassure you?" Without waiting for an answer, she walked naked into the living room and retrieved her bra and top.

As she returned to the bedroom, he stared at her shamelessly, and she tingled as she felt his eyes on her. "The last time I caught you staring at me like that I was reading the guidebook at Sizun. But if I recall correctly, I was fully clothed."

"I was watching your acrobatic French lips and listening to your sweet voice. You were seducing me without even realizing it."

Sitting on the edge of the bed, she turned her pants right side out. "I'll remember that the next time I want to seduce you. I'll read to you from a guidebook."

"Try doing it naked next time."

"Oh, I can do a lot of things naked. You have no idea. But driving isn't one of them." She pulled her top over her head and ran her fingers quickly through her hair. As much as she hated to leave him, she was in a hurry. Returning the car later than she had promised was unthinkable.

While tying her shoes, she said, "We can come back here after dinner. By the time I'm done with you, you might wish you got seduced and abandoned." As she left the bedroom, she stopped, turned back to him and said, "Come around 7:30. And wipe that silly smile off your face."


In the roundabout at the edge of Sainte-Anne she made two playful circles like a child on a carousel before turning off toward Auray. She imagined taking this route many times in the weeks and months to come, as she rejoiced in the success of her mission. For the moment, she had it all. But not without a little touch of guilt, assuaged quickly by Jocelyne's words: if Anne was honest with him and he went along, Anne could see him temporarily with a clear conscience.

93

When Anne entered the apartment, her mother came out of the kitchen carrying her purse. She glanced at her watch and said, "Six fifty-seven. You're always on time. How's the gas tank?"

"Around half. I only went to Sainte-Anne." As if it were not obvious.

Brigitte smiled and added, "You look radiant, even with your hair all over the place. I assume everything went well."

"Yes, Mom. Very, very well." No time to explain. No need to explain.

Very, very well indeed.

Anne took a quick shower and began to make dinner using leftovers from lunch. When he arrived, she sat him at the kitchen table and poured him a glass of cider, which he nursed while she finished preparing dinner. She glanced at him from time to time and smiled. From the way he was looking at her, she could have still been naked.

She served him and sat across from him.

"What kind of fish is this?" he asked.

"In French it's *Saint-Pierre*. In English it's John Dory."

"Sometimes I think you know more English than you let on."

"I cheated. I looked it up before you got here. I bought this fish at the market this morning, just before I saw you. If I hadn't bought it, I wouldn't have seen you. I've never been so grateful to a fish."

"This morning," he said, "I thought I'd never see you again. It seems like a long time ago."

She finished a bite of John Dory, satisfied that it had just the right amount of sorrel. "In a way it was a long time ago. When you went to the market, did you think you might run into me?"

"The thought occurred to me, but I put it out of my mind. If I'd seen you before you saw me, I don't know what I would have done. Probably just stand there with my tongue hanging out."

"You wouldn't have looked any sillier than I did, staring at you like a dimwit."

"You were the most beautiful sight I'd ever seen. You still

94

are."

She set down her glass and peered across the table at him through narrowed, accusatory eyes. "You are such a bullshitter. Don't ever stop."

After dinner, she packed an overnight bag and they returned to his house. Once inside, they exchanged a glance and headed for the bedroom.

When Anne awakened in the morning, he was already up, the aroma of fresh coffee in the air. She dressed and found him in the kitchen.

He took her in his arms, kissed her and said, "I was hoping to make love again this morning, but I didn't have the heart to wake you up."

"We have the rest of the day, if your schedule isn't too full. I thought I should hang around for a while, so you can't complain you were seduced and abandoned."

After breakfast, they went for a walk on the long, broad beach at Erdeven, each with an arm around the other, watching children play in the surf. Then back to bed.

At mid-afternoon, she emerged from an unplanned siesta. She longed to awaken him but amused herself with the idea that she had worn him out and he needed to recover. She arose quietly and put on his robe and slippers.

As a guest in his home, she felt constrained not to enter any room into which she had not been invited. But she considered the circumstances of her presence there and decided she had earned the right to nose around a bit.

She discovered his work area in a room with a desk and a double bed. A stack of file folders lay on the desk next to a computer. Examining the keyboard, she noted the absence of keys for accented letters in French, and that some keys were in unfamiliar places. On the wall behind his desk, notes in esoteric English words, probably legal terms, were secured to a bulletin board by push pins. A wooden bookcase against the wall to the right of his desk held very few books— mostly dictionaries, some law books and two of the

95

novels she had sold him when they first met.

A dark brown hardbound book caught her eye. The fabric of its cover was frayed, and the letters on its spine were worn off except the English word *Brittany*. She gripped the book by its threadbare cover and pulled it carefully from the shelf. Thumbing through it, she saw the usual old photos of Bretons in traditional costumes: women in black dresses and white *coiffes* gathering seaweed, and men in wooden clogs arranging fishing nets. She turned back to the inside front cover and saw a bold stamp "Los Angeles County Library." Why did he bring such an old book? She could not ask him without revealing her indiscretion.

She put the book back on the shelf and as she turned to leave the room, bumped the computer. The screen saver went off and the screen lit up, revealing an email. Spotting her name in the message, she started reading. It was an inexcusable violation of his privacy, worse than going through his books, but she could not stop.

John,
That's so cool that you and Anne are back together. You sounded like shit when you called last week. I was gonna come there and slap her around for breaking your heart, but now, from your description of her, I think I might fall in love with her myself. Keep me informed.
Michael

Description? She found the arrow keys and scrolled down to the message from John that Michael had replied to. Now, there was really no stopping.

Hey Mike,
Guess what? Anne came here yesterday and said she wants to see me again. I'm in heaven. This chick is amazing. Really smart and a load of laughs. After she dumped me and you asked what she looked like, I didn't want to talk about it. I'll send you a photo when I have time, but now that she's back, I can tell you she's easy on the eyes, more of a natural look than a supermodel. Very little makeup. Nice

96

complexion, greenish eyes and golden brown hair. She wears it long, down to her shoulders, not all chopped off like a lot of the women here. Slim, but shapely. And there's the French thing, which you'll never understand because I don't either, even though the women here all have it. They're elegant but not showy, seductive and standoffish at the same time. I can't describe it.

More later.

John

Although she could not translate every word, she understood enough to warm with guilty pleasure. She thought of an exchange years before with one of her English teachers. When Anne had grumbled about how hard the class was, her teacher had said, "It's important to make the effort to learn English. Someday it will help you when you least expect it." Rummaging around on the sly in an American lover's computer was probably not the sort of thing her teacher had in mind.

The dates and times on the emails revealed that John had written and Michael had replied that morning before she had awakened. She noted that John's message to Michael said nothing about her having spent the night with him. Nor did he mention her fabulous ass or any other fabulous part of her body, which he had been getting to know with apparent approval. She appreciated his discretion.

She was tempted to print the message and keep it as medicine for whenever she needed a morale boost, but her breach of etiquette was already serious enough, and the sound of his printer might wake him up. She thought of forwarding it to herself, but remembered that a little arrow would appear on the message and betray her misdeed, even if she deleted the forwarded message from his Sent folder. So she contented herself with reading his description of her one more time. And smiling one more time.

A closer inspection of the living room confirmed her impression that he had rented the house furnished and decorated. Nothing in bad taste, but nothing inspired. She allowed herself to imagine for a moment the things she could do with this room if this were her house. A bookcase on the far wall, for example.

Passing a door that appeared to open into the garage, she mused about what she might find in his collection of tools. But she thought it unlikely that he had brought many tools with him from California, and the tools already in the house would reveal nothing about him.

Instead of opening the door to the garage, she headed back to the bedroom to see if he was still asleep, thinking of naughty things she might do to wake him up.

## Chapter 15: The Blue Nets

In the weeks that followed they were inseparable. This man who had walked into her life from so far away sensed her needs, understood what gave her pleasure. Her days were brightened by thoughts of him, the anticipation of seeing him.

On days off, they set out on day trips, driving, hiking, exploring, following mysterious signs and tips from waiters in cafés that led them to places she had never seen: a dolmen in a forest, a quiet pond, a remote chapel, a classic old farmhouse.

From time to time, a moment of curiosity about what had brought him to Brittany arose and passed quickly. If there was any chance she might marry him, she would have to know. But for now, what did it matter? Those simple and glorious days and nights were the happiest she had known, not to be tainted by worry about the next day or week or month. And if he harbored any regrets about accepting a temporary relationship, he did not share them with her. He seemed as happy with her as she was with him.

With the passing of days, Anne's search for a husband took its place without protest among those tasks that must be attended to someday.

In late August, she took him to Concarneau for the annual *Festival des filets bleus,* the Festival of the Blue Nets. The Festival had started in 1905 to show the town's solidarity with fishermen hurt by the sardine crisis and evolved over the years into a celebration of Breton culture.

They listened to bagpipes, Celtic harp, and *bombarde.* She explained to him that the *bombarde*, a wind instrument that looked like a small oboe, was rarely played solo. It took so much lung power that from time to time the bagpipers distracted the spectators while the *bombardiste* caught his breath.

As they watched a parade from the sidewalk, he seemed so absorbed taking photos that he barely acknowledged her presence. Families in Breton costumes marched by: the men in colorful vests and black hats trailing ribbons. Women wore traditional black dresses, some with white aprons, others brightened with plastrons of yellow, blue, and red. Lace-trimmed white headdresses, each part of Brittany with its own style, completed the costume. Anne pointed out the regions each *coiffe* represented: the tower of starched lace from the Pays Bigouden, the swirls and loops of the Aven, the simple white cloth of Auray. She thought of the old book about Brittany that she had found in his study. By now, she could well have seen it under circumstances more respectable than sneaking around his house while he slept. But the time did not seem right to ask him about it.

As they walked along the street with others who had come for the festival, he said, "This is a long way from California."

Was he going to say why he had left? What could she say to encourage him? "Do you miss it?"

"No. I'm just thinking about how Brittany already had a rich culture when Californians were still living on acorns."

She could guess where this was headed. It would turn into yet another exchange in which he waxed lyrical about Brittany while she defended California, a place she had never seen. "Don't forget that in 150 years, while Brittany essentially stood still, the United States went from nothing to the richest and most powerful nation on earth. Brittany produces more than just crêpes and vegetables now, but there's still no comparison." Their debate, while good-natured, was getting more animated, loud enough that people around them were sneaking looks at them.

He had not finished. "If you value tradition and culture over wealth and power, we aren't even close. The oldest culture we have in California, aside from Indians, is a string of Franciscan missions from the late 18th and early 19th centuries, made of dried mud, most of them half-destroyed by earthquakes."

"For someone so critical of his native state, you know a lot about it." It was almost a platitude, but if she could keep him talking about California long enough, he might tip his hand and say why he had moved.

"I think it's from living in France. I like old stuff, you know, history, prehistory. In California, everything is too new."

"You're such a malcontent. But if you weren't, we never would have met." She was pleased with herself for stifling an impulsive remark that he liked her because she was old stuff.

He slipped an arm around her waist. "As long as I'm with you, I'm not a malcontent. So when do I get to see you in your Breton costume?"

"I don't have one. Those clothes are very expensive. I'll bet you don't have a Franciscan robe." As preposterous as the suggestion was, she had to throw something back at him and perhaps get him back on the subject of California.

"Are you kidding? It's not just a robe. There's a belt made out of rope," he said, gesturing toward his waist. "The end of the rope dangles from the waist and has three knots in it. Those three knots stand for poverty, obedience, and chastity. I have a hard time with all of those."

"I'll allow you one of the three. Keep enough money so you can stay here and obey me. As for chastity, if you ever take that up, I'm history."

He laughed.

She tried her best under the circumstances to sound threatening. "You think I'm kidding?"

After the festival, she took him home but did not stay. An important brief was due when the office opened in the morning, which meant he had to finish it by Monday afternoon. He had been working on it most of the weekend and would not have taken the time off but for the Festival. Anne preferred not to stay at his house while he was working. He was not available to her, and she did not like to hear him speaking English. Not only did he sound like a stranger, she was appalled by how little she understood. It was worse on week nights. His arrangement with his firm required him to be available during business hours. Five pm in California was 2:00am in Brittany. If the phone rang late at night, he got up to answer it and upon hanging up, sometimes worked for several hours. But he had one rule that he never mentioned to his firm: if the phone rang while they were making love, he ignored it.

She was not ready to introduce him to the rest of her family and have to endure well-meaning but annoying questions about their relationship and whether she ever planned to get married. It was different with her mother. He had met her, and it seemed natural to invite him occasionally to the apartment for dinner. When Anne told him she appreciated the respectful attention he gave to her mother, he said, "It's an old American trick. If I can get close enough to your mother, you won't leave me again, because you're too kind to hurt your mother. Of course, it's risky. If you decide again to stop seeing me, I'll lose two women, not just one."

He packaged the comment with a disarming little smile, but if she ignored the smile, he sounded dead serious.

On the other hand, she enjoyed showing him off to her friends. She was proud of his skill in French, his inexplicable love of Brittany, and the ease with which he met new people. Sophie told Anne several times that she wanted to meet him, promising Anne she would take his measure and render her opinion. With some trepidation, Anne accepted a dinner invitation from Sophie and her husband Michel.

That morning, Anne stopped into the *pâtisserie* up the street from the bookstore to buy pastries to take to Sophie. Madame Laennec, the wife of the baker, greeted her. After some small talk, Madame Laennec said, "I've seen you with that nice American who comes in here. He speaks such good French. He told me he learned in Bordeaux." Anne smiled, but offered no details. The town was too small to keep secrets.

Michel answered the door. John and Michel had barely finished shaking hands when Sophie burst out of the kitchen, went straight to John, grabbed him by the shoulders, and kissed him on both cheeks. She looked him up and down and, without letting go of him, turned to Anne and said, "He's even sexier than how you described him!"

John looked beseechingly at Michel.

Michel shrugged. "Get used to it."

Two other guests, who had been sitting in the living room enjoying Sophie's performance, came over for introductions.

Over aperitifs and at dinner, the others asked John about California, his year in Bordeaux, and his impressions of Brittany. After those subjects were exhausted, the conversation turned to old times and old friends. They spoke of couples they knew that had formed and broken up and assured each other that the circumstances leading to those breakups did not apply to anyone present. The discussion of couples segued into a lively debate on the nature of love. Michel, who by now was a bit tipsy, asked, "John have you ever been in love?" It appeared to be Michel's well-intentioned if clumsy way of bringing John back into the conversation.

John cast a quick and uncomfortable look in Anne's direction and said, "I think I'm falling in love with Sophie."

Michel smiled with apparent pride. "Sophie scores again! Tune in next week when she goes to the finals."

When the laughter began to subside, Sophie said, "You both have excellent taste in women, even when you're drunk. Everyone go to the living room. I'll get the coffee."

As she drove them back to his house, Anne said, "I hope you weren't too bored when we talked about old times."

"No. It was fine. Everyone made an effort to include me."

"Do I dare ask what you and Sophie talked about when she dragged you into the kitchen?" Anne could imagine, but she wanted to hear it from John.

"She said she told you to sleep with me. But not in those exact words."

"That's what I figured. What did you say to that?"

"I said 'I owe you big. She's very good.'" He put his hand on her thigh.

"You did not! Did you? You did! Now I'll never hear the end of it. I warned you about her."

Anne glanced away from the road long enough to see that he was watching her with great amusement. As they approached the turnoff to Sainte-Anne-d'Auray, she picked up his hand and set it back in his lap. "Just a few more minutes."

On awakening in the morning, she turned to him and saw he was still asleep. She watched his lips as he slept, wanting to brush them with hers, to make him dream of her. Thoughts of the previous evening made her smile, then brought on a twinge of sadness.

They would have breakfast together and talk about how to spend another carefree Sunday, as Anne continued on this indulgent detour from what she believed to be the path of her life. This day would come and go and move them closer to their eventual breakup. Was that how it had to be? Was it what she really wanted?

He began to stir. His eyes opened, and he turned to her with a bleary-eyed smile. His smile faded as he ran a finger under her eye. "Why are you crying?"

"I'm not crying. The sunlight made my eyes water a little. But I'm glad you woke up. I missed you."

He slid closer to her and kissed her. "I'm right here, not just to kiss you and make love with you, but for anything you ever need."

How could she let such a man get away from her? Should she tell him what she had been thinking? Raise his hopes? Or worse, learn that he was satisfied with their temporary arrangement? No. Why look for trouble? Why risk ruining the day? "Right now I need a chocolate croissant. Let's get dressed and walk to the *boulangerie*." She got out of bed and headed for the bathroom.

One day in September, Bernard called to tell Anne he had an appointment in Vannes and asked if they could meet for lunch. Anne and her brother were not close and rarely saw each other outside of family gatherings. She surmised he had something on his mind.

## Chapter 16: A *Galette* and a Memory

The day their father moved out, Brigitte took Anne and Bernard to visit their aunt and uncle and cousins. When they returned, it appeared to Anne that little had changed, until she gathered the courage to look in the garage. Laid out carefully on the workbench, she found a note and an array of tools: a hammer, two screwdrivers, a measuring tape, a pair of pliers, an old hand drill with a set of bits, and an assortment of wrenches. "My Dear Anne," read the note. "These are for you to keep. I love you. Dad." A month passed before she touched the note or the tools.

Anne and Bernard stayed in the house with their mother for three years. Every other weekend their father dutifully picked up the two children and took them on a drive, to lunch or wherever else he could entertain them for a few hours.

It was not long before Bernard began to complain, accusing their father of pathetic attempts to atone for what he had done, of boredom, of lost Saturdays. Anne joined in. The problem came to a head during dinner one evening. When Brigitte told them their father would pick them up at ten that Saturday, Bernard said defiantly, "I'm not going."

Anne was emboldened by Bernard's refusal. "Neither am I."

Brigitte picked up the carafe of water and slowly filled her glass. "I understand you may not want to, but you are both going."

Bernard pushed his chair away from the table and crossed his arms in front of him. "I hate going there. He's a pain in the ass and I'm bored to death."

"Bernard, watch your language."

"He's right." Anne said. "He tries to be all Mr. Nice Guy and pretend nothing's changed. And now we have to put up with Florence – ." She caught herself, but it was too late.

Bernard uncrossed his arms and turned to Anne. "Nice going, big mouth!"

"It's all right," Brigitte said. "I know about her."

Anne yelled back at Bernard, "Don't call me big mouth! I

hate that! As if you're such a saint!"

"You shut up! What do you know? You're barely out of diapers."

Anne turned to her mother and said, "See why I don't want to go with him? He's a total creep, just like Dad. I'm not going, with him or without him, and you can't make me."

Brigitte raised her voice just a bit. "You're both going and that's that."

Bernard jumped up and charged toward the front door.

Her words crisp and clear, Brigitte said, "If you go out that door, don't bother coming back. It will be bolted from the inside. A few days sleeping on a park bench or in a homeless shelter might teach you to appreciate what family you have left."

Bernard stopped and stood motionless facing the front door, while Brigitte resumed eating her dinner. Anne watched him and waited, awestruck at her mother's words. After what seemed like ten minutes, he turned around and returned to the kitchen table.

Brigitte spoke in measured tones, looking first at Anne, then at Bernard. "I know it's hard to understand right now, but it's important for you to see your father. When you're older, you'll be allowed to decide for yourselves how often. But for now, you'll do as I say, and there will be no further discussion."

As tolerant as Brigitte could be of her children's outbursts, they both knew that when she declared how it would be, that was how it would be.

When Anne was fourteen, Brigitte announced that she had taken over a bookstore in Auray and they would move to an apartment just above the store. Anne was unhappy about leaving the house and her friends in Rennes, but the move solved the problem of having to visit her father so often and see Florence, whom Anne held responsible for her father's departure. Auray was an hour and a half from Rennes by train, so her father's apartment would now be more than just a ten-minute bus ride away. The next year, Bernard went away to university.

One day when Bernard was home for vacation, Anne was in

the kitchen eating lunch and reading. Brigitte had stayed in the bookstore after closing for lunchtime, to catch up on some paperwork. Bernard came in, made himself a sandwich, and sat down at the kitchen table across from her. He appeared to be angry about something.

"You don't look happy," Anne said.

"I called Dad," Bernard grumbled. "Florence answered. She gives me such a pain. All that phony, 'How are you? It's good to hear from you' crap."

"Why did you call him?"

"For money. I hate to ask him, but I hate to ask Mom even more." Brigitte rarely mentioned money, but she did make comments from time to time about what they could not afford.

"What did he say?"

"He asked me how I'd spent the last money he gave me. I said if 'I have to submit a report and show you receipts, forget it.' So he said, 'OK, we'll forget it.' Then I got pissed. I said, 'It must cost a lot to maintain your stable of bimbos,' and off we went. I don't even know which of us hung up on the other."

"What do you mean 'stable of bimbos'?"

"You know. His mistresses. All those sluts he was out screwing while he pretended to be a loyal husband and father."

Anne concealed her shock as best she could, too proud to tell Bernard she had never suspected. As skeptical as she had been about the excuses for her father's absences, she had tried hard to believe them and not delve any further, lest she learn something she would rather not know. "Oh. Yeah. That's what I thought you meant."

Bernard's revelation left her smoldering. It was too much to keep to herself, but there was no one she could tell; it was too shameful. After two days of lonely misery and mounting anger, she called her father.

When he heard her voice, he said, "Hi Sweetheart."

She shouted into the phone, "Don't call me sweetheart! How could you do that to Mom? You didn't deserve her. You don't deserve me. I don't ever want to see you again!" She slammed down the phone. *I will not cry. He will not make me cry.*

The phone rang. She waited for the answering machine to pick up.

"Anne, please. Pick up the phone."

She left the kitchen and closed the door behind her, still hearing his voice through the door. After enough time had passed, she returned to the kitchen and erased the message.

She refused to visit him or even speak to him. This time, her mother finally said, "You're old enough to decide for yourself."

Anne met Bernard in Vannes at the Crêperie du Golfe. She ordered a *galette complète* and a bowl of cider.

After the waitress picked up the menus, Bernard said, "When we were kids and the family went to a *crêperie* for dinner, you always ordered a *galette complète*."

Anne shrugged. It was not like Bernard to remember such a detail. Perhaps he was warming up to tell her why he had called. She was not about to wait until he got around to it. "So what's on your mind?" she asked.

"I was in Rennes last week and dropped in on Dad. He said he hadn't seen you in a while."

Was that why Bernard had called? Because their father had asked him to? "I hope you're not planning to lecture me about poor, neglected Dad. He never comes to visit me and I'm tired of always being the one to make the trip. And if I go there, it's such a chore to be polite to Florence."

The waitress set two bowls on the table and filled them with cider. When she had gone, Bernard said. "Mom told me you've been seeing an American."

So that was it. She would do her best not to disappoint him. "We were about due for another family scandal," she said. "I suppose it was my turn to provide the material."

Bernard was used to his sister's sharp tongue and took her sarcasm in stride. "It hasn't caused a scandal that I'm aware of, at least not yet. I hope you're not getting serious about him. I don't want you to get hurt."

108

"I appreciate your concern, but there's no need for it. John is good to me and I enjoy his company. And he's a big improvement over most of the Bretons I've dated."

Bernard took a sip of cider. "I shouldn't be surprised that you've taken up with a Californian. You've been threatening to run away to California ever since you got that book. If you moved there, Mom and Dad would be very unhappy."

"Don't count on it. Mom would miss me, and I'd miss her. That's one reason I'd never move there. But Dad wouldn't even notice I was gone. Try it. Tell him 'Anne married an American and moved to California.' He'll say 'Anne? Anne who?'" Suddenly uncomfortable, she shifted in her chair.

"It's still that bad?"

Her silence answered his question.

"He doesn't bother me so much anymore," he said. "When something comes up between us, we have a big argument, we don't speak for a while, then it passes."

"At least you get a reaction. I used to yell at him, and he'd just look at me like I wasn't even worth a response. I don't want to talk about him. It's making me mad."

"As you wish," Bernard said, followed by an awkward pause in the conversation.

As they fidgeted and played with their cider bowls, Anne tried to steer the conversation away from their father. "How are you so sure John will leave?" She would never admit to Bernard that her own biggest fear was that John might move back to California.

"Why would he stay here? I just read an article about California in *L'Express*. They have everything there: sunshine, beaches, mountains. The state is rich and its economy is booming. Los Angeles is the city of the future. The entertainment business is there. Trade with the Pacific Rim passes through there. What does Brittany have to offer him? He'll get tired of it. He just wants some company and whatever else he can get until he decides it's time to go."

She found his concern touching but patronizing. "Since when is it a sin to want some company? As for whatever else he can get, he's already gotten it. And if I have my way, he'll get a lot more of it."

Bernard smiled and shook his head in amusement. "I used to think it was my job to protect you since Dad wasn't around. But I was too busy being pissed at everyone. Now, I want to take care of you to make up for letting you down years ago."

"Don't blame yourself. Protecting me wasn't your responsibility then and it isn't now. Besides, in a way it was easier for me than for you. I was closer to Mom, and as for you and Dad . . . ."

The waitress appeared with their meals. Anne stared at her *galette* for a moment, trying to remember the family going out together in happier times.

"After Dad moved out, I was mad at Mom for a while," Bernard said. "I thought she must have disappointed Dad somehow or he wouldn't have left. With Dad it was simple. He abandoned us. He only cared about himself and not his family. I told him that more than once. Oops. I'm sorry. We weren't going to talk about him."

"Just tell me how he reacted."

"Mostly he got mad. I told him he couldn't handle the truth, which led to another shouting match. Sometimes I wonder how a kind, gentle person like Mom managed to raise two such mouthy kids."

"We felt safe with her. She let us speak our minds."

"Up to a point," Bernard said. "She knew when to let us unload and where to draw the line. Remember the time she threatened to lock me out of the house?"

Anne smiled and nodded, recalling how shocked she had been.

"She would have done it," he said. "I had a lot more respect for her after that. I'm glad you're living with her. I'd hate to see her living alone after what she went through."

"She has Charles. They see each other quite a bit."

"That's fine as long as she's in Auray and he's in Nantes. Weekends and vacations are mostly fun. It's daily life that's the challenge."

"Why? Do you get bored with your family?" Anne had little

sympathy for people who had what she wanted and did not seem to appreciate it.

"Sometimes. When I see an attractive woman in a café, I start imagining how she'd be in bed, then I think of what Dad did and Marie looks better all of a sudden."

Bernard continued, "Once, I started talking to a woman at a café in Rennes. She was lonely and available and didn't care that I was married. It was a moment of truth for me."

"I hope you're not going to tell me – "

"Unless you don't want to hear it."

"I didn't, but it's too late now." Anne could guess what was coming and was sickened by the thought of it.

"Marie and I weren't getting along at the time, so I thought I'll show her. I went with the woman to a hotel. Afterwards, she started talking about the next time we see could see each other, about taking a vacation together. I could see she was needy and probably unstable. But mainly I thought about Dad's philandering and knew I could start following his example."

Anne jumped to the defense of her sister-in-law, a sweet, self-sacrificing person who deserved better. "You should have thought about Marie and about Dad before you screwed that slut!" Now, every time Anne saw Marie, she would think about what Bernard had done and have to keep silent about it.

Bernard took a quick, uncomfortable glance around the terrace and said, "No need to preach. I know it was a mistake. And it was the only time. I wanted to get rid of her without a scene, so I made a date and stood her up. I got nervous. I mean, I could have destroyed my marriage and for what? A few minutes in bed with some woman who meant nothing to me. I asked Marie to go with me to a marriage counselor, and we managed to work out most of our problems. It still isn't perfect, but what marriage is? I stayed away from Rennes for six months and I never went to that café again. By the way, nobody knows about this except you. When Marie and I were having problems, she asked if I was seeing another woman. I lied. I said I was tempted because she kept turning me down, but that I had never done it. Stay away from married men. They lie."

How true, Anne thought. How painfully true. Time to change the subject.

"Did Mom ask you to talk to me about John?" It seemed unlikely, but why else would he have brought it up?

"No. It was my idea."

"It's not the best idea you've ever had, my dear brother. Let me give you some perspective. You have a spouse and two great kids to fill your evenings and weekends. I don't." Nobody had the right to judge how she lived her life. If she wanted to see John, she would damn well see him. Someone fortunate enough to have his own family had no right to lecture her, not even her brother. "Can you understand how much it means to me to get up in the morning and have something to look forward to other than work? John is more to me than just sex and company. He's affectionate. He listens to me. He takes care of me. If I'm down, he cheers me up. Not only am I happy when I'm with him, we never run out of things to do together. We visit places I haven't been in years and when I go with him, it's like I'm seeing them for the first time."

Bernard seemed taken aback by the intensity of Anne's retort. "Like where, for example?"

Anne thought for a moment. "OK. Here's one. On a drive we took in the Black Mountains, we passed a sign pointing to Spézet. He said, 'Let's go into Spézet.' Other than a pretty chapel on the outskirts, there is nothing in Spézet. It's a clean, pleasant village in the middle of nowhere, and there is nothing in it, at least nothing I could see. We go into a café and he tells the bartender he'd like to meet someone in the *Cercle Brug ar Menez*."

"The what?"

"My point exactly, Mr. Born-and-Bred Breton. For your information, it's a Breton dance troupe that's one of the best in Brittany, and he knew all about it. You get the idea? Maybe there's no future for me with John, but for now, my life is rich and fun and full."

"Well, little sister, enjoy it while it lasts. As for Mom, she seems to like him. She says he's charming. They say that's why Americans are so successful in business. They act like naive little kids and turn on the charm and before you realize what's happening, you've sold them whatever they wanted for half its value and they're gone."

"Do you really believe that?" She was sick of self-styled experts criticizing Americans.

"How would I know what to believe? I don't know any Americans."

"It's about time you met one. You're in luck; I happen to have one in stock."

"Good. Dust him off and bring him to dinner at my house on Sunday. That way the rest of the family can size him up too."

They paid the check and left the restaurant. Bernard walked with her back to her car. As she opened her car door, he asked, "Are you disappointed by what I told you?"

"Frankly, yes. But don't worry. Your secret is safe with me."

Bernard was right; it was time for John to meet Bernard and other family members. She could guess how it would go. He would make a good impression; he always did. The relatives at Bernard's house would tell others about John. Those who had not met him would ask, "What is Anne up to now? There have to be ten thousand eligible Bretons; why an American? Is she that desperate?" She had heard enough family gossip over the years to know what was being said and who was saying it. This time though, the prospect of stirring up some chatter was more amusing than annoying. She was developing a taste for defying expectations—even her own.

## Chapter 17: Uncle John

The following Sunday she picked him up and drove him to Bernard's house, where she introduced him to Bernard, Marie, and other assembled relatives. Brigitte was spending the day with Charles and his family, and Jocelyne was with Philippe's family that day, so Anne would have to wait for Jocelyne's assessment of John. Today's guests included one of Anne and Bernard's cousins, his wife, their three children, and Marie's parents.

After a few minutes of general conversation with those who had already arrived, Anne suggested to John and Bernard that they adjourn to the lounge chairs on the veranda, where they could converse away from the others and keep an eye on the children. The edge of a forest marked the boundary of the backyard, where the children were playing. A short path led from the yard through the forest, down a gentle hill to a stream.

Anne sat quietly while John and Bernard warmed up with safe topics such as the weather, the economy, and some brush fires in California that had been in the news. She doubted they would have any problem breaking the ice, but she stayed long enough to make sure they got off to a good start. She excused herself and went to the kitchen to help Marie.

At first, Anne felt guilty in Marie's presence, as if guarding the secret of Bernard's transgression made Anne an accomplice. But she managed to put it out of her mind.

She glanced at Bernard and John through the window from time to time, looking for signs of how the conversation might be going. They were sitting close together, looking intently at each other, one or the other nodding occasionally.

After a few minutes, Anne no longer saw the children in the yard and asked Marie, "Where are the kids?" Bernard and Marie had two children, Yann and Justine, ages seven and ten. Justine had an opinion about everything and was always ready to express it—just like Anne at that age, Brigitte had noted.

Marie excused herself to check on the children. Through the kitchen window, Anne saw her speaking to Bernard. On returning to the kitchen, Marie said, "They went down to the stream. It always makes me a little nervous when they go down there alone, but there's never been a problem." They resumed dinner preparations.

Five minutes later they were interrupted by a disturbance in the backyard. Through the window they could see the children running out of the forest into the yard. One of the children was yelling, "A snake is killing Yann!"

Anne and Marie ran out of the kitchen in a panic to the backyard. Bernard was standing in the yard, the frightened children crowding around him, the equally frightened adults gathering behind the children. John was behind Bernard, trying to work his way through to Yann.

On arriving at where she could see what was happening, Anne recoiled in horror. A snake slightly less than a meter long was wrapped around Yann's arm and hand, waving its head menacingly. Yann was crying loudly, and Justine was saying over and over, "I told him not to pick it up!"

All the adults and children stood paralyzed—including Anne, who was terrified of snakes. She watched John as he squeezed between Bernard and the children and reached out quickly to grab the snake behind its head. As he unwound the snake from around Yann's arm, he spoke calmly, promising Yann he would be fine. Yann stopped crying and John stepped away from him, raised the snake to his own face and looked at it closely, turning it sideways to him, then facing him. The snake flicked its tongue at John's face.

Marie yelled at Anne, "Is he crazy? Doesn't he know that snakes are poisonous? I'm going to call emergency!"

John announced, "It's just a grass snake. It's harmless."

Cries arose from the adults, "A harmless snake? There's no such thing! Who is he kidding?"

John spoke some more reassuring words to Yann and turned to the adults, all of whom took a step back. "Look," he said, "It has a narrow head, a round eye and no fangs. If it were venomous, it would have a slit pupil, a triangular head, and two long fangs at the top of its mouth. Who wants to hold it?"

The adults yelled almost in unison, "Not me!"

115

Anne was close enough to see the snake was grayish green with black markings here and there and patches of pale yellow. She started to go closer for a better look but stopped.

Justine stepped up, determined to prove her courage to the adults and buttress her authority over the younger children. "I'll hold it." If John could hold the snake, so could she.

John showed her how to take the snake with one hand behind its head. "Even though it's not venomous, it has little teeth it can scratch you with, so you still have to be careful."

"It smells bad," Justine said.

"That's one way it protects itself," John explained. "We'll wash our hands when we've finished with it."

"Are you going to kill it?" Bernard asked.

"There's no reason to kill it. We're going to let it go. Yann, show me where you found it and we'll take it home. Its parents are probably worried about it." Yann marched off into the woods, followed by Justine with the snake, then John, then the rest of the children.

Anne, Bernard, Marie, and the other adults stood on the lawn looking sheepishly at each other. Anne could guess what they were thinking: Americans are even stranger than we thought. Let them think what they wanted. At least John had known what to do while the rest of them stood helpless.

"Bernard," Marie asked, "What would you have done if John hadn't been here?"

"I would have remembered I was late for an appointment in Paris."

While the adults were laughing at Bernard, John and the children reappeared. Justine proclaimed, "Uncle John helped me hold its head when we set it on the ground. It turned around and looked at us before it slid off into the bushes."

Yann added, "And when it looked at me it smiled!"

Anne turned to John. "Well done, Uncle John!"

John was beaming. He seemed to like his new title.

At dinner, Marie asked, "John, how did you become such an

expert on snakes?"

"I grew up in the country and snakes came onto our property, so we had to learn which ones were harmless. We used to catch them and play with them for a while and let them go. When I came here and got a house in the country, my neighbor must have thought I had grown up in a big city, so she warned me to watch out for snakes. I thought it would be a good idea to learn about the local species."

"I suppose it's like wild mushrooms." Bernard said. "Make a mistake and you're dead."

"Not necessarily dead, but it's not a chance worth taking." John said. "I told the kids if you're not sure it's harmless, don't pick it up."

Anne imagined her relatives telling those who were not present all about John and the snake, no doubt embellishing the story for dramatic effect. The more dramatic the better. She was proud of him.

After dinner, Bernard took Anne aside and said, "I'm not sure I gave you good advice. First of all he seems very solid. Second, he's obsessed with Brittany. Third, his French is phenomenal. Fourth, he doesn't have a single positive thing to say about Los Angeles. It's hard to imagine he'll ever move back."

Anne was triumphant. "It sounds like he charmed you too."

"Yeah. Like he charmed that snake and all the kids."

As she was driving them home, Anne said, "When I saw Yann with a snake wrapped around his arm, I almost fainted. Marie was so scared she crossed herself, and she's an atheist. You made quite an impression."

"It was nothing. I saw right away it was harmless."

"Harmless or not, it scared me to death."

He reached across the console. "No it didn't. I can feel your heart beating."

"That's not my heart!"

"Close enough."

117

"Don't distract the driver."

He put his hand back in his lap. "Seriously, now that you can tell the difference, why don't you just decide not to be afraid of harmless snakes?"

"That's easy for you to say. I've been afraid of snakes as long as I can remember. Not like you. You don't seem to be afraid of anything. Or maybe you have some phobia you've been hiding from me."

"Maybe I do. Let me think a minute." He was silent for a moment, then said, "I can think of one thing I'm afraid of."

"Will you tell me what it is?" She glanced at him and saw he had turned serious.

Looking straight ahead, he said, "Losing a woman I love."

Another one of his mysterious little tidbits about his past that he would probably not explain, like in the boat, when he had mentioned his ex-in-laws and changed the subject. It was time to press the unspoken boundary around his past. "Has that ever happened to you?"

"Yes," he said, "and it's going to happen again."

His words stopped her cold. Who was he talking about? Certainly not her. As close as they were, as much as she cared about him, as much as he excited her, they did not love each other. Their relationship was temporary. Someday it would change and they would become the best of friends. But who else could he mean? She started to ask but stopped, afraid of what she might hear.

In the bookstore the next morning, Anne had time to puzzle over John's comment that he had lost a woman he loved and that it would happen again. Perhaps he was expressing a general pessimism about relationships, a fear that if he married again, it would end badly, like his first marriage. Anne could only assume it had ended badly, and that from one passing reference to his ex-in-laws. But it occurred to her that some dismal event ends all marriages, whether divorce or, as everyone professes to hope at the moment of their wedding, by death. Perhaps John had reason to be pessimistic.

But what if he had someone in particular in mind? What if

Anne was the woman in question, the one he loved and was afraid of losing? That could only mean he thought he loved her. The very idea, as improbable as it seemed, gave her an unsettling thrill.

As she puzzled over this little mystery, she began biting her knuckle and becoming annoyed with him. Why did he do that? Why did she let him get away with it? If he had something to say to her, he should find the courage to talk to her and stop dropping tantalizing little remarks and slamming the door.

Passing the nature section, she pulled out a book on the fauna of Brittany. In the index, she searched for "Grass snake." Turning to the page, she found a photo of the snake and its scientific name: *Natrix natrix*. She studied its face, its inscrutable smile, the black and yellow bands behind its head where John had held it in his confident grip. She felt strangely drawn to it, yet still afraid of it.

October brought the first of fall weather. Chilly days and rain showers kept them indoors more of the time, where they read together, watched movies, and entertained friends. As perplexed as she was by their conversation in the car leaving Bernard's house, she did not bring it up again and neither did he.

They planned to go for a drive on the next day of fair weather before the onset of winter. After several days of rain, Brittany's capricious sky cleared, and they set out into the Ille-et-Vilaine southeast of Rennes to the Roche-aux-Fées, the Fairy Rock.

He seemed never to tire of visiting megalithic monuments. For Anne, who had grown up in their midst, they were as everyday as sunshine and freeways were to him. They had gone together to visit some of the local sites, including the cairns at Locmariaquer at the mouth of the Gulf and on the island of Gavrinis. Both were chambers of vertical stones with a ceiling of flat stones and covered by a mound of small rocks.

John admitted to occasional solo visits to the famous rows of tall stones, known as menhirs, in the fields around Carnac. It was not at all obvious why a man from California should be so enchanted by rows of rough stones, but whenever he suggested they visit a megalithic site, she went along graciously, proud that he appreciated her heritage and hoping to rekindle in herself some enthusiasm for these wonders built by a lost civilization.

As they neared the Roche-aux-Fées, she reached into the glove compartment and pulled out his well-worn guidebook, the same one she had read from at Sizun shortly after they had met.

He saw her thumbing through the guidebook and said, "Better keep your clothes on or we'll never get there."

"Is that all you ever think about?" Considering the amount of time they spent in bed together, much of it at her instigation, he could ask her the same thing.

"I'm with the sexiest woman on the planet; what do you expect me to think about?"

"Shut up and listen," was the best she could toss back at him after such a compliment.

She read from the book. "The Roche-aux-Fées is an unusually large chamber enclosed by walls of upright stones supporting a roof of horizontal megaliths, some of which weigh forty metric tons. Archeologists estimate it was built between two and three thousand years B.C. and theorize that it might have been a burial chamber. According to legend, it was built by fairies who carried the stones in their aprons, thus its name. Whatever its builders intended, Bretons of more recent times have spun up their own legends about the Roche-aux-Fées. On the night of the new moon, lovers can test their compatibility by walking around the outside counting the stones, the man walking clockwise and the woman walking counterclockwise. They hope, on returning to the starting point, to have each counted the same number or close to it."

They entered the parking lot, and Anne put the guidebook back into the glove compartment. As she got out of the car, the sun warmed her face. She resolved to enjoy it while it lasted. They walked together from the parking lot, up the path across a lawn that led to a grove of trees surrounding the Roche-aux-Fées. She slipped an arm around John's waist. He put his hand on her shoulder and gave it a gentle squeeze.

She saw a couple approaching from the opposite direction. Anne recognized the man. Short of taking an obvious detour across the lawn, there was no way to avoid him. As the two couples neared each other, the man gave Anne a self-conscious look of recognition and a muted *bonjour*. She gave him an icy *bonjour* and kept walking.

When they were far enough away, John said, "Would I be out of order to ask who that was?"

Someone Anne was not happy to see. "An old boyfriend."

"From your tone of voice and the look on his face, I don't have the impression you parted friends."

"That's an understatement. It's the closest I ever came to killing someone." *Why did I say that?* Now he would ask her to tell him the whole sordid, humiliating story, and how could she refuse, after what she had just said?

"Do you want to tell me about it?" Right on schedule.

John's disarming way of asking the most personal of questions made her want to tell him everything, sometimes against her better judgment.

# Chapter 18: Mr. Wrong

When Anne was thirty-two, she met a new salesman for Editions Guillemot when he came to the store. His name was Pierre. He asked her to lunch, which she thought at first was to encourage her to order more books from his company. They got along well, very well, and he came to see her whenever he was in the area. Lunches and drinks after work became dinners, movies, then overnight stays in his hotel room. They began to speak in general terms about marriage and children.

Pierre lived in Saint-Malo, on the northeast coast of Brittany. She asked about his parents. They lived in Dinard, in the Côtes-d'Armor, not far from him. Anne told him she would like to meet them. Pierre said they wanted to meet her too. He promised to arrange a visit, but put it off several times, pleading work commitments.

About four months after meeting Pierre, Anne began to wonder if there might be another reason he put off her visit. She thought there might be something he was embarrassed about, probably nothing that would bother her, perhaps a shabby apartment or a family member who drank too much. She decided to ask him, but to wait for the right moment, when the question would not sound accusatory.

Before that conversation could take place, Anne received a call at the store. A woman said, "I'm sorry to bother you, but I'm trying to reach Pierre Garnier. By any chance have you seen him today?"

Anne's instinct told her to say as little as possible. "Are you from Guillemot?"

"No, I'm his wife. It's rather urgent."

Anne's stomach knotted. She gasped for air and struggled to sound like nothing was wrong as she gathered her wits about her. "I haven't seen him."

"If you happen to see him or hear from him, would you ask him to call his wife immediately? Our son is in the hospital."

"Have you tried his cell phone?"

"He left without it this morning. That's how I found your number."

Anne hung up the phone and sat down, dizzy, breathing hard. *That son of a bitch!* A wife. A son. How many other children? It all made sense now, why she could not visit him at home. How could she have been so gullible?

Her face burned. What would she say to him when he called next? Maybe his wife would tell him of their conversation and Anne would never hear from him again. So much the better. No. *He can't get away with this.* She had to do something, to say something. Call his wife and tell her. Call his company. *Think, Anne, think.* A customer came in. She went through the motions.

Her mother must have suspected Pierre was married, but had said nothing. Jocelyne had sounded skeptical the second or third time Anne had told her that Pierre had cancelled plans for her to visit. Anne had not wanted to hear it. Now she could not face either of them. At six o'clock, she closed the store, went to her bedroom to get her purse and a sweater, and told her mother she was going out to dinner. She drove aimlessly, finally turning onto the Quiberon Peninsula. The west side, the Wild Coast, matched her mood. She parked and walked past a sign warning of the terrible fate to befall anyone who might venture down to rocks pounded by the surf. Watching the waves break, she imagined how a scorned woman might come here to end her misery. She would not give Pierre the satisfaction. She would make him pay, somehow.

She would have called him to tell him the game was over, but she had only his cell-phone number and his cell phone was securely in his wife's possession. Waiting was not her style, but she had no choice.

Anne drank little alcohol. Tonight, though, she needed help. Once safely at home, several shots of *Fine de Bretagne* put her to sleep.

Pierre called the next day and said he would come by the store that afternoon. His words, his tone gave away nothing. If his wife had told him of their conversation, he did not let on. Anne planned her ambush.

There were no other customers in the store when he arrived.

123

She was at the front, rearranging books on a display table. When he went to kiss her, she turned her head and stepped to one side.

"Is anything wrong?" he asked.

"I'm concerned about your son. Is he OK?" She glanced at him just long enough to see his look of surprise, then resumed working as she waited for his answer. This was going to be good.

He regrouped quickly. "Yes, he's fine. How did you know?"

"Your wife sounds like a nice person. I'd like to meet her sometime. I'll bet she'd like to meet me and your other mistresses, too." She finished arranging the books on the table, walked over to the outside of the counter as if he was not worth much attention, and picked up a book she had left there to be shelved.

He stayed next to the table where she had been working. "I was going to tell you. Our marriage has been over for years. I didn't want to leave her because of the kids. I didn't want to tell you until I got to know you better. By then I was in love with you and it was too late to tell you without hurting you. I didn't know what to do."

Anne was ready for him. "You didn't know what to do?" She turned to face him. "Let me help you. You can get out of my sight and out of my life and stay out! Starting now! Then I'll decide at my leisure how much I want to tell your wife about your escapades. I suppose I could take a tour of the other bookstores in Brittany and find your other mistresses. They might like to be enlightened too. And maybe your kids, however many there are, should know what a worthless excuse for a father they have."

A glint of fear pierced his self-assurance, as he realized he risked losing more than just Anne. "Anne, you don't understand. There's nobody else. My wife and I haven't made love in years."

"That's hardly a problem since you manage to get laid elsewhere with no difficulty. How many are there? This club that I've joined, how exclusive is it?"

"Don't talk like that. There's only you. I swear." His facade was starting to crumble.

"A lie is a lie, whether you tell it to one woman or ten. You're a liar and a disgusting son of a bitch! Now get out of here!"

He made no move to leave. "Anne, I would never do

anything to hurt you. I love you." He took a tentative step toward her, then a step back, as if he was afraid to come too close to her.

"You don't love me and you never have. You don't even know what the word means. You lied to me to screw me. It's as simple as that. And I was too stupid not to see it."

"It's not like that at all."

"It's not? Explain it to me."

"I've never met a woman like you. I didn't want to ruin everything at the start by telling you I was married. I needed time to straighten things out first."

"Just what does that mean 'to straighten things out'?" Anne was smoldering. She could barely restrain herself. But she wanted him to dig the biggest hole possible before she buried him.

"Divorce my wife."

"And you had that planned for when, exactly?" She looked at the book she was holding, turned it over, and pretended to study the back cover.

"As soon as possible. We've been working on a settlement. I've been looking for an apartment to move into."

He had been such a brilliant liar, but he was losing his touch. Now, as if he had not humiliated her enough, he was treating her like a complete idiot, expecting her to buy that shopworn line. She had heard enough.

She slammed the book down on the counter and shouted, "Get the hell out of here! Get out of my life! It's over! Do you understand? Finished!"

"Anne, calm down! Listen to me."

"Out! Now!"

He started toward her, looking desperate. Now it was Anne's turn to panic. She grabbed the book from the counter and threw it at him. He stopped and ducked, then took another step toward her. She looked around for something else to hurl at him and spotted the pole for adjusting the awning. She stepped around the end of the counter, grabbed the pole with both hands and swung it hard at him, the steel hook on its tip just missing his face. She started to swing again, but he turned and dashed out of the store. She ran to the door

125

and locked it behind him.

The pole slid from her hand and clattered to the floor. Gasping again, she backed against the wall to steady herself, watching the bookshelves across the room tip one way, then the other, like the horizon from a boat. She slid down the edge of a bookcase to the floor, shaking at the thought of what she might have done to him. A customer tried to open the door. Anne stared straight ahead, drained, paralyzed. Time passed. Another person tried the door. A few seconds later, the lock turned. Her mother entered the store to find Anne sitting on the floor, the pole beside her, an open book face down on the floor.

## Chapter 19: A Pastry and a Megalith

They sat on a bench, facing the massive stones of the Roche-aux-Fées. Anne waited uneasily for some reaction, but so far, nothing. The longer the silence, the more she regretted telling him the story. She should have said Pierre was a classmate or a customer.

She tried to decipher his expression. He was staring straight ahead, pensive, intense, his eyes narrowed and his lips pressed together. "What are you thinking?" she asked.

His face softened, and he put an arm around her. "I'm sorry. It took me a minute to suppress the urge to chase down Pierre and kick the crap out of him. I was hoping you were going to say you split his head open."

"Sometimes I wish I had. I've never been so furious in my life."

They sat silently for another moment. What was he thinking now? "Are you disappointed to learn how naive your girlfriend can be?"

"My girlfriend is anything but naive; that's what I don't understand. She's one of the smartest, most perceptive people I know. Nothing gets past her. And yet you didn't suspect." He was his usual tactful self.

"I should have suspected, but I didn't. Everybody saw it but me. Jocelyne tried to warn me, but I wouldn't listen. Sophie didn't say anything, which for her was saying a lot." Now, having told John the story, all she could do was try to explain it away. "He always had a plausible excuse for why I couldn't visit him at home or meet his friends or his family. But I didn't want to see it. I thought I was in love with him. I was blind." And desperate to get married, she had since realized.

A couple strolled past them with three children. The father said to the mother, "Shall we count the stones?"

The mother replied, "Don't you think it's a little late to find out we're unsuited for each other?"

John and Anne looked at each other and laughed, both of them welcoming the relief from a tense conversation. The father turned to them and said with mock solemnity, "Do it now, before it's too late." The mother smiled. The family moved on.

"I don't get how someone can do what Pierre did," John said. "Maybe if I were French, I'd understand, or maybe that's just a stereotype."

It was the first time he had ever said anything critical of the French. He had been married to a French woman, Anne assumed. Was there a connection? She wanted to ask him, but as always, his silence and her sense of discretion kept his marriage off limits. And yet if she could stay on the subject of marriage, he might reveal something. "I know we have that reputation," she said, "but I can only speak for myself. I don't care how many people do it, men who cheat on their wives are lowlife scum, and women who knowingly go along with them aren't much better. Think of the damage they cause to the man's family."

"Let's walk," he said. They got up and strolled along the paths around the park. "Why do people like Pierre bother to get married?" he asked. "Why don't they just stay single and hop from bed to bed as they please?"

"Oh, that's not hard to figure out. They don't want to be alone. They want children. Men want a wife to cook, to clean house, to do their laundry. Women want a husband to support them and protect them. Not only that, we live in a world of couples. Single people don't fit. But some people want it all, the stability of marriage and the excitement of an affair. They want to be married but can't live with the monotony of it." Once again, effortlessly, he was drawing her out, avoiding any talk of his own experience. She could imagine what he did with witnesses in court: put them at ease and sit quietly while they told everything.

"Do you think marriage has to be monotonous?" he asked.

This time she was ready. "Why are you asking me about marriage? I've never been married and you have. You know more about it than I do."

"I'm hardly an expert. I wasn't married very long and I was studying all the time, so I wasn't much company. Marie-Clo had issues besides boredom."

128

Anne was stunned by her success. He had actually acknowledged the existence of his ex-wife. Now she had a name, and Anne had an opening for a point-blank question. "What were her issues?"

"Some people expect marriage to solve all their problems, to make them happy. People with expectations like that are doomed to disappointment."

He was dodging the question by slipping back into generalities. Stay after him. Change tactics. "Those expectations might be a bigger problem for French people. We're easily bored. Maybe that was her problem. You, on the other hand, you never seem to get bored. All your wife would have to do is hand you a creme puff and park you in front of a megalith. You'd be happy for hours." Too late she realized she had led him away from Marie-Clo. He was going to escape again.

He smiled and said, "You think you're kidding, but you're not far off. It's one of the great things about living here. For me, simple things like eating a pastry and looking at megaliths are exotic. But I expect you need more than that."

"I need more than a pastry and a megalith, but I don't ask for much. I just want a family of my own, a man who loves me and is good to me." She was uncomfortable talking to him about her ideal husband, so she turned the conversation back to him, hoping that one more nudge would open him up. "What about you? You told me you didn't know what you wanted in your life. Do you ever think about that? One of these days, pastries and megaliths won't be exotic anymore. Then what?"

They had been strolling with his arm around her back, his thumb hooked in her waistband. He stopped, dropped his arm to his side, and looked across the road to the field on the other side. Still staring off into the distance, he said, "I try not to think about the future. We agreed you won't be a part of my future, so I'll just stay with you until the day you tell me 'I've met my future husband. Let's try to be friends.' That's when I'll have to face where I am and what I do next." They resumed walking, this time without touching.

"Don't assume I'll be telling you that anytime soon," she said.

129

"Men are not lining up at my door with engagement rings." From the moment she had set down the conditions under which she would see him again, this was the first time either of them had ever mentioned the inevitable end. Thoughts of their future made her turn away, back to his past. Perhaps the door to it was still ajar. "Apparently you weren't happy with your life before you came here."

"If I had been, I would have stayed there."

She glanced quickly at him and looked away, still trying to sound offhand. "Do you want to tell me about it?"

"Not right now. I'm still thinking about what you went through with Pierre. Even after all the time we've spent together and as much as we've talked, there's still a lot we don't know about each other."

Exasperated, she stopped on the path and turned to face him. How could he have the nerve to speak of how little they knew about each other? "What more do you want to know about me? What's left to tell? You've seen where I live, where I work. You've met my mother, my brother, my friends. My niece and nephew both worship you. I've just shared with you the most humiliating experience of my entire life. But you . . . " She caught herself once again. What right did she have to be angry at him? As frustrating as it was when he held out on her, she had no right to fault him for it. She had set limits on their relationship and so could he. The best she could do was finish the sentence and let the matter drop. " . . . you don't seem to like talking about your past, about your life in California."

His expression revealed nothing. "You know what's important about me. I have no wife and no kids, and you're the only woman in my life. The rest is just boring details." And that, by his tone of voice, was the end of it.

Boring details. Like everything she had told him about Pierre. Just boring details.

As they walked past the Roche-aux-Fées on the way back to the car, he said, "Maybe we should count the stones."

"It's not the night of the new moon," she said indifferently.

"We could come back. But we might discover something we don't want to face."

"What? That we aren't compatible?" In her mood of the moment, she did not need an old pile of rocks to tell her that.

"No. That we are."

His games were getting tiresome. He was leading her in circles, dropping tidbits and clamming up, again and again. It almost seemed he was trying to get back at her for the limits she had insisted on. This was going nowhere. It was best not to respond.

After an awkward silence, he added. "Let's go back through Rennes and you can show me where you used to live."

## Chapter 20: Time Running Out

At 12:30 on the day of Jocelyne's wedding, Anne closed the store for the day and threw together a quick lunch. Sitting in this familiar kitchen where she had eaten alone or with her mother thousands of times, something was off in her world. Since her visit with John to the Roche-aux-Fées, their tenuous relationship seemed even more fragile. His reluctance to talk about his past puzzled and annoyed her more than ever. Was he hiding something big? Something more serious than just a failed marriage?

She went to her bedroom and changed, putting herself together carefully: a black, knee-length sheath dress, panty hose, heels, the works. From her jewelry box she chose a pendant set with an oval amethyst, an heirloom from her grandmother. John had never seen her dressed up, at most in work clothes: a skirt or dressy pants, a businesslike top or blouse, and sometimes a blazer. Outside of work, casual pants or blue jeans, a plain top or sweater.

She examined herself front and back in her full-length mirror. Satisfied with what she saw, she went to the car and headed north to Sainte-Anne-d'Auray.

When she stopped in front of his house, she started to get out of the car, but he came out, closed the front door, locked it, and turned to walk to her car. It was the first time she had seen him in a suit, other than in the photo she had found on the internet right after meeting him. She thought it might be the same navy blue suit. He wore a white shirt and a blue tie with a red and white geometric pattern. He seemed older, more poised. And handsome. Very handsome.

He got in the car and leaned over to kiss her. She turned her head and offered him a cheek. "Don't smear my lipstick." While he was attaching his seat belt, she added, "You look very distinguished."

"And you, *Mademoiselle*, you are stunningly elegant."

She smiled and they set off for the Church of the Holy Cross in Nantes, to the wedding of the last of Anne's close single friends.

She navigated the familiar streets of Nantes looking for a

parking space. Neither had said a word about the question he must surely have on his mind: why was Anne not a bridesmaid in the wedding of one of her best friends? Unless he asked her point blank, she did not plan to tell him, and maybe not even then. She had already told him enough—too much. She spotted a space and pulled quickly into it.

They walked to the church, where they met Brigitte and Charles. Anne introduced John to Charles, who cheerily greeted John in what sounded to Anne like good English. Typical Charles, she thought, reflecting on the authenticity of his charm, on how pleased she was that he and her mother had become a couple. John answered him in English, speaking so slowly and clearly that even Anne understood. Mr. Charming meets Mr. Considerate. The four of them entered the sanctuary, filed into a pew, stood for a moment, and sat.

Soon the church filled with organ music, and the bridesmaids started down the aisle: Jocelyne's younger sister, still respectably single at age twenty-five, and two other women, both in their thirties: one divorced and one who had been living with a man for several years.

As they entered one by one, Anne began to feel left out. Yet it had been her choice. When Jocelyne had asked her, Anne had agreed at first, but that same evening, she pictured herself in front of a church full of witnesses, her unmarried status on display for everyone to see, no prospects in sight. She found the courage to call Jocelyne the next day and tell her how she felt. It would have been an awkward conversation, but Jocelyne replied with her typical grace, "I assumed you'd tell me if you didn't want to. I understand. It's OK. Really." If Anne had known she would be escorted by a boyfriend, she might not have felt so pitiable.

All the bridesmaids and groomsmen had entered and taken their positions. A dramatic change in the music signaled the impending entry of the bride. Everyone stood as Jocelyne came down the aisle on her father's arm in a classic long, white satin dress. John leaned over to Anne and whispered, "She's a knockout. If they split up, I want her. You can have Philippe." Amused in spite of her edginess, Anne responded with an elbow to his ribs.

As the ceremony progressed, Anne began to sense the time running out on her arrangement with John. What did he have to offer her besides some fun and company? Someday he would have to return to California, if only to see his parents and check in at his firm. At that moment, would she invoke their agreement and end their relationship for all time? If not, how long would she wait for him to come back? And why would she wait to resume a dead-end relationship?

If he were Breton, she could imagine making a life with him. But he was not Breton; he was not even French. At first, the idea of a foreign lover had excited her. But now as she found herself among her friends and family, her fellow Bretons, she knew more than ever that it was where she belonged.

As they filed out of the church after the ceremony, smiling and approving guests assured each other that Jocelyne and Philippe had chosen well. Even with his obsessions with soccer and rugby, Philippe was a good man with a good job. Born and raised in Nantes, he was a solid Breton and a good match for Jocelyne.

At the reception, John was his usual poised and friendly self as Anne introduced him to friends and relatives. At times, when the brouhaha and movement of people edged him out of her conversations, he spoke to others on his own, finding things to talk about with apparent ease. The superficial American, friendly with everybody but hard to know. After all this time, how well did she really know him?

During dinner, while Philippe danced with Jocelyne's sister, Jocelyne came to their table. Anne introduced her to John and watched them as they greeted each other. After some light conversation, Jocelyne asked Anne if she would allow her to dance with John. Good. Let them get acquainted. Before Jocelyne had met John, she had encouraged Anne to keep seeing him. What would she say now?

As Anne watched them dancing, engrossed in conversation, a hand touched her shoulder. One of the groomsmen, a friend of

Philippe's whom she had once met briefly, asked her to dance. Jean-Yves was a bank manager in Nantes, friendly, good looking, not pushy. He asked about her bookstore, where she had lived and gone to school. Maybe some decent, eligible men were left after all. Anne stole a look whenever she could at John and Jocelyne. They appeared to be far from running out of things to talk about.

Later, while Anne danced with John, he asked her who she had been dancing with. He listened to her answer but did not comment. After a few moments, she said, "You're not saying much. Are you bored?"

"No. I was thinking; that's all."

"About your own wedding?"

"Among other things, yes." He sounded wistful.

"Will you tell me about it?"

"Yes, but not tonight. It's too dismal a story to tell on a happy occasion like this."

How could she argue with that? Insist that he tell her about his divorce or his wife's death while celebrating her dear friend's wedding? She almost asked when he would tell her the story, but backed off once again.

On the way home in the car, the highway took them through the suburbs of Nantes into dark, open country. For the first few minutes, neither spoke.

As they passed the turnoff to Saint-Nazaire, she asked, "What did you and Jocelyne find so riveting to talk about?"

"A little of everything. I like her. Philippe is lucky."

"But you aren't. All you have is me."

"What do you mean?" He sounded surprised.

Her impulsive burst of sarcasm opened the valve to what had been building all afternoon and evening. "Oh, I'm handy to satisfy your little needs, someone to go out with, to cook for you, to screw when you get the urge. You have everything you want. And me? What do I have? I am sick to death of this life! I want my own family, a husband, children."

He started to speak, but she cut him off.

135

"And you know what really pisses me off? I bare my soul to you and you tell me nothing. You pretend to care about me, but you treat me like a stranger, like you don't trust me. What are you afraid of?"

At first he said nothing. He looked out the window at the passing forests, fields, gas stations.

"I'm talking to you! You have nothing to say to me?"

He chose his words carefully. "If I react to that rant, I might say something I'll regret. What did I do to deserve that?"

How could he stay so calm? She wanted him to react, to show her he was listening, that he cared what she was saying. Another jab might do it. "Apparently you weren't listening."

Still no reaction. He looked at her, studying her, as if trying to grasp what was happening. She expected he would think for a moment and tell her what she had heard before: how wonderful she was, how much he cared about her, how he hated the thought of losing her.

"I know we can't go on much longer like we have," he said, "not for you and not for me."

"And why not for you? You have everything you want."

With that, he exploded. "What the hell do you know about what I want? All you seem to care about is what *you* want. But since you're so sure you know what I want, please tell me, so we'll both know!"

She had finally gotten to him, finally gotten a rise out of Mr. Cool. "I know more about what you *don't* want: to leave your family, your country, your friends. In spite of all your big talk about living here, you're not about to throw all that away on a whim to move to the other side of the world, marry, have children, make a life here."

"Since when have you ever wanted to talk to me about marriage?" he shot back, louder now. "You haven't the slightest idea of whether I'd ever marry you because you rejected me as a possible husband from the moment we first met. As for this life you're so sick of, let me remind you it's exactly the life you asked for! You laid out your conditions and I agreed to them, because that's all you were willing to give me. Let's have some good times now and ignore the future, while you stayed free to look around for a better prospect. Those were *your* terms. Remember?"

"And you couldn't agree with them fast enough. My terms suited you just fine!"

"That is total bullshit and you know it! And how do you suppose I felt last week when you lectured me about what you wanted in a husband as if I didn't exist. Not that you give a good goddamn about my feelings. But OK. You want to change the deal and talk about marriage? Let's talk about marriage. Suppose I asked you to marry me right now."

It was an obvious smokescreen. He had no intention of ever marrying her, even if he thought she would consider it. "I'd say you're insane."

"That's outrageous! You tell me you'll keep me around for your temporary entertainment until you meet a Breton who's willing to put up with you then toss me aside like an old sock, and now you lay into me because you've somehow decided I'll never marry you, but the instant I mention marriage, you tell me I'm insane. You are really getting tiresome!"

"OK," she said, "While I'm getting tiresome, let's take it all the way. Let's go to the City Hall on Monday and get married. Then what? Will you sell your house in Los Angeles? Will you tell your parents and your employer and all your friends that you're not coming back? And how will you earn your living? Don't plan on working in the store. There's barely a living for two of us."

"You are really off the deep end! Why don't you try being honest for a minute, or is that too difficult? Your little snit has nothing to do with where I come from. There's something else." He was agitated now, looking at her, out his window, and back at her.

"Oh, this is going to be good. I can hardly wait to hear it." She was glad to be driving. It gave her an excuse not to look at him.

"Slow down and stay in your lane. You'll kill us both!"

"Not a bad idea. I wouldn't have to listen to you preach anymore."

"You've done your share of preaching; now you can shut up and listen. I don't even care if you want to hear it." He took a

137

breath and went on. "You can just keep taking the easy way out, writing me off so you don't have to think about what makes a real relationship. And when they next guy comes along, you'll do the same thing. He won't be perfect either, but with him it won't be so simple. You won't be able to dismiss him because he's a foreigner."

"So tell me, Mr. Fortune-Teller, what will I do with him?" she said in the most sarcastic voice she could muster. "I'd take notes if I weren't driving."

"Oh, nothing original. You'll do what women do. You'll convince yourself that once you marry him, you can change all the things about him you don't like. But you can't do that with me. You can't change where I was born."

"So I'm supposed to ignore all your faults because you're American? That's convenient." Now she had him. Let him argue his way out of that.

"Convenient for *you*. It lets you keep me outside your little fence without ever facing whatever it is that stops you from staying with a man—me or anybody else."

What an obnoxious know-it-all he was. "And what do you suppose that is? Since I'm stuck in church, I may as well hear the whole boring sermon."

"I don't pretend to know, and I'm getting to where I don't care. Why don't you stop wasting your time with me? You can marry some Breton, and go to work finding fault with *him*. But if he has any balls at all, he won't put up with your bullshit. He'll look somewhere else for a woman who accepts him as he is and where will you be then? Home chasing screaming kids around the house while your dreamboat is off somewhere in the sack with his mistress."

Her stomach tightened. Her eyes burned. How could he say such a cruel thing to her? She wanted to scream at him, but gripped the steering wheel hard, determined not to let him know he had gotten to her.

But he knew. As the headlights from a passing car lit her face, he could see he had gone too far. He looked out his window again and turned back to her, his voice softer. "I'm sorry. If you only knew . . . . " She thought he was about to lapse into silence

138

again after dropping yet another tantalizing tidbit. Not this time. "You can't imagine what torture it is to sit on the sidelines, watching the woman I love wait for the man of her dreams, knowing it will never be me."

Incredulous, she looked at him.

"No need to look so puzzled," he said. "You heard me right. I don't know when it hit me. Maybe the first time we kissed, maybe at the café in Plumergat, maybe the moment I walked into the store and first saw you. I almost said it in the car in the forest coming back from Huelgoat. When you laid out your conditions, I would have agreed to anything to keep seeing you. After that, I could never tell you how I felt. You think I've been holding out on you? You're right."

She was afraid to speak. She no longer knew him.

He was shaking his head, beyond anger now. "After all we've shared, as close as I thought we were, I'm still just an obstacle, standing between you and the life you want. I don't know what else to do, what else to say. Loving you is ecstasy one minute and misery the next. I don't know if I can take any more." He exhaled loudly and turned to stare out the window into the emptiness of the night.

She drove on in stunned silence, feeling her careful control eroding, the balance between them shifting. His words in the car leaving Bernard's house came back to her now, telling her that someday, once again, he would lose a woman he loved. So it was Anne after all. But how could he love her knowing he could be cast aside at any time? He had stayed with her, put his life on hold to be with her, dreading the day he knew would come.

"I don't know if I can take any more." he had said. Was their time together coming to its inevitable end? Was he ready to leave her behind and move on? He was giving her more than tantalizing little tidbits now, but the more he said, the less she understood.

Taking the exit to Auray and Sainte-Anne, they entered a roundabout and headed north. She turned onto his street and stopped in front of his house. Across the road a dog barked. She turned off the motor and the headlights. The barking stopped. He made no move to get out. Neither spoke. Minutes passed.

139

If he got out of her car and went into his house, it could be the end of them. She would go home to an empty apartment and be alone, so alone, tonight and the endless days and nights to follow.

More silence. She could feel him withdrawing again into himself, into that dungeon where he kept his past. She had to know what he was thinking, as afraid as she was of the answer. "Do you want me to get out of your life so you can find a woman who's not such a headache?"

He was facing the windshield, toward the dark country road outside. "You are a headache; I won't argue with that. But if you want to unload me again, it won't be so simple. You've gotten under my skin big time. There's my problem."

"May I stay?"

He gave her a quick nod. "I'll open the garage."

She kept an overnight bag with a change of clothes at his house. As she waited for the garage door to roll up, the odd thought occurred to her that if they went out the next day, someone might notice her in blue jeans carrying a black sequined purse.

Once inside the house, she put her arms around him and kissed him on the cheek. He held her, sliding his hands over the satin back of her dress. "It's late," he said. "Let's go to bed. We can talk more in the morning when we're both calm and rested."

As much as she regretted her angry outburst, she was more drawn to him now. Instead of giving up on her, instead of shutting her out as her father had, he had met her passion with his own, even told her in a moment of exasperation—perhaps regret—that he loved her. One more night together, but how much longer? Something had changed between them.

She came out of the bathroom into the bedroom to find him standing in his underwear, holding his pajamas, looking lost. Their boundaries had been battered by an argument that had pulled them apart, then left them in a fragile truce, a new divide between them. What could they expect from each other now? Small wonder he looked lost.

She took his pajamas from him, set them on a chair, and pointed to the bed. While he got in, she pulled her nightgown over

140

her head and got into bed next to him.

In the past, in the warm afterglow of making love, they had often talked, rambling and uninhibited. Yet even at those times, certain subjects had tacitly remained off limits. Until tonight.

"Why is my past so important to you?" he asked. "Why do you keep asking me about it?"

"Because I care about you."

"You care about me to a point." The Man Who Never Complained was starting to grumble.

"What could you possibly tell me about yourself that's more personal or more painful than what I told you about Pierre? It's not fair to shut me out."

He rolled over onto his back and felt around under the covers for her hand. He found it and took it in his. She laid her head next to his shoulder and nibbled at it, waiting for him to speak. Minutes passed.

Without moving, he asked, "What do you want to know?"

"Why you abandoned your old life and moved here."

"Stop me if I bore you."

"Don't worry." She listened in rapt attention to every word.

## Chapter 21: Love and Loss

"When we first met, my sordid past wasn't a proper topic of conversation. Even when we got to know each other better, I couldn't bring myself to say much. I wanted to tell you more, but the best I could do was drop little bits and change the subject."

So he knew he was doing it. She started to say something about it, but did not want to give him any excuse to stop.

"Where to start? I got married when I was barely 21. It wasn't really my choice. I got her pregnant."

John met Marie-Clothilde when he was a student in Bordeaux for a year in his university's education-abroad program. She was a political science major with an eye on a career in the diplomatic service. They were both twenty. She was like no other girl he had ever known: mysterious and alluring, distant yet seductive. He was mesmerized.

John and Marie-Clo were careful, but not careful enough. One day she announced that her period was overdue. A test confirmed she was pregnant. She was not Catholic enough to reject fornication, but too Catholic to abort. At least that was what she told him. John was far from ready for fatherhood, but could not bear the thought that someone else would raise his child.

His mother and father were as shocked as hers, but both sets of parents agreed to help John and Marie-Clo financially until John finished school. They married in Bordeaux that summer, and he brought her back to Los Angeles. His parents accepted her uncritically and anticipated the arrival of their first grandchild.

One day, when Marie-Clo was seven months pregnant, John came home after class to find Marie-Clo upset.

"The baby hasn't moved all day. I'm worried."

John called the doctor, who agreed to squeeze them in between appointments that afternoon. The time in the waiting room seemed endless, as Marie-Clo sat quietly with a hand on her belly, hoping to detect some movement. While she was on the examining table, John watched the doctor's inscrutable face. Finally,

142

deliberately, the doctor put his stethoscope down and after a glance at John, said to Marie-Clo, "There's no heartbeat. I'm afraid it's all over. I'm sorry. Would you like some time alone together?"

John nodded and the doctor left the room. John sat on the examining table next to Marie-Clo and held her.

"I didn't want this baby," she said. "Now I want it more than I ever wanted anything in my life." She wiped her eyes with the heel of her hands.

Now and over the months that followed, John was so preoccupied with comforting her that he had little time or energy to take care of himself, to understand and come to terms with his own emptiness.

Marie-Clo went from depression to rage and back again. After a few months, she settled down and found a job at the French Consulate. She welcomed the job initially as a step toward the diplomatic career she had aspired to and given up when she became pregnant. But the work was clerical and routine, and the position offered no serious possibility of advancement. She stayed with it to occupy herself and help support them, working while he went to class and studied, consoling herself with making friends among French people living in Los Angeles. Those friends and her colleagues at the Consulate became her social life, while John spent his days, evenings, and weekends consumed with his studies. They lived parallel lives and, without the baby to hold them together, drifted apart.

A few sessions with a marriage counselor revealed that Marie-Clo blamed the baby for derailing her education and career, and was in turn wracked with guilt over her anger at her dead baby. Rather than confront the issue, she searched for someone to blame for everything wrong with her life. She did not search long. It was John, after all, who was responsible for her pregnancy, John who had forced her to give up her own ambitions and leave her country, her family, and her friends.

Just how far they had drifted came home brutally to John when he discovered Marie-Clo was having an affair with a man who had come to the consulate to renew his passport. When John

143

confronted her, she ended the affair, and John tried to put aside his hurt. But he could not keep up his studies and give her enough attention to win her back. More sessions with the marriage counselor failed to heal the widening breach between them.

When Marie-Clo announced to John that she was leaving him to return to France and resume her studies, he tried half-heartedly to dissuade her. As much as he still cared for her, he was worn out.

They wrote to each other until their letters degenerated into an endless argument. John concluded it was time to move on and filed for divorce. Once their divorce was final, he and Marie-Clo abandoned all contact with each other. Even so, John did not forget the support and understanding her parents had given him, regardless of their motives, and he continued each year to exchange New Year's greetings with them, never mentioning Marie-Clo.

He finished law school, passed the bar exam, and taking a job with a small business-law firm, worked hard to become the best lawyer he could be. On the advice of older lawyer in his firm who had become his mentor, he set aside some of his earnings for investment. John saved and invested well and his portfolio grew. A series of superficial relationships met his need for sex and companionship, but he avoided dating any woman who, like Marie-Clo, might lead him again to abandon his good sense.

Then one Saturday, when John was working in his yard, he heard his neighbor Frank fall off a ladder. John hopped over the fence, splinted Frank's broken arm, and drove him to the emergency room. As the attending physician worked, John watched, enchanted. Diane M. Orsini, M.D. declared the lab coat of this energetic and attractive brunette not quite John's age. It was a slow day in the emergency room, and John chatted with Dr. Orsini while she worked. When she sent Frank to be x-rayed, John asked her if she could take a coffee break with him.

They sat across from each other at the end of a long table in the hospital cafeteria. "I appreciate the way you're handling Frank, Doctor. He's not especially brave. I could see him relax while you were talking to him."

144

"Thanks, but you're not my patient, so call me Diane. And what do you do, sir?"

"I'm not your patient, so call me John," he said, and added with some trepidation, "I'm a lawyer."

She was unfazed. "Don't sue me for the bad coffee, OK? I just work here." A pause. "A lawyer. Too bad. Lawyers and physicians don't usually get along."

"You're right," he said, "This coffee is awful." As they each took a sip of awful coffee, he groped for something more intelligent to say. The best he could conjure up was, "How do you deal with the stress of your work?"

"Stress? What stress? I love it. It's always exciting." Indeed, she seemed invigorated by the mere mention of her work. "And the rare times it slows down, I get to have bad coffee with charming lawyers." A quick little smile. "OK, this is the first time. But I hope it's not the last."

As they talked, John gazed at her, mesmerized not only by her riveting brown eyes, her long chestnut hair and flawless complexion, but also by her intelligence and humor. As she spoke, he felt himself emerging from the emotional dead zone in which he had existed since Marie-Clo left him.

Lest he get his hopes up and be disappointed, he wanted to ask Diane point blank if she was available and interested. "Now that we're on first names, may I ask you a very personal question?"

"Why don't we have dinner tomorrow night and you can ask it then?" she said. "But I have to warn you; there are certain things I never do on a first date."

"Such as?"

"Accept a marriage proposal."

John stared at her, stunned and fascinated. He retorted as best he could. "You wouldn't want to marry me anyway. I'm damaged goods."

"Oh, this I have to hear. Try to shock me. Just try."

He doubted he could rise to her level of outrageous, but accepted the challenge. "I've been married twelve times."

Diane was not to be outdone. "Finally a man with some

experience! I'm so sick of thirty-five-year-old virgins who live with their mother. We're gonna get along just fine."

At dinner the following evening, John did not propose marriage, but he did propose another date, which Diane readily accepted. Her intensity and uninhibited wit excited him, as did her frenetic need to live for the moment. When he walked her to her door on their third date and kissed her goodnight, she put her arms firmly around him and backed into her apartment, dragging him with her. In the morning, he awoke to find Diane sitting on the bed offering him a mug of coffee. She did not give him time to finish it.

During the next five months, they saw each other whenever their respective schedules permitted. She entertained John with tales of the emergency room, which he found fascinating. He in turn regaled her with his accounts of life in France, where she had never been, saying as little as he could about Marie-Clo. One Sunday afternoon, when they were lying in bed after making love twice, Diane sat up abruptly and announced she wanted to go for a drive. He called her a hyperkinetic nymphomaniac. She took it as a compliment. He assured her it was. They drove an hour and a half up the coast to Santa Barbara for dinner, during which John proposed and Diane accepted. They set a tentative date for their wedding.

After a few weeks, John noticed that Diane was less available. She seemed to lose some of her fire, which was not all bad; sometimes her energy wore him out. And then one morning, she showed up at his house at 3:00am. At first, he thought nothing of it. Several times, she had dropped in on him after work at odd hours of the night, telling him, "I'm too hyped up to sleep." He quickly learned that her solution to the too-hyped-up-to-sleep problem would make it worth his while to stumble through the next day exhausted. This time, she was not hyped up. She was more serious, more somber than he had ever seen her. He asked her what was wrong.

"It was a slow shift tonight. I had time to think and I finally came to terms with something I haven't wanted to face. I'm not ready to get married. I'm not ready to settle down. I misled myself and I misled you."

"We can put it off," he said. "I'm in no hurry."

"I don't know if I'll ever be able to live a normal, domestic life. It's just not me, at least not yet."

He sensed something ominous, that she had more to say. He did not want to hear it, but he had to. "What are you trying to tell me?"

"I love you and I respect you. We've had wonderful times together. But I'm not ready to limit myself to one man." And in case he had not understood, she added, "I hope we can stay friends."

As he began to comprehend what was happening, he stared at her, unable to speak.

"I'm sorry," she said. "You won't believe me now, but I really do love you. Give me a chance to prove it." She pulled him toward the bedroom.

He went along passively, still in shock. When it was over, she dressed, kissed him and said goodbye.


He sat in the living room reliving their torrid, frenetic months together. At dawn, he called the office and left a message that he would not be in. He had always looked forward to his work day. Not today.

Diane called him a few days later to check on him. It was a tense but civilized conversation. She did her best to convince him that she still loved him, and asked him to call when he was ready to see her as a friend. That time never came.

John went from disbelief to despair. Marie-Clo's departure had been tempered by the realization that a stormy relationship had ended, that his best years were ahead of him, that he would recover and move on. This time, he had no such consolation. He could not imagine ever meeting another woman who could measure up to Diane.

His motivation and ambition began to wane. Each day's challenges, which he had met with energy and enthusiasm, became oppressive.   Daydreams of the life he had planned with Diane flooded his thoughts and crippled his concentration: places they would go together, the family they would raise together.   Even his own house made him think of her and his dream of moving her into it: the kitchen where they cooked, the patio where they ate, the bedroom where they made love.

Morose moods began to morph into visions of places he might escape to, where memories of Diane would not arise at every turn.   As the days passed, even as Diane began to fade from his daydreams, visions of escape became more intense, more intrusive. He knew they would not go away, that he had to do something, to go somewhere.

He imagined going to live in France, a place just exotic enough, where he knew the language and customs.   But where in France?   Bordeaux held too many memories, and he could not risk crossing paths with Marie-Clo.   He recalled a trip he had taken to Brittany when he was a student in Bordeaux, a pilgrimage to places he remembered from a book he had read as a child.

What he had seen on that trip enchanted him.   He explored the southern coast: the old inner city of Vannes, the rows of ancient stones in the meadows around Carnac, Pont-Aven with its rushing stream and water wheels, the fortified town on an island in the bay of Concarneau.   He turned north into the Argoat, Brittany's interior, passing through villages stuck in time, exploring hills and forests, rivers and glens.

Thoughts of Brittany sent him to the library and the bookstore, where he read everything he could find.   It all pulled him in the same direction, toward Brittany with its history of a fiercely proud people scraping out a living from the land and the sea, its distinctive language, music, dances, and costumes.   Brittany would be perfect, he decided: rich in history, prehistory, and scenic wonders, but largely rural and undiscovered by American tourists.

His closest friends were surprised that John, who was everyone's paragon of stability and responsibility, would consider such a thing.   But when he awoke one morning, his decision was made.

148

The goal of living in Brittany restored his spirit, turning his thoughts away from Diane and back toward work—and his plan. He tried working at home two days a week, to see whether telecommuting was feasible. It was.

Finally he presented his partners with what he wanted to do and a carefully thought-out plan showing how the change would benefit the firm. They could sub-let his office or fill it with an additional lawyer. He would need fewer support services. He could trade tasks with the lawyers in the firm who wanted to do less paperwork and spend more time in court. The management committee, after giving due consideration to John's years of hard work and dedication, agreed to let him try it.

He rented his house to a friend, leased a house in Sainte-Anne-d'Auray, and moved.

Then one day, with nothing more on his mind than buying some books, he walked into the Librairie Renaud and first laid eyes on Anne.

She lay quietly beside him, touched by all he had shared with her. At last he had opened up and let her in. At last she understood what had brought him to the moment they met.

Thinking again of that moment, she said, "When you first came into the store, I remember a strange look on your face, like you thought you were in the wrong store. What was going on in your head?"

"I was spellbound. There you were behind the counter in command of an army of books, looking at me with those sparkling green eyes. I could hardly talk. It was all I could do not to stare at you. You caught me peeking at you later, remember? When you came closer, I tried to sneak a look at your ring finger."

"I was doing the same thing. I remember you took a book from me with your left hand; was that on purpose?"

"Good catch. I kept coming up with more books to ask you about. I was ready to buy every book in the store until I got up the courage to ask you out."

149

"While you were thinking of more books to buy, I was thinking I could seduce you, sell you 100 books, then send you on your way."

"You've only sold me about ten books so far, but you did seduce me. Does this mean if I buy ninety more books I'm back on the scrap heap?"

On a mirthful whim, she rolled over, half on top of him, grabbed his wrists and pinned him to the bed. "Who seduced whom?"

"*You* seduced *me*. You came here on the pretext of wanting to talk, you flashed me a gorgeous smile, you came into my house and kissed me passionately. What did you expect to happen?"

"I don't recall much resistance." She let go of him and lay back down, sensing this was her chance to ask him everything, before he clammed up again. "The book about Brittany, it's the one that's on your bookshelf, isn't it?"

"It shouldn't surprise me that you've been snooping through my books, given what you do for a living."

"You wouldn't tell me anything, so I had no choice. How did you manage to keep a library book? Did you steal it?"

"There was this gorgeous librarian who seemed to like me. She noticed that I checked it out several times. When the library was getting rid of old books, she retrieved it and gave it to me."

"How old was she?"

"Really old, maybe twenty. I was ten. Why are you smiling?"

"It's a cute story." She wanted to tell him about the California book her father had given her, but it was more important to keep him talking.

After a strategic pause, she asked, "Why didn't you want to tell me about Marie-Clo and Diane?"

"At first it was because I came here to get away from my old life. If I talked about it here, it would follow me here. Then, I was afraid you'd wonder what was wrong with me that makes women leave me when they really get to know me." He lay on his back, facing the ceiling. She could tell this was still hard for him to talk about.

150

"What they did says more about them than it does about you."

"Maybe so, but our relationship is fragile enough. I didn't want to give you a reason to end it."

"Why are you so sure I'll be the one to end it?"

"That's our deal, isn't it?"

"No. That's not our deal." In spite of the agreement she had extracted from him, she had not assumed she would be the one to break it off. "You could decide you've had enough long before I even think about ending it. You talk like you've committed to stay with me until I decide to go off and marry someone else no matter how long that might be. And what if that never happens? Whatever it is you want from me, if you decide you're not getting it, you're free to go anytime you want. We aren't chained together."

"I wish we were. I don't want to lose you."

The air in the bedroom was chilly. She rolled onto her back and pulled the blankets up to her neck. "I understand the fear of losing someone. I can't get the idea out of my head that you'll go back to California and I'll never see you again."

When she awakened at midmorning, he was still asleep.

She lay in bed, staring at the ceiling, stricken with anxiety.

## Chapter 22: A Plan of Action

She slipped out of bed, put on blue jeans and a sweater, and sat outside on the veranda behind the house. Across the back fence, a flock of blackbirds swirled over the pasture and disappeared into a cloudy sky. A neighbor's cat climbed into her lap. As the cat curled up and began to purr, Anne stroked its long, brown fur and lamented. *I'm ruining my life. Whenever happiness is in sight, I run the other way.*

Anne had rejected every man she could have married, always enumerating her reasons with irrefutable clarity. And now, with a man who attracted her like no other, the pattern was repeating. She could run again, but from what? There was no escape. Whatever it was that pushed her away from other men would follow her now, as it always had. Somehow John knew it too; he had said as much the night before on the road from Nantes. Through the ups and downs of their relationship so far, John had been constant. Anne had been the one to come close then pull away, just as she had done with other men, all of them French. John was right. His nationality was just an excuse.

What was her problem? Bad luck? Bad timing? Was she too aloof, too desperate? If she was doing something wrong—pursuing unsuitable men, for example—Sophie or Jocelyne, both of whom were candid with Anne, would have told her.

She lifted the cat off her lap and set it on the ground and left John a note telling him she had gone home to take care of a number of unstated pressing obligations and promising to call him later in the day.

Jocelyne was in Spain on her honeymoon, and despite a gnawing sense of urgency, Anne could not bring herself to intrude upon Sophie's Sunday dinner with her family. When Anne called later in the afternoon, Sophie asked about Jocelyne's wedding, adding, "Don't mind the racket in the background. "We're playing Scrabble and Stéphanie is arguing with Michel about the word he just put down. So what's up?"

Anne sidestepped Sophie's question about the wedding and went to the point. "Can you come here for lunch tomorrow? I'd come there, but I have to work all day and I really need to talk."

"Anne, what's wrong? You sound terrible. Of course I can."

"Go back to your family. I'll see you tomorrow."

On hanging up, Anne pictured Sophie, Michel, and their children playing Scrabble together, spending Sunday afternoon in the warmth and security of family. Now more than ever, Anne longed for what she did not have: the strong presence of a husband, the innocence and wonderment of children.

She missed John already, but was not ready to face him. She kept her promise to call him, even with some misgivings about where the conversation could lead. He asked her if she was getting her work done.

Knowing he would be too discreet to ask what she had to do that was so urgent, she said only, "Yes," then carefully turned the subject away from her. "What are you doing today?"

"Frankly, I've been wondering why you dashed off without even saying goodbye, especially after all we shared last night. You sound a little off this afternoon. Is anything wrong?"

"No, of course not," she said, and promised to call him the next day.

On Monday, Sophie arrived at the bookstore just as Anne was closing for lunchtime. They walked to the Crêperie Alréène, where she had gone with John for their first lunch.

After they had ordered, Sophie said, "I bet all the women at the wedding fell in love with your gorgeous hunk of a boyfriend!"

Anne appreciated Sophie's effort to cheer her up, but it was futile.

Anne's silence turned Sophie serious. "Something's wrong between you and John, isn't it?"

Anne told Sophie about the wedding and their argument afterward, about how they made up and her panic on awakening.

When Anne had finished, Sophie said, "It sounds like you're getting ready to dump him."

"Up to now we've been able to live for the moment, to be together and enjoy each other. But it isn't working anymore. I knew this was where we'd end up, but I refused to think about it. So did he. Now it's caught up with us. I can't stop worrying about what happens if he moves back to California. As for him, he's tired of being with me knowing what's just under the surface, dreading the moment it'll pop up again and ruin everything."

"Why do you have to assume he'll go back? If you keep insisting it's just temporary between you, he probably will; why would he stay? But if he thought you were really serious about him, he'd find a way to stay."

Anne, who had sought Sophie's help in sifting through her confusion, found herself turning impatient and skeptical. Sophie's assessment sounded too simple, too certain to be correct. "I doubt it," Anne said. "John will leave me eventually just like my father did." She took a sip of cider and asked, "Are you still thinking of remodeling your kitchen?"

Sophie sat up and fixed her eyes on Anne. "Do you realize what you just said?"

"I asked if you were still thinking of remodeling your kitchen."

"Before that."

"All I said was John will leave me."

"After that."

"Just like my . . . father . . . " She sat stunned, speechless. Why had she not seen it before now? She caught herself staring at Sophie, who was waiting for some reaction. "You don't think . . . "

"I've wondered for years."

"Why didn't you ever say anything?"

"It was just a thought, and it didn't seem to matter so much. But John's different." Sophie stopped and looked away.

"Sophie, what are you trying to tell me?"

Sophie turned back to Anne, as serious as Anne had ever seen her. "You're about to throw away something really good. You light up when you talk about John like I've never seen you do. And I understand why; he's a gem. He's not like other men. You can't let

154

him get away."

At home that evening, Anne replayed again and again what Sophie had said. "You're about to throw away something really good." She tried in vain to dismiss the words as just another of Sophie's dramatic flourishes, but the afterimage of Sophie's tone and expression would not allow it. Anne awoke in the middle of the night hearing the words again. "He's not like other men. You can't let him get away."

In the morning, Anne considered for a moment telling her mother what Sophie had said, but could think of no way to phrase it without implying that her mother had some responsibility in the matter. She went so far as to think her mother would have little to offer, having failed to hold onto her own husband. But that thought too was quickly dismissed, leaving Anne feeling guilty for entertaining such an idea, however transitory. Her mother was blameless, Anne reminded herself.

When she called John that night as promised, he asked her to go with him the following evening to see a movie they had talked about. She accepted with mixed feelings, fearing he would sense something was off and ask what was bothering her.

When he drove her home after the movie, he stopped in front of her apartment and said, "You're not yourself lately. I'm getting worried. Are you upset about something I said Saturday night? Are you trying to get up your courage to tell me it's time to stop seeing each other?"

His bluntness surprised her. Anne had been so mired in her own anguish that she had given little thought to what John might be feeling. Her standoffishness had disturbed him more than she had realized. She hastened to reassure him. "No. No. Of course not. I'm just having a hard time lately. I'm not sure why. I didn't mean to take it out on you. I'll get over it."

Jocelyne called the next morning to tell her she and Philippe were back from their honeymoon in Spain and suggested they meet for lunch.

Anne's uneasiness mounted as lunchtime approached. Since Anne had met John, it seemed her two best friends—two women with nothing but Anne in common—had been giving Anne the same advice without ever speaking to each other. What would Jocelyne say now?

Anne asked Jocelyne about the honeymoon, not really wanting to hear about it. Yes, she was happy for Jocelyne, but wishing her friends well as they married off was wearing thin.

Jocelyne disposed of her honeymoon in a few words and changed the subject. "Something's bothering you; I can tell. Do you want to talk about it?"

"I didn't want to burden you with my problems right now. I figured you'd be preoccupied with settling in, getting used to married life."

Jocelyne shrugged. "Actually it's nice to get out of the house for something other than work." She noticed Anne was biting her knuckle and asked, "Is it John?"

"John and every other man I've known. It seems I blame them all for what my father did to me."

Jocelyne looked pensive for a moment, then asked, "What did your father do to you?"

"He proved to me that men couldn't be trusted."

"All men?"

"Maybe that's not fair. There must be a man out there I can trust." Anne felt like one of Jocelyne's students, forced to think, pursued relentlessly when trying to evade an important issue.

"And if you ever meet him, will you trust him?"

"Maybe not. It seems I expect every man in the world to behave like my father."

"Suppose for a moment that's true. What does that mean for you? A lifetime of dumping men before they can leave you?"

The next morning, Jocelyne called her with a name and phone number, which Anne dutifully wrote on a scrap of paper. For all her impatience and determination, it took her an hour to summon the courage to make the call. She made an appointment for Monday afternoon.

She sent John an email. "I need a few days to myself. Be patient with me. See you soon. Hugs and kisses."

Later, she saw John's reply. "I miss you. I'll wait for you. I love you."

There it was again, that troublesome little word. He had used it once before, in the car after the wedding. As affectionate as he was, he had been careful not to go too far, not to say the word that would threaten their delicate balance. Now, almost in desperation, he had written it. She had never said it to him. As much as she cared for him, as much as she wanted to be with him, as much as they had become part of each other's life, she did not know if she loved him— or if she ever could.

Monday afternoon, Anne drove into Vannes. She entered an office building and found her way to the door she wanted. "Odile Laborde, Ph.D." Apprehensive but resolved, she opened it.

Dr. Laborde seemed ageless, older than Anne but perhaps younger than her mother. Her gentle manner tempered a strong presence. She showed Anne into a softly lit room with two overstuffed chairs and a couch. The couch seemed too cinematic. Anne chose a chair.

Dr. Laborde sat in a chair opposite Anne and said, "Would you like to tell me what prompted you to call?"

Anne wanted to get started—and finished. "I've been seeing an American man and trying not to fall in love with him. I'm losing the battle. He's everything I've ever wanted, but we have this problem."

Dr. Laborde nodded, signaling Anne to continue.

Anne told Dr. Laborde about meeting John, about leaving him and coming back to him, about their argument after the wedding, about how she felt the following morning. She spoke of previous relationships, how they started with excitement and anticipation and ended in indifference and disappointment. At the end of the session, she made another appointment for Wednesday

157

afternoon and walked out relieved to have avoided for the moment the issue that had brought her here.

As Anne approached Dr. Laborde's office on Wednesday, she was every bit as apprehensive as when she had first come here. Today there would be no more skirting the big issue. Like learning to go off the high dive, there was only way to do it.

She opened with, "I should tell you about my family background."

"Please do."

Laboriously, Anne plodded through her childhood, her relationship with her father, her parents' separation and divorce, her anger on learning of her father's affairs. She finished with her conversations with Sophie and Jocelyne and sat silent, drained, waiting for some comment from Dr. Laborde.

When enough time had passed to know Anne had finished, Dr. Laborde said, "It sounds like you took what your father did very personally, like he did it to you too, not just your mother."

"He did it to all three of us. We were like nothing to him. All he cared about was finding a new place to stick his dick!" She stopped, ashamed of what she had just said. "I'm sorry. I shouldn't have said that."

Dr. Laborde remained impassive. "Why not, if it's how you feel?"

"I'm not usually so crude."

"You're safe here. You can say how you feel any way it occurs to you. Go on."

It had all come back, the helplessness and anger Anne had felt when her parents had announced their separation. "When he left, I was furious at him. I was determined to punish him for it. But I was eleven years old. There wasn't much I could do, other than shut him out of my life. It only got worse when I learned about all his affairs."

"How would shutting him out of your life punish him if he didn't care about you?" Anne, who had an answer for everything, was stumped. She groped for a response but found nothing. After a long pause, Dr. Laborde added, "So now you expect all men to behave like your father."

Somehow Anne had hoped to hear that her problem had nothing to do with her father. But Dr. Laborde's blunt summary left her no escape. She studied her fingernails, bit her knuckle. Her eyes wandered around the room, oblivious to whatever they saw. She wanted to protest, to say we're wasting time. She had heard of people spending years in psychotherapy. Anne had neither the patience nor the money for that. She told Dr. Laborde she wanted a plan of action, something dramatic she could do to move things along.

"Twenty years won't be undone in one day. But let's explore that. What action might you take? What occurs to you? Don't reject anything."

Anne came back to what she had done before. "Go see my father and tell him off, make him understand what he did to me."

"You've done that before. Did it help?"

"No. It made it worse."

"Suppose you went again to talk to your father, what else might you say to him?"

John's latest email disturbed her. "I can't stop thinking about the last time you were distant with me and what followed. I miss you. I need to talk to you. I need to hold you. I'm afraid I told you too much."

She was determined not to hurt him again, but what she was about to do would take all of her attention, all of her strength. What she had set in motion had been too long in coming; she would allow nothing to distract her. She replied, "John, I miss you too. I'm working through something and I need some time. Please believe me that I'll come back to you. Give me a few more days. Please trust me."

Then she called her father.

A few minutes after noon on Saturday, she arrived at her father's apartment in Rennes. At the front door, she scanned the column of buttons set in a shiny brass plate, each with a name on a label next to it and found "GOUDIN, Jacques." She stared at the name for a moment. It was not as if she could back out now; they were expecting her. She pressed the button. With a buzz and a click, the door unlocked. She took her time walking up two flights of the winding staircase, noting that the leafy pattern in the aging beige wallpaper in the stairwell had faded almost entirely away. She had not been here in many months.

At the end of the hall, the door to the apartment was ajar. Florence, her father's sometime mistress and now wife, opened it as Anne approached. They exchanged a formal two-cheek kiss. The same with her father, who greeted her with, "It's good to see you, my dear. It's been a long time."

Anne fumed. *It takes one lousy little hour to drive from Rennes to Auray on a modern four-lane, toll-free highway. And the train and the telephone, great inventions. Maybe I should tell him about them.* In spite of her annoyance, she kept her sarcasm to herself. She was determined not to sabotage her mission by lapsing into her old ways.

A veneer of innocuous conversation at lunch helped Anne conceal her anxiety over what was to come. By the time they had finished discussing the weather, the municipal elections, fuel prices, and trends in the book business, they were finishing their coffee. Florence cleared the table and excused herself. As dense as Florence could be, she was capable of understanding that Anne had come to see her father and not her. Anne thanked her cooly for lunch. As Florence left the dining room, she closed the door behind her, as if she sensed something important was about to happen.

It was time for Anne to get down to business, quickly, before her courage failed. She looked her father in the eye and asked, "Why did you leave Mom?"

Suddenly, he looked ten years older, sad, defeated. One little question from Anne seemed to hit him harder than years of her angry tirades.

He pushed some breadcrumbs around on the tablecloth and looked back up at her. "Your mother and I agreed never to involve you and Bernard in our problems. I would like to talk to you, but I want to respect that agreement."

With that, Anne exploded. "Don't treat me like a child! I am thirty-three years old, in case you've lost track. I have a right to know. It's *my* life we're talking about, not just yours. Why do you suppose I'm an old maid twenty-one years after you bailed out to go off on your little adventures?"

The anguish on his face stopped her. She took a deep breath and looked down, grasping the edge of the table to steady herself. She had not come to berate him again; she knew it would accomplish nothing. She looked back up at him. "I'm sorry," she said. "I'll keep my mouth shut for a change. It's your turn to talk. Don't worry about your agreement. Mom will never know."

He looked toward the dining-room door then at the window, as if seeking to escape once again from his daughter's fury. There was no way out. "It isn't news to me that you're still angry with me, not just for leaving your mother, but for leaving all three of you. So many times I wanted to talk to you. I never knew what to say. And I didn't know how you would react."

"What did you think I might do?"

"Something like you just did, or worse. You've never been afraid to speak your mind, not even to your parents."

"I came here and I'm asking you," she said. "I need to know."

He shifted in his chair, moved his coffee cup to one side and began haltingly. "Your mother was—is—a wonderful woman, attractive, responsible, loving, dependable, faithful. Everything a husband could want, except . . . " He stopped and searched for the words.

Anne prodded him. "Except what?"

"That was the problem. Life had no more surprises, no excitement. Everything was predictable. I suffocated. I started to look for adventure with other women. Little by little, your mother figured it out. When she confronted me, I didn't deny it. She already knew, but it still hurt her. I offered to leave, to do whatever was necessary for her to divorce me. I offered to give her everything. She asked me to stay a little longer for you and Bernard. But I

161

couldn't live like that. I couldn't ask her to live like that. Every time I came home, she would know. I knew I wasn't going to change."

He spoke as if he had finally been given permission to tell the truth after a lifetime of lies. "I lied to Florence like I lied to everyone else. When she found out I had a wife and two children, she was horrified. She said she refused to destroy a family, even for me. She begged me to go home to my family and never see her again. For a while she refused to see me."

Anne was aghast. Did he just say that Florence refused to see him when she found out he was married? Why had nobody ever told her? After all those years, now to see Florence as a well-meaning victim was almost more than Anne could absorb.

There was more. "Eventually, we figured out that if she and I never saw each other again, it would make no difference; I'd just go after someone else. I cheated on her too, before I married her and after. I'm not proud to tell you this. But you already knew most of it. Your father, I'm afraid, is a self-centered bastard. I'm grateful that you and Bernard turned out so well in spite of me. Your mother gets all the credit."

She had not expected him to open up as he had. At most, she had hoped for some attempt to explain his behavior. But at least words would flow.

"I'm not so sure I turned out all that well, in spite of Mom's best efforts."

She came back to the bombshell he had dropped on her. "You should have told me the truth about Florence. Leaving me to think it was all her fault wasn't fair to her or to me. I used to think if I was mean enough to her, she'd go away and you'd come back." They sat for a few moments in silence. It was her move again. She was not sure she was up to it. It was too hard, too threatening, too painful.

He gave her an opening. "All of that happened years ago. Why did you come and ask me about it now?"

She got up from the table and paced a few times across the end of the dining room, stalling, deciding whether to tell him about John. She made up her mind and turned to him. "There's a man I've

162

been seeing. He's a wonderful man, and we're made for each other. He loves me more than I thought any man could love me. I'm afraid if I let myself love him, he'll leave me."

"Like I did." His voice was tentative, his defenses down, his excuses exhausted. The voice of a failed father wanting to make amends but not knowing how.

Anne nodded slowly, reluctant at first to speak, fearing what might emerge. But she had resolved when she came here to hold nothing back. "You showed me how it felt to be loved by a man. Then you left me."

Her father stood up, walked over to the window and looked out. What could he be thinking? He turned back to her. "Whatever regrets I may have about what I did—and believe me, I do have them—what's done is done. What can I possibly do about it now, after all these years?"

As she listened and watched his face, it was clear he wanted to know. The moment was upon her; it was too late to back out. Summoning all her courage, she asked him—begged him—for what she had desperately needed for so long. "Tell me you didn't leave because of me. Tell me I'm worthy of a man's love. Tell me . . . just tell me you love me!" Her voice broke as her eyes filled with tears of despair.

Through her tears she saw him coming to her, crossing the divide between them. With his arms around her, he said, "I love you, my dear sweet little girl. I love you so very much. And I have missed you. Oh God how I've missed you!" He held her while he regained his composure. When he was able to speak again, he said, "I'm looking forward to meeting this man. Does he have any idea how lucky he is?"

With her cheek next to his, the aroma of old wool and shaving cream carried her back to her childhood, to sweet memories of the happy times they had lived together, and she mourned the years they had lost.

On the way home, she took a detour to Nantes. It was out of her way, but she needed time to absorb all her father had said to her,

163

about himself, about her mother, about her, and about Florence, time to comprehend what had just happened, what Anne had finally found the courage to make happen.

Already, warm feelings toward her father were giving way to new moments of bitterness, and she found herself slipping back into the confusion that had beset her for so many years. Dr. Laborde was right when she warned her that talking to him would be only a first step, that regardless of his response, twenty years would not be undone in one day. But at least, Anne had taken a step.

Anne was not one to waste time and had already decided on her next step. What she was about to do was almost as risky as what she had just done. She needed a few more minutes to get up her courage again.

She walked past her old apartment on Rue Gambetta, remembering those bygone days, the failed relationships, the men she had tried to love but rejected. Crossing the street, she entered the Botanical Garden, sat on a bench, and took another moment to select her exact words. She called John on his cell phone, resolved to say the words before she changed her mind.

He answered.

"I called to tell you I love you." A moment of silence told her he was taking in what she had just said. For that matter, so was she.

He regrouped. "It's disconcerting to be loved by an invisible woman. Where are you?"

"In Nantes. I had lunch with my father." It was too soon to share the details. "And where are you?"

"On the beach at Erdeven. I've been trying to work, but all I can think about is you. So I'm sitting here watching a man and his daughter tossing a beach ball back and forth. When are you coming back?"

"Right away. I want to see you. I'll come straight to your house."

"Be careful on the road from Nantes. There's a warp or something that puts you in a bad mood."

She heard something odd in his voice. His facetious warning

did not square with his serious tone. "I'll be careful," she said. "What's so fascinating about a man and his daughter playing with a beach ball?"

After a few seconds of silence, he said, "My baby that died . . It was a girl."

## Chapter 23: Too Much Alike

The hour's drive from Nantes to Sainte-Anne-d'Auray passed quickly. She was eager to see him. On arrival, she saw he had opened the garage for her and pulled her car in next to his.

He greeted her at the door from the garage into the house. "Did you tell your father about me?"

"Yes. He said you're a lucky man."

"He's right—most of the time."

She sensed a reserve, as if John was not fully present. It was not like him; he had never been moody around her. She did not mention it right away, hoping the specter of their short separation would fade and his mood would pass. "I needed some time alone," she said. "There was something I had to do. I was afraid if I was too comfortable, I wouldn't do it. I'm OK now."

"Will you tell me about it?"

"Soon. Not right now." It was the first time she had refused him an answer. As satisfied as she was with what she had done, she was not ready to share it with him. She had taken on as much as she could handle and wanted to put it behind her for the moment. She would tell him in due course.

The longer they were together, the more subdued he became. In bed, she snuggled up to him and kissed him. He held her and stroked her hair, but said little and showed no interest in sex.

While she was dressing in the morning, he went to the *boulangerie* to buy bread and croissants. She made coffee and set the kitchen table. As they sat down to breakfast, she did her best to appear upbeat and optimistic, hoping his mood had changed. She asked, "What do you want to do today?"

"This afternoon I'm going to visit some friends in the Côtes-d'Armor for two days. I was lonely and I didn't know if—when— you would come back. You can come with me if you want." The invitation sounded lukewarm.

"I can't. Mom is staying in Nantes tonight and I have to work tomorrow morning. Did you really think I wouldn't come back?"

"The thought occurred to me. You tried to reassure me. I appreciated that."

"But you didn't believe me."

"You came back the first time. The second time at least you stayed in touch. The third time, who knows?"

"Are you so sure there will be a third time?"

"I'm not sure of much of anything anymore."

"Are you going to get upset with me every time I need a few days to myself?"

"How can I answer that when I have no idea why you stayed away from me?"

She knew he would not let go until she gave some explanation. "OK. Listen. I have some problems with my father. It's very hard for me to talk about right now. It's too raw. I'll tell you about it later. Please try to understand."

He stared silently into his coffee bowl. She waited in vain for him to speak. After another minute of silence, she reached across the table, put a finger under his chin and lifted his head until he looked at her. "Talk to me John. You're worrying me. What's going on in there? A week ago, you shared your life with me. A few days ago, you wrote 'I love you' in an email. Today, I barely get a 'good morning.' Are you mad at me?"

He reached for the bread basket and asked absently, "Would you like another croissant?"

"No!" she shouted, overcome with frustration. "I would not like another goddamn croissant! I would like you to talk to me! Is that too much to ask?"

He looked at her, saying nothing, showing nothing. Now it came back to her, trying to get some response from her father by speaking sharply to him and getting even angrier when he refused to react. Yelling at John was every bit as futile.

She changed her tone. "What do you want from me? Do you want an apology? Do you want me to go away and leave you alone? Tell me what you want. I'm listening."

He took a croissant, tore it in half, and dropped half back

167

into the basket. He stared at the other half for a moment and set it down on his plate. "I can't stop thinking about what you said at Huelgoat. If it's inevitable that you're going to leave me, it might be better just to get it over with. I hate the thought of it, but I hate this uncertainty even more. We're both obsessed with protecting ourselves from losing the other."

Anne did not know what else to say. As she was starting to progress, he was slipping away from her. She searched for the strength to hold herself together and do what she could to help him, but a numb sense of futility overtook her. All she could think to do was suggest they take a walk. He agreed.

They walked down the road toward the village, through the courtyard of the Basilica, into a park past a statue of Saint Anne standing with her daughter Mary. As they passed, Anne looked beseechingly into the face of her saint. *I need you! Help me!*

They sat on a bench. Neither had said a word since leaving the house. She was losing him. Almost in desperation she said, "I told you I loved you and now you'll barely talk to me."

He said nothing at first. After a few minutes he finally spoke, almost in a monotone. "Two women loved me and left me," he said. "Telling you about them brought it all back. Then when you stayed away from me, I thought it was over, that you decided our time was up."

"If our time was up I wouldn't be here."

A group of people arriving for mass approached them. He waited until they had passed. "You're here now, but for how long?"

She felt their carefree, just-for-now relationship crumbling. What more could she say? What more could she do? She looked at him and saw him staring blankly ahead. "Let's go back," she said.

At the house, she gathered her things and said, "Go see your friends. When you come back, if you want to see me, you know where to find me. I won't call you. Take some time to figure out what you want."

She backed her car out of his garage and drove down the road where weeks before she had started to regret her decision to leave him. This time, she was starting to regret coming back to him.

168

In the store the next day, few customers came in, and all the paperwork and stocking of shelves was quickly finished. Anne wandered around restlessly, dusting here and there. What John had said, as perverse at it was, was starting to make sense. They were too much alike in their fear of being left, each poised to leave before the other—a preposterous reason to throw away the best relationship she had ever known. Yet she saw no solution.

Yes, she could buy time by telling him about Dr. Laborde, about how her troubled relationship with her father had tainted her view of men, but she barely understood herself what she was embarking on; how could she explain to him? This path she had started on, how rocky would it be? How long the journey? Where would it lead? Would it bring her back to John? Or would she learn that she had been right all along, that loving him could lead to no good?

And how would he react? He might well decide she was too troubled to love, too temperamental like Marie-Clo, unwilling to commit, like Diane.

What to do? Telling him what she was doing was risky, but concealing it would be impossible; he would read her moods and know something was up. Yet she dreaded losing him completely. Then it came to her: hold onto him by doing what they had agreed. Become friends. They could wind down their troublesome passion for each other and enjoy each other's company without the conflicts that always lurked, ready to pounce.

At 6:00 she closed the store and left to pick up her mother at the train station. She considered telling her mother what her father had said, aware that it might be a touchy subject for her mother. Brigitte rarely mentioned her divorce, and Anne always assumed she preferred not to talk about it.

As Anne arrived at the passenger-loading area, Brigitte was coming out of the station. On the way home, she asked about John.

"We saw each other yesterday morning. He left in the afternoon to go visit friends." Her tone betrayed her.

169

"It sounds like it's not going well."

"I can't hide anything from you. But then neither one of us could ever hide much from the other. Even when I was little and you made excuses for Dad, I could tell you were lying." The segue was forced and she knew it, but it nudged the conversation in the right direction. She thought of her parents' agreement and her implicit promise not to tell her mother that her father had breached it. She knew her parents would never talk to each other about it. Anne was not ashamed to be looking out for herself, even if it meant breaking a promise. It was long overdue.

Brigitte seemed to welcome the chance to talk. "I tried to protect you and Bernard. Whatever your father's faults, he was still your father."

They stopped for a red light.

"He told me you had no faults."

"What?"

"I went to see him on Saturday. I cornered him. He told me he left you because you were the perfect wife. I swear I'll never understand men."

Her mother looked surprised. "He said something like that when he was getting ready to leave. I thought he was feeding me a line, trying to deal with his guilt. The light's green."

Entering the Place de la République, Anne pulled into a parking space. Brigitte reached for the door handle.

"I was sure it was my fault," Anne said, "that he left because of me."

Brigitte let go of the handle and turned back toward Anne. "Because of you? Where did you get that idea?"

"I made it up. I didn't know why he left, so I concocted my own reasons. We were so close. I adored him. Then he left. I didn't know what I did, or if I did anything. I just felt like, well, if we were close and he left, I must have disappointed him somehow. I thought maybe he got bored with me. I didn't know what to think."

"I remember days when the two of you spent hours together fixing things around the house."

"I get so sad when I think of those days. I wanted them to

go on forever. I think that's why when he left, I got so mad at him I didn't want to see him."

"I know. I did what I could to keep you and Bernard from pulling away from Dad. Everything I read said to encourage children to spend as much time as possible with the absent parent. That's why I insisted that you see him even when neither one of you wanted to. I even met with him to talk about what to do, but nothing seemed to help. I've often wondered if I should have told you the truth. It's so hard to know how honest to be with children, how much they can handle. Even as vocal as you could be, I was never sure what was really going on in your little head."

If her mother remembered her agreement with her father, it was not apparent.

Anne glanced at her watch, picked up the parking disk, rotated it to show the time, and tossed it on the dashboard where it would be visible through the windshield.

Brigitte asked, "Is there some connection between your lunch with Dad and your problems with John?"

"Maybe. Before I talked to Dad, I stayed away from John for several days while I got up my courage. He didn't take it well."

"Is he possessive?"

"No. Just insecure. He thinks I'll leave him. Maybe he's right. Maybe I will. I never know what I might do where men are concerned."

"Every time you've had problems with men, I wished I could do something, say something, and make it OK. It's hard for parents to accept that we can't assure our children's happiness."

"You can't. My life is my responsibility, not yours. You've done everything you could possibly do. Now it's up to me."

In the past when Anne's love life had gone sour, she called Jocelyne or Sophie for advice and sympathy. But she had subjected both of them to enough of her self-pity. She saved it all for Dr. Laborde.

At her next session, Anne told Dr. Laborde about confronting her father, about staying away from John, about John's

171

pulling away. When she had finished, she asked, "What should I do?"

"I can't tell you what to do, but I can help you find your own answer. What do you want to do about him? What occurs to you?"

"Dump him, marry him, become his best friend without ever touching him again. I don't know. I don't know. I don't know."

"What do you suppose he thinks you're feeling right now?"

"When I saw him last, he knew I wasn't pleased. I told him I wouldn't call him."

"Do you miss him?"

"Yes. I miss him. I miss him a lot."

After leaving Dr. Laborde, Anne walked aimlessly around the old city. Vannes had survived World War II spared from the devastation suffered by Lorient, Brest, and other port cities of Brittany. The old city center with its narrow streets and half-timbered buildings seemed timeless, like it would survive all adversity.

As she walked and pondered what to do next, she found herself more confused than ever. When raindrops began dotting the sidewalk, she headed back to her car, reaching it at the beginning of a downpour.

She pushed her dripping hair off her face, wiped the rain from her eyes, and started home. At a red light, she sat mesmerized by her windshield wipers as they swept one way, then the other, then back again, clicking and moaning at the end of each cycle.

Anne had never been blessed with patience and was already regretting telling John she would not call him. She thought of their previous separation and how he had written to her after promising not to call her. A real letter, not just an email. He knew how to get her attention.

At home, she ran a towel through her hair, changed to a dry sweater, and sat down at her desk. She wrote:

John,
I miss you.

172

Anne

She sealed and stamped the envelope and looked out the window. The rain had stopped. She walked across the wet pavement and cobblestones of the Place de la République to the mailbox in front of the City Hall and double-checked the pickup times. Her letter should arrive the next day.

The following morning, while Anne was working, John called. "I miss you too. I want to see you."

## Chapter 24: Perfect Friends

They met that afternoon at the Café du Guesclin, across the square from the bookstore. After their last frustrating conversation, she was not ready to go to his house or invite him home. When she arrived at the café, he stood and greeted her with a kiss on each cheek. She ordered coffee and turned to him and saw that humorless look she had noticed when they first met, this time underscored with a certain intensity. Where to start? "Are you in a better mood?" she asked.

"I'm thinking of how much I missed you and how much I'm going to miss you if we can't solve our problem." Strong words. Dark, pessimistic.

"Our problem? What do you think that is?"

"When you called me from Nantes, you said 'I love you.' Did you mean it?"

She nodded. He seemed to know where he was headed. But wherever they were headed, she would insist they start from the same place. "When you said it to me in the car coming back from the wedding, and when you wrote it in your email, did *you* mean it?"

The waiter arrived with her coffee. John paused until the waiter had left. "I meant it. And I don't know where we go from here. I love you and you say you love me, and in spite of that it's still temporary. One day you'll serve me notice and it'll be over. I can't live that way anymore. That's our problem."

She tried to unwrap a sugar cube but her fingers were not obeying. "I said you'd get tired of it before I would. I warned you." Why was it so difficult to remove the paper from a sugar cube, something she had done thousands of times?

He took the cube from her, unwrapped it, put it back in her hand and stared off across the square. Turning back to her, he said, "That's right. You warned me, like you warned me at Huelgoat, like you warned me when you came back to me. You warned me and I didn't listen, until you wouldn't see me or talk to me for a week. I had time to think. I started to see what was happening, where I was headed, and I didn't like what I saw."

"What did you see that you didn't like?" She stared at the sugar cube for a moment and dropped it into her coffee.

"The prospect of having the same conversations with a series of women and ending up a lonely old man."

"I don't think you have to worry. You'd be quite a catch."

"So we're back to 'You'll make a wonderful husband for some lucky woman' again. Some lucky woman but not you." He was more direct today, more willing to expose the cracks in their fragile relationship.

"What do you want me to do? Do you want to change our deal? Shall we call it off? Is that what you want?" Her words came out like a challenge. Not what she had intended.

He picked up his spoon, rolled its handle over in his fingers several times, and set it back down next to his cup. "I haven't been completely honest with you, but I didn't realize it until a few days ago. I agreed not to expect anything long term from you, but I didn't stop hoping. I thought if we stayed together long enough, you might start to think we could have a future after all. But it isn't going to happen. You are who you are and I love you the way you are. But the way you are excludes me. If that isn't a problem, I don't know what is."

She felt the ground shifting under them. She knew Dr. Laborde was right that working through her past would take time, that confronting her father was only a first step. She had barely started, and he was not going to wait with endless patience. Nor could she ask him to; he had enough misgivings about her already. What could she say to him now? Nothing. Cover as best she could and honor their agreement.

"It sounds like it may be time to become friends." She said it without much conviction, with no pleasure.

He picked up her sugar wrapper and turned it over as if the solution to their problem were to be found there. "I was afraid this was where we were headed, but I hoped you wouldn't agree so quickly, that maybe you'd change your mind."

"I don't see a way around it. We've had wonderful times together and I don't regret a minute of it. But now you've changed.

175

You want more than I can give you. I'm sorry."

"Don't be sorry. You gave me a part of your life and I'll always be grateful for that. But it's not enough. Not anymore. If I can't have your body and soul all to myself for a lifetime, I'll have to do what I did before and take what you're willing to give me. Your friendship is better than nothing."

He was right. It was best to salvage what they could. "You've been one of the greatest joys of my life," she said. "It can change between us, but it won't end completely. I won't allow it."

"Just so you don't ever think this was what I wanted, I still think you and I are perfect for each other."

"We are. Perfect and perfectly impossible. I've known it almost since we met. Now let's try to be perfect friends."

"I'll try my best to be your perfect friend, but I don't know if I can stand to see you and not touch you."

"Touch me now," she said.

He brushed her cheek with his fingertips and set his hand on hers on the tabletop and asked, "How long until we see each other?"

"A month?"

"Too long. Three weeks?"

"Three weeks."

Yet again, they had set conditions that would keep them from a life together. This time they had gone further. This time they had agreed to stay away from each other, to cool their passion for each other. Now she could think only of what she was giving up. No more leisurely walks in each other's arms. No more blissful hours of making love, giving each other such intense yet sublime pleasure. No more uninhibited, aimless conversations afterwards. No more feeling his warmth next to her in bed. *He's right; we really are perfect for each other, like we were created to be together. If only he were French.* Her heart ached.

It was too much to keep to herself. When she got home, she called Jocelyne and told her what she and John had agreed to.

Jocelyne, ever the optimist, said, "At least you know you'll still see him."

"It'll be so strange to see him now."

"Until you get used to it. I'm betting he could be a very good friend. Before long you'll be going to each other for advice on your love lives. Listen. I've got an idea. Jean-Yves is coming for dinner Saturday night. Why don't you come too?"

Anne thought of the handsome, gracious man she had danced with at the wedding. "I'm not ready for another man."

"It's only dinner."

With some misgivings, Anne accepted.

Anne could not sit still. She went to the car and left Auray. As she entered a roundabout, a sign beckoned her toward a turnoff: "Sainte-Anne-d'Auray➜." After two more circles in the roundabout, she took a different turnoff and found herself at the dock where John had taken her soon after they met, back when every little touch was a thrill. She headed north to Plumergat, stopping by the café where they had gone after rescuing Christine and talked for so long, falling in love with each other without realizing what was happening.

Leaving Plumergat, her car seemed to find its own way. It took her to the rolling meadows around Carnac, to the rows of tall stones brought there by a mysterious prehistoric people. As the sun descended to the horizon, she watched its changing light on the gray stones. They turned crimson, then black as darkness swallowed them. An overwhelming fatigue seized her.

Three weeks. Three interminable weeks.

Two days later while Anne was at work, a letter from John arrived. No doubt another one-line note telling her he missed her. How well she could understand missing someone. She opened the envelope and unfolded one handwritten page:

Dearest Anne,

When I told you I didn't know what I wanted in my life, I did not tell you the truth. I knew exactly what I wanted but had to pretend I didn't.

I wanted to know that twenty years from now you and I would be sitting together in front of the fireplace on a rainy evening, reading and talking and enriching each other's life. I wanted to see your sparkling eyes and dazzling smile on the faces of our children. I created this dream that I knew was impossible and then I tried so hard to put it out of my mind.

Somehow I'll live without making a life together, without making a family together, but only because I don't have a choice. No matter what happens, I'll remain your stalwart friend. And I'll cherish as a friend what you've shown me as a lover: your wisdom, your wit, your grace and style.

I've loved and lost before and I've survived. But right now, life without you feels like no life at all.

All my love,

John

She looked up from the desk behind the counter at the door he had opened to enter and illuminate her life, at the bookshelves and display tables in the room, at her world of books, at the store that had brought them together. Nothing in any of her books could assuage the despair of finding the man of her dreams and watching him slip away.

The door opened and a customer entered. Anne put the letter back in the envelope and hid it in the back of a drawer. At 12:30, she closed the store and took the letter up to her bedroom, closing the door behind her. She took the letter out of the envelope and read it again.

How could she tell him she had created the same dream about him? And like him, she had tried so hard to put it out of her mind.

After dinner, she sat at her desk and reread John's letter. She took out a sheet of stationery and started to write:

Dearest John,

I . . .

On a new sheet, she started again.

Dearest John,
　　　When I read your letter . . .

She put down her pen and reached for the phone, held it a moment, started to punch in his number but hung up. She turned in her chair and surveyed her room, now smaller, now lonelier. On her dresser a framed photo of the two of them in front of the Roche-aux-Fées. On her bookshelf, *English for Dummies*. In the bottom of her closet, the brown suede hiking shoes she had worn when they climbed to the top of the Roc Trévezel and kissed, and all the rest of Brittany faded away as she lost herself in his embrace. She put the photo in a drawer under a folded flannel nightgown.

　　　Time to move on.

　　　Dinner with Jean-Yves was not at all like dinner with Paul. Jean-Yves was soft-spoken and gentle. Jocelyne had no doubt briefed him.

　　　He called her the next day and invited her to join him for a movie during the week.

　　　When he took her home after the movie he limited his goodnight to a handshake. She liked him. He sensed he should not move too fast. They made plans to go out to dinner together the following Saturday.

　　　The day after the movie with Jean-Yves, a woman came into the store and approached Anne. She looked familiar.

　　　The woman said, "I know it's been a while. You might recognize me if I poured a bucket of cold water over my head. I'm Christine." She showed Anne a note she had made about a book on sailing off the coast of Brittany. Anne did not have the book in stock but said she would order it for her.

　　　"Have you seen John recently?" Christine asked.

　　　Anne sensed the question might be more than just casual conversation. "Not for a while." The less she said about him to Christine, the better.

　　　"If it's not indiscreet, do you know if he's seeing anyone?"

179

"Not that I know of." Her suspicion had been correct. Now Christine would ask her for John's phone number. Anne would have to give it to her or lie and say she did not have it.

But instead, Christine reached into her purse and took out a pen and note pad on which she wrote her name and phone number. "Would you give him this and tell him I'd be happy to hear from him?"

Christine had left Anne no real choice other than to pass the information on to John. But she was afraid if she called him, he would hear in her voice how much she missed him. And now Christine, whom he barely knew, might see him before she did. She fingered Christine's note and turned to her computer to compose an email.

> "Christine came to the store to order a book. She asked me
> to send you her phone number and tell you she'd like to hear
> from you. I think she has the hots for you, so be warned."

Anne feared her attempt at humor might fall flat, intended as it was to cover her own jealousy. That Anne had no right to be jealous was all the more reason not to let it show.

> He replied later, "Thanks for the info. I'll give her a call. I

miss you." Not terribly chatty, which told Anne that his interest was piqued and he did not want Anne to know it.

Saturday evening, before Jean-Yves was to pick up Anne, Jocelyne called.

"Don't worry about John. He appears to be surviving. Philippe and I saw him today in Nantes at La Cigale, having lunch with a woman."

Only nine days after he had last seen Anne and seven days after sending his letter, John was having lunch with another woman, and at La Cigale, no less, the most famous restaurant in Nantes. Who could it be but Christine? "Did you meet her?"

"No, but I got a good look at her. John came over to say hi, but she stayed at their table."

"What did she look like?"

180

"About thirty, blonde, pretty."

Christine was a brunette. It was someone else. Anne winced with jealousy. It gave her no comfort that she had no right to be jealous. "Do you know who she was?"

"No. We didn't talk long. It was a little awkward. John said what a good time he had at the wedding and that was about it."

Christine would have some competition. And while two attractive women competed for John, like it or not, Anne would fade quietly out of the picture.

## Chapter 25: An Ideal Husband

When Jean-Yves picked her up, he greeted her with a kiss on each cheek. When he took her home, he kissed her lightly on the lips. She appreciated his restraint but felt deceitful. Her promise to herself not to think of John at moments like this was proving hard to keep. The right moment for her to invite him in for a drink came and went. She got out of his car.

When Christine's book arrived, Anne called to tell her, adding, "I gave your number to John," hoping Christine would take the bait and tell her if she had heard from him.

"Thank you. He called me. He said he's seeing someone and doesn't date more than one woman at a time. But he offered to meet me for coffee, 'platonically for the moment,' was the way he put it. We sat in a café and chatted for forty-five minutes and that was that, although he said he'd keep my number. Do you know anything about this mysterious other woman?" Anne noticed that since Christine had gotten past her initial embarrassment at the carelessness that had almost cost her her life, she was not at all shy. John's lunch companion at La Cigale, whoever she might be, would have some competition.

Anne said, "Rumor has it she's a blond. That's all I know."

When Christine came to the store to pick up her book, they had lunch together at Anne's suggestion. Better to keep the enemy in view. One of them anyway. During lunch, Christine recounted part of her conversation with John, enough of it for Anne to understand they had addressed each other with the formal *vous*. Without prompting, Christine commented, "Talking with a man who saved my life, it seemed like I should call him *tu*, but I didn't want to sound too forward. I wanted him to change to *tu* so I could, but he never did. I thought because he's American, maybe he didn't really understand the difference."

Anne knew better. That was one French mistake he never made. *He's keeping his distance. Good.*

The days crawled.  Anne was apprehensive but eager as her rendez-vous with John approached.  When she arrived at the Café du Guesclin, he was already there, at the same table.  He stood and kissed her on each cheek—like a man would greet his sister.

After some pleasantries, she asked, "I've never stayed friends with a former lover.  What are the rules?  Are there any forbidden subjects?"

"Only one that I can think of.  If you sleep with another man, I'm not ready to hear about it."

"OK.  We'll stay off that subject.  Are you seeing another woman yet?"

"It's only been three weeks."

"Who did you have lunch with in Nantes?"

He smiled.  "It was a woman, as near as I could tell.  I watched Jocelyne from across the room to see how long it would take her to call you."

She laughed.  "If you aren't sure it was a woman, you couldn't have gotten very far."

Now John was laughing too.  "You never miss a straight line."

It came back to her now how much he appreciated her.  He had been her friend all along, not just a lover.

She hoped they could stop making each laugh long enough for her to get him to talk.  "So do I get to hear about this woman for whom you rejected poor Christine?"

He laughed again.  "It sounds like a cabal of women is spying on me.  I sort of like that idea.  She's Catherine's sister."  Catherine and her husband ran a bed and breakfast where John stayed before moving into his house.  John had made friends with them—as he seemed to do with everybody—and had taken Anne to their house for dinner.  "When I told Catherine that you and I were no longer together, she invited her sister and me to dinner.  During dinner, we talked about having some errands in Nantes and agreed to go together.  And while we're nosing into each other's private life, what about you?  Are you seeing anyone?"

"Our friends are taking good care of us.  I've gone out twice with Jean-Yves. He's the man I danced with at the wedding while you were dancing with Jocelyne."

"I remember. I was insanely jealous."

"Bullshit."

"You know me too well."

They were more relaxed with each other than she had expected, although she noticed that he was fiddling with his coffee cup.

"So did Jocelyne set you up with him?" he asked.

"Only after I told her about our new arrangement. Does this blond from La Cigale have a name?"

"Vanessa. What else did Jocelyne tell you about her?"

"That she was pretty. Do you like her?"

"It almost sounds like you want me to get involved with her. Are you feeling guilty?"

"Feeling guilty?" She glared at him, incredulous. "What the hell are you talking about? Feeling guilty for what? For trying to take an interest in your life as any friend would? How could you say such a thing to me?" She was almost shouting. "If that's the way you talk to your friends, this is not going to work!" Reaching into her purse, she pulled out enough money for her coffee, dropped it on the table, and walked away. She had barely crossed the square and reached the sidewalk when a hand touched her shoulder. She turned and found herself in John's arms.

"I'm sorry," he said. "I'm having a hard time with this. I can't just turn it off. It's going to take time."

"I know," she said. "It's hard for me too." A moment passed and they were kissing, too passionately for the sidewalk in front of the *pâtisserie*. *Let people talk. I don't care.* They were alone together on the planet, holding each other desperately close. Friend or not, she wanted him. She knew he wanted her too, but was too proud to say it. She spoke softly in his ear, and they walked—almost ran—to her apartment.

For a few intoxicating minutes they were lost in each other, giving no thought to what would follow. When it was over, they lay

184

side by side in silence. She longed for the afterglow, the easy chitchat that had always followed making love with him. This time, there was only tension, a sense of dishonesty.

"We can't do this," she said. "I can't date one man and sleep with another."

He nodded half-heartedly.

She glanced at the clock. "I think you should leave now. I don't really want you to, but I don't want to have to explain this to my mother when she closes the store and comes upstairs."

"I understand. I mean I understand about your mother. I'm not sure I understand about us."

"I'm not sure I do either." She thought of the previous week, of how the mounting anticipation of seeing him made her regret that their days as lovers were over. "This may be all wrong," she said, "but I'm thinking if we saw each other more often, this wouldn't happen again."

"I suppose it's worth a try," he said. "How long?"

"Two weeks?"

He gave her another half-hearted nod, which told her that becoming his friend was going to be a challenge.

Anne took the train to Nantes to meet Jean-Yves for lunch and to see an Impressionist exhibit at the Musée des Beaux Arts. She planned to return to Auray late that afternoon. A day in Nantes was a welcome break from Auray. It did not matter to her that she had seen and done everything in Nantes many times during her student years and those that followed. She enjoyed its spacious but walkable city center, its shops, cafés, and restaurants—as long as she was not alone.

While they were strolling around the museum, Jean-Yves invited her to stay in Nantes for dinner. What else he would suggest after dinner and how she would she respond? She excused herself, went to the end of a hall outside the restrooms, and called John.

"Have you kissed Vanessa?"

"Uh, yes." He sounded suspicious.

"On the lips?"

"Yeah, but I couldn't help it. It was our third date and I was running out of excuses."

She smiled, thinking of how much she loved his sense of humor. "Just a dry little kiss, or a big French one?"

"That's very personal! A big French one."

She looked around to be sure nobody else was near her and turned back toward the window. "We agreed to stay off this subject, so you don't have to answer, but have you slept with her?"

"I'd like to, but I'm afraid I'd say 'Anne!' at the wrong moment."

She gave up trying to be serious. "Oh? And when would be the *right* moment?"

"I suppose when I'm making love with someone named Anne. Weren't you listening all those times? Why are you asking me these questions? Are you trying to decide whether to sleep with Jean-Yves? Don't answer that! I don't want to know."

"I was just curious."

"While you're curious, would you like to know the real reason I haven't slept with Vanessa?"

"I suppose."

"She's not you."

She told Jean-Yves she had to be back in Auray that evening.

On the train, she replayed her conversation with John and smiled. Her smile faded as she tried to understand the confusing swirl of her emotions. One thing was certain: if she called John every time a man made an advance, her wedding would be a long way off.

In her sessions with Dr. Laborde, Anne confronted her latest challenge. How could she let Mr. Perfect Future Husband continue to court her while she held him off and slept with her former lover, who was supposed to be her platonic friend? But answers eluded her. The more she delved, the more laborious the sessions became.

She told Dr. Laborde, "With John, once we agreed on the rules, I never had to worry about what it might turn into. I never had to think about how good a husband he might be. I didn't have to

186

anguish over questions like 'Will he propose? If he does, what will I say? If I marry him, will he be faithful?' Most of the time it was refreshingly simple. Was it good because it was temporary? Because it wasn't for real? Because we never had a chance to get tired of each other?"

And in the following session, "Maybe it wasn't so simple with John. With other men I was cautious; I didn't want to make a mistake and marry the wrong man."

"Are you saying you weren't cautious with John?"

"I was at first, but once we agreed it was temporary, it was safe. I relaxed and it crept up on me. When I realized I loved him, it scared me away. I think it scared him too."

"Why do you think it scared him?"

"He said the more he loved me, the more he was afraid of losing me."

"So where does that leave you?"

Anne stared at the hardwood floor and at the off-white walls. "It leaves me stuck. It seems I can't love a man unless I know I'll never marry him. So what do I do, marry a man I don't love? Or forget about getting married and move in with John?"

"For two sessions now, you haven't said a word about Jean-Yves."

"Jean-Yves. I need to see more of him. I've been neglecting him."

Anne preferred to see Jean-Yves in Nantes, far from reminders of John. When she called Jean-Yves to arrange a visit, he said, "You're always welcome to stay here—with no obligation. I have a guest room."

"I'll let you know when I'm ready for that."

They agreed to have dinner together. He would pick a good restaurant and make a reservation. When he insisted she would be his guest, she was relieved not to worry about how expensive it might be, but still uneasy. It almost felt patronizing, like he assumed that because she worked in a small bookstore and lived with her mother, money was an issue for her. Was he trying to show her he could

187

offer her financial security?   Although financial security had its appeal, becoming dependent on a man did not.  Money was never an issue with John; they always worked out with no difficulty who would pay for what.

She chided herself for analyzing too much and resolved to stop looking for trouble.

Anne and Jean-Yves arrived just as the restaurant was opening for dinner and were seated in a private corner at the end of a row of booths.

They looked at the menu and ordered, then reviewed the day's activities: a bike ride along the Erdre River, lunch in the historic Quartier Bouffay, and a nostalgic visit to World of Books, where Anne had worked years before.  When there was nothing left to say about the day, the conversation stalled.  The waiter saved them by arriving with the next course and announcing in some detail what he was serving.  During another lull in the conversation, Anne looked up from her plate and caught Jean-Yves gazing wistfully at her.  She smiled self-consciously and turned her attention back to her meal.

It was clear he liked her, but why?  Had he thought about how compatible they might be over decades of marriage?  Or was he in too much of a hurry to get married just to find his place in life, to have a family?  She was curious why he had never married, but they had not gotten far enough to have that kind of conversation.

Anne could scarcely complain about his motives; hers were similar.  Jean-Yves looked good on paper: handsome, refined, well-employed.  Best of all, he would not leave her to go home to the other side of the world.  And then she started what she had vowed never to do: comparing Jean-Yves to John.

The two men were about equal in the looks department.  Both were employed and appeared solvent.  How were they different?  Jean-Yves was an eligible suitor; John was not.  Jean-Yves had his roots in Brittany; John did not.  John had an air of mystery and adventure about him and a devilish sense of humor that brought out Anne's best as they bantered with each other.  And when she tried to imagine being married to Jean-Yves, she sensed a boredom

188

so intense it would drive her to crave an affair. Since an affair would forever be out of the question for her, she would be trapped.

Actually, it was much simpler than all that. When she thought of Jean-Yves, she often segued into thinking of single women she could introduce him to. When she saw John, she wanted to rip his clothes off.

She looked back up at Jean-Yves. He was pushing food around on his plate. She asked him if something was wrong.

He said, "Sometimes I wonder why you keep seeing me when your heart doesn't seem to be in it."

Her lack of enthusiasm was more apparent than she had realized. "Right now, I don't know where my heart is."

"I suspect it's in Sainte-Anne-d'Auray."

"It won't be for long. I just need some more time." There was something about Jean-Yves, a childlike sensitivity perhaps, that made her careful not to be too blunt with him. "I really like you and I appreciate your patience with me. I didn't think it would take me so long to get over John."

The chef stopped by their table to greet them. Anne complimented the chef, and after a few more pleasantries, he moved on to customers at another table.

Anne hoped the chef's visit had distracted them from the subject of John, but Jean-Yves was not ready to not drop it. "Do you know if he's seeing anyone else?"

"Jocelyne and Philippe saw him with a woman at La Cigale. I don't know if he would have told me. And there's another woman he and I know who might have designs on him."

"He seems to be popular. Does it appeal to women that he's American?" Although she could not blame him for trying to understand the competition, talking to him about John was making her uncomfortable, as if it were disloyal to both of them.

"I was curious at first," she said as casually as she could, trying to redirect the conversation with a jab at stereotyping. "But his nationality is no big deal. He's no different from any other man I've known." She was dismayed to have led herself into such a lie.

"Does he know you're seeing me?"

189

Jean-Yves seemed to be seeking reassurance that he was still in the game. He had a right to know.

"Yes. But I don't tell him much about us."

"You don't tell *me* much about us either."

The harder she tried to change the subject, the more he pursued her. She searched for something that would satisfy him. "I like seeing you. I enjoy your company. That's all I can say right now. I think you'll make a wonderful husband for some lucky woman." The words slipped out before she could stop them, the same words she had said to John.

Jean-Yves looked crestfallen. "It sounds like you don't consider yourself a candidate."

"Forgive me. It was intended as a compliment. It's just that . . . for now . . . " There was nothing more she could say.

"Maybe we should stop seeing each other until you decide what you want."

"I know what I want: to get married and have a family with a man like you." At least let him know she was not writing him off.

"Is that really what you want? You already have a man like me who wants to get married and have a family and it doesn't seem to be enough."

A strong statement for Jean-Yves, daring her to tell him he was not for her, a warning, perhaps, that he would not wait forever for her to come around.

Two good men wanted her and she was rejecting them both. How many more times would she tell a man he would be a wonderful husband for some lucky woman? Why not her? Jean-Yves would marry her in a second; he had said it almost in so many words. Everything seemed to be in their favor: a common culture and language, no fear of long separations. *I should just marry him and try to be happy. I would have what I want. But what if Jean-Yves is right, that I don't know what I really want?* Jean-Yves would be an ideal husband—just like her mother was an ideal wife. The thought made her shiver.

## Chapter 26: Not a Customer

On a slow afternoon in the bookstore, Anne caught up on paperwork, an endless stream of orders, invoices, government forms. She was interrupted when a woman entered the store, an attractive woman about thirty, blond hair, brown eyes, and an elegant but natural look. She was dressed stylishly but not ostentatiously. Her white pants and dark green sweater flattered an enviable figure. They exchanged a *bonjour* and Anne resumed her work behind the counter. But the woman came to the counter and asked tentatively, "Are you Anne?"

At first, Anne thought nothing of the question. Customers often sent their friends to the store with instructions to ask for Anne. But something about the woman, perhaps an uneasiness in her voice and stance, did not fit her appearance. Anne studied her more closely. This was not a customer.

"My name is Vanessa Deternay. Do you know who I am?"

There could be only one Vanessa in all of Brittany who would come to the bookstore looking so ill at ease and ask for Anne by name. "I can guess," Anne said cautiously.

"You're wondering why I'm here."

"I assume you're not looking for a book."

"I hope you don't think I'm out of line coming here." Vanessa seemed nervous, unsure of what to say next.

"No, of course not." Anne rose from her chair as she spoke. For some reason, she wanted to put Vanessa at ease, as if she were a guest in her home.

"Now that I'm here and talking to you, I'm not really sure why I came. At first I thought I would walk in, browse a little, check you out on the sly and leave. But as soon as I saw you, I had to talk to you. I have to be honest with you. I like John very much. He seems to like me and keeps seeing me, but it's like he's just passing the time with me. I know it's because of you; he doesn't try to hide it. I needed to see you and find out what it is about you that makes him so—I don't know how to say this—that makes him so loyal to you."

191

"I've wondered myself." Anne was uncomfortable talking about John with Vanessa, but was disarmed by her guileless manner. "I assume he's told you it's over between us."

"Yeah, but he doesn't act like it. I wouldn't waste my time on a man whose heart belongs to another woman, but he seems special."

"He is." Anne regretted her words the instant they escaped from her mouth. *When will I learn to shut up? Why am I encouraging another woman to court a man I love?* It gave Anne no comfort that she had given up any claim to John. She contemplated Vanessa's face, her figure, her engaging simplicity. Anne wanted John to be happy, even without her. If Vanessa could make him happy, Anne should not stand in her way.

Anne looked past Vanessa out the front window, not knowing what else to say or how to extricate herself from this uncomfortable conversation.

"I'm sorry," Vanessa said. "I shouldn't have come here. I'd better go." She said goodbye and went out the door through which John had first walked into Anne's life months before.

Anne sat down, looked at the door, down at her work, then at the door again. Memories welled up of her first encounter with John, their furtive glances at each other, their cautious conversation, their first lunch together. As she started to drift into other memories, she caught herself and resumed her work. A few minutes later the door opened. Startled, Anne looked up. A woman, a regular customer, entered the store. Anne exhaled, greeted the woman and reached behind her for a book the woman had ordered.

More customers came to distract her from thoughts of Vanessa's visit. So John could not let go of Anne in spite of all that had happened. It was too much to keep to herself, yet too much to share with a friend. She called him the following morning, not at all sure of what she would say.

"Did you hear about my visitor?"

"Just a few minutes ago. She didn't want to tell me; she knew I wouldn't like it. But she didn't want me to hear it first from you. She said she wanted to find out what it was about you that I find so irresistible."

192

"She said something like that to me. I assured her I had no idea."

"It's your books, my dear. I'm surprised you haven't figured that out."

"My books? What a disappointment. I thought it was something else."

"Let's stay off that subject. I might get turned on and come over there. I could embarrass you in front of your customers."

"Why would you do that when poor Vanessa is pining away for you? What are you telling her, that you took a vow of chastity? I hope you don't show up for your dates in a Franciscan robe."

"I'll try that if she gets too aggressive. Thanks for the tip."

"If you put her off too long, she could run out of patience. Just some advice from a friend who wants you to be happy."

"I appreciate your concern. I'll have to take my chances."

## Chapter 27: The Pretense of Friendship

In her next session with Doctor Laborde, Anne lamented that she and John were making no progress in reordering their relationship. They could not even talk on the phone without flirting. As she tried to picture her next meeting with John, all she could see was the two of them in bed again.

"It isn't working and it isn't fair to either one of us. As long as we have a date to see each other, we just look forward to it and keep our lives on hold. In the meantime, we're both missing out on other relationships. Women are circling him like vultures, and he keeps shooing them away. Even though I'm a little jealous, I'm starting to feel sorry for them."

"What do you think you should do about it?"

"I'm thinking of telling him we can't see each other until I decide we can handle just being friends."

"You sound unsure."

"I still love him."

"Maybe you always will." Not what Anne needed to hear.

"Jean-Yves is patient with me, but for how long? At this rate I'm going to lose both of them." Anne stared silently for a few minutes at a painting of a pastoral scene on the wall behind Dr. Laborde. "I'm curious what my mother thinks, but I don't want to worry her. I thought she would be the first to say, 'Why are you getting involved with an American. It's risky.' But no. Nobody seems to have a problem with him but me."

"What does your father think?"

Her father? It had never occurred to her to confide in him. "I haven't asked him. Now that he's decided he has a daughter again, he says all he wants is for me to be happy. If John makes me happy, that's good enough for him. It's convenient. It lets him off the hook for messing me up." Anne was dismayed by her burst of bitterness. She had spoken to her father several times since she had confronted him: polite, adult conversations. But now, she was near the end of the session, and what to do about John was more pressing.

When Anne did not pursue the subject of her father, Dr.

Laborde asked, "How is it going with Jean-Yves?"

"He's exactly the kind of man I've been waiting for, but I'm nowhere close to wanting to marry him."

"What's the problem?"

"Something's missing."

"Are we back to our old ways?"

"I hope not. But I won't know until I get some distance from John. I haven't given Jean-Yves a fair chance."

Anne was convinced she could go no further with Jean-Yves while she continued to see John, even on the pretense of friendship. It was time to act. More contemplation would lead to more equivocation.

She walked to the park bench where she had returned John's first call months before. What she was about to tell him was better said face to face, but she knew that seeing him could lead to another impulsive romp in bed together. She took her phone from her purse and glanced around the park, noting how much less inviting it was this time of year. The trees were leafless, the sky overcast, and the fine gravel of the park's walkways wet enough to stick to her shoes. A man sat reading a newspaper on a bench thirty meters away. People passed in front of her from time to time as they walked through the park on their way somewhere else.

Satisfied she had enough privacy, she called John. When he answered, she said, "I don't think it's a good idea to see each other tomorrow."

"Why not? I've been looking forward to it."

"I've been looking forward to it too, but we're not ready."

"Suppose I promise you we'll meet at the café and just talk and nothing else?"

"It's too soon."

"When? Another week? Two weeks?"

"I think I should just call you when I'm ready to see you."

"How long will it be? I need to know. I can't just live my life not knowing when—or if—I'll ever see you again."

If she had stopped to think before calling him, she might

have guessed he would be hurt, that he would not make it easy for her. She tried to reassure him. "Can't you trust me to call you? I thought we had an agreement. Are we friends or not?"

"Yes we have an agreement, and it's even worse than our last agreement." By now he was talking loud enough that she had to turn down the volume. "The longer we're apart, the more I want to be with you, and not just to shake your hand and talk about the weather. You and I belong together. I know it and you know it, but you keep fighting it. This isn't just about me, Anne, or about Jean-Yves either for that matter. He'll fall in love with you and propose to you and you'll run for your life."

What gave him the right to lecture her like that? "I'm amazed you want to see me when all you can talk about is what's wrong with me. I think you prefer me the way you think I am. You want a woman who won't commit so you can act like you're ready to settle down and blame her when it doesn't happen. And you know what else? You're using me as an excuse to keep your distance from Vanessa—and Christine too." She saw two women approaching on the path in front of her and lowered her voice. The women neared her, too involved in their own conversation to care what Anne was saying or how loud she was talking.

"That's what you want to think," he said, his tone increasingly petulant. "It's not the first time you've pushed me away and blamed me for it. But you're right about one thing. I've never had to face the prospect of settling down with you. You've never allowed me to think about it for even one second."

"Stop preaching to me! I'm sick of it! Why did I ever think we could be friends? You think you – "

He interrupted. "If we can't be friends, it's not because of me. I agreed to stay away from you for weeks at a time. I agreed you're free to see Jean-Yves or anyone else. I agreed to everything you wanted and now you tell me I have to sit by the phone and wait for you to call. How many of your other friends would put up with that?"

He was exasperating. "Don't be ridiculous. My other friends have nothing to do with us. We can't pretend we don't have a

196

history. And you know exactly what'll happen if we see each other again too soon. If we do again what we did last time, forget being friends. It'll never work. Look what's happened already. We indulged ourselves one time even though we both knew better and now we're yelling at each other." As she spoke, she got up from the bench and paced around, startling a flock of pigeons milling about, hoping for a handout. She sat down again and the pigeons reconvened at her feet.

"I didn't exactly rape you," he said. "I was perfectly capable of sitting on my side of the table and behaving myself. I still am."

She started to hang up on him, but could not let him say such a thing to her and get away with it. "So that's my fault too, is it? Don't kid yourself. You don't have any more will power than I do. Don't put me down for wanting you. I'm not ashamed of it. But it has to stop. You know it has to stop. I thought we agreed."

"Sure we agreed. Just like we agreed last time. Just like we always agree. You decide how it's going to be and I can take it or leave it. And now here we go again. If I want to see you at all, it's when *you* decide and I have nothing to say about it."

It was pointless to continue the argument. "I guess we've said it all," she said.

"I guess we have."

She dropped her phone into her purse and looked at the pigeons on the ground in front of her, concerned only with their own hunger, indifferent to Anne's distress. Spotting a rock next to her foot, she picked it up and threw it hard into their midst. Some of the pigeons burst into the air; others waddled disdainfully away, their beaks stabbing the air in front of them. Anne looked up and saw a man about John's age staring at her from a few meters away.

"What do you think you're looking at?" she snapped. "Mind your own damn business!"

He turned abruptly and walked away.

Anne had a date the next day to meet Jocelyne for lunch. It came at a good time. No sooner had they taken their seats in the restaurant than Anne began ranting about John, about how unreasonable he was, about how he said he wanted to be friends but was not willing to leave her alone long enough to make it possible.

It was not until Anne stopped her tirade that the waiter dared to approach the table. After they ordered, Jocelyne, always the voice of reason, said, "I've never seen you like this over a man. You've gone headlong into new relationships, then cooled off and decided it wasn't so great after all. Now you say you want out of this one, not because you're tired of John, but because you aren't. I can't keep up with you."

"It didn't work out they way we thought. I figured we'd have a good time for a while, then get tired of each other and part company."

Jocelyne nodded. "I remember."

Anne went on. "That's what made it safe to keep seeing him. We had a great time together. But it's over. It didn't end because we got tired of each other, but it's still over. It had to end. I mean, seriously, can you imagine how I could ever marry him?"

"I like John and I think in many ways he's good for you. But if you think there's an insurmountable obstacle, there must be one." It did not escape Anne's notice that Jocelyne did not answer her question. John had charmed her like he charmed everyone else.

"Jean-Yves is good for me too. I have to give him a fair chance. If I get closer to him, I can let go of John."

"OK, but if it doesn't work, try not to hurt Jean-Yves. He's a good man and he really likes you."

The next morning Anne called Jean-Yves and asked him, "Are you free this weekend?"

"Yes and I'd like to see you."

"I'm ready to stay over, and not in the guest room."

On Saturday afternoon, Anne closed the store and ate a quick lunch. Her mother drove her to the station. As the train carried her to Nantes, she tried to imagine the evening, the night. She searched for some sense of anticipation, some excitement. Nothing. It will come, she thought.  Give it a chance.

Jean-Yves met her at the station.  They went to the Ile de Versailles and walked around the Japanese garden.  Anne held his hand and walked close to him.  After dinner, they went to his apartment on Cours Cambronne, one of the more stylish residential streets in Nantes, where two rows of elegant apartments faced a park in between.  Anne stood in his living room and looked out the window at the trees in the park.

He put on a CD of love songs and poured drinks for both of them.  As they sat together on the couch, he put an arm around her and she snuggled up to him, sipping a short glass of Pommeau.  As they sat quietly and listened to the music, the alcohol warmed her hands and face but did not accomplish much else.  When the CD ended, he led her by the hand to his bedroom.  She followed, docile, like a virgin about to be deflowered, submitting, but without enthusiasm.  He went into the bathroom to change.  She put on a nightgown and got into bed.

Jean-Yves came out of the bathroom in pajamas, dimmed the light and slipped into bed beside her.  He kissed her.  She stroked his hair.  He slid his hand down to her chest.

Anne tensed.  He pulled his hand away and asked, "Are you OK?"

She was not OK.  Definitely not OK.  What was the point of submitting passively, of deceiving him?  It was demeaning to her and unfair to him to pretend.  She had succeeded so far in keeping John out of her mind, but now it was impossible.  From the moment she and John had gotten back together, she never doubted that she wanted him and that it was right.  Tonight, with Jean-Yves, it was wrong.  "I'm not ready.  It's still too soon.  I'm sorry."

"Whatever you say.  I have no desire to make love with a woman whose heart is elsewhere.  But I think it's time you decided what you want."

"I know it is.  Right now I think I should go to the guest room.  I'm sorry."

"You don't need to keep apologizing."  It was her fault he was irritated.  She knew it was unkind to go this far with a man and stop him.

Alone in Jean-Yves' guest room, Anne lay in bed thinking about John, about the hold he had on her, trying to understand it. *I know it will never work, but I can't put him behind me. Why do I fight it? What am I afraid of? What should I do?* She lay in bed tossing, turning, and fretting, falling at last into a fitful sleep.

When she awoke, she lay in bed, dreading having to face Jean-Yves. She got up, dressed, and went into the kitchen to make coffee. Jean-Yves came in the front door carrying a bag from the *boulangerie*. They sat and ate breakfast of coffee and croissants.

"I didn't sleep well," he said.

"Neither did I."

"It's time to level with each other. It's obvious you don't have the same feelings for me that I have for you." He looked at his plate as he spoke. It was apparent he had rehearsed his speech. "I thought if I was patient and understanding, you'd come around. But I don't think you ever will. I'm not even sure it's about John. If the chemistry isn't there between us, we should stop pretending."

She heard a bitterness she had not heard before. He was right. The chemistry was not there, at least not for her. "I thought if we saw enough of each other, I would change. I was wrong. I think I should go now."

## Chapter 28: A Dark Forest

Jean-Yves drove her to the train station. She kissed him on both cheeks and apologized again. Standing alone in front of the station, she watched him drive away.

She had come to Nantes when she was eighteen, in love with Jean-Louis. As she drifted away from Jean-Louis, she threw herself into a student's life of classes, studying, parties, new friends, boyfriends. She met other students in cafés, where they took on heady issues of politics, literature, and cinema. She had worked here, played here, become an adult here.

Most of her friends who still lived here led different lives now, orderly married lives, socializing with other couples. Nothing was left for her here, and now she was returning to Auray to the life she had led before she met John. Her mother and her bookstore. A lonely life leading nowhere. Picking up her bag, she turned and trudged into the station.

On the train, she took her phone from her purse and started to call John. She wanted to talk to him, to hear his voice. She thought ruefully of their last conversation, of how it had turned so quickly into an argument despite her assurance that she would call him when the time was right. He would have none of it, and how could she blame him? What kind of friendship was that? And now, how could she call him without even knowing what to say? What did she want from him? Sympathy? Friendship? Affection? Something more? She stopped the call.

It was too soon to tell Jocelyne what had happened; Jocelyne was close to Jean-Yves, and Anne was feeling too much a failure to face her.

Sophie called and had barely said two words before Anne began pouring her heart out. When Anne had finished, Sophie said, "Oh, Anne. I'm so sorry for you. I wish I knew what to tell you."

"You could give me the best advice in the world and I'd probably do the opposite. I make one bad decision after another.

I'm at the end of my rope."

"Well, I do have some advice for you and I hope you'll take it. I was calling to tell you that Michel and I bought a package tour for five days in Rome, but now he has a crisis at work and can't go. We prepaid the whole thing and if we don't take the trip, we forfeit the money. Why don't you and I go together? I already arranged for the kids to stay with my parents."

"Thanks, but Italy is a little too romantic for me right now. Why would you want to spend five days in Italy with a sourpuss?"

"It's impossible to stay a sourpuss in Italy, even in the winter. Come on. It's just what you need. I don't want to go alone, and Michel will be relieved that he didn't keep me from going."

"I suppose some time away would do me good—women only. I've had it with men. I'll ask my mother if she can cover for me in the store."

Brigitte readily agreed. She told Anne she was happy to see her get away. Anne knew her mother was worried about her.

Anne was starting to think her mother had reason to worry.

They flew from Lorient to Rome, changing planes in Lyon. After checking into their hotel, they consulted their maps and guidebooks to plan the next day's activities, taking into account a gusty, icy wind. They decided to skip the Forum and the Colosseum unless the weather improved. Even indoors, they would not have time for everything they wanted to see.

Buoyed by Sophie's enthusiasm, Anne put aside thoughts of the dismal state of her love life. Not only was it hard to remain a sourpuss in Italy, it was almost impossible not to have a good time in Sophie's upbeat company.

While out sightseeing, they stopped into a *trattoria* for a quick lunch. Sophie glanced around the dining room and reported to Anne, "That gorgeous man over there is staring at you. I think he's got the hots for you. Shall I clear out of our room for an hour?"

Anne shot a quick look at the man and said, "No, it's you he's hot for. I can tell. He's the type to go for redheads."

"I got it!" Sophie said, "Let's take him to our room and do him together! Not a word to Michel!"

Anne laughed out loud. "We agreed no men this trip, remember?" Every time she thought she had heard Sophie at her most outrageous, she went one better.

On the last day, when returning to Brittany was upon them, Anne found herself sinking again into a funk. While visiting the interior of Saint Peter's, she was strangely unmoved by its opulent grandeur. Sophie noticed. "Your mind seems to be somewhere else today. Let me guess. John or Jean-Yves? Or the man in the *trattoria*?"

"John, Jean-Yves, it doesn't matter. I can't win. The one who excites me will leave me someday and the marriageable one feels more like a brother. Forget the man in the *trattoria*. He's probably married and has six kids."

"You have so many men in your life. How to decide between all of them."

"I don't ever have to decide. I just turn them all away," Anne said bitterly.

After lunch, they started to walk back to the hotel. On the way, a small bookstore caught Anne's eye. She asked, "Do you mind if we go in here for a minute?"

"Not at all. It's a chance to warm up a little. It's freezing out here. Hey, maybe the owner is thirty-five, handsome and single. Miss Anne, prepare to meet the man of your dreams!"

Anne shook her head. "Another foreigner is the last thing I need right now."

The owner, who wore a wedding ring and appeared to be in his sixties, heard them talking and greeted them in fluent French. Anne told him about her bookstore and asked how independent bookstores were faring in Italy.

"We have the same problems you do: competition with the big chains, the Internet, with electronic media. What we can offer is personal service. I know my customers and what they like. They read a book and the next time they come in they tell me about it, then

I share their opinions with others. And our location is crucial. The people in this neighborhood like to read and would rather walk here, chat a bit, and buy a book than take the bus to a big store where nobody knows them."

"It's the same in Auray. So far it works, but I don't know for how much longer."

While the bookseller tended to another customer, Anne browsed a bit among the books. Although she did not know Italian, she understood many words from their similarity to French and Latin. She picked up a copy of Dante's *Divine Comedy*, which she had studied in her comparative literature class. She opened it to Part One, The Inferno. When the other customer left, Anne asked the bookseller to read the first lines to her in Italian and translate them for her. He obliged.

> Nel mezzo del cammin di nostra vita
> Mi ritrovai per una selva oscura
> Che la diritta via era smarrita.

> In the middle of the path of our life
> I found myself in a dark forest
> For I had lost my way.

When he finished, she said, "It wasn't so depressing when I read it for class."

"It sounds different at different times of our lives," he said. "When we think we have lost our way, it's especially poignant. But don't forget the end. Listen." He turned to the end and read,

> E quindi uscimmo a riverder le stelle.

> And then we emerged to see again the stars.

"No matter what happens to us, no matter what hell we go through, at the end of our journey we emerge to see again the stars. Whatever is troubling you, *Signorina*, you will find your way through

204

it. You will emerge to see again the stars. You must trust me about this."

After leaving the store, Anne said to Sophie, "Dante wrote those words for me. I see you and Michel and your kids and I can't imagine anything better. I say that's what I want for myself, but I can't seem to stay on that path. I keep losing my way. I envy you."

Sophie shook her head. "It's not that simple." Sophie rarely revealed her serious side. Even with Anne she most often showed her bubbly, ribald public persona. Not now. "Yes, I have a good husband and two sweet kids, but sometimes I feel like I've lost something. I catch myself daydreaming about when we were young. Remember the excitement of discovering love and sex and not knowing what life had in store for us? We think we want to know where we'll end up, and when we find out, the excitement is gone. Why do you think I'm so nosey about your love life? You may not have the life you think you want, but from where I am it seems exciting."

"It's not exciting anymore, if it ever was. Men come and go and what am I left with? All I want is to go home to the same man every night. At least that's what I thought I wanted. I don't even know anymore."

Brigitte picked them up at the airport. After dropping off Sophie, they headed home, talking of their plans for the afternoon. Anne was tired from traveling and looked forward to a restful day at home. Brigitte planned to meet her friend Gabrielle in Vannes and attend a lecture sponsored by the Coastal Conservancy.

After some conversation about Anne's trip, Brigitte asked, "Have you heard from John?"

"No. Why? Have you heard from him?"

"Yes." There was something odd in her mother's voice, as if she was holding something back.

"Just 'Yes'? Is that all?"

"No. It's not all. He's going back."

"He's going back? Where? To California?"

"Yes."

"For how long?"

"To stay."

## Chapter 29: Back to the Devil

Anne gasped. It was a moment before she could speak. "How long have you known?"

"He stopped by the store the day before yesterday to say goodbye. I wasn't looking forward to telling you."

"You don't believe we're just friends, do you?"

Her mother kept her eyes on the road. "It doesn't matter what I believe. Look into your own heart."

Her own heart. What did she know of her own heart? Only that it was hurting. "When is he leaving?"

"I don't know when exactly. He said in a few days."

"Did he say anything about me?"

"Just that he hadn't told you."

"How did he seem?"

Her mother said simply, "I've seen a happier face on a basset hound."

Anne caught herself biting her knuckle. A vague sense of loss was growing, now turning into panic as the realization took hold that he was leaving without seeing her, without even talking to her. He might already be gone.

*He can't do this to me. He can't just abandon me as if it I counted for nothing!* Never again would a man leave her without being called to account. She reached into her purse for her phone but saw they had arrived at home. It was just as well. Whatever she had to say to him, it should be said in private. As soon as her mother stopped the car, Anne leaped out and started across the street, disregarding an approaching car. The driver honked, braked, and yelled at her as he passed. She went up to the apartment, into her bedroom and closed the door. Without even taking off her coat she picked up the phone.

His machine answered.

"John, it's Anne. I have to see you before you go. Please call me!" *His answering machine is working. He must still be here.*

She called his cell phone. Another recording, another message.

She opened her bedroom door just as her mother appeared,

carrying Anne's suitcase. One look at Anne's face was enough. "Take the car. I'll have Gabrielle pick me up."

Anne grabbed her purse and keys, kissed her mother, and ran down the stairs out the door to the car. She headed out of Auray, speeding toward Sainte-Anne along the road that had taken her to him so many times.

A sign in front of his house greeted her: "For Lease." She rang the doorbell. No answer. She pounded her fist on the door. Still no answer. While standing at the door at a loss for what to do next, she heard a cheery "*Bonjour, Mademoiselle.*" John's neighbor, a fortyish woman who had greeted Anne in the past, was standing in her front yard. The woman was often outside and started conversations with neighbors and visitors. Anne had wondered if the woman was lonely and if she had designs on John.

"Has John moved out?" Anne asked.

"I don't think so. He was here earlier today."

"Do you know where he went?"

The neighbor hesitated.

"Please tell me," Anne implored. "I have to see him before he leaves!"

The neighbor had seen Anne's car pull into his garage and had seen her leave in the morning—but not recently. Anne could see the woman's face soften. "He said he was going to the Finistère one last time and something about the Monts-d'Arée. He left about forty-five minutes ago. He's such a nice man. I'm going to miss him."

The Finistère! Where France was closest to America. Where the mouth of the dragon pointed him toward home. The end of the earth. The end of them. Anne knew why he went. He was taking their trip alone, to prove he no longer needed her.

It would not be so easy. She would find him, and he would have to face her.

Heading west toward Quimper, lost in her thoughts of John, Anne paid little attention to the speed limit. Why did he not tell her?

What would she say to him if she found him? What did she want from him? What could she offer him? Conversation over coffee every few weeks? A dead-end relationship that neither of them wanted anymore? Why would he stay for that? One minute she was furious at him for planning to leave without a word to her, the next minute berating herself for refusing to so much as meet him for coffee. She knew only that she had to find him, to see him before he left.

North of Quimper, she left the main highway at Le Faou and raced up the road to Sizun, retracing the route they had taken months before. At Sizun she saw no sign of him or his car in the village or the churchyard. She headed east, past Commana to where the road veered north and ascended the ridge under the west face of the Roc Trévezel. The rocky ridge they had climbed together from the other side towered over her. Cresting the hill and passing around the north end of the ridge, she turned into a roundabout then onto the road south to the trailhead. She arrived at the parking area and saw there were no cars there, nor was anyone visible on the trail or on the ridge. A hasty U-turn took her back through the roundabout. She turned onto the road to Huelgoat, her tires squealing on the pavement.

She passed through the center of Huelgoat, across the bridge and up to where they had parked before. At the top of the hill, she could see the parking area. No cars. Her heart sank. She parked in front of their picnic table and turned off the motor. The chase was over. If he had come here, he was too far ahead of her. Even if she went on to Saint-Herbot, the last stop on their trip, she would not catch up to him.

She realized now that dashing here to look for him had been pointless. She could have waited at his house, called him again, or returned to his house later. By now he could be back in Sainte-Anne-d'Auray, assembling his luggage and heading for the airport. Not that it mattered. Even if she went back to his house and he was there, even if some days remained before his departure, he was done with her. She had pushed out of her life the one man who could make her life complete.

Now she would do what she assumed he had done, follow the path they had taken together, this time alone, then let him go for all time and never come here again. She got out of her car and buttoned up her coat. At the far end of the parking area, she stepped onto the trail they had taken together. She wandered down the hill, past the Trembling Rock, on down to the short path that led to the river and the Virgin's Kitchen, the path on which they had shared a blissful moment without a thought of what was to come. This place—their place—was different now. The barren trees gave no shelter from the cold, overcast winter sky whose dull light left the moss on the boulders of the Virgin's Kitchen forlorn and colorless. As she neared the Devil's Grotto, she shivered at the sound of the icy water rushing below her.

Stopping at the ladder that had taken her down into the Grotto with John, she laid a hand on the cold steel railing and steadied herself against a boulder. Memories rose up, one after the other, memories of glorious times, times that she had doomed to remain only memories, never to be lived again. She saw the two of them walking together on the beach, eating together, making love, making up after arguments, their long, meandering talks, the banter, the laughter, the warm presence of a strong, gentle man who loved her and would do anything for her. All gone. All lost. As if it had been only a dream. *How could I do this? Why did I turn away the man I love?*

She left the ladder and headed for a path that curved up the hill to the parking area, a more direct path than the one she had taken with John. After crossing the footbridge over the river, she stopped and looked around at leafless oaks and beeches towering over her, suddenly haunted by the echo of Dante's words, read to her just the day before by a kind Italian bookseller:

In the middle of the path of our life
I found myself in a dark forest
For I had lost my way.

For I had lost my way.

For I had lost my way.

She plodded in misery up the hill until the parking area came into view. She stopped and stared. It took her a few seconds to realize what she was seeing.

## Chapter 30: Come with Me

At the far end of the small parking area, she saw her car from the driver's side. A man was sitting on its hood, reclining against the windshield, his hands behind his head. It could not be John. He was forty-five minutes ahead of her, so if he had come here, he had left before she arrived.

And yet it was. Somehow she had arrived before him. When he had seen her car, he could have left. But he waited. Why? Perhaps to hear why she had come here, what she would say to him now after refusing to see him.

As she took a tentative step toward him, dry leaves crunched under her foot. He sat up, turned toward her, and slid to the ground. But he stayed by her car, waiting for her to come to him. She walked slowly across empty parking spaces, his somber expression more visible as she approached. She stopped a meter or two from him, trying to read his mood.

Whatever it was she had come in a frenzy to tell him, this was her time. How would she even explain her presence? "I looked for you at Sizun and the Roc Trévezel," she said. It sounded so lame, but it was all she could think to say.

His tone was measured, detached. "I started at Saint-Herbot. I thought if I took our trip backwards, it would help free me of the spell you cast over me."

"Were you going to leave without saying goodbye?"

"I couldn't leave without seeing you. But I dreaded saying goodbye."

"I knew you would leave." *Stupid! Why did I say that?*

"Please don't start that again," he said. "I am so sick of that routine. You believed that because you wanted to. As long as you thought I'd leave, I was no threat because it was never for real. But it *was* real. I'll tell you how real it was. I would have stayed in Brittany the rest of my life for you. I would have left everything, my family, my friends, my country. But no matter what I said, no matter what I did, it was never enough."

How could she take back those hurtful words? "I'm sorry, I

meant – "

"I know what you meant; I've heard it before and I don't want to hear it again. We've had our fun, and now it's over. It's not what I wanted. I hate what's happened to us. But that's where we are."

They stood still, apart, like strangers. She pushed the strap of her purse higher on her shoulder, just for something to do with her hands, hands that did not have permission to touch him.

As he had done months before, he was speaking with no fear of saying too much, knowing it was all over between them, even their attempt at friendship. But this time, he was not going to tell her how wonderful he thought she was.

"You're free," he said, "and I'm done hoping I could be more to you than someone to pass the time with. When you broke our last date and told me not to call you, I had to face reality. We can't even be friends; we failed at that too."

Was this why he had waited there when he found her car? For the pleasure of telling her she had made a mistake and hearing her admit it? He did not have to tell her; she already knew. "Not seeing each other was a bad idea. I was wrong. We could try again."

"Try what again, some other deal to keep us together and apart at the same time? No. It's better this way. I'll be gone and you can do what you want with your life without me around to get in your way. You can marry Jean-Yves or someone else or even stay single and carefree. It's none of my business anymore."

She stared at him in disbelief, trying to comprehend how he could be so cold to her. "So we just forget each other as if nothing ever happened between us? Is that what you want?"

"All I want now is a clear conscience, to know I didn't keep you from the life you always hoped for." He looked to one side. "I've said enough. I've said too much. This is not how I imagined saying goodbye to you."

It was not what she had imagined either. Saying goodbye for all time had never entered her mind. She had imagined only that they would be friends on her terms, and he would go along just because that was the way she wanted it. But he was done with her self-

213

indulgence. She had no answer to what he had said, no explanation. Nor did he seem to expect one. There was nothing left to say, nothing left to do. This was where it would end.

She reached into her purse for her car keys. All that they had shared since their first encounter had been reduced to basic etiquette: how to say goodbye like civilized people, an act that would fix their last memory of each other. They stood still for a moment, neither one making the move or saying the words that would separate them forever.

In that moment, a breeze whispered through the trees around them and brushed her face. Something struck her. It was as if her saint was speaking to her. *This is your last chance, Anne. Don't give up. Don't let him give up. If you lose him, what will you have left? Fight for him, Anne. Fight for him!*

As the breeze blew on past her, she dropped her keys back into her purse, determined to find better words, words to keep him there, to keep him talking to her. "Why are you going back? Is it because of your family, your job?"

"Because of you. As much as I love Brittany, I can't stay here and not be with you. Everywhere I go, everything reminds me of you, of places we went together, of things we did together. And your name is everywhere. Saint Anne, Anne de Bretagne, Sainte-Anne-d'Auray. I can't even look at my own address without seeing your name and where you live. My only chance of ever putting you behind me is to go back to where I'm not surrounded by reminders of you."

"Will you ever come back? Will I ever see you again?"

"I'll come back someday. Brittany is too much a part of me to never come back." He stepped away from her car toward her, close to her, a mournful look on his face. "I'll come to visit your mother. You'll be married. You'll have children. We'll meet for coffee while your husband's at work. You'll have a few little wrinkles, some gray hair. Your exquisite little behind will be bigger, but not by much. And you'll still be beautiful and I'll still love you and it will break my heart to see you."

How more clearly could he tell her it was over? Even

214

admitting he still loved her, he had erased himself from thoughts of her future. For him, their days of passion were memories and nothing more. How to stop him? Just say it. "I don't want you to go."

"It's too late. I've made all the arrangements. Everyone is expecting me."

And so it would be: his friends and family thrilled to have him back. Anne would be left behind, a minor character in his tales of life in Brittany. Now, it was her turn to do what he had done months before: tell him what she felt for him, not to change his mind—it was too late for that—but so he would know that she would not forget him. "I've ruined everything. Most women can only dream of a man like you. I had you and I drove you away."

"And what if I stayed? Would anything change, or would you start in again blaming me for standing between you and the life you want? I refuse to start the same dance again: together, apart, together, apart. You're the best thing that's ever happened to me and now I have to get away from you. Just think. I'm going to live in another country to get over a woman I love. Does that story sound familiar?"

It hurt to hear him speak with such despair. It was her fault he was suffering, just as it had been months before, when she had told him they could no longer see each other. *Why do I punish him for loving me?*

The words came back to her. *Don't give up, Anne. Don't let him give up. Fight for him, Anne!*

What else could she say that might change his mind? Even in desperation, she knew not to make empty promises that he would not believe. "If you stayed, it would be different. Today when I thought you were gone, I realized how much you mean to me, and not just as a friend. For the rest of my life I'll never forget how I felt today when I thought I'd lost you, that I'd never see you again. If you stayed, I would try hard to trust you, to trust myself to stay with you. Please don't give up on me. If you still feel anything for me, don't give up on me!"

He looked down, back at her, and off into the bare forest.

215

No man had ever heard her speak with such humility.

They stood alone and silent, not touching, on a cold winter day at the edge of a forest in a remote village at the end of the earth. She stared at the brass buttons of his navy blue jacket, wanting so much to know what he was thinking but afraid to ask.

He broke the long silence. "Are you still seeing Jean-Yves?"

Did he actually care or was he just searching for something to say? "No. And Vanessa? Does she know you're leaving?"

"She knows and she's glad to be rid of me. She ran out of patience, just like you predicted. I didn't tell Christine. If you talk to her, tell her goodbye for me."

More silence. Anne had nothing left to say. She had laid herself bare and said it all. Now it was his turn. Now, for the first time since they had met, it was all up to him. She half-expected him to say nothing, to get in his car and drive away.

Instead, he looked at his watch and said, "I'm getting hungry. You didn't happen to bring me a sandwich, did you?"

In his dour mood, why would he ask her for a sandwich? Was he mocking her? No. Not at all. He was remembering the first time they had come here. Was he offering her a glimmer of hope or just a more gracious goodbye? "I didn't bring anything," she said. "When I heard you were leaving and I couldn't reach you by phone, I went straight to your house. I called your cell phone, but – "

"I didn't turn it on. I didn't want to talk to anyone."

"We could go into the village to a restaurant."

"I need to do something first."

"What?"

He took her in his arms and held her tenderly, his cheek against hers, as he had done so often. She longed for those times when his warmth and attention with no other motive made her want him. He was so subtle, so fine.

She wrapped her arms around him and pulled his body tight against hers.

A mother and her young daughter walked by. "Mommy, what are they doing?" the girl asked.

"They're giving each other a big hug because they love each

216

other."

"They must love each other a lot. That's a long hug!"

Anne smiled. A long hug indeed. The longer the better.

They walked down the road to a quiet street next to the lake and sat on the terrace of the Crêperie du Chaos, warmed a bit by a bright December sun that had come out just for them. They were the only customers willing to brave the cold and sit outside. When she ordered a *galette complète* and a bowl of cider, he said, "The same for me." The waitress left them and he added wistfully, "That's what we both ordered the first time we had lunch together." For many minutes they were silent. He held her hand lightly and played with her fingers, as if he were fondling gold coins from someone else's treasure, knowing he would have to give them up.

"Why didn't you tell me you were going to leave?" she asked.

"Once I told you, it would be real. It would be final. I don't know if I would have told you if you hadn't found me here. I still don't know why you came here."

"I had to see you and talk to you before you left."

"Here I am," he said. "Say whatever you want."

She stared out across the lake. What could she say that she had not already said? But if she had learned anything in the past few hours, her only hope was to say it all, even at the risk of more rejection. "I still love you and I don't want you to leave. But after the way I've treated you, I don't have the right to ask you for anything."

"How can you ask me for anything if you don't know yourself what you want?"

"I know what I want now. I want *you*."

"That doesn't tell me much. What crazy conditions would you come up with this time?"

"I don't know. I don't know. I just want to be with you. I feel like we can figure this out." He was making her grovel, and for what? He was going to leave no matter what she said or did. They would finish lunch and go their separate ways, after one long hug in the parking lot and one last *galette complète* together.

217

The waitress brought their *galettes*. He stared at his as if seeking counsel from the egg yolk staring back at him. He looked up, out across the lake. What was he thinking?

With his gaze still on the lake, he said, "You could come with me."

"Come with you? Back to Sainte-Anne?" She did not understand.

He turned to her. "No. To California."

Come with him to California? She could hardly believe what she was hearing. "Do you mean that? For how long?"

"Long enough for you to get the idea out of your head that I'm some foreign freak who came here to ruin your life."

Bitter words, spoken with the indifference of one who has nothing more to lose. He was in control. She could meet him on his terms or be left behind. It was time to let go. The more she had tried to control her life and the men in it, the more her life had slipped away from her.

"Don't say that. You didn't come here to ruin my life. But I seem to have done my best to ruin yours."

He waited until a noisy motorcycle had passed by on the narrow road next to them. "You can't ruin my life unless I let you. We make our own lives or we ruin them. Nobody forced us to stay together as long as we did."

We make our own lives or we ruin them. So clear, so simple, so obvious. And so hard to see.

She took another step onto the path that had appeared in front of her. "If I go, how long will you want me to stay?"

"As long as you want, or until I decide to throw you out. Remember when we first met?" he said. You told me you wanted to see California, and I offered to show you around. I don't recall withdrawing the invitation. Maybe I'll even include free room and board. But it's not a big house; I can't promise you a separate bedroom."

He was starting to sound like his flirtatious old self. She followed his lead. "So it's not free after all."

He smiled and looked down at her feet and ran his eyes

218

slowly up to her face, like she had done to him in the café in Plumergat. "I haven't forgotten what's under that coat. I'm sure we can arrange the terms of payment."

"I've never sold my body. The idea is rather exciting. I wonder how much I could earn?"

"Probably a fortune, but don't be in a hurry to change your profession; your mother still needs you in the bookstore." He glanced at her plate. "Your *galette* is getting cold. And I'm getting horny."

She flashed him her most seductive smile, one that had never failed to get her way with him. "There's a treatment for that. I read about it in a book."

He leaned over, put a hand behind her neck and kissed her, their first kiss in weeks. She caught a trace of grilled buckwheat and salted butter. For an American, he tasted a lot like a Breton.

As heartened as she was by his brief displays of affection, she knew that kissing and flirting would not solve their problems. It was time to drag everything out into the open—now—while he seemed willing to talk. "If I went with you, what would happen after I came back here? Would you stay there?"

"I don't know what I'd do. But I know one thing: I won't come back to resume the torture. If, at the end of your stay, you say to me, 'Thanks for your hospitality. Now I have to get back to Brittany and find myself a husband,' don't expect to see me again."

His words were blunt, but at least he was talking to her. She had to keep him talking. "If I accept," she said, "what will that say to you about us?"

He thought for a moment. "Maybe nothing. Maybe just a few more weeks together. Or it might tell me that we still have a chance."

"If I spend a month or two with you there, and after that I tell you, as you put it, 'Now I have to get back to Brittany and find myself a husband,' will you hate me for it?"

"Is that what you think you'll do?" By now, nothing she might do was likely to surprise him—or her.

No more masquerade, no more games. Let him see the real

woman he had fallen in love with. Gesturing back toward the woods, she said, "A few months ago, barely 100 meters from where we're sitting, I told you the more I saw you, the more I would like you and the more I'd want to run away from you. I didn't know at the time how true that would turn out to be. I didn't just like you more; I fell in love with you and it scared me so much I had to pretend it couldn't last. And you aren't the first. It's finally becoming clear to me what I've been doing most of my life, and every time I think I've made some progress, I screw up again. I don't know how you put up with me as long as you did. I don't blame you for wanting to leave."

The waitress cleared the table and brought coffee. He took his time unwrapping a sugar cube, no doubt stalling for time to think. "A few minutes ago," he said, "barely 100 meters from where we're sitting, you asked me not to give up on you. The truth is, before I found your car, I had given up on you, as painful as it was. I thought I might find the courage to come see you for a few minutes, say goodbye, and probably never see you again. And now here you are, asking me not to give up on you. But you won't . . . " His voice started to break. He cleared his throat and continued. "You won't give me a chance. You say you love me, you ask me not to give up on you, but you keep treating me like second-class merchandise."

"I can change," she said. "I know I can. I'll do whatever it takes." But she knew it would take more than swearing to her good intentions to bring him around. She considered telling him about Dr. Laborde, but it was too risky, his reaction too unpredictable. What else could she say to convince him? "I'll come with you to California."

"Don't decide now. I don't want you to say you'll come and change your mind later. I'm leaving on Christmas Day, so you have a few days to think about it. It was the only flight I could get."

They returned to the parking area on a path through boulders and trees along the river. As she walked through the forest with him, the rush of the river, the sunlight through the trees, and the warmth of his hand all gave her hope that she might yet emerge to see again the stars.

On returning to their cars, they made plans to have dinner together at his house. She drove ahead of him leaving Huelgoat. As they approached the main highway, she spotted the dirt road into the forest where he had parked and kissed her months before.

On a playful whim, she pulled onto the road and stopped, checking her mirror to make sure he followed her. She got out of her car and into his. The door had barely closed and he was leaning over the console, kissing her. She let herself go, drawing life and hope from him. While she was fingering his belt buckle, he moved his hand down to her thigh and slid it under her skirt. Just when she could take no more, he said, "Let's go. We can be at my house in an hour."

"I can't wait that long. Let's pretend we're American teenagers and do it in the car."

"How do you know about American teenagers?"

"I read a lot. I run a bookstore, remember?"


When she arrived at home, Anne hoped she could slip in, shower, and change clothes before crossing paths with her mother. No luck. Anne was hanging up her coat in the hall when her mother stepped out of the kitchen.

"Hi Mom. How was the lecture?"

"It was good. We enjoyed it." Brigitte glanced at Anne's wrinkled skirt and said, "May I conclude that your day went well?"

"I found him and we sort of made up."

"Sort of?"

"He invited me to go to California with him." Her coat fell off its peg.

"Really! For how long?"

Anne bent down to pick up her coat. "As long as I want."

"Are you going to go?"

"I haven't decided." She fumbled with her coat, trying again to hang it.

"If you decide not to, ask him if I can go in your place."

"Are you kidding? I don't dare leave the two of you alone

together."

At his house at the end of the evening, they lay in bed side by side, contented and exhausted. Before drifting off to sleep, Anne thought of the statue of Saint Anne in the park nearby and spoke to her. "You gave me another chance. Don't abandon me now. I need you more than ever."

## Chapter 31: To America

Anne arrived at Dr. Laborde's office fired up by all that had happened and the urgent decision that faced her. "I can't stay away from him, but the problem is still there. I'm in love with a man I'm afraid to marry. I told him if we both tried, we could find a way to stay together. I meant it when I told him I'd try, but I don't know what to do or if we really have a chance. I suppose the worst that can happen is I get a trip to California. He even offered to pay my airfare. I don't know why. Either he can't let go of me completely, or he's just being his usual generous self. Whatever his reasons, I'd be crazy to turn it down. But it still feels like a huge decision, like if I go there, there's no turning back." She stopped to catch her breath.

Dr. Laborde allowed herself a rare smile, apparently amused by Anne's excitement. "When you think of John in California without you, what do you imagine?"

"Nothing. It's a blank. Just that he's away from me, out of my reach. While he's here, I'm more in control. I can see him face to face. I mean, look what just happened. On an insane impulse I tracked him down to the far end of Brittany. He admitted he still loves me and invited me to go to California with him, and all that was after he decided he was done with me. Just seeing each other made all the difference. But if he's in California and I'm here, it's different. He's beyond my reach. I'm powerless. Maybe that's one reason I've been so obsessed with the idea that he'll leave me and go back there."

"You don't like feeling powerless."

"No."

"Why do you suppose that is?"

"I don't know. My friends—my close friends who are honest with me—tell me I like to be in control. I've just accepted that's the way I am. I've never wondered why."

Dr. Laborde gave Anne a moment to figure it out for herself. When Anne said nothing, Dr. Laborde continued, "How did you feel when your father left?"

"Sad. Sad and helpless. I would have done anything to keep him from leaving, but there was nothing I could do. My parents just announced he was leaving and he left. I didn't understand why." She stared at the painting on the wall. "I lost control of my life. And I've been trying ever since to get it back."

After another pause, Dr. Laborde prompted her. "Do you think it would help you to see John in California, to get an idea of the life he wanted to leave?"

"I'm afraid of what I might see. He's never said a kind word about where he grew up. There wasn't even a bookstore, only a little public library that he liked to go to. When he went to the library, he stopped at a bakery nearby and bought a creme puff. The way he talks about those creme puffs, you'd think it was the only pleasure he ever had. After I heard that story, I understood why he can never walk past a *pâtisserie* without going in."

"Or a bookstore," Dr. Laborde added.

She wanted to call him and say she would go to California with him, but something held her back. She knew what Sophie would say: "Go!" Jocelyne, who at the beginning had encouraged her to keep seeing John, would no doubt say the same thing. But maybe not. The stakes were higher now.

She called Jocelyne, whose logic was as compelling as ever. "If you go, what's the worst that can happen?"

Anne thought a moment. "I'll be hopelessly in love with him, I'll come back, he'll stay there, and I'll never see him again."

"And if you don't go?"

Anne was surprised to hear herself laughing at the utter simplicity of it all. "I'll be hopelessly in love with him, I'll never see him again, and I'll miss a free trip to California."

"And John will miss out on something he wants very much."

"What would that be?"

"He wouldn't have invited you if he didn't want you to come."

The next day, she drove him to the end of the Crozon Peninsula, to the Pointe de Penhir, where the west end of Brittany jutted into the Atlantic Ocean, where the dragon pointed its stony tongue at North America. Lofty cliffs descended to rocks over which waves from the open sea broke in breathtaking displays of nature's power. They sat on a rock facing the ocean, huddled together against a cold December breeze.

"Is the coast of California anything like this?" she asked.

"In places," he said, as if the comparison was of no interest.

"It sounds like you know it too well to appreciate it. Maybe I should go with you and form my own opinion. Do you really want me to go?"

"If I didn't, I wouldn't have invited you." He looked at her expectantly.

"I'll go," she said.

He smiled and gave her shoulder a little squeeze.

Anne wanted to appreciate the roar of the surf below, the brisk salt air, the terns circling and diving, but now that her trip to California had become real, the fears she had voiced to Dr. Laborde surfaced anew. How different would he be over there? What would his parents think of her? His friends?

In the days that followed, she found him more reticent, causing her to wonder if he regretted inviting her. Then to her surprise, he told her he had negotiated with his landlord to keep the house for a few more months and had taken his car off the market. Anne refrained from commenting on the mixed message he was giving her, leaving with no promises made, saying little, yet not pulling up stakes completely.

Calls to airlines confirmed what they had suspected: there was no space on his flight or any other reasonable flight until the end of the holidays. It was just as well, they decided. John would be too busy when he first arrived to spend much time with her. He was especially concerned about his job. It made more sense, they decided, for Anne to defer her trip for a month or two so John could take care of as much business as possible. They spoke of her staying a month. She did not want to leave her mother alone with the bookstore for longer than that.

She promised to check on his house from time to time and drive his car. If he did not come back, how would he dispose of the rest of his things and sell his car? She wanted to tell him he could count on her to help him even if it did not work out between them, but she did not want to speak of the possibility.

While running errands, he stopped by the apartment while the store was closed for lunch. Anne was buoyed by his visit and found herself in a playful, optimistic mood. She unfolded a map of Brittany and spread it out on the kitchen table. "Look at the west end of Brittany," she said. "What do you see?"

He looked puzzled. "A jagged coastline, bays, peninsulas, towns. Why? What am I supposed to see?"

"Look at the whole west end. What it is shaped like?"

"Don't laugh, but it looks to me like the head of an animal," he said, running his finger down the jagged coastline on the map.

"What kind of animal?"

"Is this a test? Is there a right answer?"

"Yes it's a test and yes there's a right answer."

He looked again and ventured, "A dragon?"

She smiled triumphantly. "That's the right answer." There was no need for them to count the stones at the Roche-aux-Fées.

He still looked puzzled.

"I'll explain it to you when you come back. If you don't come back, you'll never know."

Shortly before he was to leave, she made a date to take John to Rennes for lunch with her father and Florence. That morning, John called Anne to ask what he should wear. She suggested a sweater and sport coat. He called back in a few minutes and asked what color sweater. She was surprised by how nervous he seemed. Almost as nervous as she was.

Her father and Florence answered the door together. The two men shook hands, eying each other cordially but cautiously.

As they sat conversing in the living room, Anne watched her

father's expression change as he listened to John. Finally, he asked John, "Would it be indiscreet to ask where you're from?"

"California."

At that moment, John realized that Anne had not told her father that he was American. Anne and Florence looked at each other and laughed. The oversight was not accidental.

On the way home, John asked, "Do you think he was as nervous as I was?"

It was a good sign. John would have no reason to be nervous unless he had something to lose. "I know he was nervous, and not just about meeting you; he never knows what to expect from me."

He laughed. "Neither do I! I can barely imagine having a daughter like you. You must have been impossible."

"I had reason to be. You're going to ask me why, aren't you? I'll tell you. When my father moved out, I was already mad at him for leaving us, then I found out he'd been cheating on my mother. Nobody told me at first; everyone thought I was too young. When I finally learned what he had done to my mother, I was furious and I let him know how I felt."

John nodded, looking pensive. Finally he said, "I'm thinking about your rant at the Roche-aux-Fées about adulterers. At the time I thought it was only about Pierre. If you ever get married, your husband won't have to worry too much about you."

"Not only that, if he ever cheated on me, he'd be likely to lose a vital organ. You can guess which one."

"I'll remember that," he said, crossing his arms in his lap, "in case I ever need to know."

She invited him to join her mother's side of the family on Christmas Eve for mass, followed by dinner at their apartment. Dinner was not over until late. After midnight, Anne and John sat with Bernard and Marie, drinking and chatting. Jocelyne and Philippe sat across the room with her parents. The children moved together like a whirlwind about the apartment, pleased to be allowed to stay up late and excited by thoughts of the presents they would receive in the morning.

For a moment they hovered around Anne and John. Yann said to John, "Remember when I caught the snake? I wasn't afraid! Every time I go down to the stream, I look for it, but I never see it."

Justine declaimed, "That's because he talks all the time, so he scares it away."

"I do not!"

"Snakes can't hear." John said. "They don't have ears. They can feel the vibrations from your footsteps, so they still know you're coming. But you won't see it for a while. Right now it's underground, sleeping away the winter."

Justine turned to the other children and announced, "Uncle John's from America. He knows all about snakes. He isn't afraid of them. I'm not afraid of them either!"

"Uncle John," Yann said, "When are you coming back from America?"

John picked him up, set him on his lap and said, "I don't know, Yann. Soon, I hope."

"Good!" Yann slid off John's lap and ran to join the vortex of children as it spun off to another room.

As Anne watched John's exchange with Yann, it occurred to her that if John balked at coming back to Brittany, she could call him and put Yann on the phone.

When the children had left the room, Anne said quietly to John, "Come with me." She took him to her bedroom, closed the door, and handed him a book, its tattered and taped cover emblazoned with its title: *La Belle Californie.*

"This book doesn't look like you brought it up from the store this afternoon."

"My father gave it to me for Christmas, twenty-three years ago today, when I was ten years old. I got it out this morning to look at pictures of places I've always wanted to see." She took the book from him, opened it and turned the pages. "You've probably seen all these places many times: San Francisco, Yosemite National Park, Hollywood. I hope we can go to some of them." Each photo she showed him was marked with a yellowed and crumbling piece of paper.

Before he could answer, she said, "As rejected as I felt during all those years, I treasured this book . . . " Her voice caught. She paused. "I treasured this book as a sign that my father still understood me, that somehow, in spite of his absence, he might still care about me."

He took the book from her, turned it over, thumbed through it, and set it down. What could he say to such a revelation?

"So you see," she said, "A book brought you here, and because of a book I said yes when you asked me to lunch. Take your worn little Brittany book to California with you, and look at it whenever you think you might not come back."

That night, when the other guests had gone, and John and Anne left to go to his house, John said goodbye to Brigitte. After a proper two-cheek kiss, John gave her a spontaneous American hug. Brigitte hesitated a moment, then hugged him back. She did not know if she would ever see him again.

The next morning, Anne was calmer than she had expected. Two months, after all, was not so long, and her own ticket was securely in her possession. She drove John to the station in Auray to catch the high-speed train to Charles De Gaulle Airport outside Paris.

When his train arrived, she helped him carry his luggage aboard. Before she stepped back down onto the platform, he kissed her and said, "If another American comes into the bookstore and invites you to lunch, don't go!" She would miss his silly sense of humor. It had raised her spirits so many times.

Although they talked by phone and emailed each other, his absence set off bouts of insecurity that seemed to validate her fears. He was so far away. She coped by keeping busy, working extra shifts to give her mother some time off in anticipation of Anne's absence.

Anne turned her attention to finding temporary help so that Brigitte would not have to run the bookstore by herself. She called Monsieur Renaud, who had started the store. When Monsieur

Renaud had retired, Anne's father had arranged to buy the store for Brigitte as part of their divorce settlement. Monsieur Renaud admitted to moments of missing the store and was happy to help.

With that problem solved, Anne went to work on her English. She had studied English in school because it was required. Some things were easy. There were fewer conjugations to learn, for example. But others were hard. Phrasal verbs, for example, were ridiculous. If *over* means *above*, and a friend invited her to his house by saying "Come over," did he expect her to fly there? Or just climb over the fence? And how did anyone know whether a building burned down or burned up? And the pronunciation: the "th," the "r." What bizarre sounds.

In middle school, she went to England on student exchanges. When she went back years later as a tourist, she was able to speak and understand, but only simple sentences. As a teenager and young adult, she had gone through a phase of watching classic American movies. "Citizen Kane," "Gone with the Wind," "Casablanca," among others. Without subtitles, she would have understood little; spoken American English was as incomprehensible to her as Breton. When her English teacher had told the class that Americans change a "t" to a "d" between vowels, she did not believe it—until she heard it for herself in a movie. And how could they understand each other when nobody moved their lips? She did well enough in her English classes, but took no more than were required.

Then she met John.

Over the previous months, when she had asked him to speak English with her, he obliged, and was careful to speak slowly and clearly. He understood about learning a foreign language. But they always slipped back into French. It was easier and it was what they were used to speaking with each other. As soon as she decided to visit him in California, they tried to speak more English in the few days they had left. He was more patient with her than she was with herself.

They worked on pronunciation, which she could not get from books. He helped her as best he could, but their practice sessions sometimes degenerated into good-natured arguments.

"*Thing.* Not *sing.* Touch your tongue to the tips of your upper teeth and blow. It's simple." He demonstrated.

"No it's not. It's hard. Why do you have such crazy sounds?"

"How do you suppose French sounds to Anglophones? What about your silly "r" down in your throat? And words like *brûlure* and *sérurier*? They're impossible to pronounce."

"If they're impossible, how did you manage to say them both just now?"

"Years of practice. And how do you justify your preposterous genders? They serve no purpose whatsoever except to mess up Anglophones. And there's no logic to it. When I learned that the French word for vagina is masculine, I almost gave up."

She bought English-teaching software and worked with it, watched American news programs on the internet, and rented American movies, listening carefully while reading the French subtitles. When she learned a word and later encountered it in her reading or in a movie, she knew she was making progress.

Sometimes, on her days off, she went to John's house, opened all the shutters, and spent a few hours there alone, reading and studying amid reminders of their past: the couch where they sat when she told him they had to stop seeing each other, the places on the floor where her bra and top and his shirt had landed the first time they made love. But as the days passed, her time alone in his house forced her to face the possibility that they might never be together here again.

At the start of her next session with Dr. Laborde, Anne sat without speaking, not knowing where to begin. After a few minutes of uneasy silence, Dr. Laborde asked, "Can you tell me what you're feeling right now?"

"I'm nervous about my trip to California."

"What is it about the trip that makes you nervous?"

Anne pondered. "I don't know what John will be like over there. How can he not be different? And he'll be in charge. It's his country, his city. He'll know everything and I'll know nothing. I'll be under his control."

"You don't like that idea."

"No. I like being in charge. There's another thing. I always thought of California as paradise. When I was a child and got sad or lonely, I escaped by daydreaming that I was a glamorous movie star in California."

"So when you get there and see it's just more of the real world with all its problems, you'll lose something."

"Not only that, I'll have to face what to do about John. He won't put up with my indecision forever. If I pull away from him again, he'll give up on me for good. He won't even want to be friends."

"Are you afraid you might lose him?"

"I'm afraid I've already lost him. I believe he loves me. I also believe that he meant what he said: that loving me has too high a price."

"That sounds a lot like what you've said about him: that you love him but he's too risky."

"I don't know. I always thought I was afraid he would go back to California. But there's something else. How I feel about John is more intense than how I've ever felt about a man. That John's roots are on the other side of the world adds to the attraction and to the fear. It scares me to feel that way."

"We've talked a lot about the fear. Maybe it would help to talk about the attraction."

Under Dr. Laborde's gently prodding, Anne began to open up again. "He enriches my life. It's almost like my excitement when I started college. New worlds opened up to me. After college, until I met John, I thought I was a sophisticated, cosmopolitan intellectual because I had finished college and liked to read. When I met him, the outside world came to me. He started to stir up feelings I never knew were there."

"Feelings like that special bond you've mentioned?"

"Exactly. I don't understand it, but no matter what happens, even if twenty years from now I'm married to another man and he's married to another woman, I'll think of John and that connection will still be there. It goes beyond friendship. It goes beyond lust. We're in sync with each other. As close as I am with my mother and my best friends, John and I communicate in ways I've never known before and can't really explain. You'd expect language to be a problem because French isn't his native language, but it's not. It almost helps us communicate. Because we speak French, he expresses himself in a way that's simple and direct and uninhibited. He doesn't play games. When he's ready to talk, he's right there, out front."

The weeks leading up to her departure passed slowly. As the day approached, she found herself rereading old emails from John, browsing her diary, coming to grips with a potpourri of emotions: anticipation, excitement, anxiety. So much was at stake. At the end of this trip or soon after, she would come to the moment of truth, the decision—perhaps the most important crossroad of her life.

Even apart from John, she was about to visit for the first time the land of her childhood dreams. She saw herself as a Jew going to Jerusalem, a Muslim making the haj to Mecca.

Her mother drove her to the train station, kissed her goodbye and said, "Send me a postcard from California. This time I'm serious."

The train left Auray and sped through the Breton countryside. When it stopped at Nantes, Anne had a moment of thinking she was about to miss her stop, then settled back into her seat and smiled, thrilled to be going out into the world beyond Brittany, beyond France, beyond Europe. After Nantes, the train picked up speed: 250 kilometers per hour or more. The landscape passed her window like a movie shown too fast, as if her life were suddenly on fast-forward. From time to time they entered a tunnel with a *thud* and a sudden change of air pressure.

During the flight she watched a movie, then tried to read, but the only book that could keep her attention was a guidebook on

California. She smiled as she imagined seducing John that evening by stripping naked and reading to him from the guidebook. For most of her hours in the air, she was lost in reverie, trying to imagine the month ahead.

The woman in the seat next to her asked, "Is this your first trip to California?"

"Yes," Anne replied, "if I don't count my dreams."

As the plane descended into Los Angeles, she saw the vast, flat expanse of a city that stretched like a carpet beyond the horizon. John was down there somewhere. This was his city. As they continued to descend, she could make out an endless grid of perpendicular streets lined with individual houses, many with swimming pools. The sight was depressing. Millions of people lived down there, oblivious and indifferent to her existence. She felt small and lost, until she wheeled her suitcase out of U.S. Customs, into the California sun and John's waiting arms.

## Chapter 32: City of Angels

They sat for a while in his car in the parking structure, kissing and holding each other.

He said, "I'm thinking of the last time we came back from Huelgoat."

"If you tell me that making love in the car in an airport parking lot is the custom in this country, I'll believe you. But I'd still rather take a shower first."

"It's not a custom yet, but we could start it."

He drove out of the airport and into a city that radiated youth and energy. Cars everywhere. Little things caught her attention: the position of the traffic lights, road signs displaying Spanish names of streets and cities. Sepulveda, La Tijera, Sacramento. "I've been studying English," she said. "Was that a mistake?"

They turned onto a large highway—five lanes in each direction. A range of mountains loomed not far in front of them. She thought of the Roc Trévezel in Brittany where they had first kissed, a pathetic 384 meters high.

On the highway, she saw more cars and not much else. He pointed in different directions. "Santa Monica and the ocean are that way. Beverly Hills is over there. Those buildings are Century City, where my office is." After a few minutes, he turned off the highway and into a residential area. Houses of all styles: Spanish next to Tudor next to Moorish. Some looked like factories with stark white walls and steel railings. He pulled into a driveway and stopped.

"Here we are."

She got out of the car and saw trees, wisteria vines, pansies, bougainvillea. She heard children playing nearby. It was a simple, Spanish-style stucco house with a red tile roof, big enough, but not grandiose, much as she had expected, from photos he had shown her.

He carried her suitcase to the bedroom and showed her empty drawers and closet space and the rest of the house. Three bedrooms, one of which was his study, and another a guest suite with its own entrance, occupied by his friend Michael, who rented the room and took care of the house in John's absence. Michael was away for a few days. She imagined that he and John had arranged it that way.

He made them a light dinner and helped her unpack and get organized. He showed her what she would need for breakfast, figuring that because of jet lag, she would wake up before he did.

At nine o'clock she told him, "I'm fading fast. I have just enough energy left to attack your body before I fall asleep."

"I didn't dare hope for tonight. I thought you'd be too tired."

"You underestimate me."


She awoke in confusion, trying to figure out where she was. The clock said 5:20. She slipped out of bed and put on a robe. While John slept, she wandered around the house, examining pictures on the walls, electrical outlets with slits instead of holes, doors with knobs instead of levers. She looked out the front window at a dark street, quiet until a helicopter passed noisily overhead.

The details brought home to her that she was in a foreign country: the light switches, the window hardware: a lever latch and a crank, not the ornate oval knob of French windows. No shutters. She stopped to think if she had ever slept in a house without shutters.

This is what he left to come to Brittany. How attached was he to this place? How much of his dismal description of Los Angeles would turn out to be accurate?

Suddenly she was hungry. She made coffee and toast and sat down to breakfast, lost in her thoughts. When she heard water running, she left the kitchen, strode into the bathroom, dropped her robe and nightgown on the floor and stepped into the shower with him. Running her hands over his wet skin, she said in passable English, "Good morning, my love."


Later, they went for a walk in his neighborhood. People walking, some jogging. He greeted each of them. Each in turn smiled and said, "Good morning."

She said, "You seem to know everybody."

236

"I've never seen any of them before."

"In France, strangers don't greet each other on the street."

"Yeah, but in France, I get a *bonjour* and *au revoir* from every toll-booth attendant and shopkeeper, even from you. Remember?"

"How could I forget? One *bonjour* and look where I end up."

Later, when they left by car to go sightseeing, John stopped at a gas station. As he pulled up to the pump, she asked, "May I do it?"

"Sure." He handed her his credit card.

After studying the instructions on the pump, she inserted the card and filled the tank. Getting back in the car, she said, "Thanks."

"For what?" He pulled away from the pumps.

"For respecting my need for independence."

He stopped before entering the street. "Independence? Right after we met, you told me all you wanted in life was to get married. Now you're telling me you want to be independent."

"In the best marriages, both spouses maintain some independence from each other."

"Didn't you tell me that if your husband got too independent, he'd risk losing a vital organ?"

"That's not the kind of independence I meant, Mr. Smarty. Let's get going. I've waited twenty-three years to see this city. That's long enough."

They drove to the university he had attended, where they parked and walked among Romanesque brick buildings. The scale of the campus made her feel small. Just about everything did in this country.

He sympathized. "When I started here, I was eighteen. I was one little student from the country, lost among 25,000. On the first day I had my first French class. The instructor spoke only French. I didn't understand anything."

"But you figured it out. Listen to yourself now."

They returned to the car and headed west. He drove past an immense military cemetery to a boulevard divided by a wide grassy area and a long row of gnarled and leafy coral trees. An endless stream of Saturday-morning joggers ran along the grass, enjoying the sun and the cool air of late March. Cafés full of people spilled out onto the sidewalks.

Anne looked in vain at the sides of buildings for a street sign. Finally she spotted a sign on a post on a corner. Makes sense, she thought. Not as picturesque as the blue plaques with white letters on the walls of corner buildings in France, but easier to see while driving. Another Spanish name, San Vicente Boulevard. It ended at an avenue bordered by a narrow park atop a cliff. Ocean Avenue. Finally an English name. More joggers followed a path among palms and other trees she did not recognize. Joggers were not unusual in France, but here it seemed like the whole city was doing it.

They left the car and walked across the park, dodging a jogger as they crossed the path. A disheveled man in dirty clothes rummaged through a trash barrel, rising to drop an aluminum can into a plastic bag hanging from a rusty shopping cart. She caught herself staring at him as they walked, surprised that such a thing was possible in a place like California.

At the edge of the park, they stood at a railing at the top of a cliff. Below them, cars hurried up and down the coast on a highway next to a long row of houses, separated from the water by a hundred yards of sand. From the park she could see the entire bay. He pointed out the Palos Verdes Peninsula on the left and Point Dume, north of Malibu, on the right. Below them to their left, a pier reached out over the water.

Anne was no stranger to scenic coastlines, but this one was different. She sensed the tension between the huge city crowding the coastline and the sweeping vista of the bay. They walked to the end of the park and down to the pier. She noticed people fishing from the pier and asked John what kind of fish they caught.

"Nothing you'd want to eat," he replied. "The storm drains dump pollutants and trash from the whole west side of the basin into the bay. From time to time, they post warnings on fish that might be carrying something disgusting." She began to understand why he preferred the coast of Brittany.

Their next stop he called the Venice Boardwalk, where they

walked not on boards but on asphalt. An endless row of souvenir shops bordered a walkway populated by people of every size and shape, in various states of dress and undress. Anne saw multi-colored hair, tattoos, every imaginable body part pierced and festooned with hardware. She was disgusted one minute and fascinated the next. But then, every country had its weirdos. On the bike path nearby, a parade of bicyclists competed for space with skaters, joggers, and children on tricycles. He sensed when she had seen enough. They headed for Hollywood.

She ignored the tourists and freaks (most of whom seemed tame after Venice) and studied the stars on the sidewalks of the Walk of Fame, asking him about some names she did not recognize. In a moment of chauvinism, she lamented the absence of French singers, actors, and directors.

He said, "We saw Maurice Chevalier's star. Doesn't he count?"

"We sent you Chevalier; you sent us fast food. We're even."

## Chapter 33: A Taste of Ginger Ale

The next afternoon, Anne got ready to meet his parents and have dinner at their house. It one of the moments she had feared. How could she possibly show them any substance when she could barely express herself in the simplest of sentences? She would be judged, and not fairly. Sensing the futility of trying to show much personality verbally, she thought hard about her clothes, her hair, her makeup.

She asked John what to wear. He said "dressy casual" in English and tried to express it in French. When she asked for an example, he said it was how she dressed for a shift in the bookstore. She settled on a beige skirt, a maroon sweater and a blazer. Turning to jewelry, she laid out the four sets of earrings and necklaces she had brought with her. She tried each set on, examining herself carefully in the mirror. Asking John what he thought turned out to be a waste of time.

"You'd have to make a conscious effort not to be gorgeous, and even then I'm not sure you could pull it off."

"You're not helping. But thanks. I need all the encouragement I can get right now."

In the car, she asked, "What did you tell your parents about us?"

"Only that we spend a lot of time together."

"Did you at least tell them I was French?"

He smiled. "Maybe."

"What should I call them?"

"Bill and Mary. Do you want to know which one is which?" He seemed to find it amusing, taking Anne to meet his parents. Or else he was as nervous as she was and covering it better.

"I think I'll be able to figure it out. I'm a foreigner, not a half-wit."

"Oh Anne!" his mother exclaimed, "It's so nice to meet you! We've heard so much about you!" and gave her a hug and a kiss on the cheek.

Reminding herself not to offer her other cheek, Anne mumbled a timid "Hello." She was surprised by the effusive greeting. Did his mother think she was meeting her next daughter-in-law? Were all American women so enthusiastic and outgoing?

His father was friendly but more reserved and limited his greeting to a handshake. Anne thought he looked a lot like John, except for his lips. Both of his parents appeared youthful and in good physical shape for their age. They were dressed tastefully but simply.

Anne sat with John on a couch in the living room where a tray of cheese and crackers awaited them on the coffee table. John had already warned her to expect a salad at the beginning of the meal and not at the end and to set her bread on her plate and not the tablecloth, but he had said nothing about this curious practice of serving cheese with aperitifs. For that matter, aperitifs were limited to juices and soft drinks. With some misgivings, Anne tasted ginger ale for the first time in her life and was pleasantly surprised. Not that it mattered. If she hadn't liked it, she would have lied.

When Anne did not understand something or groped for a word, she glanced toward John, who fired off a quick translation. They asked her about the bookstore and her education. Their questions reflected their knowledge of Brittany. It was clear they had done some reading.

During dinner, the conversation turned to news of people who, John explained, were members of his parents' church.

"Remember Gordon Johnson?" Bill said. "He died last week."

John seemed unmoved. "His son Fred and I used to misbehave in Sunday school. The teacher threw us out of class more than once."

Anne glanced at Mary and thought she detected a fleeting look of disapproval.

After another minute of church talk, Bill said, "Anne doesn't know these people. Let's talk about something else."

To which Anne replied, "I did not know that John went to church," followed by an impish smile in John's direction.

His father laughed. "Not always willingly. He used to tell us he was going to change religions. Something about worshiping rocks."

"He still worship rocks." Anne did not have to look at John to know he was amused.

"He said he learned about sacred rocks in a book he found in the library. He spent a lot of time in the library."

John chimed in, "I didn't go there to read. I was in love with the librarian."

"And all these years I thought he went there for the books," Bill said. "Now he seems to prefer bookstores. And now I'm wondering if he goes there for the books." He winked at Anne.

As the evening progressed, Anne found she was able to express herself simply in English, but it was hard. She felt stressed, under scrutiny. And she could not get a sense of his parents. She saw them behind a paradoxical wall of relaxed formality. Their body language disclosed nothing.

A few days later, they went for dinner to the home of some friends of John's from high school. They greeted Anne like a celebrity, but spoke no French. Anne managed to communicate with them in basic English, but at dinner she could not keep up with the conversation.

She retreated into the silence of an outsider, which allowed her to watch and listen to John as he spoke with ease in his native language, unfettered with concern for errors of grammar or pronunciation. She heard strange words and sounds coming from him. He had known these people long before he met her. She sensed the depth and strength of their connection.

On the way home, he said, "I know that was hard for you.

"They were charming, but I still felt stupid, like a curiosity."

"Take it a day at a time. Remember, when I arrived in France, never having been out of the U. S., I had to cope with a new language and a new culture. So I understand."

"You understand to a point. When you were a student, you were young and flexible."

As they got ready for bed, Anne was about to tell him she wanted to go right to sleep. She was tired and felt like a stranger, not inclined to make love. Then it came to her. She had the power to make him hers alone and exclude the entire English-speaking world. And she did.

When John was about to leave for work the next morning, Anne was just getting out of bed. He said, "Michael probably came back last night. I'd thought you'd like to know, in case you planned to go to the kitchen in that sexy transparent nightgown. He's usually finishing breakfast about now."

"I'll get dressed first, at least until I have a chance to size him up."

"And if you like what you see?"

She kissed him, turned him around, and gave him a gentle push. "You're going to be late for work."

As John had warned her, when Anne went to the kitchen, she found a man sitting at the table, drinking coffee and reading the newspaper. He looked up at her and smiled. "Good morning, Anne. I'm Michael." He stood and shook her hand and sat back down.

She put bread in the toaster and poured herself a cup of coffee. Michael resumed reading his newspaper. While Anne was waiting for her toast, she was able to sneak a look at him. A sport coat over a sweater half-concealed a bit of a paunch. John had nothing to worry about. She took her coffee and toast to the table and sat.

Michael put down his newspaper. "Forgive me for staring at you. John's been telling me for months how pretty you are."

Anne looked down at her plate, at a loss for the proper American response to so blunt a compliment. "John should not lie to his friends," was the best she could come up with. She had imagined she would be under scrutiny but had not expected Michael to be so direct with her.

Michael took a sip of his coffee. At first, neither knew what else to say. Anne tried again. "I thought I would meet you before today."

"I've been staying at my girlfriend's apartment, but after a few days, her dog got jealous. Well, I have to go to work. It's been nice meeting you." He got up and started to leave the kitchen. Stopping at the door, he turned back to her. "I suppose John has already told you, but he's very happy you're here."

John had told her in his own way. Yet every bit of reassurance was welcome.

## Chapter 34: She Seems Nice

Dear Mom,

I am stunned by the expanse of this city. It's so big it's divided by a range of mountains that are twice the height of the highest mountains in Brittany. There are buses and a few trains, but mostly everybody drives everywhere. And all the drivers seem in a big hurry. According to John, the biggest hazard is young mothers in their SUVs, taking their kids to soccer practice while drinking coffee, putting on makeup, and talking on the phone. I haven't seen one yet. I think he's putting me on.

People are more open here than in France. Strangers strike up conversations on the street, in restaurants, everywhere. In a restaurant last night, a woman at the table next to us asked me what I was eating and how I liked it. When she heard my feeble English, she asked where I was from. When I told her, she said, "If you're French, you must be a good judge of food." Then she ordered the same thing. That led the people at both tables into a conversation about restaurants, weather, traffic, just about everything. This may be why we think Americans are superficial. French people are simpler; they aren't open, but they don't pretend to be. Americans are always smiling and friendly, but I wonder how much they are keeping to themselves.

John's parents are a little like that. I wanted to know what they thought when John told them he had taken up with another little French girl. What did they think of Marie-Clo? Of course, I didn't ask. They seem to accept me without really knowing me. It's like if I'm good enough for John, I'm good enough for them. I suppose that's better than rejecting me. But I would have preferred that they keep their distance and reserve judgment until they knew me better. Their approval would mean more, assuming John and I ever get to the point where their approval would be important to me. We'll see them one or two more times before I leave. John saw them once without me when he had a meeting near where they live. I asked him what they said about me. They told him, "She seems nice." So that's all the impression I made.

Everywhere I go, I hear people speaking Spanish, and a lot of the place names are in Spanish. The seat of the neighboring county is called Santa Ana. Saint Anne follows me everywhere.

I prefer daily life in France. People are not in such a hurry and take the time to enjoy the little things: meals, conversation, family.

We're leaving tomorrow by car for San Francisco. I'll tell you about it when we get back.

I miss you.

Love,
Anne

## Chapter 35: The Golden State

They left early and headed north on the coast highway. As they passed through San Luis Obispo, she asked him what the name meant. Discovering a city named after Saint Anne had whetted her curiosity about all the Spanish place names.

"It's named for its mission, like a lot of the towns along this highway. This one is for a French saint: Saint Louis Bishop of Toulouse. Ever heard of him?"

"Just because I have my own saint who protects me from the likes of you doesn't mean I know them all."

"Who protects *me* from the likes of *you?*" he asked.

"You're on your own."

It was like old times, cruising and needling each other.

They stopped for lunch at a restaurant along the coast highway. As they ate, Anne noticed a middle-aged couple in the booth across from theirs and watched while the waiter took their orders and left them to sit in silence. How many years had they been together? What had attracted them to each other? Had they already said everything they had to say to each other?

After responding to a text message from the office, John turned to see what Anne was looking at. She did not have to explain her fascination.

He frowned. "Is that how all married couples end up?"

"I hope not. I never got to see my parents arrive at that stage. Your parents seem happy enough."

"If they weren't, they wouldn't tell me. Protestants don't complain; we just accept our lot in life."

"If all married couples ended up as bored as they are, I don't know if it would be worth it."

"Here's an idea. What if every marriage ended when the youngest kid was grown. Then the husband and wife would have to decide if they got enough from the relationship to remarry each other." He took a bite of his sandwich.

"What about people who have nothing more to say to each

other? Would they stay together out of habit?"

He finished his mouthful. "Or out of fear of being alone. Nobody wants to be alone. Even with my parents together and lots of friends, I felt alone much of my life. The only time I really felt connected to someone was when I was with Diane. Until I met you, of course."

"Of course." She saw a chance to nudge him in relative safety. "If we're still together in twenty years, will we be like them?"

"There's only one way to find out."

Typical John reaction: neutral, tantalizing, revealing nothing. Anne looked again at the couple.

"See any action?" John asked.

"They're eating and talking. I think they're comparing their meals."

"Let's remember that if we ever get bored with each other. We can always talk about food."


San Francisco struck her as more like a European city. Its center bustled with people day and night, in sharp contrast to the unfashionable downtown of Los Angeles. The city's steep hills afforded a view from just about everywhere—of the bay, the bridges, the skyscrapers.

John called Michael to check in. They chatted briefly. When he hung up, he said, "Michael said to tell you he misses your breakfasts together."

So did Anne. Michael typically left for work later than John. They had gotten to know each other in spite of Anne's halting English. She found him warm and sensitive, and quickly understood why he and John were such close friends.

Leaving San Francisco two days later, they entered the Central Valley and crossed a vast plain almost all devoted to agriculture. She saw vineyards, almond orchards, cotton fields, other crops she did not recognize. On the east side of the Valley, they ascended into the mountains on a winding road and entered Yosemite National Park.

The next day, he took her to Glacier Point. After walking a few minutes from the parking lot, he told her to close her eyes. He guided her to a railing and set her hand on it. Keeping his arm around her, he told her to open her eyes. She gasped. The railing stood at the edge of a cliff, 3,000 feet straight down to the valley floor. Across the valley, another sheer rock face was punctuated by waterfalls plunging from the rim to the base of the cliff. On the valley floor, a river meandering through a flatland of forests and meadows collected the runoff from the falls. Opposite their viewpoint, huge granite formations posed, as if to mock the man-made pretension to grandeur of the great cathedrals of France.

She stared awestruck. The photos in her book did not do this place justice. Brittany seemed so small and insignificant and so far away. At moments like this, it was hard to imagine he would ever come back.

They returned to the car and descended into the valley, where the views from the valley floor to the tops of the granite formations were almost as breathtaking as the view from Glacier Point. They parked and walked to the bottom of a huge waterfall, swollen by the spring thaw. The swirling mists in the canyon below the fall drenched them and spawned a magnificent rainbow. As they stood next to the raging torrent that carried runoff from the waterfall, he took a handful of her soaking wet hair, held it in front of her face, and shouted over the roar, "A little shorter, *Mademoiselle?*"

On the last day, they drove to the Mariposa Grove of Big Trees. Anne had seen California coast redwoods growing in France, but nothing had prepared her for the size of the giant sequoias. She tried in vain to take a photo that would give an idea of the height of the trees, but had to settle for one that John took of her standing in front of the base of one of the largest ones. Reviewing the photo on the camera's screen, Anne said, "I've never looked so thin."

Leaving Yosemite, the road led them out of the mountains back down to the broad, flat floor of the Central Valley for the trip home. In the car, Anne asked, "The places we've seen on this trip, did you show them to Marie-Clo?"

"Most of them."

"What did she think?"

"I don't really know. She was more inclined to criticize than to say what she liked. She didn't say it was ugly and boring, so maybe she liked it. She rarely showed appreciation for anything, like it would give away control or that she would owe me something in return for showing her a good time. I don't know. I never understood her."

"I haven't said much either. The way you talk about California, I'm almost afraid to say anything positive about it."

"Try me."

"I think I like it better than you do."


They joined Highway 99 at Fresno and continued south toward Los Angeles. Along the highway, mile after mile, she gazed out the window at open farmland, orchards, dairies, agricultural buildings of all sizes and shapes, trucks and trains carrying produce, cattle, sugar beets. The scale of its agricultural operations was as grandiose as everything else in California. It was not long before the monotony of the scenery, the long, straight, flat highway, and the hum of the car's motor put her to sleep.


She awoke, sat up, pushed her hair away from her eyes and asked, "Where are we?"

"We're just starting into the mountains between the Central Valley and L. A. We'll be home in about two hours, depending on traffic." The multi-lane highway rose from the flat valley floor, curving into a draw in the mountains that loomed ahead of them.

The highway took them deeper into the mountains where lush fields of purple lupine and golden poppies carpeted green hillsides. He told her she had come at a good time, that in two weeks the flowers would be gone and in a month the hills would turn brown as cardboard.

She could see he was ready for a break. "Would you like me to drive?" He pulled off the highway, briefed her on the route ahead, and told her to wake him up if she needed help.

He watched as she pulled onto the highway and got her bearings. Tense at first, she began to relax as she found her place among the speeding cars, the trucks, the motor homes. The highway rose and descended through steep valleys, curved along sparsely wooded mountains. It was not long before he fell asleep. From time to time she turned her gaze from the road ahead to glance at him.

So little had been said about what this trip would mean to them. Was this visit the last flourish of a doomed relationship, or did he have hopes for them that he had not shared with her? When it came time for her to leave, would he tell her, "It's been fun. Now you can go back to Brittany and find yourself a husband."?

For her part, would she come to her senses, put this whole escapade behind her, go back and marry Jean-Yves to have a family, to find her place in society? However unexciting Jean-Yves might be, he was a decent and stable man. What more could she want?

She thought of her talk with John at the Roche-aux-Fées about marriage, about the choices people make that change the course of their lives, about what they give up for what they think they want. What did she really risk with John? A clash of cultures? Long separations? Or was it all her imagination, excuses she made to avoid a decision? Was it time to stop wavering, time to tell him she was his if he wanted her?

No. Not now. Better to make the most of their remaining days. The moment of reckoning would come soon enough.

As she passed a family in a dark green SUV towing a boat on a trailer, she found herself reminiscing. When she was nine years old, her father took her to the Lac de Guerlédan and taught her to fish. Her father said, "When you feel a little tug on your line, don't react. Wait for a stronger, steadier pull. That will mean the hook is set firmly in the fish's mouth. If you pull on the line too soon, the fish will escape."

Whoever had taught John to fish had taught him well.

He woke up before they were out of the mountains, while they were passing a bulldozed hillside at the end of a treeless housing tract. She pulled off the highway and John took the wheel. After

251

another forty-five minutes, they rolled into his driveway.

The day after their return, they stayed home to recover from their trip. He needed to catch up on a few things, including assembling a cabinet he had bought for his business files. Anne could not help but wonder if buying furniture revealed anything about his intentions, whether to stay in California, to keep the house and return to Brittany temporarily, or something else. But she kept her thoughts to herself and offered to help him assemble the cabinet.

They took turns reading the instructions to the other, an undertaking made easier by a French translation for the Canadian market. She made him laugh by reading the French instructions with an American accent. But her levity did not last long.

She set the instruction sheet down on the floor where they were sitting and working. "When I was a little girl, my father let me help him with jobs like this. I was his pal. We had so much fun together. I adore my mother; she's my best friend. But right now he's the one I miss."

"What would you like say to him?"

"That I love him and I miss him."

"Do you know his phone number?"

"Yes."

He looked at his watch. "It's 8:00 pm in Rennes. Come with me." He led her by the hand to his study, sat her in front of the phone and went out, closing the door behind him.

## Chapter 36: Dear Dad

As she sat and stared at the phone, she remembered sitting on a bench in the Botanical Garden of Nantes after confronting her father, mustering the courage to call John and tell him she loved him.

She dialed and took a deep breath. Her father answered, and she said the words that rolled back the years.

At first he said nothing.

"Dad? Are you there?"

"I'm here. And I miss you so much."

On hanging up, she sat for a moment, then turned to John's computer. She and her father had only recently started to email each other—for the most part short, cordial messages.

Dear Dad,

It was good to talk to you. I have to admit it was John's idea to call you when I told him I missed you. At first, I didn't want to bother you. I'm still getting used to the idea that you have time for me. I write that not to hurt you, but to face what we too recently discovered: that I thought you wanted nothing to do with me, and you thought I wanted nothing to do with you. So many years of suffering alone by both of us. I hope that's behind us now.

Hugs to both of you.

Love,

Anne

That afternoon, while Anne was sitting with John at the kitchen table finishing lunch, the phone rang. John went to answer it, and Anne carried the lunch dishes to the sink. She heard the name "Diane" and could not resist turning to look at his face. Big smile, animated voice. What Anne was hearing was not sitting well, but it was too late for a    discreet exit. From what she was able to understand, John had seen Diane since he had come back. She would insist on hearing every detail, even if it proved to her that John was as untrustworthy as every other man. As he talked to Diane,

Anne's annoyance turned to indignation, her indignation to anger. She managed to maintain her composure long enough to confirm what she had understood.

He covered the mouthpiece and said, "It's Diane. She wants to come by this afternoon at 3:30 and meet you."

Anne bit her knuckle and stayed as calm as she could until he got off the phone.

## Chapter 37: Two Women

"I didn't understand everything," Anne said, "but it sounded like you saw each other before I arrived."

"We had lunch together once. That's all."

"And the rest of the afternoon? Did you have a good time?"

"What are you talking about? It was nothing!"

"Nothing? You have a little tryst with your former fiancee, the great love of your life, as if I didn't exist, and you have the nerve to tell me it was nothing? When she gets here, you can have her to yourself, since that's obviously what you want! Don't worry about me. Not that you ever did!"

She stomped out of the kitchen and out the front door, slamming it behind her. She took off, walking furiously, paying no attention to the direction she took.

So that was his agenda. Show off his French girlfriend to everyone, make Diane jealous so she would come back to him, then dump Anne to get even with her for leaving him. Well it would not work. She would not go quietly. She would meet Diane at the door and tell her off, then pack up and go home.

As Anne walked and calmed down, she regained a measure of reason. Her melodramatic scenario spun up in a fury made no sense at all. If in fact John wanted to settle scores with women who had left him, he would have started with Diane. Anne had no intention of telling John what she had imagined; why make a bigger fool of herself than she had already?

Instead, she would meet Diane and assess for herself whether she was a threat. Anne might have more to learn about American men, but she knew she could read another woman.

She arrived at a boulevard where she recognized nothing. A sympathetic drugstore clerk let her use the phone. John arrived in five minutes.

In the car, they were silent at first. Anne had said what she had to say. And although she was past her initial fit of jealousy, she was not done. He still owed her an explanation.

"I was wrong not to tell you I had seen Diane," John said. "I

255

didn't tell you because I didn't want to alarm you. I know what you must think, that if I had nothing to hide I would have told you."

"That's exactly what I thought."

"I made a mistake, OK? I can understand you're not happy about it. But it was no reason to blow up like you did. What do you want me to do about it?"

"When she arrives, leave us alone together without talking to her first."

He looked surprised. "If that's what you want."

"That's what I want."

"You might regret it. Once you start her talking, it's hard to shut her up."


As Anne prepared herself for Diane's visit, important decisions faced her. Pants or skirt? Makeup or no makeup? Dazzle Diane with French elegance? No. It was an impromptu visit in John's house in a city where nobody dressed up for anything. Stay casual. Let them both think the visit was no big thing. She decided on form-fitting blue jeans, a light green sweater, and a touch of eye shadow. No lipstick.

As she dressed, she practiced what she would say, searching for the right English words and becoming more and more apprehensive. Yet again, she had spoken too soon and would have to deal with the consequences. She could tell John she had changed her mind about seeing Diane alone, but she was too proud; it would look like she knew she was wrong.

Just before Diane was to arrive, Anne took a book into John's study and sat in his easy chair while he busied himself in the kitchen, but by the time the doorbell rang, she had not so much as opened her book. She put down the book, got up, and waited until she heard a woman's voice inside the house, feminine and confident—more confident than Anne was feeling. Anne stepped into the hall and examined Diane while walking casually toward the entryway.

Diane was taller than Anne and shorter than John, with fine features and a flawless complexion. Long brown hair pulled back.

Although she appeared to be slim, she wore a loose dress, so evaluating her figure would have to wait. This, thought Anne, was the woman who had penetrated John's defenses. This was the woman he was ready to marry with no pregnancy to force the issue. Anne tried not to compare herself, a small-town French bookseller, to a successful American physician.

Diane was asking about his family. He asked about hers. Each sent greetings to the other's parents. Anne arrived just as the initial pleasantries were concluding.

Diane did not wait for introductions. Extending her hand, she said, "Hi Anne. I'm Diane. It's so good to meet you." Diane's smile was as warm and confident as her voice.

Anne was not prepared for this frontal assault of friendliness. She played it safe with a simple "hello," followed by a nervous attempt at returning Diane's smile.

"I just remembered I have to call a client," John said. "Excuse me for a few minutes. The coffee should be ready. I'll come back as soon as I can."

Diane appeared to study him for a moment, as if sensing some tension. When John left them, she turned to Anne and smiled again.

"Come to the kitchen," Anne said, gesturing toward the door next to them and the table just inside the kitchen, well aware that Diane had known the way to the kitchen long before Anne did. She poured coffee for both of them and sat, still unsure of where to begin. This was what she had insisted on in an impulsive moment of self-righteousness.

Diane, who many times each work day started and commanded conversations with strangers in distress, many of whom barely spoke English, noticed Anne's discomfort and took the lead. She spoke slowly and clearly, opening with, "What is your impression of Los Angeles, so far?"

"It is very big." Start simple. "Much more big than my town."

And so it went, Diane asking thoughtful questions and listening carefully to Anne's halting answers.

Even so, it was an effort for Anne to keep up her end of the conversation. After enough time had passed that she could include John without losing face, she excused herself to check on him. He was still on the phone. Apparently he really did have a client to call. She returned to the kitchen and asked Diane, "Do you want to walk?"

"Good idea," Diane said. I haven't been in this neighborhood for a long time." It seemed to Anne that Diane's last comment was intended to reassure her. She left a note for John.

They walked for a few minutes in awkward silence under a clear blue sky. People walked by in short sleeves in spite of the cool air. Anne, who had been so quick to question Diane's motives, was increasingly disarmed by this poised, gracious woman. Diane glanced around at their surroundings. She must be thinking how close she had come to marrying John and moving here.

Anne took a stab at restarting the conversation. "It is strange to hear of you in France and now to know you."

"I don't know what he told you about me, but I feel like I already know you. Careful!" she said, touching Anne's arm and pointing to the sidewalk where a section of concrete was raised and broken by a tree root.

"John told me today that he has seen you." Anne wanted to absolve Diane of complicity in John's transgression. By now, it had become clear to Anne that Diane was not judging her. Perhaps seeing her alone was not such a bad idea after all.

"He didn't tell you until today?" Diane was more serious now as she became aware of Anne's suspicions.

"No."

They stopped and watched for a moment as a squirrel with a tangerine in its mouth dashed across the sidewalk, a crow in hot pursuit.

"I called him just to say hello, and we decided to meet for lunch. I told him to tell you. I'm surprised he didn't. All he could talk about was you. I've seen him in love, so I know the signs."

"You have seen him in love with you."

Diane looked sad for a moment, perhaps regretful.

Anne had pictured Diane in a white lab coat, curtly snapping orders to the hospital staff. Yet this energetic, accomplished woman was showing her a soft and sensitive side. Anne began to understand why John had wanted to marry her.

They walked on under liquidambar trees sprouting new leaves. As they approached the end of the block, Anne asked, "Did John talk much to you of Marie-Clo?"

"Not much. Whenever she came up in a conversation, he told me as little as he could get away with and changed the subject. He insisted he had put all that behind him. I believed him because I wanted to, but as I think about it now, I'm not so sure. She stopped and turned to face Anne. "When we had lunch last month, I teased him a little about his weakness for French women. He talked a lot about you, but he didn't say a peep about Marie-Clo."

"A what?"

"A peep, the sound of a baby bird. It means he didn't say anything about her. I'm sorry; I need to be careful about using expressions like that."

"No. Please use them. I must learn."

They resumed walking and retreated to more mundane subjects.

At the end of Diane's visit, they walked her to the door and stood on the porch while Diane got in her car. John put a hand on the back of Anne's neck and gave it a squeeze. "Do you feel better now?"

"She's very nice. You have good taste."

They waved at Diane as she drove away.

"I know," he said as he put his arms around her.

He smiled and took her hand to lead her into the house and to the couch, where he sat her down and pulled her close to him. They sat in silence for a moment, as if they both wanted to talk about Diane but were reluctant to start.

"I'm sorry I blew up at you," Anne said. "I was feeling a little insecure."

"It's OK; it got me all nostalgic for our drive home from Nantes. So what did the two of you talk about all that time?"

"About you."

"And?"

Anne weighed carefully what she was about to say. As risky as it was to tell him, her observation was too important to hide. "She still loves you."

He looked skeptical. "Did she say that?"

"No. But I can tell."

"It amazes me how women think they can read each other's minds. To me, it's simple: if she loved me, she wouldn't have left me."

"You're a man. You don't understand women. If I tell you she still loves you, you can believe me."

He gazed across the room, long enough to make Anne think that once again, she had said too much.

"Let's assume you're right," he said. "Does that bother you?"

"A little. But she said something else that bothers me more."

"What?"

"That you've never gotten over Marie-Clo."

He shrugged and said nothing.

They invited his parents to dinner. Anne was determined to impress them, well aware that as a French woman she had a reputation to live up to. She spent a tense day cooking, summoning John when she needed a missing ingredient or help converting measurements and grumbling from time to time about American resistance to the metric system.

Although Anne's English had improved, her conversation with his parents remained superficial. She appreciated their compliments about the dinner but was puzzled by how effusively they were expressed. For the most part, Anne remained in the background, serving and clearing dishes. John's interaction with his parents was much like it had been when Anne had first met them: polite, superficial conversation about people, family, the weather.

From what she could observe, John's maintained a cordial

but casual relationship with both of them—very different from the extremes of her relationships with her own parents. And although she was a stranger to them, they appeared to accept her uncritically, as if there was no reason to know her better. Perhaps he had told them their relationship was temporary. They remained a mystery to her.

She thought of how John and her mother had become good friends, but only cautiously, over several months. Her mother, perhaps aware of how fickle her daughter could be, had been careful not to get too close to Anne's previous suitors. Perhaps his parents were doing the same thing.

At the end of the evening, they walked his parents out to their car. Mary said, "Anne, it's been so nice meeting you! Have a safe trip back and come see us again soon."

Bill gave Anne a hug and said, "Or we could come visit you in Brittany."

"Yes. Please come," Anne said, suspecting that Bill was talking with no intention of ever actually doing it. Or was Bill assuming John was going back to Brittany to live? It occurred to Anne that John might have said something to his parents about his intentions. Whatever he had said, it had to be more than he had told Anne.


When his parents had left and Anne and John were washing dishes, she asked him if he missed his parents when he was in France.

"Sometimes. We wrote. We called each other. They have an active life, a wide circle of friends. They raised me to be independent. Maybe they were more successful than they intended. I don't think they ever imagined I would go live in a foreign country."

Was this a hint that he was planning to move back to Brittany? "You did it once for a year and once for five months. I wonder what they imagine now." More to the point, Anne wondered what John imagined now.

261

## Chapter 38: An Unlikely Ally

Since her conversation with Diane, Anne's persistent fear that John might not return to Brittany now had company: a nagging disquiet about Marie-Clo, made worse by John's reaction when she told him what Diane had said. Later, when she had tried to pursue the subject, he said, "You wanted to know about her, so I told you everything. There's nothing more to discuss."

Anne pondered what to do, giving serious thought to doing nothing at all. Who knew what digging into John's past with Marie-Clo could lead to?

She started to call Jocelyne to seek her wise counsel but thought of someone else.

She called Diane and told her she wanted to see her before she left, a sentiment Diane echoed. They compared their schedules, looking for a time when John would be at work. The best they could arrange was to meet on Diane's lunch break, subject to last-minute cancellation if the emergency room got too busy.

Anne took a bus to the hospital, where the volunteer at the desk paged Diane and directed Anne to a waiting area across from the desk. She sat with grim-faced people, many of indiscernible ethnicity. Hospitals are the same everywhere, she thought—the smell of alcohol, worried people waiting, others in blue scrubs dashing about. It was ten minutes before Diane appeared, wearing a white coat bearing the name "Diane M. Orsini, M.D." stitched in blue thread over the breast pocket. She slipped a stethoscope off her neck, stashed it in a coat pocket, and greeted Anne with a hug.

Diane explained that she was working on an elderly man who had just arrived in a diabetic coma and she needed to stay available. So they went to the hospital cafeteria where they each got a yogurt and coffee in a paper cup. They sat at a table by a window. Anne wondered if this was the room where John and Diane had gotten acquainted, but did not ask.

"It's good to see you, Anne," Diane said, "but I suspect from your tone of voice on the phone that this is not just a social visit."

Anne herself could not categorize her visit. If the two women were not friends, what were they? It almost felt like a visit to Dr. Laborde. "Please excuse me for thinking only of myself. You have been kind to me."

"Don't mention it. When I have a problem and need a sympathetic ear, I'll call you and talk you to death."

"Talk you to death?" It seemed an odd thing for a doctor to say.

"Ah! There's another expression for your collection. It means I'll talk until you wish you were dead so you don't have to listen anymore. Didn't John warn you not to get me talking?" Diane was showing another side of her personality. Today she was more frenetic, like John had described her when he first spoke of her. "Anyway, what's on your mind?"

Knowing that Diane could be called away at any moment, Anne went right to the point. "What did John tell you of his marriage?"

Diane took a sip of her coffee and made a face. "I'm sorry the coffee's so bad. I gave up complaining about it." Looking up from her coffee cup, she said, "He told me Marie-Clo got pregnant, they married in a hurry, she came to L.A., the baby died *in utero*, and she left."

"The same what he told to me. Did he say if he was sad about the baby?"

"He pretended not to be, but I never believed it. I remember one time when the subject came up, and he said as little as he could. He was like a patient trying to con me by withholding important information. So I pressed him a bit. He said if they had planned and wanted the baby, and if it had been born normally and died later, it would have been much worse."

Diane took another sip of her coffee and went on. "I thought it was telling that he referred to the baby as 'it,' although he must have known its sex. I always suspected it was a boy and he had imagined all the things they would do together. He was too young to get married, and losing a baby was more than he could handle. Knowing John, he probably gave all he had to taking care of Marie-

Clo. He's such a giving person."

Anne was surprised that John had not told Diane that the baby was a girl. But it made sense. Taking about the baby as "she" and not "it" would make her human, the loss harder to bear. And he had only told Anne on a whim, while sitting on a beach watching a girl playing with her father—right after Anne had told him she loved him. She wanted Diane to know that the baby was a girl, but it was not her place to tell her.

Diane glanced toward the door, as if she expected someone to come looking for her. Anne sensed they were running out of time. "One time when we argued and he was angry, he said women try to change men. If I ask him that he talk to Marie-Clo, do you think I try to change him?"

Diane reflected a moment. "No. I don't think so. It's more like you're helping him learn to be more comfortable with himself. Do you know if he has any contact with her?"

"He has said not since fifteen years."

"Maybe it's time. Excuse me a second." Diane answered her cell phone and spoke briefly. She said to Anne, "I have to go. I'm sorry. I'll call you." A quick hug and she was gone. Her words stayed behind, still resonating.

Yes, Anne thought. Maybe it's time.


When John came home from work, he asked Anne about her visit with Diane. "Did you talk about me again?"

Anne was far from ready to bring up Marie-Clo with John. "Do you think we have nothing to talk about but you?"

"OK. So what did you talk about?"

"Girl talk. Nothing that would interest you."

He took the hint and let it drop.

## Chapter 39: Time to Go

They had settled into a daily routine, almost like a married couple. John went to work and Anne cooked, washed dishes, cleaned a bit between the housekeeper's visits, emailed and called home. She explored the neighborhood on foot, studying the houses, their landscaping and curious mix of styles. Other times she walked to the boulevard and looked in store windows. In the evening, they ate the dinner she had prepared and talked of how they had spent their days. She had time alone and time with him, a man to talk to in the evenings, to compliment her on her cooking, to share her bed. One thing alone was missing: any vision of what lay ahead for them.

When he was not working, they visited friends and went for drives. When he took her to places that were not in her guidebook—the Watts Towers, the Lake Shrine, the Palos Verdes Peninsula—she sensed he knew his city better than most others who lived there. Either his attachment to it was stronger than he admitted, or he knew it so well it was time for him to move somewhere new.

But their time together was nearing its end.

Three days before Anne was to leave, a malaise descended on the household. Michael stayed in his room most of the time he was home, leaving Anne and John alone as much as possible. She knew it was time to face what her departure would mean to them, but had not found the courage to bring it up. Nor had John.

In the afternoon of the second day before her departure, she was reading a book on the living-room couch, a novel in English that she had found on John's bookshelf about a young American man and a French girl in France in the 1960s. John came into the living room and sat on the couch beside her. She closed her book, marking her place with her thumb. He often took a break from his work to sit with her and talk, but today, his approach was more determined, his expression more resolute. She knew this was the moment. A stab of anxiety told her she was not ready.

Before he could speak, she said, "I'm having a hard time with this book. The author uses too many words I don't know. And I can tell it's going to end badly. It's obvious he's going to leave her, but she doesn't want to believe it. She thinks he's going to take her back to New York with him and marry her, and she'll live happily ever after."

"It was a doomed relationship from the start. She was a lower-class girl. Neither one had money. Flying was a lot more expensive back then."

Her thumb slipped out of the book, causing her to lose her place.

He went on. "It's different for us. Whenever we're apart, we can be together on a day's notice." His tone was upbeat, but his message was not at all reassuring.

She set the book down on the couch next to her. "Is that the kind of relationship you want?"

His eyes narrowed, as they did when he was unhappy about something. "Of course not. Even when we lived fifteen minutes away from each other, I hated it when I couldn't see you."

"So when are you coming back?" There was no time left to do other than meet him head-on, to force the issue.

"I don't know yet. Maybe we shouldn't try to make any big decisions before you leave. We can talk after you go home."

"What about your house in Sainte-Anne and your car? What are you planning to do with them? Right now, you're paying for nothing."

"I'll come back and live there, or I'll come back to sell the car and finish moving out of the house. It depends on what we decide."

"Don't waste your time and money coming back if it's just to clean out the house and sell your car. I'll do it for you if it comes to that."

"You would?" He seemed surprised.

"Sure. It would be good for me. I have a lot of memories in that house. If you don't come back, it'll be good catharsis."

She had half-expected he would try to put off any serious discussion until she was gone, and knew now that she would have none of it. If she left with nothing decided, she would be helpless again. Without her in his house, in his bed every night, he might

266

decide that even if he loved her, she was more trouble than she was worth. Leaving to go back with nothing resolved was not good enough. "Why would I wait for you if you might never come back?"

"Because you love me." He seemed more confident, negotiating with her in his own territory.

"That doesn't mean I'll wait for you forever."

"There was a time when I thought I would wait for *you* forever."

"But now you won't, is that it?" She did not like the turn the discussion was taking and had no intention of concealing her displeasure.

Neither did he, it appeared. He frowned and fiddled with a pillow next to him, but did not answer her.

"So where does that leave us?" she asked. "You here and me in Brittany and nothing decided, no plans, nothing. Did you invite me here just to deliver on an offer you made when you barely knew me?" She picked up the book and tossed it noisily onto the coffee table. "I didn't track you down to Huelgoat like a madwoman just to . arrange a vacation."

Her sarcasm did not pass unnoticed. "What do you want from me?" he asked.

"I want to know where we're going, what was the point of all these months together."

"I'd like to know that too, but you still won't come out and say what you're willing to give me. Even after you tracked me down to Huelgoat like a madwoman, nothing really changed; we just went back to where we were before. You asked me not to give up on you and for all I know, I'm still just someone to pass the time with while you wait for Mr. Right."

She started to bite her knuckle, but stopped and put her hand back in her lap. "What do you want me to say? That we should get married?"

"The last time I mentioned marriage, you told me I was insane. You talk like you're not getting something you want from me, but you won't tell me what it is you want, and I hate guessing games. Maybe you should just come out and say it."

"Maybe *you* should."

"I invited you here, didn't I?"

"I didn't come just to see California. I could have booked a tour and avoided complications."

Now he was looking straight at her, his eyes narrowed again. "I used to be an obstacle. Now I'm a complication. What will I be reduced to tomorrow?"

"Can't you just tell me what you're thinking instead of rehashing old stuff? Can you tell me what you feel for me, what I am to you?"

"Every time I tell you how I feel about you I live to regret it. I'm afraid to get my hopes up."

How could she blame him? She had given him ample reason to be wary. What would it take to reassure him, to convince him that her vacillation was a thing of the past? The bland assertion "I know I used to avoid commitment, but that's behind me," seemed too simple to be credible. Nothing better came to her. In frustration she raised a hand briefly as if to make a point, then dropped it back in her lap and said, "We're getting nowhere."

He turned away from her and stared out the window next to the couch.

At a loss for what else to say, she got up from the couch and went to the front door. She stopped and turned to look at him. He was still on the couch, watching her now, waiting for her next move. She knew better than to dash off in a snit again. Instead, she turned toward the door and opened it, stepped out onto the porch and closed the door gently behind her.

She pondered what to do next, and wandered up the driveway to the backyard, where she sat on the back steps. After a few minutes, she heard the gate open, but did not turn to look.

A voice said, "It may be none of my business, but there was no way I could avoid hearing the two of you." Michael sat down on the step beside her. "I didn't have to know much French to figure out what it was about."

Anne stared into the yard, embarrassed that he had heard their argument, but calmed by his presence. Two evergreen pear trees and some ferns in front of a weathered wood fence bordered a small patch of scraggly lawn. If John decided to stay here, she would buy him the American version of *Gardening for Dummies* as a goodbye present.

Whatever her problems with John, everyone here, his family, his friends, even his ex-fiancee reached out to her and supported her. She wanted Michael to know she welcomed his help. "When a man will lose a woman and he says he loves her, it may be the business of his friend. Did I say that correctly? Did you understand?"

"I understood perfectly. I also understand that he's scared. He's afraid he's going to lose you."

"He is not more scared than I am."

"Anne, what do you want him to do?"

With little time to decide, all she could think of was what she wanted at this moment. "I want that he promise to me that he will come back in Brittany. Today, that is all I want. If he will not promise, it will be finished."

"You want him to return to Brittany and resume where you left off?"

"No. It must change. Both of us must change."

"It seems to me you've been helping each other change. You both have a lot invested in this relationship. It would be a shame to give up now."

She was touched by his concern, by his encouragement. "I cannot give up. He is all I have now. But I do not know if he wants me still." She chose her words carefully, speaking slowly, hoping her halting English words expressed her thoughts. "I have seen that he has a very nice life here. He could have any woman. Why would he come back to Brittany and—how to say this?—be again with a difficult woman like me? No. I know what will happen. I will go back, and I will marry with a man that I do not love."

Michael leaned forward, resting his arms on his knees and his chin on his arms. They both stared ahead, into the yard. "If you do that, he'll pull back into his shell and just work all the time. He used to be fun, always up for a good time, a drive up the coast, a bike ride, getting together with friends. When Diane left him, he turned into a

269

different person."

"And he went to Brittany."

"And he met you, and he was his old self again—until the two of you . . . " He turned to her. "When you leave, if he believes you still love him, he'll go back."

"And you will lose your good friend."

"I'll see him at your wedding."

She picked up a twig from the step next to her and snapped it. "You are more optimist than I am."

They sat without speaking. A hummingbird appeared, hovered over the lawn for a moment and took off. It came back, hovered another moment and took off again. Sophie would say it was a sign.

"Where is he?" she asked.

"Sitting on the front porch, staring off into space, trying to decide if life is worth living. At least that's what his face looks like."

Leaning toward Michael, she kissed him on the cheek. He smiled at her as she got up. Armed with Michael's encouragement, she walked back up the driveway to the front porch, thinking of what she had just said: "I cannot give up. He is all I have now."

She found John sitting slumped in a wrought-iron chair at a café table on the porch. Stepping up to the porch, she stood behind him and rested her hands on his shoulders. He pulled a chair over next to him. She sat down.

"I'm sorry," he said.

She took his hand in hers.

"I have some big decisions to make. How long will you wait for me?" he asked.

"How long do you need?"

"Two or three months."

"Then what?"

"I'll decide what to do. I know one thing: if I come back and it's more of the same, it won't last long."

"I know."

They sat quietly, holding hands. A squirrel ran up the trunk of a birch tree on the lawn in front of them, stopped on a branch to stare at them for a moment and disappeared up into the foliage.

"I always thought we were destined to be together," he said, "But I can't shake this terrible fear that we're going to fail."

"Because of me or because of you?"

"Until I came back here, I thought it was because of you. Now I don't know anymore. As much as I miss Brittany, I'm comfortable here. I'm over Diane. I like not having to work in the middle of the night. It's easier to get things done here. And no matter how much I work on my French, it's not my native language, so it's harder. While you're here, I have it all. After you leave, I don't know what I'll do. We still have a lot to work out. I don't know where to start."

"We have to start somewhere. And soon. I can't leave my mother alone with the store any longer."

"If you'll give me some time, I can get things in order here and decide what to do, whether to come back. If I do, we can spend some time together, and we'll have to make a decision. Then I'll stay or leave. I don't know."

They sat a few more minutes.

"We can't go on like this," she said, "not knowing what's next. We're both wearing out. Promise me you'll come back. I don't know what'll happen after that, but I can't wait for you unless I know I'll see you again."

He looked pensive but said nothing.

Another nudge. "Promise me."

He turned his gaze across the street to a group of children playing hopscotch on the sidewalk, then back to her. "I'll come back. I can't say for how long, but I'll come back. Then we'll see."

She laid her head on his shoulder. The children across the street abandoned their hopscotch game and ran off. She thought of what she had said to Dr. Laborde about how in John's presence she could reach him and persuade him. She stroked his thigh. "I know you hate to be seduced and abandoned," she said, "but that's what's about to happen to you. I'm going to give you something to think about whenever you start getting the idea you can live without me."

## Chapter 40: Home Again

The night before her departure, as John slept beside her, thoughts of the uncertainty that lay ahead kept her awake. Anne did not doubt that he would keep his promise to come back; he always kept his word. But he had promised her one trip back to Brittany, nothing more. And after seeing him at ease in his country with his friends and family, she knew that his next stay in Brittany could be short indeed.

The hours in the air and on the train passed quickly as she crossed back over the divide between his world and hers.

Outside the train station in Auray, she waited for her mother to pick her up. A car stopped in front of her. Anne looked inside and recognized Sophie, who explained her presence. "Monsieur Renaud is sick today, so your mother had to stay in the store. She thought you might be a little fragile and didn't want you to have to take a taxi." She helped Anne load her luggage into the back of the car.

Once they were on their way, Sophie looked expectantly at Anne and said, "Well?"

"Well what?" Anne replied, knowing exactly what Sophie meant. "We slept in the same bed, if that's what you're asking."

"What a story! What an adventure! My sheltered, provincial friend flies to the other side of the world to make love for a month with a handsome foreigner and comes back to her quiet little life in Brittany. You're so sophisticated now; you're going to be bored to death with all of us."

"Sophie, stop! That's not all we did."

"Of course not. You had to stop every now and then to eat and sleep and go sightseeing. I hope you took some good pictures. How many movie stars did you meet?"

"Oh, dozens. I lost count." Anne was exhausted, disoriented. As she looked out of the car, little things like narrow streets and road signs in French appeared so strange. This was her home, yet now it struck her as a foreign country. She was not quite ready for Sophie. Even at thirty-three years old, more than anything Anne wanted to see her mother.

When Sophie dropped her off, it was late afternoon. Anne waited in the downstairs hall and when there were no customers, walked into the store. Her mother looked up from her work and returned Anne's smile.

"I made *cotriade* for dinner," Brigitte said, "just so you'd know you're really back in Brittany."

A customer came in, and Anne left the store to take her luggage upstairs.

She called John to tell him she had arrived safely. On hanging up, she looked around the apartment. How strange it seemed, at the same time familiar and foreign. Everything was undersized, especially her bedroom. Her life was larger now.

She opened her book *La Belle Californie* and turned the pages, looking at photos, this time of places she had seen for real. She was no longer a wide-eyed little girl gazing awestruck at pictures of fairyland. California was no longer just a dream, a lonely child's escape. She was growing again; her life was changing. Her book, that precious gift from her absent father, brought back his words, "I love you, my dear sweet little girl. I love you so very much. And I have missed you. Oh God how I've missed you!" She closed the book, lay down on her bed and fell asleep.

She awakened to the aroma of authentic Breton fish stew. Her mother's *cotriade* was one of Anne's favorites. She got up carefully and looked in the mirror, not surprised to see her eyes puffy and the side of her face red from sleeping motionless on it. She brushed her hair and made her way to the kitchen table.

Brigitte served the *cotriade* and poured cider for both of them. "I can only imagine the condition you're in. Would you rather not have to talk?"

"You know me better than that," Anne mumbled through a haze of fatigue. She and her mother had emailed and spoken often by phone while Anne was in California, so it was not as if Brigitte needed to hear details of the trip. But Anne had something on her mind.

Taking a spoonful of broth, Anne said, "I keep comparing myself to Diane and coming up short."

"Do you think she might regret what she did?" It was not her mother's style to comment without first encouraging Anne to talk.

"Maybe. And I have a paranoid thought from time to time that she was so nice to me as a way of getting close to him again."

Brigitte had stopped eating and was staring off into space, appearing to gather her thoughts, much like John often did.

"Mom, you're trying to decide whether to tell me something, right?

Brigitte smiled. "You're reading my mind again. Sometimes you're scary."

"You can lay on the motherly advice while I eat. Pass me the bread. As long as you keep making your *cotriade*, I'll never move to California."

As Anne took another spoonful, Brigitte said, "You can't compare yourself to Diane or anyone else. You're in a class by yourself. John knows that. Everyone seems to know that but you."

In the morning, Anne opened the store and got quickly back into her routine, taking charge, feeling competent again. As she worked, she continued to marvel at all that she had seen and done.

## Chapter 41: Stepmother

Anne called her father to tell him she was back and wanted to visit him. Florence answered. When she asked for her father, Florence said, "He's away on business. I don't expect him back for several days. I'll tell him you called."

Anne saw an opportunity to make amends without losing too much face. "May I take you to lunch? Just you and me?"

A moment's hesitation told Anne that Florence was surprised by the offer.

"Yes," Florence said. "I would like that."

Anne and Florence had not been alone together in years. When Anne was fourteen, Florence had taken her to the fair. Florence had tried hard to show Anne a good time, but Anne had been as difficult as possible. Later, she told her father that Florence had been mean to her. Florence must have spoken to her father about it too, because never again did anyone suggest that Anne and Florence be alone together. For the most part, Florence stoically endured Anne's insults and tantrums. Once Anne had grown up enough to restrain her hostility, she and Florence settled into a distant formality.

They met at a restaurant in Rennes. When they reached the end of small talk, Anne was ready to raise the stakes. "When I came to see you and Dad last October, before the time I came with John, Dad told me you had asked him to stop seeing you and go back to his family. That was the first I knew. I'd always blamed you." Anne hoped her words sounded the way she intended them: as a confession, not an accusation.

Florence did not seem surprised. "It was easier to blame me than to blame him. It's hard to stay angry at someone you love."

"I wish he'd told me before. I'm embarrassed when I think of how I treated you all those years. You didn't deserve it." Just admitting her behavior was hard enough. Anne was not yet up to an outright apology.

275

"You didn't know. And you coped the best you could. It might have been harder for you than it was for Bernard." She paused while the waiter removed their empty plates. "The two of them fought and argued. You wouldn't believe some of the things they said to each other. But they got it out. Eventually they were able to make peace." Florence reached into her purse for a mirror, quickly checked her teeth and the status of her makeup, and put the mirror away.

"Every time I blew up at Dad he didn't react. It was like he didn't care." As they talked, Anne marveled that she was confiding in Florence, something she had never imagined possible.

"He cared. A lot. He held his tongue because he didn't want to hurt you any more than he already had. He knew that in spite of all your bravado, you were a sensitive child."

Never before had Anne allowed herself to notice how wise and articulate Florence could be.

"That sensitive child seems to have grown into a confused and headstrong adult. It's so hard to change how I see my whole life."

"You're trying. That's what's important. Not only for yourself, but . . . " Now it was Florence's turn to decide how much to share with Anne.

Anne prodded her. "But what?"

"I was never able to have children of my own. When I married your father, I hoped you and I . . . I was so naive." Florence stopped, put a hand to her face and looked away.

Anne rested her hand on Florence's arm and said, "It's not too late."

The waiter arrived to clear the table and take their order for coffee.

"From what your father tells me," Florence said, "you and John are quite serious about each other."

"Serious, yes. What else, I don't know. He promised me he'd come back, but he didn't promise he would stay."

"Anne, it may not be my place to offer you advice. You can tell me if you don't want to hear it."

In the course of this lunch together, Florence, whom Anne had considered her arch-enemy, had become someone whose advice Anne would respect. "I want to hear it."

"Don't blame John for what your father did. I can tell you have something very special. Don't throw it away."

"No," Anne said. "This time I won't—if it's not too late."

A few days after her lunch with Florence, Anne's father called her with a surprising request: that Anne meet him and her mother at her apartment the next day at 6:30, a time he had already cleared with her mother. Later, Anne asked her mother why he wanted to see them.

"I have no idea." Brigitte said. "He called me and asked if he could meet with us. He said it wouldn't take long. Maybe he wants to buy back the store and you and I can both retire."

## Chapter 42: No Regrets

Anne waited nervously with her mother for her father to arrive. The buzzer sounded. Anne answered the door and showed her father to the living room. As far as she knew, her father had not been to the apartment since he bought the store for her mother. It was odd to see him in her mother's space. She tried to remember the last time her father and mother had seen each other—a few years before perhaps, at Justine's school play.

He and Brigitte exchanged pleasantries and broke some tension with light conversation about Bernard's children. While her parents were talking, Anne flashed back to the day twenty-two years before when her parents announced to her and Bernard that they were separating. That sense of impending doom was absent, but why he had come remained a mystery. Beset with her usual impatience, she shifted in her chair, anxious for him to get on with whatever he had come for.

Instead, he asked Anne about her trip to California. She promised to come see him and bring her photos. It was as if he was getting up his courage, but for what? Beads of perspiration appeared on his forehead.

He cleared his throat, turned to Brigitte and said in one breath, "Brigitte, I am very sorry for what I did to you and the children. Is there any chance you could forgive me?"

Brigitte, obviously surprised, looked at Anne as if seeking her counsel.

For once in her life, Anne was speechless.

Without waiting for Anne's reaction, Brigitte took charge in her own elegant way, turning back to the man who had cheated on her and left her. "I forgave you long ago. There's no point in regretting or bearing grudges. I survived. I'm fine. What's most important is that we created two wonderful children."

It was only when her mother spoke of Anne and Bernard that Anne realized her father had been speaking not only to her mother, but also to her. She knew this was difficult for him. She admired him for it. And as she watched and listened to her mother, Anne hoped she would learn someday to be as gracious and generous of spirit.

While Brigitte saw him to the door, Anne went to her bedroom window. She was not surprised to see Florence waiting in her father's car. Florence looked up at Anne and waved. Anne smiled and waved back, as if to say thank you.

Anne was not yet ready to talk to her mother; there was too much to say, and at the same time too much that words could not express. An unfamiliar feeling welled up, the weight of years lifting from her. Her mother, a kind and generous woman, humiliated by her father for having been the best wife and mother she could be, had been made whole, her honor restored.

Anne's vision of her life was changing. She understood now that when her father left, she took upon herself the burden of protecting her mother from blame for her father's departure. But what else could she do at age eleven other than take the blame herself? If her father's departure was Anne's fault, it could not be her mother's. At long last, with the help of Dr. Laborde, and now with her father's belated contrition, she felt herself rising above her past, breaking free of the bonds that had held her back.

When had her life started to turn around? Twenty-one years after her father left, on John's veranda, she realized she would lose John and every man after him if she could not summon the courage to confront her demons. Why had she done it for John and no man before him? Because when this unassuming man from far away had walked into her bookstore, somehow he knew he had discovered a woman worthy of his love. After she pushed him away, he took her back and forgave her. And when she expelled him for the last time and he was about to leave, when he found her car in the Tall Wood of Huelgoat, he waited there for her. After all the pain she had caused him, of all the less troublesome women who could have been his, he waited for her.

As these thoughts rushed by, she lay on her bed staring at the ceiling. Paint was peeling in the corner. Easily fixed. Scrape, sand, prime, match the top coat. A faucet washer in the bathroom had been vibrating noisily. She would fix that too.

What was her mother thinking now? Anne got up off her bed and went out of her bedroom. Her mother's bedroom door was ajar. Anne knocked lightly.

"Come in," Brigitte said.

She found her mother sitting on her bed, her back against the headboard. Brigitte smiled as Anne sat on the bed beside her.

"Remember when you and Dad announced to us that he was leaving?" Anne said. "You came to my room and sat on my bed."

Brigitte nodded. "I thought the world was ending. Having you and Bernard kept me going. I couldn't imagine I would ever have a life of my own again, but I do. I have a wonderful life. This evening it came home to me just how lucky I am."

Brigitte looked at the ceiling and said, "Some paint is peeling. I've noticed it in several rooms."

"I don't know how much longer I'll be living here," Anne replied, "but I'll patch it before I leave. And Sainte-Anne's only a few minutes away. I'll come back."

"You will if you want a paycheck." Her mother knew to stop there and let Anne say what both were thinking.

"I can't imagine John would have a problem with a working wife."

Brigitte looked at Anne and said, "A working wife?"

"I'm just musing. He has a few things to clear up when he comes back. And when I get my hands on him, I'll make sure he remembers all the reasons he can't live without me."

Brigitte smiled and glanced at the clock on her night stand. "Are you as hungry as I am?"

"Ravenous. Let's make some dinner."


In its visible details, Anne's life had not changed: work, visits with friends, Sunday dinners with family. The days passed as they always had. In the course of those days, Anne revisited many times her father's words and her mother's response. A new serenity came over her, as the wounds from her past healed and closed, freeing her to move on.

280

Now, with every day of John's absence came bouts of impatience, of wanting him now, to have her last chance to repair the damage she had done. Every morning before breakfast she checked her email for a message from him. Every afternoon, when she thought of him awakening to morning in California, she never strayed far from a phone, hoping he would call. When they spoke, each asked about the other's parents, the other's work, the weather—innocuous, almost platonic exchanges in which they avoided the only topic that really mattered: when was he coming back and what would happen after that.

After almost two months, Anne's patience—always in short supply—ran out. It was time to call him on his promise, to ask him to set a date for his return. She thought of how she might bring up the subject, knowing that if she pushed him too hard, he might balk.

In the afternoon of a day off, in the privacy of her bedroom, she called him. "You've been away from Brittany so long; I thought I should tell you that a beautiful Bretonne is living for the moment you return. But enough about my mother. When are you coming back?"

When he stopped laughing, he said, "As soon as your mother breaks up with Charles."

"Oh, shut up! I miss you. Get your buns over here!" Bantering with him made it easy for him to avoid a serious answer, but it was either that or beg, which she refused to do, or give him an ultimatum, which was too risky.

"When did you last check your email?" he asked.

"When I got up this morning."

"Look again."

And there it was: a forwarded message from Air France confirming his flight in three weeks.

The countdown began. He would come back, days would pass, and one of them would say, "It's time to talk." If they could not come to terms, he would leave, and she would slip back into her old life. She knew now how much was missing from her life before him and how much richer her life could be.

On the day of his arrival, she arose early and went to work preparing his welcome. She headed for his house, stopping by a florist on the way. First opening all the shutters, she arranged red roses in vases in the living room and kitchen. She thought of putting flowers or dried lavender in the bedroom but decided against it. It was still his bedroom. She did not have the right to make it more feminine. Not yet.

Trying not to think too much about the bedroom, she walked around the house, looking for any detail she might have missed. It was his house, not hers, but if she had her way, he would scrutinize her homemaking skills as never before.

While inspecting the kitchen, the refrigerator caught her eye. She had forgotten all about it.

She dashed off to the market and bought milk, cheese, butter, eggs, apples and strawberries, carrots and radishes, bottles of Plancoët water, of cider and Muscadet. She stopped at a *charcuterie* to pick up a roasted chicken for dinner. She was too distracted to cook, and once John was back, she doubted they would stay long in the kitchen.

Later that afternoon, she stood on the platform, pacing and looking up the track, waiting for his train. The loudspeaker broadcast its cheerful four-note tune that called attention to an announcement. "High-speed train 5236 from Lille and Paris Charles De Gaulle, destination Quimper is entering the station." Her heart beat faster.

The train made its energetic entrance, its swept-down nose sniffing the track ahead of it, rolling so fast into the station it seemed it would never deign to stop in her little town. It slowed at last to an impatient halt. Doors opened with a hiss of compressed air, and passengers began to step off the train. She looked one way then the other.

"Anne!"

She turned and saw him in a doorway. She went quickly to his door, took a suitcase from him and wrestled it to the ground. He stepped down carrying two others, set them down and threw his arms around her. He kissed her long and hard while air currents stirred up by the departing train blew her hair into his face.

She held him close, lest he slip away again.

As she drove him home to Sainte-Anne-d'Auray, he looked through the car window at the passing countryside as if it were his first time in Brittany. He walked through the house inspecting each room, wearing that beatific little smile she had first seen when she had caught him staring at her at Sizun.

## Chapter 43: Unfinished Business

The next morning, she awoke and turned to find he had already risen. She lay in bed, smiling, thinking of how she had ambushed him outside the bathroom door after his shower, grabbing his arm and throwing him onto the bed, about how he awakened her at 4:00am, complaining of jet lag, only to learn that jet lag was not the only thing on his mind.

Her campaign to keep him in Brittany was off to an auspicious start.

They spent their first days as they had before, living for the moment, deferring talk of the future. At long last, Anne knew that she was his for the asking. Yet his intentions remained a mystery. He was attentive, affectionate, and more inscrutable than ever.

She had seen the good life he had in California. Would he decide to go back, even if it meant losing Anne? His speech in the market about sacrifices was a long time ago, when losing Diane was fresh, when living in Brittany was new, before Anne had rejected him a second time. As much as she wanted to move things along, if she pushed him and he was not ready, events could take a bad turn. After one failed marriage, he had risked again and been hurt again, first by Diane, then by Anne herself. Would he balk at yet another commitment? And if he married Anne to keep from losing her, would he want children? What scars remained from the baby he had fathered and lost?

With no occasion to celebrate, he took her to dinner at his favorite restaurant in Sainte-Anne-d'Auray. After dinner, they strolled around the grounds of the Basilica in the remaining daylight of a summer evening, the forecourt a riot of color from beds of flowers set out for the tourist season.

They sat on a bench next to a flower bed, facing the immense facade of the Basilica. He said, "We have to talk."

"I know." Anne had learned that when he got around to an important subject, it was best to say as little as possible, lest he retreat once again into silence.

"I haven't been looking forward to this," he said. "I'm afraid of where this could lead. Each time you draw me back in, you turn and run again."

As she had surmised, her changes of heart had done their damage. Her gaze fixed on the bell tower of the Basilica, she ventured, "Do you think I'm still the one who might give up?"

"Isn't that how it's always been?"

"It used to be. But now I think you're the one who's having second thoughts," she said.

"Oh? And why do you suppose that is?"

It was finally time to say it. "Marie-Clo."

He sat up and turned to her. "Are you out of your mind? She's ancient history."

She had touched a nerve. "I'm not so sure. Before I left Los Angeles, I asked you to promise me you'd come back. You kept your promise. You've been back three weeks and we've gone back to where we were: seeing each other and nothing resolved." She stopped and waited for his reaction, but he remained impassive. She went on. "And we'll keep on like that until we break up for good, unless you do what you have to do."

"And what might that be?" He sounded impatient, like he thought she was concocting yet another excuse.

"Find Marie-Clo. Talk to her. About everything. About your marriage, your separation, and about your baby. Tell her what you felt when the baby died and when she left. And ask her to do the same."

He turned away from her, then back to her. "This was Diane's idea, wasn't it?"

"So what if it was? What difference would it make?"

"None. It would still be a terrible idea. I don't want Marie-Clo to know I'm in France. You don't know her. It's asking for trouble. He stood up and began pacing in front of the bench. "Why is this so important to you?"

Anne started to stand but thought better of it. Sitting gave her more authority. "Because she's between us now. And if there's a chance for us, I want all of you—in the present with me. Part of you is stuck in the past. I don't want her specter in our bedroom. I want her out in the light, like Diane. And even if you and I never –" It was too hard to say. "It's not just for me that you have to do this. It's for yourself."

"What makes you such an expert on what's wrong with me and what I should do about it?"

The more he protested, the more she knew she was on the right track. How could she break through his resistance? A candid answer, perhaps. "I told you what happened when you were gone," she said, "about how my father apologized to my mother. I didn't tell you how important it was to me, how it freed me to live my life. I want you to be free to live yours."

He stopped pacing and faced her. "If I do what you ask, what will happen between you and me?"

"What do you want to happen?"

"Here we go again. And this time Michael's not around to mediate."

"What do you think Michael would say?"

He sat down and resumed staring at the facade of the Basilica. "He'd take your side. He adores you."

"Would he be wrong?"

"I don't know. He wants us to succeed."

"So do I. So does everybody else. Will you do it?"

"I have to think about it. I probably couldn't find her if I wanted to."

His tone made her think of her brother when her mother asked him to clean his room.

The next day after closing the store, she went to his house, unsure of what to expect. She was barely inside when he came out of his study and started in, without so much as a *bonsoir*. "I lost contact with Marie-Clo's parents. Every year since the divorce, I sent them my greetings for the new year. But two years ago, the envelope was returned undelivered. So today, I searched on the internet for Marie-Clo, for her parents, for her sister, for two of her friends, and for one of her cousins and found nothing. The friends and cousins are all women, so they probably married and changed their last names. I suppose the next step would be to go to Bordeaux, to talk to the neighbors and whoever lives in the house."

She was taken aback by his apparent change of direction.

"I know you and Diane talked about Marie-Clo," he said. "She wanted me to do the same thing, to find Marie-Clo and talk to her. She never actually said 'I want you to do it,' but she dropped hints. I didn't want to. I wonder if that was one reason she had second thoughts about marrying me."

"Maybe that's why my conversation with Diane annoyed you. It must feel like two women are plotting against you."

"You may be plotting against me, but you're both trying to help me. So right now it feels more like making love with two beautiful women at the same time."

"Something you're an expert at?"

"In my dreams!"

"Does that excite you, the idea of having sex with Diane and me at the same time?"

He looked wistful. "I've never done a threesome. If I ever did, I would be smart to include a physician. It would likely give me a heart attack."


As John prepared for his trip to Bordeaux, Anne tried to picture herself in Marie-Clo's position. How would she react to contact from John? From what little John had said of her, she was self-centered, quick to anger, and unforgiving, although Anne surmised that John's description of her might well be tainted by the bitterness of their separation and divorce. She tried to picture Marie-Clo. John had kept no photos of her—one more way of turning the page on that chapter of his life.

"What was she like, physically," she asked.

"A little shorter than you, short dark brown hair, brown eyes."

"Pretty?"

"When she was cheerful and affectionate, she was pretty. But when she was in a fury, I have never seen a woman so ugly."

He called Anne from his hotel room in Bordeaux. "I don't have much to show for this morning. Marie-Clo's parents have moved. The new owners seemed to want to help me, but have no forwarding address. I left my card with a note and asked them to pass it on to anyone in the family they might hear from. I did the same with the neighbors, one of whom actually remembered me. None of them knew where Marie-Clo's parents moved to."

"What was it like to see her house again?"

"Like seeing a place I had dreamed about. At the end of the school year, after my dorm closed, I lived there for several weeks while we planned the wedding. I should say while *they* planned the wedding. I was in a fog most of the time, like I was watching a movie of someone else's life. Today, when a stranger answered the door, it seemed like part of my past had vanished. I've got to think of what else I can do here."

"Have you thought of checking the records at the university?"

"I'm going there this afternoon."

That evening, he called again to tell her he had gone to the suburb of Talence to the university and found no information on Marie-Clo after graduation. He spent the rest of the day walking streets where he thought her friends had lived, looking for something familiar, finding nothing.

He took the train back to Brittany the next day.

Two weeks passed. No word from Marie-Clo's neighbors or anyone else. No call. No email. No letter. Nothing. Occasional new ideas all led nowhere. His search for Marie-Clo had become an obsession, driven now, it seemed, not by a desire to please Anne, but by his own need.

While John was deciding where next to direct his search, he went for an afternoon to help a friend clear brush from his property. Anne stayed at John's house to do laundry and make dinner. She had been spending more and more time there. She liked the space, the openness.  It was the kind of house she hoped to live in someday with her own family—a simple white house with a gabled slate roof near fields and woods, walking distance from the village, neighbors just close enough.

While she was folding towels, the doorbell rang.  She went to the front door and opened it.

# Chapter 44: Out of the Past

There in the summer sun stood an attractive woman, not quite as tall as Anne, short, dark brown hair lightly streaked with gray, intense brown eyes with the beginnings of dark circles underneath.

The woman asked, "Is this the home of John Becker?"

"Yes," was all Anne could think of to say.

"Is he here?"

"No." Taking refuge in the forms of basic etiquette, Anne extended her hand. "I'm Anne Goudin."

"Marie-Clothilde Brossard," she said, confirming what Anne already knew.

Meeting Marie-Clo with no warning had caught her off guard. She had assumed that if John located Marie-Clo, he would go to meet her, away from Anne. Yet here she was, standing in front of her. Careful not to betray the importance of this moment for her, Anne said, "Please come in. I was about to make some tea. Would you like to join me?"

"No, thank you." Marie-Clo took a card from her purse and handed it to Anne. "Would you please ask John to call me? My cellphone number is on the card. I'll be staying at the Hotel Gwened in Vannes tonight and tomorrow."

"Yes. Of course."

Anne realized that Marie-Clo was taking care to say as little as possible. She could not know who Anne was or what she knew and sounded doubtful that Anne would deliver the message. As Marie-Clo turned to leave, Anne said, "John will be glad to learn that you were here."

Marie-Clo stopped and turned back toward Anne. "Are you his wife?"

"No." *Not yet, anyway.*

With Marie-Clo gone, Anne's composure began to dissolve. She sat down in the chair next to the front door and took stock of what had just happened. Her hands were shaking and her heart was pounding. She had actually met the infamous Marie-Clothilde

Brossard, the former flame and wife of the man she loved.

With the few words they had exchanged, Marie-Clo had remained cooly polite, giving no hint of the histrionic personality that John had described. But Anne did sense an artful seductress; it was not hard to imagine a youthful John falling madly in love with her. And now? Where had she traveled from to find John? Why had she shown up unannounced? And, most important, how would John react to her?

Anne called John and dutifully delivered the message. Fifteen minutes later, he called back. He had talked to Marie-Clo and arranged to meet her for dinner that evening in Vannes. He asked Anne if she would stay at his house that night. There was no need to ask.

He came home and showered. Figuring he might need some moral support, Anne hung around the bedroom while he dressed. "It must have been strange to talk to her again," she said.

"It was downright surreal. How was she with you?"

"Polite but wary. It was obvious she wanted to know who I was but didn't dare ask. I told her as little as I could."

"She said you were kind."

"I tried to be. It was strange for me too."

Before leaving for the restaurant, he said, "Should I wake you for the report?"

"I'll be awake." Wide awake.

John left and Anne made some dinner for herself. She tried to read but could not concentrate. She thought of going for a walk, but felt the need to stay at the house, as if it were threatened and she had to guard it. It had been her idea for John to find Marie-Clo and dig up their common past. But now they were alone together. She knew that John still had feelings for Marie-Clo, feelings he had long repressed. What would happen between them when they saw each other for the first time in fifteen years? What was happening between them right now?

John did not return until after midnight. Anne turned off the television, which she had been staring at blankly. He sat on the couch next to her.

"You look drained," she said.

"I am."

He and Marie-Clo had talked for hours over dinner. When the restaurant closed, they walked around the old city. Anne knew it well, its narrow streets, its half-timbered houses. Marie-Clo told him she had kept in occasional touch with a friend from *lycée*, who had lived next door to her in Bordeaux. The friend's parents had asked her to tell Marie-Clo about John's visit and to pass on his contact information. When she heard that John was looking for her, she drove straight from Paris to Sainte-Anne-d'Auray to John's house, stopping only to refuel and to check in at her hotel. Knowing Marie-Clo, John figured she had calculated the dramatic effect of showing up without calling first.

Marie-Clo had finished her degree in political science, worked for the government, then left to join a political consulting firm in Paris, where she still worked. She had remarried and divorced after three years. She had no children. She asked John about his life since their last contact. He told her about his work and his family, and about where he lived.

When he had finished, she asked, "Why were you looking for me?"

"I wanted to know where you were, how you were, what you were doing. And I thought it might be good for both of us to talk, rather than live the rest of our lives with the bad feelings we parted with."

She looked wistfully at him, making him think he had said too much.

Anne did not want to interrupt the narrative but could not resist asking, "Did she say anything about the baby?"

"I don't think she was going to," he said, "but I asked her if she ever thought about her. She said 'sometimes,' and tried to change the subject. I said 'I try to imagine how old she would have been and what she would be doing now.' I could see Marie-Clo was starting to cry, so I didn't tell her that when I try to imagine our daughter, she has no face. Next thing I knew I was crying too."

"How did the evening end?" Anne asked.

"Not well. I felt sorry for her. I managed to rebuild my life. I found Diane; I found you. She, on the other hand, doesn't have much to show for her life, other than her work. So when she put an arm around me as we walked, I put mine around her. It seemed like a comforting, conciliatory gesture. Big mistake. After a moment, she stopped, turned toward me, and kissed me."

"On the lips?"

"On the lips. A serious French kiss."

Anne winced "Are you giving me these details to make me regret putting you through this?"

"I'm giving you these details because I don't want to hide anything. There's more."

Anne took a breath and said, "Go on."

"I pulled away from her as diplomatically as I could. I was standing there on the sidewalk, trying to decide how to deal with her. Then she asked me to go back to her hotel room with her."

"What nerve!" As hard as Anne was trying to keep him talking without interrupting, she could not help herself.

"I suppose I can't blame her for asking," he said. "I had told her almost nothing about you or about our relationship. I told her I couldn't because of you, and she lost her temper. She yelled at me, 'Why did you bother to come looking for me just to reject me one more time? You are as self-centered and insensitive as ever!' Finally, someone on the second floor leaned out the window and asked us to take our domestic problems elsewhere. Because it was late, I walked her back to her hotel. She ignored me all the way back and didn't even say goodnight."

"How did it feel when she kissed you?"

He gave Anne a look that betrayed his reluctance to tell her. "It was as if no time had passed, like we were on the streets of Bordeaux and I was twenty again. I have to be honest with you. It felt good. Good and terrible at the same time, like she was casting a spell on me, something, I might add, that she always had a gift for."

"I should have stopped to think about how difficult this

would be for you," Anne said.

"You were right to push me. I had to do it. When she started pulling away from me and when she left, I couldn't admit I still loved her. It hurt too much. When I first met her, up until our baby died, she made me feel things I couldn't even imagine before. And she knew how to play me. If she had asked me to climb to the top of the Cathedral with her and jump, who knows what I would have done? She kept me off balance. I think her unpredictability was one of the things about her that excited me. But it made her impossible to live with. It all came clear to me tonight."

"I suppose she'll head back to Paris in the morning."

"Maybe, but it wouldn't be her style to leave without a scene. Nothing would surprise me. We'll see." He glanced at his watch. "It's almost 2:00am. Let's go to bed."

During breakfast the next morning, the doorbell rang. They looked at each other.

"There she is," he said, "right on schedule."

Anne set down her coffee bowl. "And you called her unpredictable."

He went to the door. Marie-Clo stood glowering, her arms crossed in front of her.

"I want to speak to Anne."

"Wait here."

He closed the front door, went to the kitchen and said to Anne, "She wants to talk to you."

"To me? What should I do?"

"It's up to you. If she gets too worked up, you can call me and I'll take over. Or I can just tell her to beat it."

Anne had not imagined that she might become a player in this drama. She had expected John and Marie-Clo to meet and talk and that would be all. But since it was she who had set in motion the events leading up to this moment, how could she refuse? "No. I'll talk to her. How do I look?"

"You don't have to impress her."

Anne shook her head. "You'll never understand women.

294

Stay here."

She went out of the kitchen, closing the door behind her. After a quick stop in the bathroom for a look in the mirror, she opened the front door.

Marie-Clo went straight to the point. "I came to ask you to stop seeing John. I know I hurt him and I want to make it up to him. I know what he needs. I know how to take care of him."

Anne said, "That's out of the question."

"Just listen for a minute. I know I'm the one he loves. He's loved me for years. He wouldn't have come looking for me if he didn't still love me. How long have you known him?"

"That's none of your business."

Marie-Clo paused. It seemed she was not used to boundaries so firmly set and so calmly enforced.

"OK. Listen. I want just three months with him. Not even. Just two months. After two months he can choose between us."

Anne held her ground. "He's already chosen."

"How can you say that? You couldn't even stop him from going to look for me."

As much as she wanted to break off this pointless argument, Anne could not resist setting Marie-Clo straight. "If you must know, finding you was my idea. I thought it would be good for both of you."

While Marie-Clo stood dumfounded, Anne said, "I'm sorry to end this discussion, but I have to go to work. Good day." She closed the door and heard Marie-Clo's rapid, angry footsteps on the gravel and the slamming of her car door.

John came out of the kitchen. "You were magnificent!"

Anne took a moment to compose herself. "I understand now. I understand everything."

"What did you expect? I was twenty. I was horny. I was an idiot."

## Chapter 45: On the Mountain

Two days after Marie-Clo's last visit, John asked Anne to reserve her next day off for an outing. She asked where they were going. "You'll see," was all he would say. Her next full day off was three days away. When Anne begged her mother to cover her shift the next day, Brigitte's poorly concealed smile made Anne wonder if her mother knew what John had planned.

They left early the following morning and headed west on Route 165 under a moody Breton sky that clouded and cleared, that threatened rain and recanted. As they crossed into the Finistère, Anne relived for a moment the sense of doom that had shadowed her when she had come here alone on a cold winter day, desperate to find him, fearing it was too late. Now it was summer again, a balmy day in spite of the threat of rain.

So far at least, they were following the route they had taken on their third date—toward Sizun, the Roc Trévezel, and Huelgoat— the day they had first kissed, the same route she took later in the winter of their relationship. Now, it almost did not matter where they were going, as long as they were together. She watched southern Brittany roll past her: gentle hills, farms surrounded by forest. They passed a turnoff to Concarneau, where she had taken him to the Festival of the Blue Nets many months before.

Until they followed the highway north at Quimper, Anne did not dare guess at where he was taking her and why. When he took the exit at Le Faou toward Sizun and the Monts-d'Arée, an idea began to form. She did her best to hide her excitement.

He parked, and they walked in silence up the rocky path, their way brightened by gorse bushes ablaze with yellow flowers, to the top of the Roc Trévezel. As they stood together on Brittany's backbone, Anne thought of all that had passed between them in the many months, almost a year, since they first came here together— their separations, their reconciliations, their struggles to rise above the past and stay together.

He turned to her and asked, "Do you love me?"

"You know I do."

"Enough to marry me?"

Anne's heart filled with joy. She threw her arms around him, pulled him tightly against her and murmured in his ear, "Yes, my love. Yes, yes, yes."

They held each other a very long time.

As they started back down the path, she asked, "Did you tell my mother what you were going to do?"

"I only warned her that you might ask her to cover your shift today. I know how impatient you can be."

"She probably figured it out. Did you plan something else for today?" As if anything else were necessary.

"Since we're in the neighborhood, I just thought, out of respect for tradition, that we might pay a visit to the Virgin and the Devil."

As they reached the bottom of the path and crossed the road to the parking area, he said, "After knowing me two weeks, you declared it would never work. It seems you've changed your mind."

"I was too much of a coward to try. We'll make it work. I'll do whatever it takes."

"Even living in California?"

As much as she hoped he would never ask that question, she was ready for it. "Maybe part of the year."

"That's too bad," he said. "I don't want to live in California any part of the year."

"Nice ambush. I hope you're proud of yourself."

"Very proud," he said, pressing her against the side of the car with his body and kissing her.

While he started the car and backed out, she said, "There's something I want to ask you. After we're married . . . That sounds so strange. It's the first time I've said it. After we're married . . . I'm getting used to it. After we're married, I want to keep working. May I assume that's OK with you?"

"I hope you will. Some men are turned on by models and actresses. Me, I have a weakness for booksellers."

"I'll never understand men."

297

"You no longer have to. Just me."

"How many children do you want?" she asked.

"Two."

"Me too. At my age, I barely have time for two."

"You have time for anything you want."

She reached across the console, took his hand and squeezed it. "I have what I want."

They parked at the edge of the forest of Huelgoat. Anne got out of the car and looked over the railing through the lush greenery of oaks and beeches now fully leafed out, down at the path she had walked up months before to find him sitting on the hood of her car. She thought of how lost she had been up to that moment.

Remembering the bookseller in Rome and his kind words of encouragement in her time of despair, she said aloud, "And then we emerged to see again the stars."

John looked at her, down at the path, then back at her. He smiled and nodded.

It did not surprise her that he understood. Through the ups and downs of their relationship, across the divide of an ocean and a continent and of language and culture, somehow, almost from the moment they had met, with or without words, they understood each other.

Together now, they walked down the hill past the Trembling Rock to the path along the river past the Virgin's Kitchen to the Devil's Grotto. Down in the Grotto, they stood at the railing, their arms around each other, gazing at the torrent below them.

When it was time to leave, he gestured toward the ladder, sporting a mischievous little smile. She returned his smile and started to climb, thinking of their first visit to the Grotto, her ascent, his admiring gaze, and the wrenching conversation that had followed. She thought again of the tortuous journey they had taken since that day, and the new journey now ahead of them. Proud and confident, she stopped, looked down at him and asked, "How's my ass? Still fabulous?"

## Chapter 46: Epilogue: Two Glasses of Cider

*Sainte-Anne-d'Auray, France*
*22 years later*

Anne takes off her reading glasses and sets her book down on the table next to her. She gets up from her lounge chair on the veranda and walks into the house. John sneaks a look, as he always does, observing that her figure has suffered little from age and two babies. She knows he is looking, and he knows she would be disappointed if she turned around and caught him with his eyes still in his book.

After Juliette, their first daughter, was born, they bought a house on the outskirts of Sainte-Anne-d'Auray, not far from the one he rented when he moved to Brittany twenty-three years before. In spite of suburban sprawl, they still look out on a cow pasture over the back fence. Juliette has just left for Los Angeles for a year of college, to the great delight of John's aging but mostly healthy parents. He and Anne agreed he would speak English to their children. Juliette is proud of her bilingual skills and sometimes called to him in English to impress her friends when he picked her up at school.

Laurie, on the other hand, begged him not to speak English to her in front of her friends. She studied Breton in school and will deign to teach her parents a few words when they ask. Last week they took her to Nantes for her first year of college.

Beguiled by Jacques's charm, John has managed to forgive Anne's father for his misdeeds. Florence, who did her share of forgiving, died several years ago. Anne was at her bedside constantly, trying to give Florence the daughter she wanted but never had. Jacques moved another woman in within months after Florence died. There was speculation in the family that he was seeing her even before Florence got sick.

Brigitte, who at seventy-seven is still elegant, warm, and wise, refuses to retire. As much as John adores her, sometimes he thinks she's a little too perfect, and he has come to understand how Jacques

299

might have felt he couldn't measure up. She has an employee now, and Anne works in the bookstore from time to time. With the girls away, she will spend more time there. She loves the bookstore and speaks wistfully of the days when it was the center of her life, as the passage of time helps her forget how lonely she was before she met John.

John has managed to stay employed, in spite of moments of insecurity with his firm. Every time a new management team takes over, his arrangement is scrutinized. During one of those nervous moments, he took a job teaching Anglo-American law at the University of Nantes. That led to some lucrative French clients, which he is now in charge of. He figures he'll need to keep working for a few more years, if only to finance their trips to Los Angeles.

Anne and John have had their difficulties —not surprising for two headstrong, passionate people from different hemispheres. Their arguments, no matter how loud they get, never last long. Their path to the altar was so rocky that neither ever takes the other for granted. John remembers what Anne said when he proposed and she accepted: that she would do whatever it would take to make it work. He would do no less. They never doubt they were destined to be together.

He remembers well their wedding: standing in the Basilica in front of the congregation watching Anne coming down the aisle on her father's arm in her simple off-white Breton wedding dress, her lustrous golden-brown hair adorned with a *coiffe* in the style of Rennes. Those flamboyant loops of starched lace dazzled every American present, including John. Even back then, traditional Breton wedding dresses and *coiffes* were mostly relics, rarely worn. Anne told him later that marrying an American in one of Brittany's most sacred sites demanded a nod to tradition. She added, "I thought you would like it." He did.

From time to time, they speak of their conversation at the Roche-aux-Fées so long ago about surviving the routine of marriage, of the ever-present challenge of leading a life rich with variety while remaining faithful to one person. There is no escaping that much of married life is routine: getting the kids up and off to school, making

300

sure they do their homework, paying the bills, housework, calling the plumber when there is a problem not even Anne can fix. Yet married or not, it is mostly of those mundane things that everyone makes their lives. When Anne and John wash the dishes together, they think of it as a date, almost a dance, and they move together in harmony.

Sometimes they muse about going back to the Roche-aux-Fées on the night of the new moon to count the stones, but they always agree there is no need. It would only confirm what they already know: that the spirits of the people who put up those stones thousands of years ago somehow arranged for them to meet and stay the course together.

Every year they celebrate their anniversary with their own ceremony. They drive to the Monts-d'Arée and kiss on the Roc Trévezel, then walk through the forests of Huelgoat, listening to the spirits whispering through the trees. Leaving the Devil's Grotto, he still sends her up the ladder ahead of him. She always obliges. The dirt road into the forest between Saint-Herbot and the main highway is partly overgrown now. Sometimes they stop there for another kiss. For the rest of the celebration after the kiss, in recent years they have found it more comfortable to restrain themselves until they are back at home.

From time to time they ask each other what they did to deserve such happiness. Anne tells John he paid his dues when he lost Marie-Clo, Diane, and his first daughter, who died nameless. John reminds Anne of her struggle to forgive her father and rise above her past. They renew their resolve to savor their time together, well aware that in this life, every pleasure is temporary.

Anne returns to the veranda with two glasses of cider and sets one on the table beside him. She asks, "What are you thinking about?"

"About you."

She smiles, and little crow's feet brighten the twinkle in her eyes. After all these years she still asks, even though his answer is always the same.

301

Because she knows it's true.


— END —

# GUIDE TO PRONUNCIATION FOR ENGLISH-SPEAKERS

Argoat (ahr go AHT)

Auray (oh RAY)

Aven (a VEN)

Boulangerie (boo lahn ZHREE)

Charcutier (shar koo TYAY)

Coiffe (kwahf)

Commana (cuh mah NAH)

Concarneau (kohn kar NOH)

Côtes-d'Armor (coht dar MOR)

Cotriade (Coh tree AHD)

Crêperie Alréène (kreh pree ahl ray EN)

Du Guesclin (doo ghek LAN)

Finistère (fee nee STAIR)

Galette Complète (gal ett kohm PLET)

Gavrinis (gav ree NEES)

Goudin (goo DAN)

Grotte du Diable (gruht doo DYA bluh)

Gwen Ha Du (gwen ah DOO)

Hennebont (en BOHN)

Huelgoat (well go AHT)

Ille-et-Vilaine (eel ay vee LEN)

Jean-Louis (zhahn LWEE)

Jean-Yves (zhahn EEV)

Jocelyne (zhoh SLEEN)

Laborde (lah BORD)

La Cigale (lah see GAHL)

303

Les Halles (lay AHL)

Locmaria (luck mah ree AH)

Locmariaquer (luck mah ree ah KAIR)

Lycée (lee SAY)

Marie-Clothilde Brossard (ma ree kloh teeld bruh SAR)

Ménage de la Vierge (may nazh duh lah VYAIRZH))

Menhir (men EER)

Monts-d'Arée (mohn dah RAY)

Morbihan (mor bee AHN)

Nantes (nahnt)

Pâtisserie (pah tee SREE)

Perros-Guirec (pair ohs ghee REK)

Place de la République (plass duh lah ray poo BLEEK)

Plumergat (ploo mair GAHT)

Pointe de Pen'hir (pwant duh pen EER)

Quimper (cam PAIR)

Rennes (ren)

Roche aux Fées (rush oh FAY)

Roche Tremblante (rush trahm BLAHNT)

Roc Trévezel (ruk tray vuh ZEL)

Saint-Gildas (san zheel DAH)

Saint-Goustan (san goo STAHN)

Saint-Herbot (san tair BOH)

Sainte-Anne-d'Auray (san tan doh RAY)

Sizun (see ZUHN)

Spézet (spay ZET)

Vannes (van)

# ACKNOWLEDGMENTS

These people each contributed in some way to the realization of this book:


Anna Maria Angelini
Jacqueline Belin
Bernard Casabianca
Nathalie Casabianca
Anne Castagnaro
Laurence Denié-Higney
Annlee Ellingson
James B. Gabrielson
Kristin Gabrielson
Joelle Juillard
Pamela Klein
Eric Lafayette
Andreas Merenyi
Nicole Ransac-Vivaldi
Lynette Berg Robe
Ellen Ruben
Nancy Schlothauer
Alex Spataru